Waiting On My Cue

Author:

Belinda S. Hunter

Waiting On My Cue

Belinda S. Hunter

Hunter.belinda99@gmail.com

Belindahunter335@yahoo.com

www.waitingonmycue.com

Adnileb Publishing

This is a work of fiction. Any names, places, events or characters are only the figment of the authors imagination or used fictitiously.

ISBN: 978-0-615-78376-5

Printed in the United States of America

Acknowledgements

First and foremost, I have to thank my heavenly father before anyone else. Thank you for always keeping me, even when I'm not deserving. You never cease to amaze me.

I would like to thank my biggest supporter literally, my mother Lurlene Miller. I still hear her heartfelt words that really made me want to complete this when she said, Lynn finish your book. You have been wanted to do this for years, I will support you in anyway, just finish it!

A special thanks to my children, Dontavius Gist, Dweshun Adair, Tiffanie Adair and Jamarris Adair who has had to deal with me giving them the blank stare, or a quick I'll call you back, when they would come into the room or call while I was busy writing wanting some mommy talk time. Guys, mom is free now, hopefully for a moment so hurry and bring it. Oops, the time has passed, working on novel two. But you all know that you are my first priority, so if you really need me... Forget a book.

I have to send a great big shout out my cousin Tina Parks, who encouraged me to pick my novel back up and complete it, after years had gone by without me thinking about it. And my cousin Trisha Watson, for making me believe that I was onto something when I gave her a sample chapter to read and she called me demanding the rest, as if that was really going to happen. I must acknowledge Pastor Marvin Miller, who has always felt the need to anoint me. After reading this, he's going to be throwing oil on me every time he sees me. Thank you for your spiritual wisdom. Yes, I did listen.

The clowns that have kept me on my toes, my sisters and brothers. Tiffany Miles, Priscilla Sullivan, Dante Dodd and Lamar Barton. I love you guys.

Thanks to my Virginia family, for supporting me in anyway necessary. Aunt Carolyn King, Joyce Magnum, Denise King, and Joe King, Jr. Your support and advice has meant so much to me.

A special shout out to whom unknowingly became my advisory team; Anthony Smith, Lorando Lockhart and Paul Davis. I could hit them up at anytime with questions or advice and they were always boosting me up, or telling me the dos and don'ts. Thanks for keeping it real, guiding, being patient and answering all of my questions. You guys are the greatest. Thanks for being that ear when I was in a panic about deadlines. Anthony, I took your advice and got that drink.

My ace, confidant- and friend that I would trust my life with- Tesha Foster. I wish that everyone could be blessed with a friend like you. Thank you for being the calm that helps balances my storms when I am on the war path. Your spirit keeps me close to God. You are such a sweet and humble person, and I treasure your friendship.

I have been blessed with GREAT friends, and I cannot let them go unacknowledged. Tessa Williams Hamilton, Deborah Yeargin, Shayla Simpson, Courtney Berniece Robinson, Wanda Smoot, Andrea Heard, Robbie Jones, Latorre Cooper, Tammy Gaines, Shannon Williams, Dorothy (Boochie) Grayson, and Natasha Phillips. Thank you all for the help, laughter, encouragement, and just always being there for me when I was frustrated, needing to vent, or just get out for a breather, you were always there.

My friends Barbara Bryant and Judy Thompson, we are more like sisters than friends. I value your honesty with me, even when I don't want you to be. You get under my skin and I know I get under yours. You two have been one of the greater thorns in my side. Glad that we can agree to disagree and keep it moving.

A special thanks to whom I call my very own personal geek squad. Aquandra Ballenger Few and Lori Edwards. You ladies really were the life behind making this book happen. I know you got tired of seeing me coming, but I could not have done it without you. Even when it was something that you did not know, you figured it out and made it better than I could have imagined. You ladies are definitely in the wrong profession.

And a great big shout out to my cover models Jasmine Fowler, Tiffanie Adair and Zhazamar Davis you guys rocked.
My editors, Marietta Evans, Christopher E. McCants and Tiffanie Adair, you had your work cut out for you. "Belinda, did you even try to edit at all?" Nope!!! I love the fact that you all saw my vision, and made it remain my book, my words and my story.

Joyce Mallory for always sending me a word of inspiration, just when I need it. Thanks for being so plugged in to God.

My late father, Mr. James Douglas Miller. How I wish you were here to witness this completed. I remember you sitting on my porch reading it, and looking up at me saying, "Damn baby, you wrote this?" I love you and miss you like crazy. Six years and I still tear up thinking about you. Thanks for always making me believe that everything stood still for me, and that the world revolved around me(even if it was only in our minds).

Hugs and kisses to my little princesses and soldiers whom my time has been limited with lately because I have been so busy writing. Promise, Junior, Saniya, Draylyn and Aubri Gist and Ryan, Jaishun and Akeirah Adair. GG is going to make it all up to you. I love you little people soooo- much!

And last but certainly not least, I have to thank my husband, Mr. Frederick Hunter. No matter what I set out to do he roots me on 100%. If he sees that it makes me happy… he's all for It, you are truly a sweetheart. I am so blessed to have such an amazing support team. All of my family and friends, thanks for believing in me!

Dedication

This novel is dedicated to a lady who has been nothing short of a superwoman in my life. Lurlene Miller you are the best thing to me next to God. Every survival skill that I have in me has come from you. You have showed me all aspects of how a strong woman looks, thinks, falls, gets up and finish with a vengeance. I am often told that I have a heart of gold, my simple reply is- "It was inherited." Mom I only hope to be half the lady that you are one day, you cannot be replicated.

Chapter One

(Keisha)

This poverty shit is for the birds. My mom had me standing outside of Po-Folks in this 90-degree weather, waiting on whomever she could coax into picking me up from work to get here.

This was a never ending battle with my mother; she knows exactly what time I clock out. My aunt allows her to drop her off at work and keep the car so that I will have a ride home. But more times than not, her ass is either not here to pick me up on time, or she is sending someone that I don't even know to pick me up.

I swore to myself that I will be a better mother than she has ever been. Because of all the irresponsible bullshit that I have witnessed and lived through; I know I would never allow my children to live that life.

I love my mother. I can't help but to love that happy-go-lucky-live-life-to-the-fullest personality she has. But at the same time, things that I love about her are some of the same things that I hate about her. Her care-free-spirited attitude has led her to a life of partying, hustling at its best, and has blinded her of her home responsibilities. She is always looking for her next hustle instead of getting up off of her ass and going to work somewhere.

We still live at home with my grandmother. This is probably the most responsible decision she has ever made for all of us. Honestly if we weren't with granny in our early childhood years, I most likely would have been the one raising my brother and sister.

Just a few more weeks and I will have my car- a 1994 Toyota Corolla. This old man around the corner from grannies is selling me for a $1,000. He's allowing me to give him a $100 a week because he knows my circumstances, and sees my ambition. He knows I want more. I have already paid him $700, and only owe $300 more. I could take it out of my savings account; but I don't want to empty out my account, so I decided to just wait three more weeks and pay the car off. I will then use what I have saved to pay my car insurance, and taxes, this way I will still have some change in my account.

I looked at my watch. It was a quarter till four. I have been off of work since three! Where is her butt? Just because she has no shame don't expect for me not to. Hell, I have an image to maintain.

"You're still here girl?" Samantha asked, as she came out after her shift ended.

I was hot and bothered. I wanted to ask her cock-eyed ass did she not see me still standing here. Instead, I gave her a sly smile and said, "Yes, my ride is running a little late."

She asked if I needed a ride. I declined because I knew they were on their way. I just thanked her. This was so embarrassing to me; all the other young people that worked with me already had cars. Unlike the others, I did not have anyone to give me anything. Whatever I got I had to work for it. I am a hard worker and love to make my money so don't get me wrong. It's just that it is aggravating to see how some get everything, and I am still busting my butt and got nothing but a swollen bank account.

When four o'clock came, I took out my cell phone and called my mom again.

She answered the phone while still laughing and talking to someone before she finally asked what was up.

"Where is my ride mom? I am still out here waiting," I said, shifting my weight to my left leg and hiking my slipping duffle bag back onto my shoulder.

"Oh shit, she hadn't picked you up? I asked Shelia to get you when she left the hair salon. I told her if she hadn't left by three to call me and I would send someone else. I am still playing cards. Let me see if I can get one of the guys to run and get you real quick. Hold on," she said, placing the phone down before I could even tell her that Shelia had just pulled up. When she came back to the phone she said, "Cue is going to pick you up." I put up a finger signaling Shelia to hold on a minute.

"Cue who?" I asked. I knew pretty darn well who she was referring too. My mom was a gambler, and this hot ass guy name Cue was also. I remember one night when my mother asked me to bring her wallet over to the Westside where she was playing cards. When I pulled up, Cue and all the other jocks he hangs with were standing outside of the house. I have always had a secret crush on Cue; he was one hot, sexy ass guy, but I had never said anything to him other than hi. One reason is that our paths hardly ever crossed, and when they did he always had all these other fly, high maintenance chicks on his jock. And even if this particular night had been different, he still would not have seen me. I had just borrowed my aunt's car to bring

Ma Dukes her wallet, and I was sitting behind these tinted windows looking a hot mess. There was no way I was getting out of this car. I used my phone to call her to send someone out to get her wallet and I bounced, cursing myself the entire ride back home. This could have been my opportunity to really be noticed by him. I promised myself that one day in the near future that I was going to have to get fly and ride over to see my mom while she played cards, since I now knew where the guys were when they were not clubbing.

"His name is Cue Davis. You don't know him, but he drives a black Camaro," was her reply.

"Ok," I faintly replied.

"He's good people Keisha. I would never send someone that I didn't trust to pick you up," my mom said, thinking my tone meant that I wasn't comfortable.

"I know. I am good," I told her, "love you." When I disconnected the call I ran over to Shelia's car and told her that she did not have to take me home, that one of my friends was already on her way. I told her that I thought mom had forgotten me so I went ahead and called someone. I apologized, thanked her, and then sprinted back into Po-folks to the bathroom. I took off my apron, fixed up my uniform, reapplied my makeup, and fixed my hair. The only thing I could not do was get rid of this chicken smell that was embedded in my clothes. What in the hell was I going to say to this guy? I wondered if he even knew that it was me that he was picking up. I was so nervous my hands were shaking. I stepped back and looked at myself in the floor length mirror and thought, damn, what is he going to think of me in this dirty Po-folks uniform, smelling like chicken? Most of the women he had sweating him were college students or spoiled brats who did not have to work their way through high school as I did.

I went back out just as the Camaro was pulling up. I watched as he circled around the parking lot so he could pull up in front of the door. This car was one of the sweetest I had ever seen. And just to think I was getting ready to be riding in it with Mr. Cue himself. Too bad no one would see me with him-Damn!

When he came to a stop, I walked up to the car and opened the door. I found myself staring into the eyes of the sexiest man on earth as far as I was concerned. Cue looked damn good behind the wheel of this sleek car. I said, "Hi," as I got into the car.

He held his head back laughing and said, "I'll be damned. I didn't know you were Doretha's daughter."

"How would you?" I said, with a smirk on my face. "You don't really know me - do you?"

Dang this dude was finer up close than he was from a distance. He had the sexiest sideways smile, and the sexiest dark low bedroom eyes. For someone to be as tall as he was he was not at all skinny. He was a nice sized dude. I kept glancing over at those nice broad shoulders every time I could sneak a peek. His hands were humongous. Apparently he knew that his smile and eyes were contagious as well, because he kept flashing that flawless ass smile and squinting those sexy ass eyes. I have never been anyone's one night stand and neither have I ever been one to sleep with someone from the start, but this mug here could definitely get it right now! All he had to do was place one of those massive hands on my thigh... and it would have been over.

"I know your ass Keisha. You're the one that acts like you don't know a nigga," he said, returning that same crooked smile that I had just given him. Conversation was actually pretty easy with Cue. For someone who seemed so cool and smooth at all times; he was funny as all get out. I loved his country drawl. Whenever I would see him in the club, he and his boys would always just be posted up chilling. His presence though always screamed; cool, sexy and no nonsense. We practically laughed and cracked on one another the entire ride home. He had a slick mouth, and my retaliation was just as slick. The ride home was too short for me. I wished he wasn't from the area and I could have taken him thirty minutes out of the way to get me home, rather than the ten minute route that he knew. Once we arrived on my street, I was surprised and delighted that everyone was outside, including the local "Round the Way Girls" and the "Penny Addict Drug Dealers" that stayed in my hood. After I thanked him for the ride, and he said the pleasure was all his, I stepped out with my head held high like, "Yea, I'm doing him." Everyone knew Cue's car, and the glares did not go unnoticed.

Cue and I did not exchange numbers because... *hell, I don't even know why.* All I know is that he never even asked me, and I was not bold enough to ask for his. He did say, "Well I guess I will see you at the club?" I played it over and over in my head as to why he didn't ask. I actually know that he enjoyed my conversation, and I know I am a pretty cute chick. And I kept noticing him checking me out in the car; although he was trying to do it on the sly. I don't know whether it was the gap in age, or the fact that he knew my mother was a crazy lady and would most likely have him castrated if she even thought he was doing her baby, or maybe, he was just out of my league. Whatever the reason, it bothered me, and I knew that unless I got bold and approached him myself when I would see him at the club, that the opportunity would most likely never arise because he was always smothered by so many groupies, that he couldn't see past them to see what other options were out there for him. And let the truth be told, I was just not that bold. I am old school in believing and waiting for the man to approach you. My mother always said, "If he's interested, he'll make a move. If not, whether you liked him or not, let him keep moving along. Because if you approach him first, and when things start going south, the first thing out of his mouth will be that you're the one that wanted this. I was not ready to be in a relationship." I don't totally believe that to be true, but I just cannot seem to shake it.

After wrestling with this for over a week, I decided that I would put my guard down and go to the club on Saturday. If I see him there which I was very sure that I would, I would go up to him and speak. After all, we are associates now, right? So I will just casually say, "Hello Cue, long time no see," aim at a little humor. As fly as I planned to be, just praying that he follows my lead. Yes, that is exactly what I will do.

I got up and went into the living room where my mother and some friends had a card game going on and sat on the couch. My mom was saying how the police busted up in some house and took everyone to jail, including a fifteen year old girl that had nothing to do with it; she just stayed at the house. And Cue was telling them she's a child, what the hell you messing with her for she has nothing to do with this shit. My mom said one officer told Cue that he better shut up- and Cue went ballistic. Although he was handcuffed; he kicked the police car, and kicked at the officer before he was shoved him into the rear of the car and hauled off. She was saying that someone said, "I tell you what, he left here without a bruise, so when the lawyer comes to see him tomorrow, he better not have a scratch on him!"

Needless to say, after hearing all of this with it being Saturday already, I knew my plans to approach Cue tonight at the club was null and void. I guess I will just have to wait until next week. Next week actually turned into a year for me, because that was the sentence that Cue ended up with.

I sat back in the cut with every intention of going over to speak to Cue after the crowd died down that had him surrounded. Cue had just come home from prison. This was more like a welcome home party for him than the regular Saturday night at the club. All you heard every other song was the DJ saying "Welcome home to my main dog Cue. Good seeing you back in the house man." The waitresses stayed over in that area bringing bubbly and other drinks. All eyes were on the VIP for very good reason. Cue was everything you needed to look at with his fine ass.

After a while I realized that the crowd would not die down. As soon as one set of groupies left another group filled the void. Even with his girl Mercedes by his side, he was still getting mad love from the ladies. Although they played it off as if they were just happy to see him and welcoming him home. But I knew flirting when I saw it.

I decided that I might as well bounce because I had to work in the a.m., and with Mercedes stuck to his hip, the conversation would not be the way I anticipated anyway. So I gathered my belongings to leave. As I was passing by where Cue and his crew were posted, to my surprise, we were able to briefly make eye contact. He was talking to his boy Eric as I passed. I do not know what made him look up, but he looked directly at me. I gave him a slight smile and with a sexy sideways glance mouthed real smoothly, "Welcome home." He nodded his head and gave me a knowingly smirk. He pressed those lips together as he squinted his eyes slowly looking me from head to toe and back up again.

That small gesture was more than enough for me. I played it over and over in my head. The way he squinted those eyes to look seductive, which he did achieve, and bit on that lower lip. That alone told me that he was very interested. And in due time, it would be our time.

Chapter Two

(Keisha)

Cue, my on again-off again, I'll go out on the limb and use the word boyfriend; and I had not talked in almost two weeks. I had yet again heard another rumor about him messing with another low life that's always on his jock. I am not Cue's main lady; however, I made it clear to him when he started pursuing me; that I would only deal with his current girlfriend Mercedes because she was there before me. But I certainly would not be dealing with any other groupies that are always on his jock. If it's me you want, then you better make it known, because you will not cheat on us. I know this may sound crazy, but until you have wanted someone as bad as I have always yearned for Cue, you can't say you would not settle for being second or judge me.

Finally, on Monday, I started back responding to his advances and entertaining him again. We had made plans to meet Saturday night after he returned to town from taking care of some business. He told me that he would get a room because his house was a mess from the replacement of new floors that he was having laid. He said that he would be staying at a hotel anyway and he wanted to make the evening special. He was going to get us a room at the Hyatt Regency downtown, Jacuzzi and all.

Needless to say, I was all excited for a few reasons; I love this man more than life, and we were going to spend the entire night together in a luxury hotel complete with room service and all. Not to mention that I am horny as a damn dog in heat. It has been almost three weeks!

I get a call from this tramp named Tamisha telling me that she doesn't know what Cue and I are doing, but that she just wanted me to know that she was with Cue when I called him last night. And he told her that I was calling about some marijuana. She claimed that she just wanted to know what was up, before she moved any further with him.

I was livid and wanted to kill. I called Cue, but of course I received no answer. So I sent him a text and simply said, "I will not be meeting you tonight. Tell Tamisha to meet your ass. You are full of games and I personally do not have time for your games." He only replied back and said, "Ok, what ever, believe what you want."

Later that night, I was sitting at home steaming and bored out of my mind. I sent Cue a text and said, "You may think I am crazy, because I am beginning to think the same thing. The bottom line is that I am in love with you, and I miss you so much. If you would have me in your arms tonight, I would love to be there. Please call me or text me and let me know what is up." I never heard anything back from him, so I decided that I was just going to ride out to the spot and be there when he arrives.

I got to the hotel and sat in my car to wait on Cue to arrive. Twenty minutes later he pulls into the parking lot in his black Denali. I thought, "*Here comes my baby*," and got butterflies just thinking about the fact that I would soon be in his arms again.

Cue walked right past my car and did not even notice me. I giggled to myself as I prepared to get out the car and follow him into the lobby of the hotel. When I got out of the car I noticed that his truck was still running. This told me that he would be coming back out so I decided to get back into my car and re-strategize my surprise appearance to my baby. I noticed as a car pulled in beside me and a girl got out of the car. She walked around my car, right over to Cue's truck, and got in on the passenger side.

"What the hell is going on?" I thought to myself. I looked over at the truck. I could not see her clearly inside of the truck because of the tint. However, I could tell that she wasn't robbing him. It appeared as if she had her head rested on the head rest, waiting for Cue to come back out.

My heart was beating so fast that I probably should have had a heart attack or worse. I do not know what took over my body. I got out of the car and walked into the lobby right-up behind Cue and asked, "Who is that in your truck?"

Cue, who was filling out the required papers to rent a hotel room turned his head to see me. You could tell from his eyes that he had been busted and he knew it.

"What are you doing here Keisha? You said you were done!" Cue said, rather than ask. Ignoring his question, I threw one at him. "So make me understand. You said that there was no one but me and Cedes, and then I get a call from Tamisha saying that she has been with you all weekend. And now there is another unknown female sitting in your car? Bastard, just how many women do you keep on the side?" My eyes had filled up with tears. They hadn't started rolling down my cheeks yet but I knew that I would not be able to stop them from doing so. My heart was pounding, and my legs felt as if they would desert me at any moment.

"Keisha you are the one that said you were not coming. I have wanted to see you for the past two weeks. You are the one that has been on trip mode. I can be faithful, but why should I if all you are going to do is question and believe everything you damn hear?"

He finished filling out the paper work and was now facing me with his arms crossed on his chest leaning against the wall. I just shook my head slowly at him because my voice would give away all the pain I was feeling if I dared to speak.

As the tears started to roll down my face, I turned to walk away. Cue grabbed me and pulled me back to face him. He lifted my chin and proceeded to wipe away my tears with his free hand.

"Baby don't do this, you know that I can't stand to see you cry." Looking into his eyes I could tell that he was sorry. "Keisha what can I do to prove to you that you mean everything to me? It's like I keep hurting you over stupid bitches that mean nothing to me. I have tried my best to show you that you are more than a side chick to me. You keep letting these stupid hoes come to you with bullshit, and then you take it and run with it."

"So why was Tamisha with you this weekend Cue?"

Cue shrugged his shoulders, "She asked to go. Hell, you and Mercedes both have been tripping all week. And although it may be a lame excuse, I just needed the company. That was the only reason. I didn't know what was going to happen with us because you have not been talking to me. And when you did you basically said you were done with it all. So, what did I have to lose? It was you that no longer wanted what we had."

"Cue, I can't do this anymore. I have to deal with Mercedes and that is hard enough for me. When you tell me that you and I cannot get together because you and Mercedes are going to the movies- out to eat- or whatever your plans may be, it kills me. I just take it all in stride, but now it's the other women you're asking me to deal with also?"

"Keisha, I am not asking you to deal with no other women and you knew the deal with Mercedes," Cue was saying as I cut him off.

"Yes I know the deal with Mercedes, and I have handled it very well. I am talking about the chick in your car as we speak. Tamisha, and all the others I have dealt with since being involved with your ass."

Cue just looked at me for a moment. I could tell that his mind was trying to come up with a believable reply.

"Keisha all I can say is that I am sorry. If you really look into it, we were usually always on the outs when I dealt with any of those females. I love you and I do not want to lose you."

"So- What's with the chick in the car?" I asked, crossing my arms leaning all of my weight to my left hip.

"Shit, you say the word; I will tell her she has to bounce – as a matter of fact," Cue said digging in his pocket to pull out his cell phone, he started dialing a number. "Hey you got to leave; my girl has popped up. Mmm hunh- yea- ok- I'll holla."

Do not think that it did not dawn on me that he could just call this girl up at anytime. Apparently, she already knew that he had a woman. And believe me; I knew that Cue's player days were long from being over. For some reason right now I just yearned for him more than ever. I need to be held in his arms. I do not know why I keep forgiving him. I heard stories about other women but I thought it was just hearsay, and most of the time I would act like it didn't bother me. My mom always said "If you didn't see it for yourself...then he got away with it." Plus, I had no solid proof until now.

Catching him in the act tonight hurt more than the night that Eboni and I were at the club when Tamisha first confronted me about Cue. That was over two months ago.

Thinking back to that night, along with the actions of tonight, really is a reality check. Eboni and I had not been in the club for more than ten minutes for the charity benefit that Cue and the guys were hosting. I was really feeling myself that day, and from the way all the men were approaching me, I knew they were also. I was always treated with V.I.P status anytime I came to this club, and most all clubs in the area. Although I was not the main chick of one of the biggest hustlers around; I was his chick- and everyone knew that. Even if his main girl Mercedes was in the building, I was still given a tab that was later taken care of by Cue or one of his peeps. And as long as his girl stayed on her side of the road, I stayed in my lane also.

Eboni and I had just come from outside where they were grilling everything from steaks, to corn on the cob. I must say they had a pretty good set-up going on for this charity benefit. On the outside there were three 200 pound tank grills with food covering them. Balloon rides, and the fire trucks outside for the kids activities. They also had a bingo tent on the side of the building, and inside of the club had been opened for those of us who wanted to get their dance on. Admission was twenty dollars, which included entry and food. I was tripping because if you did not know any better, you would have thought it was eleven o'clock at night inside this club instead of 5:00 pm. It was so crowded inside. As Eboni and I was making our way through the club looking fly and moving to the music, some random guy asked me if he could get a dance later tonight. I was wondering if he was talking about later tonight when the club opened back up for its official business, or did he mean later this evening? I was straight tripping.

"Sure just holler at me when you are ready." I said, as I really looked at him and wondered, "Where the hell did you come from with your gorgeous self?"

I will dance with anyone no matter what shape, size or nationality. I just loved to dance and have a partner to do it with. But this man here- I would consider taking home.

"Ok, he said, as he looked me square in the eyes. "Don't act like you don't know a brother when I come to cash in."

"Never that," I said, flirting as I proceeded to make my way through the club.

I was asking my girl Eboni, who was he, when I was nearly pulled down to the floor.

Cue, who was sitting at one of the tables, grabbed me by my arm as I was passing and asked, "Why are you talking to Marcell?"

Oh, was that his name? I thought, making a mental note to remember the name of the fine specimen that had asked me to dance and whom I had never seen before in my life. But why bother telling Cue this, he is jealous for a change.

"What?" I asked, with an annoyed look on my face.

"That boy has a girl, and I would hate for Cookie to whip that ass," Cue said, smirking.

"You have one too," I said, raising one of my eyebrows as I pulled my arm away from him and continued towards the bathroom.

"Girl you are crazy," Eboni said. "Cue has a nerve trying to ask you about another man. What- are you only suppose to talk to him and he has a woman?"

"I know right?" I replied as I entered the bathroom. He's jealous. I must admit I kind of like it, I thought to myself. Eboni went into the bathroom stall as I examined myself in one of the full length mirrors.

I was wearing some dark denim skinny jeans, a white plain t-shirt that hung off one shoulder and a bad ass pair of Hunfew shoes that I had spent too much money for. But hey... these shoes spoke for themselves, something about Hunfews that makes me crazy. This particular pair I was wearing had a five inch heel and the sole was platform. The Hunfew blue out lined the tear drop hole at the tip of the shoe. The leather covered the top part of my feet and straps of various colors took over from there, creating a boot look. I had accidently found a necklace that had all the colors of the shoe in it at Macy's. I paid extremely too much for it. But what were the chances of me finding something that matched perfectly, with a pair of shoes of this caliber without them coming together? The shoe is what made the outfit hot. And of course my small waist and thick hips showed through the loose fitting shirt that hugged my hips. I turned to the side to take a look at my profile to see if the shirt was hitting in the right area of my rear end.

Tamisha walks up and stood beside me adjusting her blouse. I briefly stopped what I was doing, and looked at her surprised. Everyone knew she had no love for me, but was madly in love with Cue. So for her to come and stand in my air space kind of threw me for a second.

"Are you still seeing Cue?" she asked me while still fixing up her blouse and looking into the mirror not making eye contact with me.

"Why?" I asked, looking at her directly through the mirror.

"Keisha, I am not trying to start anything. I just want to know if Cue is telling me the truth when he says that he is not dealing with you anymore."

I looked from the mirror to Tamisha. Is this girl trying to tell me that she is messing around with Cue again? We have been down this road in the past and she knows that Cue and I see each other. She also knows that he has a girlfriend. Why does she and all the other hoochies that claims he is messing around with them always feel the need to run to me every time their feelings starts getting involved, I have no idea. The way these hoes acted you would have thought that I was the numero-uno. I guess a threat is a threat no matter who it is. I guess they figure I am the next closest thing so why not start with me first. Apparently they knew if they went to Mercedes that Cue would probably drop their asses.

Now I'm pissed off. "Tamisha cut the bullshit. Is there something you are trying to say to me or you want me to know?" I asked, as I placed my hand on my hip.

"Cue was at my house last night and has been calling me on the regular again." She said, with a satisfied look on her face.

My heart was slowly breaking. I could feel the cracks; but I was not going to give this ghetto-non-dressing- bad weave wearing-stank heifer the satisfaction of knowing that. I was a threat, and that was why she was telling me this. The only thing Tamisha has is a nice figure. There is nothing else about her that spelled soul mate for Cue. Her ass has been in love with Cue for the past three years. I guess she is always a willing body for when Mercedes or I are not giving in to him because we are mad about one thing or another. Her dumb ass hasn't realized that yet?

"Listen, I am not Cue's woman. Cue has a woman and you know who she is. So why do you feel the need to run up on me every time Cue fucks you, I don't know. Apparently you must see me as more of a threat to you as you see his lady. What the hell am I suppose to do break up with him? I can't breakup with someone who is not my man. And if Cue is screwing you- that doesn't mean you have him honey. Get some control because you will end up getting your ass beat if you think you can eliminate all the women Cue may fuck with."

I'm just telling you because I don't want to mess with a man that is seeing someone else. You are the one that's getting all defensive," Tamisha said looking at me while placing her hand on her hip.

"You sound so stupid. Hell, you and everyone else know he's with Mercedes! So if Cue is who you really want, then you better find Mercedes and let her know that you're fucking her man and try to eliminate her. I don't really give a damn!" I turned and walked out of the bathroom steaming. Where in the hell was he? I was going to give him a piece of my mind. If he was going to mess with these tramps, at least keep them out of my face! Although I couldn't see him through the crowd, I knew he was over by the VIP section, and that is the direction I headed.

As I was making my way through the packed club, some guy grabbed my arm and pulled me to him. I jerked my arm away from him and said, "Get your hands off me!" He looked offended but what the hell did he expect, a wet kiss? Hell, he didn't know me so he should not have been manhandling me like that.

Eboni grabbed my arm and pulled me over to the side out of the traffic from everyone else.

"Keisha, you need to get it together girl, that girl is not worth all of this. If anything you need to leave Cue alone. What are you going to say? He is not your man; he is just someone you happen to be fucking. Hell, how can you confront him about cheating on you? If he will do it to her, what makes your shit so good that you think he won't do it to you?" Eboni's words stung worse than a bee, and I knew she was right. I could not do anything. I felt the tears filling up in my eyes and apparently so did Eboni, because she pulled me to her and allowed me to cry on her shoulders. Thank goodness she had pulled me into a corner, I was uncontrollable.

"Get it together Keisha, you are so much better than this," Eboni said, while rubbing my back.

"Why do I keep trust him with my heart, and he just keeps breaking it?" I sobbed, into her shoulder.

"Nonsense Keisha, if your heart was broken that would mean you'd have internal hemorrhaging.

I stopped crying, and held my head up from Eboni's shoulder and just looked at her.

"What?" I asked, shaking my head with a questionable look on my face.

"Girl, if your heart was broke, you would have internal bleeding and be damn near death. You're good, let's go to the bathroom and clean up," Eboni said, as she gave my back a pat as if saying, "Good job."

I started laughing as I pulled myself together. We headed for the bathroom to get my face back right, and then went to our table.

When we got to our table, Mercedes was sitting two tables down with her crew of friends and in Cue's lap. I was mad as hell, because I felt this was done as a shot towards me by Mercedes. They normally always sat in VIP, so why tonight amongst the pheasants? I sat there steaming while I watched her laugh with her friends, and Cue was looking a little uncomfortable as he talked to his boy Eric. It was something about the way he had his hands on her waist that bothered me.

I know that she is his woman, but I rarely see them showing any kind of affection. Just this mere form of affection I must say had me a little jealous.

"Mmm... don't they seem happy?" I said, while chewing on my bottom lip.

"Girl don't trip. Hell you knew what you were getting in when you got in it. Cue is good to you and all, but you have options; because you don't have to deal with him. And quit biting your damn lip, you look desperate and jealous!"

I quickly let my lip go and sat up straight. I had forgotten for a second who the hell I was- Eboni was so right. I did not have to deal with Cue- I choose to because I love him so much. So what- if Cue is good to me, there are plenty of brothers out there that are just as fine, have just as much to offer, and are willing to make me their number one- if given the chance. But noo... my ass couldn't see past Cue. I had the nerve to be devoted to a nigga that has a woman already. What in the hell is wrong with me?

"You know Eboni, you are so right. It's time for me to start seeing other people, because I am only getting older. I deserve a man that I can be seen with and who can spend time with me regularly. I am tired of being lonely."

"I never understood why you were so faithful to him anyway," Eboni said as she rubbed her crossed legs.

Just as I was about to answer Eboni, Russell came and pulled me to my feet and said, "Come on sexy, let's dance." I allowed Russell to lead me to the dance floor. I love to dance, and Russell has mad moves also. Needless to say, we turned it out for at least four songs back to back. Russell was one of the show boating hustlers. He was fine and he knew it. I once considered messing with him when Cue and I was going through one of our hiatuses, until I actually had a real conversation with him and realized how arrogant he was. He talked about how women suck his dick and he doesn't even fuck them afterwards; they just want to get him off. And how this nigga ain't making no money; they just perpetrating. According to him- he's the only real nigga on the streets. This fool even went on to say that even the men be jealous of him because their women be on his jock. Russell had women crazy, and I mean that literally. Russell must have a 9 inch steel dick of gold, because these hoes would cut you behind his cheating ass.

"I see your man has his Miss America with him tonight."

"He is not my man Russell, he's hers." I said, annoyed that he had labeled her so highly. "She's pretty, but she is not Miss America, you tripping."

"She isn't even pretty to me," Russell said. "Just because you have long hair, slim and light skin doesn't make you pretty. If you look at her, she is just average. Nothing stands out about her but her complexion and hair. But that nigga just an average Joe himself. He thinks she's a dime because she yellow, but she ain't shit but a nickel to me. You need to drop that nigga, hell; he can't give you nothing that I can't give you."

"Russell, you aren't shit either. Hell, the way you have these women fighting over your ass, I am not trying to get cut." I laughed, feeling good about what he had just said about Mercedes. He was right; Mercedes was skinny with no curves. She had a light complexion, pretty skin and beautiful long hair. Because she was in "Corporate America" she walked around like her shit didn't stink, and as if she was so much better than everyone else. I use to think she was so pretty too when I first saw her. But the more I saw her; I realized she had lots of flaws that didn't show from a distance. Her eyes were too huge for her small face, and her cheek bones had a manly look about them. Although she dressed nice, her clothes had nothing to hang onto. No matter how tight she tried to wear them. She looked good, but there were no curves. I figured her to be about a size 2.

"Those hoes ain't anybody to me; if I had a woman like you I promise you there would be no drama."

"That's what you all say." I started going down to the floor while doing the dog. They were playing a very old school song called the "Atomic Dog" and the beat was fierce. Russell was dipping with me and we were totally in sync with each other. We were laughing and having a great time. He had taken my mind completely off of Cue and all the non sense that had happened tonight.

When Zapps, "I Wanna Be Your Man" came on I excused myself, but Russell pulled me back to him. As we slow danced, I must say; I understood why the women went goo goo over his fine ass. He smelled so damn good. His touch was soft, and the way he moved let me know that this nigga could put it down. As he spoke softly into my ear, I felt his soft lips grazing it every few moments, as he tried to be heard over the loud music. This little gesture sent chills down my spine.

"You know I've been jocking you for a minute Keisha, he was saying. If you think I am bull shitting you, just tell me what it is I need to do to show you I am for real. You just give me the word and all these other hoes are gone.

"Just like that?" I asked, as I looked at him.

He flashed a crooked smile and said, "Just like that."

I laid my head back on his shoulder and thought about what it would be like to be his woman. He was fine, loaded and swagged out. On the flip side, he just didn't seem to have any respect for the women that he dated. I had seen firsthand when he had been busted with another chick, and he just told the one that he was supposed to be seeing at the time, that he was single for a reason.

"When have I ever told you that you were my woman? As long as I am giving you what you need, you have no right thinking you can step to me about another hoe I'm sleeping with. This is an open relationship remember." I was like dang! And all she could do was walk off with her jaws dragging on the floor. There was nothing she could say, because he spoke the truth. So the only way I could be his lady; was if he made a public announcement. Put it in the paper, on the radio, or either he put a ring on it from the jump.

The song ended and he walked with me back to our table. Britney had finally showed up. She and Eboni were laughing about something. She stood to give me a hug. As she hugged Russell, she asked for a drink. Russell took out a hundred dollar bill and laid it on the table.

Russell looked at me and said, "We'll talk." I just nodded my head as he walked off.

Britney took up the money and stuck it in her wallet.

Eboni said, "No hussy, your giving me half of that money."

"Girl I need to use this on my light bill," Britney said.

"Well you have fifty to go towards it," Eboni said as she passed Britney fifty dollars in exchange for her half of the hundred dollar bill.

Britney pulled the hundred back out of her purse, snatched the fifty from Eboni, and tossed the hundred. "Heffa you need to get your own darn hustle," she said teasingly to Eboni. "

I have one remember? I'm your pimp. You see how fast I just made that fifty bucks don't you?" We all busted out laughing.

"You and Russell were out there showing y'all asses." Britney said as she took a sip of her strawberry daiquiri. "You two had Cue *and* Mercedes watching you."

I gave Britney a high five across the table. I had really started enjoying myself. Russell, along with a lot of other guys, was constantly at our table buying drinks for the three of us; well, putting money in Eboni and Britney's pockets. We loved all of the attention that we were getting. I was showing Cue that there were plenty of others just waiting to come in the back door, as soon as he exited the front. Although I was not interested in Russell, I talked to him just to piss Cue off. He hated Russell with a passion, this much I knew.

Russell had just left our table, to no doubt go and find someone he could take home with him tonight. He sure as hell knew it wasn't going to be me.

Eric comes over and kneels down beside me and says, "Cue told me to give this to you," and passed me a wad of money.

I took the money without even bothering to count it, and dropped it in my purse. I figured it was at least enough to cover the $500 I had dropped on these Hunfew shoes I was rocking. So that was a gain for me.

"And just to help you out a little, it may be in your best interest to keep Russell out of your face." The gopher said.

"Is that supposed to be an order?" I asked, looking directly at him because he was stooped right to my face level.

"You can take it anyway you want to, but I know you are really pissing my boy off over there," he said nodding his head in Cue's direction with a slight grin on his face.

"Well your boy can kiss my ass, because if anyone should be pissed, it should be me. Yea, I know he was at Tamisha's last night she couldn't wait to tell me."

Eric dropped his head and shook it, "I don't know anything about that baby girl."

"Sure you don't Eric; I didn't expect you to. I said, being sarcastic.

Eric just laughed and stood up to leave, but not before saying, "Keep that nigga out your face." He then looked at Britney and winked his eye as he walked off.

"Eric better quit fucking with me," Britney said. She thought Eric was the sexiest man alive. And although she threw herself out there and let him know that she wanted him, he hadn't bitten. He does flirt back with her, but has never tried to get up with her. I think he's afraid of Britney frankly. I don't think that he is use to a woman that is as bold as Britney.

Tamisha walked by Cue and looked very distraught as she seen Mercedes sitting in his lap all booed up. She looked even more stupid as she walked by me. I held my hands up in an "I don't know what to tell you position" and shook my head before I busted out laughing.

"I sure hope she doesn't think that Cue is feigning after her ass just because he screwed her. Hell, he probably done screwed three other random females this week. They're going to learn," I said, high fiving Britney.

"Well one thing I can say that you have in your favor, is that Cue does care about you. You're not just a fuck to him." Eboni was saying. "I can tell that Cue really cares more about you than these other hoes that be riding his dick."

"Aaaaw Eboni, thank you sweetie," I said, pressing my lips together as I squeezed her cheeks.

"Bitch stop," Eboni laughed as she smacked down my hands. "I am not saying that is reason enough to stay with his cheating ass. I'm just saying that I can tell he cares about you alot, that's all."

I tried to conceal the smile that was threatening to come across my face. I always knew that I meant more to Cue and that I was more to him than a booty call. For my girl to know it also made me feel giddy inside. All they knew was that I would bathe this man, cook three meals a day for this man, and submit in every way, just for him to be mine. I loved Cue just that much; he was the man that I could never get tired of. He was my Knight in Shining Armor.

Eric approached our table and said, "What'cha ladies doing after the doors close, because you know their closing early tonight right?"

"Yea, we just heard after we came in that they were," Eboni said like she was upset.

"It isn't like you paid to get in anyway," Eric said to Eboni.

"Whatever nigga," Eboni rolled her eyes at him.

"Well go over to the Motorcycle Club, we're having a sip. Tell them that I said to take care of you until I get there; I should be there around two." Eric said.

"Where are you going to be until then?" I asked, looking at my watch to see if I was correct on the time. Because this club was closing at eleven tonight, and this mug talking about he will be there around two a.m.

Eric looked at me and said, "Get out my bizness shawty," then looked over at Britney and asked, "You rolling wit me?"

Britney, who was still babysitting her drink, nearly choked. She wiped her lips, picked up her hand bag, stood up as she smoothed out the front of her white lined pants that were fitting her like a glove, looked at us out of the corner of her eyes, threw up her two forefingers into a peace sign and said, Deuces.

As she walked off with Eric's hand rested on her lower back, she looked back at us with a "How you like me now" smirk on her face.

"What in the *hell* just happened?" I asked Eboni, while still watching with my mouth hanging opened as Eric and Britney walked out the door.

"Girrrrrrrl, I don't know," Eboni said chuckling. "That bitch ain't asked no questions- just bounced on our asses."

"Ain't that some shit?" I said laughing. "Wait! That heifer has my car keys!" I said, as I jumped up to go after them.

As Eboni and I were passing the table where Cue and Mercedes were sitting, they were looking. So I gave an extra twitch to my hips. No matter how tight of a jean Mercedes may try to wear to accentuate her ass, she couldn't compete with what was natural for me. Yea, I had a small waist and my booty was very round. And her man loved it.

I got outside just as they were getting ready to exit the parking lot. I was frantically waving for him to stop, but he did not see me and went on down the street. I tried calling Britney's cell phone. It just went straight to voicemail.

"What in the hell am I going to do?" I asked no one in particular. Then I thought about the fact that Cue had my spare car key. I shared this thought with Eboni.

"*Well call his ass.* Better yet you need me to go back into the club and ask for it?" Eboni said pointing her stretched out arm towards the club. "Because you know I will."

"No fool," I said, laughing. "I will text him." I said, as I took out my phone to send Cue a text.

I sent the text and ten minutes later he still had not replied. He pisses me off when he does that.

I was just about mad enough to take Eboni up on her offer to go inside and ask for my spare key, when DJ came over and handed the key to me. He turned to head back into the club without as much as a "Here you go" I said, *"Thanks!"* He just nodded.

For some reason DJ was one of Cue's friends who did not care much for me. He had never said anything bad to me or neither had I ever heard that he had said anything about me. But he never said more than two words to me and none if possible. I did notice however; that he and Mercedes always seemed to get along very well whenever we were in the club. I do not know what it was about me that he disliked and I never bothered to ask.

"He is such an asshole," Eboni said as we watched as he was walking off. "But he is a fine one."

"I know, right?" I said while also watching him walk away.

As soon as I got into my car I received a text from Cue that said "Take your ass straight home and I will call you when I leave here to tell you where to meet me." I looked at Eboni and said, "Sorry boo, but you're going to have to pick Britney up from the Motorcycle Club tonight, because I have a date."

"I need some new friends I swear," Eboni said, shaking her head in disbelief.

"But you know I love you girl," I said, nudging her cheek.

Cue was stood behind me as we rode the packed elevator up to our floor. His hands felt so good holding onto my waist. I don't know how he managed to get away from Mercedes after leaving the club tonight nor did I care. He was here with me.

Chapter Three

(Tonya)

What was to be a night of relaxation and chilling with the girls, turned into a night of; banging on doors, tire slashing and tear shedding. This bullshit is the primary reason that I do not take any crap from any man. If my best friends Mercedes and Mahogany would listen to what I have to say sometimes instead of those weak ass minds of theirs, they would realize that I do know what I am talking about. Therefore, they would not be going through all the stress and crap that they always seem to with their so called men.

They say I am hard and that I need to lower my standards because I will never find the perfect man; he doesn't exist. I say you need to set your standards higher and if the perfect man never comes, just love yourself and buy more toys. I be damned if I am going to deal with whatever and whoever just for a hard dick. At least with the toys I don't have to worry about them going down before I've got mine, nor do I have to wait in line to get laid because he's so busy sharing his peter with ten other women. That is for the weak and confused. I am neither.

Don't get me wrong, yes, every now and then I do want to go out to eat or feel the body and stroke of a warm man. Please believe, I do have one or two I can call up for that. When I am done'… home they must go. I will never allow a man to take full control of my heart and soul and do whatever in the hell he wants to with it. Simply because I am just too stupid to realize that there are plenty of other fish in the sea. The heartache will only hurt for a while, but just like everything else, this too shall pass.

And to make matters worse, yes it gets worse. He is not devoted. Cue has a lot of the things that women want in a man. He's tall, dark and handsome; I can't take that from him. He's loaded with money; he has a nice home, nice cars, and swag out of this world. According to Mercedes he has a dick that will have you talking all kind of gibberish. So tell me does all of that overshadow the fact that he is a whore and has more women than Comet has rice? He doesn't have a legitimate job. He has had your ass run to the doctor to be treated more than twice with an STD. He's spending his money on other women also, so it's not all about you boo. And rumor has it, that his main jump off has a three year old son that supposedly belongs to him. So tell me why can't my well educated, sophisticated, smart and cute best friend see that the man she calls her   -Mr. Everything- is not all that she cracks him up to be? When I tell you out of four years of college, and three years of grad school, the extent of her vocabulary is; Cue this and Cue that. Someone from the English department owes her parents some money.

Mercedes, Mahogany and I had decided that after we left Cue's charity event, that we would just chill out tonight instead of going to The Hustlers Motorcycle Club, which is where everyone went after leaving Cue's other place Club Ego. Earlier today they had sponsored a huge cookout for charity, and it had been very nice. Tonight when the club doors opened all proceeds were going towards the charity as well. I thought this was mighty big of our local hustlers to do something with their dirty money for such a good cause.

Well it took a lot of arm twisting before Mercedes agreed, because any chance she got to see Cue she was all for it. With him being part owner of the club, seven times out of ten, he was more than likely to be in the building. Then there was that 3% chance that he may not grace us with his presence. And during that time he was usually laid up with some other woman spreading the wealth. He'd come home later or the next day telling lies, knowing she believes everything that comes out of his mouth saying that he had to make a run out of town to handle some business. Those nights that he did not show up at the club were the worst, because she would just be down all night, and of course that particular night she'd claim that the club was so boring to her that she's ready to leave. Well when we presented our idea of chilling to Mercedes, she looked at us as if we were Martians.

Then she had the nerve to utter, "Why, because Tonya's mad at Eric?" And then gave me a sideways look like, "Yeah bitch I thought you were so hard and didn't care about him." My response to her stupid ass was, "Mercedes you can kiss my natural big ass, don't get it twisted, I am not you. Eric would never have anything to do with my decision as to whether I go somewhere or not. He is just a boy toy for me. I can have another him in a minute. He knows that and so do you, so don't trip."

Later while we were at the charity benefit, Cue tells her that he's not going to even make his own benefit at The Motorcycle Club. Apparently, he just had some emergency business, and I quote, "Business" come up to take care of. So she back tracked to us like she had decided that she just didn't feel up to the club scene either, so it was fine with her if we just chilled, played cards and order up some food at her house. I just shook my head as I thought to myself - this girl here! Even if I was head over hills in love with Eric, which I am, but Mercedes will never know that. He certainly would not be the cause of me wanting to stay in because I am too weak to be in the same world, less on in the same room he's in with another woman. I don't care how much I cared or how much sleep I was losing over his trifling ass, he would never know it. I would not give him that satisfaction. Mercedes and Keisha may sit around and wait on Cue, but I will never do that. If I ask you once and you give me some bullshit excuse that is it. I will flip the script on your ass. So the next time you call me wanting to hook up, I do not care if the only plan that I have for that Saturday night is to count my toes to make sure there were ten. I will tell your ass that I already had plans, hit me up in advance next time. Eric definitely had me twisted with Mercedes. He had tried those same games that Cue plays with Mercedes, on me.

We were all sitting around the card table that Mercedes had placed in the center of her living room so we could watch television while playing cards. I was straight tripping over Idris Elba with his fine dark self. I was telling them how just his accent alone could get me in the bed. Lord forbids that he lowers those eyes and look at me - it would be a wrap. I was so lost in Idris touch, accent, and eyes; that Mercedes had to do a double snap at me to answer the house phone which was ringing right next to me.

"Answer the damn phone girl," she snapped.

"Bitch, don't be hollering at me," I snapped back as I reached over to pick up the phone.

"Hello?" Silence. I could hear someone breathing on the other end of the line so I said again, "Hello?" No one responded, so I placed the receiver back on the cradle.

"Who was it?" Mercedes asked while dunking a chicken wing into ranch dressing.

"I don't know," I replied, while setting up my cards. Wow, I had a good hand; they don't even know what's about to happen to them. "Whoever it was did not say anything. I could hear them breathing on the other end, but nothing." I looked up at Mercedes and shrugged my shoulder.

"Must have been a wrong number," said Mahogany.

But Mercedes with her naïve smirking ass said, "It was Cue. He just trying to see if I was really at home tonight because I told him I wasn't going to the club. He's a trip trying to check up on me." I wanted to tell her so badly that even if Cue was at the club, which he is not, checking up on you, or even thinking about you, while you are not in his presence would have been the last thing on his mind.

Cue right now is more than likely laid up with some groupie. Cue is not worrying about Mercedes whereabouts because he has already covered his tail by telling her that he was going out of town to handle business. And if by chance Cue was at the club; she had already told him that she would not be there. He would be in hog heaven talking to whomever, and doing whatever, without her being all up his butt crack.

Sad to say, but Cue has Mercedes in a place that no man should ever have a woman. Mercedes is beautiful, has a great job, and smart when it pertains to anything but a man. Cue knew that he had no need to worry about her drifting, because whatever swag he had laid on her, no other man could even break the surface.

I believe in love. I want to love a man in a way that I can't breathe without him. However, if I can't breathe without him... you best believe he's going to be suffocating without me too. A feeling like that has to be mutual or someone is in danger. And it saddens me to know that one day Cue could just walk away from her never to look back. This would be all it would take to drive her to someone's nut house. He had the audacity to tell her during one of their heated arguments when she threatened to leave him if he did not stop the infidelity; that he loved her, but he could walk away. What tha' hell?!!!

The phone rang again and this time Mercedes nearly knocked over the table trying to get to it. Then she lowered her voice all seductively as if she had not just run a Boston Marathon to answer it.

"Hello?" I don't know what the person on the other end of the phone was saying, but I watched as Mercedes eyes went from bedroom to bowling balls. Whatever was being delivered to her ears was not something she wanted to hear. She suddenly slammed the phone down and took off running down the hallway. By the time I had gotten myself untangled of the yarn from the scarf I had started to crochet, Mercedes was already headed back up the hall full throttle.

"What's going on?" I asked, as I was slipping on my boots. Mahogany not knowing anymore than I did, had already grabbed her coat and was fastening it up and turning off the television.

"I don't know," Mercedes said, as she moved around the room clapping her hands trying to set off the key detector for her car keys. If you did not know what she was doing you would have thought that all her lights weren't on in her head.

"The only thing they said," she was saying, as she continued to clap looking under cushions for her keys. "Was that Cue was at the Hyatt with a female. That since they had me on the phone, they knew that it wasn't me."

"Wait a darn minute," I said, as I stopped fastening my coat. "You are not telling me that you are fixing to go follow up on this bull crap? Mercedes you are so much..." that was all I got out before she turned on me with a vengeance.

"Tonya I don't need your, I am so perfect when it comes down to men lecture right now! I am not you. I love Cue, and what I am going to do if he is at the towers, I have no fucking idea. But I am going to see for myself. So either you can roll with me or you can stay here until I get back. Whatever you decide though, please keep your holier than thou advice to yourself!" And with this she was out the door.

Mahogany jokingly sneered at me as she walked by and said, "Well I guess she told you". I nudged the back of her head as we headed out into the garage to get into the car that Mercedes had already begun to back out. When I saw the tears of distress silently rolling down Mercedes cheeks, I could have pulled the trigger on Cue myself at that moment. No matter how much I try to tell her, I guess she has to get sick and tired of being sick and tired before she finally wakes up. So if going to a hotel and seeing your man there with another woman was what it was going to take, then so be it.

I remember when Mercedes and Cue started seeing each other, I had warned her of how he was. Cue has always had women, even before he became the so called, "It man," Yes, I knew of a few other chicks that were also his main dish before he and Mercedes hooked up. There was one in particular that he was really crazy about, even she did not keep him from having dessert in other places. Mercedes has been with Cue for a while. He takes care of her; and he's good to her. Her claim to fame is, "These chicks are stupid because there's no way I will be kicking it with a man and know that I can't be his #1. Well I'd rather be # 9 than riding up to a hotel and finding that my man is laying up in some room here with another woman. And that's exactly what his #1 just did. As soon as we pulled around into the rear parking lot, there sits Cue's White Lexus 400, all clean and shining. And what does this dumb ass say when Mahogany points out the car?

"How do we know it's his? When they made one Lexus 400', they made a thousand more."

"Well do they make them all with custom rims and tags that say Cue dog?" was my smart answer to her dumb question.

Her response was to throw the car into park with so much force, that she almost sent me into the windshield. "Damn Mercedes, I'm sorry but is Cue really worth all of this?" Mercedes was already exiting the car with Mahogany behind her. Mercedes and Mahogany was headed for the lobby door. I reached into the dashboard and popped the trunk to retrieve the iron bat that was a gift to us from Mercedes for protection we all carried it in the trunks of our cars. We knew from past experiences, that if Cue was caught in the room with another female, and things went anyway in which they did the last time he was caught in the act, we were going to need the bat to beat him off of Mercedes ass. It amazed me at how he was the one that got caught cheating, and she was the one that took the butt whipping from him. I sat on the hood of Cue's car and watched as the two of them entered the hotel. Then I thought, go with these fools because neither of them thinks straight and you may have to tell them when to run. I caught the elevator door just as it was about to shut. I had shielded the bat on my left side so that the receptionist would not see it as I walked past her.

Looking at Mercedes, I asked, "So how in the hell are we supposed to find Cue's ass in this big hotel?"

"Cue always gets the Jacuzzi Suites, and they only have ten of them here, so we will start there," she said.

I am thinking, is this girl serious? Does she really know him like that, and does her ass really know where all of the Jacuzzi Suites are located?

As if she was reading my mind she continued... "Each floor has two Jacuzzi Suites. They are on each end of the floor, we will work our way up to the fifth," she said, as she continued to work with her phone, as if it was giving her all the information that she would need.

When we get to the first floor, Mercedes directs us up the hall to the first suite. A white man came to the door with a cigar hanging out of his mouth and a beer belly from hell, looking like he had just rocked some ones world.

"Yeah?" He said, looking Mercedes and Mahogany up and down.

"Sorry wrong room," she moved over to the next door and continued on, looking for a familiar face. Mahogany was all on Mercedes's back like she wanted to be the first to be seen when Cue was found. I don't know what she was going to do because her scary behind wouldn't bust a grape in a fruit fight.

After about twenty minutes of knocking, excuse me's, and getting nowhere, we decided to go back to the car. Apparently, Mercedes and Mahogany had already discussed their next move because without a word, Mahogany pulled the switch blade from the dash, Mercedes took the bat from my hand, and the two of them started demolishing my dream car! As soon as Mercedes hit the windshield, the car alarm started going off, as she anticipated, hoping this would lure Cue outside. Boy was it loud.

Mahogany was slashing the tires with so much anger and screaming "mother fucker, bring your ass out!" I thought to myself, what was she so upset about? Mercedes may need to watch her ass. People started peeping out their windows; some even came out onto the balconies. I scanned the ones that had emerged, praying that I did not recognize any of the faces, or better yet, that any of them did not recognize me, because this was embarrassing. Here are three educated, sophisticated, well raised women- acting straight up ghetto!

The man with the beer belly hollered, "Gal, you better leave now I've called the cops".

Mercedes in returned screamed, "You can call whoever you want to, this is my damn car. I can do whatever I want to it!"

The car is in Mercedes name, just as a lot of things that Cue purchases because he has no legitimate way of showing that he can afford to pay for all the extravagant things that he has. I have told her over and over that she does not need to let him get her mixed up in his mess. If he ever gets busted, it could possibly take her down, and she has worked hard to get where she is.

Truth be told, Mercedes makes very good money, and she could easily justify her finances and spending. But why go through all of that when she did not have to? Cue purchased the Mercedes that she cruises in around town. He gave her the down payment for the condo that she is buying. He takes her on these extravagant vacations and get-a-ways and gives her practically anything else she ask for, except the pleasure of knowing that he is solely devoted to her. After we started hearing sirens and Mercedes realized that Cue was not going to emerge, we decided that it may be in our best interest if we left. This time, Mercedes jumped in the back seat and I drove because she could not see through the tears that were rolling down her face. I glanced at her through the rearview mirror as she sat back there silently crying like a baby. I again wondered for the thousandth time how had I managed to remain friends with her naïve ass for all these years. Because believe me, Cue is not the first guy she has been stupid in love with. I wanted to turn around and just shake some sense into that hollow head of hers so badly, that it was causing me to get a headache. But like my grandmother always said, you have to know when to scold them, and know when to just let it go. Sometimes, if you don't have anything nice to say, just don't say anything at all. So I chose not to say anything and just chill. Hell that is what I was supposed to be doing tonight anyway.

Chapter Four

(Britney)

"Eric, how do you feel about what we are doing?"

"What are you talking about Britney? I love what we are doing; hell I look forward to it." Eric laughed as he pulled me over to where I was now resting my head on his chest as we sat on the couch.

"I mean how can I say it other than to just say it? This may not make much sense to you, but I am just going to tell you my feelings on this whole thing." I said, with my head still lying on his chest and my arm around his torso. I loved being here.

"I am really feeling you a whole lot. I tried my hardest to not get too caught up in you, but you made it so hard for me not to. You tell me that you want us to have an open relationship, but yet you're here all the time doing and treating me exactly how I want to be treated. So how do you expect me to separate my feelings from what we are doing, honestly? It's as if the more I try to pull back, the more you do to make me want you even more. What do I need to do because I am really confused?"

Eric shifted his body so that he was in the corner of the couch and facing me. "Britney, you chill, that is what you do. It takes a lot for me to let a woman here." Eric said, demonstrating by pounding his chest where his heart was. "But you are here, not that I don't want you there, but for a woman to get under my skin... that shit is major. You just keep playing your role because we are in a good place, no worries."

I suppressed a smile and asked all giddy, "Really Eric?"

Eric pressed his lips together and shook his head smiling. "Girl you're crazy. Now let me be honest with you. I have always feigned for you. When I would see you, Eboni and Keisha out, I would be thinking; how am I going to approach her? She's so sure of herself. You looked like you weren't for any nonsense. You had and still have a banging body, a beautiful face and you just had fun when you were out. You never were the one to just sit around and hold up the wall. Yet you had such a seriousness about you, that I wasn't sure you would buy into what I was selling."

I felt all mushy and relieved. Although Eric and I have been kicking it for a minute, and he shows me that he cares a lot about me, I have a hard time feeling secure. He has stated from the beginning that he did not want anything but to enjoy one another's company. He had told me that he did not want to be tied down. Men are made from a different kind of dirt that is most certain. I think that God went to the very top of Mt. Vernon and dug really deep to the hardest part of the clay and created these mugs.

Eric's phone rang. He used the arm that wasn't cradling me to reach over to the table to answer it. He sat up so fast that my head plopped down on the pillow. He looked over at me and mouthed, "Sorry babe."

"Man you shitting me," he said jumping up from the couch and walking over towards the window. "Whose car was that nigga in? I sure hope it was one of his and not one of mine," he said, in a hushed tone as to shield the conversation from me. I heard him say, "Yea, I'm at home. Britney's with me - but give me a minute, I'll be there." He said as he was sliding into his shoes.

"Is everything okay bay?" I asked, standing up walking over to him. He put his arm around my shoulders and kissed me. "Yea baby, that stupid ass girl done fucked up Cue's car, and he wants me and DJ to come and bring him another car. Cue needs to leave that stupid ass girl alone."

I stood back and looked at him like, What did you just say? Eric laughed, and pulled me close to him, squeezing me as he rocked me from side to side.

"No- that is your girl," I said, "You know you and Mercedes are dawgs, remember?" I muffled into his chest because he had my face buried so deep in his embrace.

"Mercedes is nothing to me but my boys' girl," he said, as he released me and headed towards the bedroom to retrieve his car keys. I followed behind him and asked exactly what happened. He explained that Cue was at a hotel with some chick and Mercedes and her girls had come to the hotel.

"You're telling me this, really Eric? You know Keisha is my girl, and you're really telling me that the man she is kicking it with is laid up with another girl, and all the bullshit she goes through with him?" I asked, picking up my phone so that I could call my girl to see if we needed to ride out and handle some business.

"Whoa killer," he said, as he took my phone from my hand and pulled me to him. "You and I have already talked about this shit. Remember when you wanted to know something a while back that went down? You and I are an item. I talk to you because you are with me, and I like talking to you. I trust that whatever you and I discuss in our conversations stays between us. I know she's your girl, but you are my girl, and I do not need you repeating what I tell you- We," he said, using his two forefingers pointing from his chest to mine, "have a code of honor."

Call me a sensitive bitch, but my eyes watered up. Maybe I meant more to him than I thought. I know that he and Tonya sees each other. She is such a hot head just like Mercedes. Tonya doesn't think her shit stinks either. But she is the only one that he told me about when we started seeing one another. I have sense copped that there are a few others like myself through Facebook. The first night we hung out together I asked him was there anyone that he was seeing seriously. He said there wasn't. Although he did have a friend, that is all that they were. He claimed that that is how they label themselves when introducing one another. This alone told me that Tonya was the one that I needed to avoid showing my emotions towards him around when we were all in the same place.

"They, who was it?" I asked, looking up at him while still in his embrace.

"DJ said that it was Mercedes, Mahogany and Tonya." Eric said, tickled by the entire situation. "I have told that dumb ass about parking his cars that everyone knows at these damn hotels."

"Why is Cue at a hotel anyway, he has his own place?"

"Because you don't take random ass to your home baby girl," Eric said as he smirked at me and pulled me to him pecking my forehead.

If this man did not want me to get emotionally attached he sure was not doing a good job at making me feel like I was just random. Here I am at his apartment, as I always am when we get busy. So was this his way of letting me know that I was not just a random chick? Or was he just that bold that he did not give a damn about me not handling a breakup well and stalking his house?

"I'll be back shortly. Give me about an hour or so- ok?" He asked pulling his torso back looking at me.

"So you want me to stay here until you get back?" I asked.

"No Britney, I want you to go home. When I get back I will call you to come back over," Eric said, sarcastically as he walked towards the coffee table to pick up his car keys. He looked back at me and said, "I will see you when I get back," and winked at me.

I stood there dumbfounded and confused. Did he really just leave me alone in his place? He was really sending me very mixed signals. You don't just leave someone in your place alone unless you are really trusting and feeling something special for them. Shoot, I thought to myself. It had been almost two years before Cue even let Keisha start coming to his spot. It had taken another year before he gave her a key and let her stay alone at his place. I have gotten farther with Eric in five months. No key, but I am alone in his pad.

I picked up my cell phone to call Keisha. I changed my mind about calling her since I could not tell her what was going on. Although it killed me to know that at this very moment, her man is at a hotel with another woman, and I had enough details for her to go and catch him red handed and could not tell her. I sat on the couch and channel surfed until I ran upon TI & Tiny

Family Hustle. For some reason this show made me think about my girl Keisha even more. I grabbed my phone and called her this time. Although we weren't blood we were thicker than Eric and I. How can he tell me some bullshit like that and expect for me not to tell my girl?

Keisha's phone just rang. I hung up when her chipper voice came across her answering machine because this was nothing that I was going to drop on her on her machine. Hopefully, she would call me back soon or else Cue would have just gotten away with his cheating once again. There would be no need in me telling her if she could not prove it, because Cue was just smooth like that. This brought me back to my affair that I am now having with Eric. How many other women does he have out there? And how am I supposed to respond if I find out that there is more than Tonya? I have paid even more attention to the different groupies that are always on Eric since we have been kicking it. They are a dime a dozen. No one suspects anything about Eric and I, except my two girls, and they don't suspect - they know.

When Eric returned three hours later, I had dozed off on the couch and was awaken by his juicy lips softly touching mine.

I stretched and said, "Hey baby." I took his face in the palms of my hands and kissed him passionately. "Is everything alright with Cue?"

Eric pulled his lips away from mine and gave me a smirk and said, "Guess who was with my boy?" He could not contain the smile that spread across his beautiful face. I sat up and looked at him and said, "Nooo, you are kidding me, what the hell were they doing at a freaking hotel?"

"Apparently, Cue had told her that they were going to do something special tonight. So he went and got them a Jacuzzi suite and ordered up food and champagne." Eric was apparently having a field day with this as he went on to tell me about the events that had taken place tonight.

I thumped him on the cheek and said, "Stop, you're tripping. How is my girl, is she ok?"

"Yea babes, she's fine. I started to tell her to call you since you were here at the house waiting on your big daddy to get back," he leaned over and kissed me. "Keisha and Cue are a trip. Those girls messed my boy car up!" Eric said as he rolled over from me to where he was now relaxed with his back to the couch, slid down, channel surfing. He kept laughing as he was telling me about the car and how Cue was behaving. Eric was all but cutting cartwheels over Cue's mishap. Hell, he was almost ecstatic. These men although very close, had no remorse.

Eric's home phone rang at 10 a.m. We had been up practically all night watching movies, playing cards and handling grown folk business. I looked over at Eric to see if he was going to wake up and answer it; he was out cold turkey. So I just lay back down because I enjoyed being at his place, and I sure was not going to mess up my invites by answering his darn phone. To my surprise an answering service kicked on. I rose up to look over at the phone, and low and behold, there sat an answering machine. What in the world? I thought to myself, who has those anymore?

I sat anxiously waiting to hear which female was calling him and what she had to say. I silently prayed that the machine did not wake him. I should have known that with what I had put on him this morning, he was indeed in a coma.

"Hey Eric. This is Mercedes, give me a call. Cue told me that you were in his car last night and that you were upset because of what we did. You know that if I had known it was you, I would not have done that."

Mercedes voice had begun to break as if she would burst out in tears at any moment. "I am sorry, but I just go through so much with Cue. I know that is your boy. I understand the need of you to sometimes use his car, but understand where I am coming from. And please don't be mad at Tonya. She is my girl just as Cue is your boy. Just like you will break a back for Cue, my girls will slash a few tires for me." She sort of giggled as she said this. "Call me when you can."

"Oh- my- goodness," I thought as I flopped back down onto the pillow. So Cue has put his act of infidelity off on Eric, and Eric was with me all night. I swear these men are a mess. And who at this age goes and takes anger out on someone's car anyway? Yet they consider themselves so classy. Please!

We are twenty four years old, grow up already. And Mercedes who suppose to be so high sudity, she sure as hell doesn't act like it with the way she goes around writing checks that her ass surely can't cash. She is always up in someone's face about Cue, and they are always busting that ego of hers. Sit down somewhere because you're making a fool of yourself girlfriend.

She wants to look down her nose at us because she and her little friends have a fucking college degree. That use to be her argument all the time, "I am in college and I have too much going for myself than to be arguing with you people over irrelevant stuff." Yet, she was always the one bringing the irrelevant stuff to light. And her college educated ass is right back here working just like everyone else. I haven't seen anything that she has that we don't have or cannot get. Hell, I have an office job as well. I have my own place, two cars, very independent and all I have is my high school diploma. While a college education is a great thing to have, it doesn't shield you from being naive to all the bullshit that goes on around you. And frankly that is what Tonya and Mercedes needs is a class of Common Street Sense 101.

And what in the hell was Keisha's ass doing with Cue anyhow? I swear I did not understand Keisha or that relationship. The last time I spoke to her, which was just yesterday, she was claiming that she was really done with his ass this time. Although I knew that was not totally true. I guess when she is sick and tired, of being sick and tired; she will finally wash her hands of him and bounce.

True, I am seeing Eric. I know that he sees Tonya. However, I do not stop... drop... and roll... every time he calls. He has called me at times and I had absolutely nothing to do, but I acted as if I did. It will not always be on his time that I see him. If you start acting like your world revolves around them and you are available every time they call, then that is exactly how they are going to proceed. Eric and I have gone as long as two weeks without even talking to one another. It seemed that whenever I called him, he never answered. So... I returned the favor. We basically texted back and forth saying, "Sorry I missed your call." And giving excuses and miss you's.

Eric and I have been seeing one another for five months now. I can honestly say that we have never had an argument. Yes, he has agitated me and I am sure I have him, but it has not been anything that we have had to have words about. We have expressed our opinions about certain things and we jokingly resolved it. Yes, he knows my feelings about him not being available when I call or need him to be. He also knows that I will not make myself available to him every time he calls if he cannot do the same for me. We both are the type of people that need our own space, and do not like being suffocated. So we are good there. We may skip a day or two without talking -no harm done. Truth is, I like Eric and I like Eric's company. As long as he continues to treat me as he does, we have no problems.

Chapter Five

(Keisha)

I turned over, and the stream from the sunlight seeping through the mini blinds warmed my face. I attempted to open my eyes but the light was so bright. I had to shut them back and give them a minute to adjust to the brightness of the sun. It took me a second to realize where I was because it was so quiet. Then, my nostrils inhaled a faint smell of Drakkur. I could not stop the beam that came across my face, nor the chill, or goose bumps that took over my body. I knew I was in bed with the love of my life, Cue.

It had been a very long night, and I had slept hard. I rolled over and his back was to me. I slipped my arm under his arm so that my hand was rested on his chest that I loved so much. I pushed my naked body into him as close as I could as if I was trying to get deep into his soul. I whispered softly into his ear, "I love you Cue," and lightly kissed the side of his neck.

He responded with, "I know, I love you to babe," as he shifted his body around to face me. He put his arm around my waist and kissed me on the forehead and said again, "I love you too babe," while looking right past me with a faraway look in his eyes.

"What's on your mind?" I asked, tugging at his goatee, while trying to push myself up so that I could look directly into his dark eyes.

He looked at me as he gently stroked my cheek, kissed the bridge of my nose and said, "Nothing, just enjoying waking up with you." He pulled my head to his chest so that we were no longer looking at one another.

Lying on this chiseled chest was what I lived for. It bothered me that my baby was still upset about the events of last night. If he gave me the word... I would kick Mercedes' ass all over Greenville County. Last night had been a world wind of a night for the both of us, physically and mentally. After I busted him in the act with some unknown female, his girlfriend Mercedes almost did the same thing with me. Mercedes and her girlfriends had decided to go on a -Find Cue Mission- I guess, and ended up at our hotel room door.

Cue and I had just got out of the shower when I heard someone banging on the door. I went and looked out the peep hole but the range was limited so I moved to the corner of the curtain. The front part of the hotel room faced the interior of the hotel that overlooked the lobby. And there was Mercedes, Tonya and Mahogany. At first, I thought that maybe someone had tipped them off that we were in this room, but I seen as her girlfriend Mahogany moved across the hall and proceeded to start banging as well. I knew then that they knew Cue was here, but they had no idea what room he was in. I closed the curtain thinking, as upscale as this hotel is, why do they not have security at the elevators? People should have to show a key or something to get up to the floors, rather than anyone just walking in and going wherever the heck they pleased.

I went and stood in the arch of the door way and said, "Cue we have company."

He was bent over the sink brushing his teeth as he looked up with toothpaste dripping from his mouth. Knowing exactly who I was referring to he said, "You're shittin' me?"

"No boo, I am not kidding." Leaning against the door frame, I explained to him what was going on. How they were randomly knocking at all doors. So this told him as well, they had not found us.

He finished brushing his teeth and wiped the excess toothpaste from his mouth, placed his hands on my shoulder as he turned me towards the bedroom and said, "Let's go to bed".

We had just lain in the bed. I was adjusting myself onto the spot where I loved nestling on his chest, when we heard glass shattering, and a car alarm go off. Cue jumped up so fast that my head flopped back and awkwardly hit the pillow. I got myself together and followed him to the balcony door. Low and behold; there was Mercedes and Mahogany destroying his car! Cue was so mad that I had to keep jumping in front of him to keep him from going outside and beating the slop out of those girls.

"Keisha move!" Cue boomed, with fire in his eyes.

"Cue, no. I will not let you go out there and end up going to jail."

"Hell, she's the one that's going to jail. She is the one out there fucking up my shit, and messing with me!"

Cue, finally aggravated with me jumping in his way, lifted my 5'9 frame away from the door as if he had just lifted a piece of paper.

"Cue" I cried, as I tugged at his arm. He just shook me off and opened the door. I headed to the balcony and peeped from the curtain that covered the slide door. I thought just because he may be caught, she will not know who was with him. Not that I cared about her finding out about me, because I would love to flaunt it in her face that I was screwing her man. Yea, the girl that you thought was beneath you is the main girl that has your man's nose wide opened. But I loved Cue too much, and I certainly would not do anything that would hurt him. I definitely didn't want to take the chance that she found out about me, and demanded that it be me or her. While I knew Cue cared about me, I can't say I would be the one to come out on top.

Thank goodness that by the time he had gotten out the door they were pulling out of the lot. Cue proceeded to go down the stairs to examine his demolished Lexus. I saw as he hit the roof with his fist, lowered his head between his arms that were both placed on top of the car, as two patrol cars pulled up behind him.

Some white man approached them, and was telling the cops who were talking to Cue, that he had seen everything. He questioned Cue as to whether it had been his wife who had demolished his car? I heard Cue say, "Mind your own fucking business," as he pulled out his cell phone and started making a call. I do not know what Cue said to the cops, but after speaking to them for maybe fifteen minutes I watched as they got back into their patrol cars and left just as quickly as they had arrived. I stood on the balcony listening as Cue stood by the battered up car, talking to his homeboy D.J on the phone telling him what had happened. He asked him to pick up Eric and go by the crib and pick up another car to bring to him. D.J who owned his own wrecker service would haul away the Lexus when they got here.

When he walked back into the room I didn't know what to say or do. I just looked at him with my tear stained face and red eyes. He pulled me to him and I laid my head on his chest.

"Baby, I'm sorry about all of that." Cue said as he stroked the back of my head.

"It's ok. So what are you going to do? Is Eric coming?" I asked, softly.

"Yea, he's going to bring me another car. He and D.J are picking up the Lex when they get here.

Cue released me and headed over to the table where the bottle of Hennessey was and poured him a shot. He came and sat on the corner of the bed. I don't know if he was more worried about her finding his car here, or upset about what she had done to his car. I kneeled behind him on the bed and rested my chin on his broad shoulder and started massaging his back.

"Baby I'm so sorry," I said softly. He turned his head a little towards me, cupped the back of my head with his hand pulling it towards him, and kissed the side of my head. He held his lips there for a minute.

"I love you baby," he said.

I really believed he did in Cues kind of way.

After about fifteen minutes there was a knock on the door. Since Cue was in the bathroom I went and looked out the curtain to see if Mercedes or one of her girl's cars were in the parking lot before I opened the door. What if those heifers had been bold enough to back track? I would be outnumbered, it was three of them and my girls weren't with me. Surely Cue wouldn't allow them lynch me I hoped. I saw Eric out there walking around the Lex. So that meant that D.J was at the door. I was thinking why Eric couldn't bring his nosey tail up to get the key? He was walking around observing the demolished car, shaking his head, laughing and taking pictures. I liked Eric but hated D.J. Simply because he hated me. Reluctantly, I opened the door for D.J hating that Cue was not in the room to break the ice of what I knew would be an awkward moment.

"What's up Keish?" D.J said to me as he stepped into the suite. I was shocked as hell; one- that he spoke at all, two- because he called me "Keish" like we were buddies.

"Nothing much, just trying to get my baby's pressure down," I said, as I closed the door and walked to the bathroom door to let Cue know D.J was here.

D.J laughed and said, "Good luck with that one." Cue came out the bathroom and dapped him up before they headed out the door. After Eric and D.J left Cue came back into the room as if nothing had happened and we had the time of our lives together.

I knew when I got involved with Cue that this was going to be just what it was; chill whenever we could and just make the best of it. I knew that he was fond of his lady, and I was not in it to take him from Mercedes. After a while of hanging out together, my holding back sex from him, playing my role and playing it so well that Cue had started falling so hard for me that he was beginning to give me all of the time he could. I stood firm in telling him that I may have to deal with Mercedes, but I do not, and will not deal with the other side bitches. Cue had gotten so into me that even when we were out in the clubs he acted like I was his main chick. I would go into the club and stay in my lane, meaning I knew that I could not be all on him, or all up in his face, because this was our down low thing and we didn't need people running back telling Mercedes. Cue had got to the point as to where he was bold and he wanted every man in the club to know that he was hitting this. So my attitude was, hey, I had nothing to lose. If he wanted to put his relationship on the line it sure as hell didn't bother me. It is what it is.

The thirsty groupies eventually realized- that it was not only Mercedes they had to respect. Some women will argue that not only do they have to be number one, but that they also have to be the only one. Well my motto is this, "If I get all the good the ride has to offer, let the main chick deal with the breakdowns." Yes, I do love Cue. I do wish that I could wake up to him every morning and know that he is coming home to me every night. But that is also what makes our coming together so special. The not seeing him whenever I wanted- not sleeping with him whenever I wanted- and- not knowing when he was going to call me at the spur of the moment wanting to get together. It actually excited me and gave me some kind of freaky rush when the three of us would be in the same club and it being his and my secret from her. I knew Cue had started to care about me more than he wanted to. I knew that no matter what happened... I had made an impact and would not be easily forgotten. He was taking care of me financially, physically and emotionally. I was good. And although I couldn't be with him as often as I wanted, when we did hook up, it was always worth the wait.

I looked at my boo sitting there as if he had the whole world resting on his shoulders. As much as I wanted to believe that it was the car that he was so upset about, I knew that he was also worried about eventually having to face Mercedes. I know that Cue loves her; although, I don't think it's the same passionate love that we share. They have a history together.

From our conversations over the past two years, I have realized more and more that "Ms. Thing," doesn't have it the way that she thinks she does. Cue at first never discussed his and her relationship or doings with me; although, I was very interested in his other life. He said what she and I do have nothing to do with what you and I do. When I am with you as long as it's all about you, then you should not concern yourself about her and I. So with that being said, I never again questioned him about the two of them.

After a while, he voluntarily started telling me things. He mostly confided in me when he was upset with her about something. I found out that she was not as fun as I am. He said that she is always so serious and whenever he tries to play with her the way he does me, she's always hollering, "Stop Cue, you are so childish." She didn't find him as humorous as I do, and Cue is a very funny person. I like to play cards and watch any kind of sport; she wanted nothing to do with either of the two.

Cue summed up the difference and what he likes about me, versus her. He likes the fact that I don't mind going out on the limb to get my fruit, where she'd rather go to the produce stand. To wrap it up in one word she's "BORING." I asked well why do you stay with her? You are not married, you have no kids together, and you have your own money. His answers were because he had so much invested in her, and he had no legitimate way of showing that he could afford to purchase some of the things he had. However, in the last year or so, he had put several things in my name as well. In my heart I knew it was more than investments that he was still with her.

Cue and I have been together for the past four years and we've had our ups and downs, but the good always has outweighed the bad. Mercedes during this time did not even know that I knew or associated with Cue. After two years of dating I became pregnant with both of our first and only child. To this day very few people know that Cue is the father of my child, besides our immediate family and closest friends. However, when I became pregnant someone leaked it to Mercedes that I was pregnant, and that they had heard that it was supposed to be Cue's.

I've known Mercedes since junior high school. I remember over hearing her and her boogie friends talking about him during computer lab every day. Mercedes and I had gone all the way through junior and senior high school together, but we were never more than associates.

We came from different sides of the tracks. Mercedes and I were each other's competition per say while in high school. She came from the side of the track that they called, "The cream of the crop." I came from the side that was called, "The bottom of the slum." She came from educated and well to do parents. My mom still stayed with my grandmother, never had a job, and my father was somewhere up north, never to be heard from again. While Mercedes did not have to do anything but go to school and get good grades and her parents saw to it that she had everything else that she wanted - from clothes to cars. I had to go to school, get good grades, and work a job because I wanted out of the hood. I worked after school in order to save up the money for the car I bought, as well as buy my own clothes. Other than the advantage of coming from an educated family, Mercedes and I were toe to toe on everything else.

The only thing that she had that I did not, was the fact that I worked for mine. We were both popular, cute and had good grades. I never said anything out of the way about her, but she forever kept my name coming from her mouth. She did not like me because I was just as pretty as she was. She made sure that I was not in her crowd of friends, and that was fine by me, because I had my own friends. Her friends pretty much came from the same background as she did or at least pretended they had it going on to keep up with her. My friends came from the same background as me, and none of them even pretended to have any kind of class. I was the only one in the group that always wanted to be, and have more. That is why I went to work every day after school, because moms and pops were not going to see to it that I was one of the best dressed and fliest girls at the school. Don't get me wrong, I loved my crew of friends because they were ride or die and not easily intimidated. As a matter of fact, they took up for me more than I took up for myself, and just like me they did not care for Mercedes or her bourgie friends.

Even though I could pretty much do as I pleased I still had morals from my grandmother, so I did not hang out all-night with guys from the neighborhood as my friends did. This gained me respect from the guys in our neighborhood. Don't get me wrong, I loved my neighborhood, and I liked hanging out in the park with everyone and tripping. However, they knew I was different. As a matter of fact one of our little nickel and dime hustlers told me one day, that I did not belong in this neighborhood. He said you are only here by circumstance; this is not your final destination. My reply was, "Let the church say amen".

Anyway, when Mercedes asked Cue about me of course Cue denied that he even knew me, less on could have gotten me pregnant. This was enough to put her mind at ease. However, it still prompted stares, and glares from her and her friends whenever our paths would cross. One day I was at the mall sitting in the food court eating, it was still early so the mall wasn't packed yet. Mercedes walked by and glanced over at me, she did not speak and neither did I. I watched as she rounded the corner, I guess she must have gotten a gust of confidence, because not fifteen seconds later she came back around the corner and headed right in my direction.

Once she approached the table where I was sitting she asked if she could talk to me for a second. My stomach started to quiver, not because I was scared of her because I would dust the floor with her ass, but I knew it was something concerning Cue and I. I did not know what it was or how I should handle the situation. I wiped my mouth with the napkin and pointed to the seat in front of me. My mouth was still full with the stir fry so I couldn't speak, well chose not to at the time anyway.

She sat down with her hands rested in her lap as she leaned back in her chair and asked, "Are you having an affair with Cue?" She did not take her eyes away from mine as if she needed to see my every reaction.

I pretended to be trying to swallow my food buying time for an answer. I lifted up my forefinger signaling to give me a minute. How do I answer this? I thought to myself. Apparently, this chick knows something; but she can't have any concrete information, because if she did she would not be asking me, she would probably be trying to attack me. Of course if she ever did find out for sure that Cue and I was indeed involved, she would not be getting that confirmation from me, and she certainly was not about to get it now either. If I wanted to be an asshole and tell her, where would that leave me? Cue-less? Hell nah, that was not about to happen.

"Mercedes" I said, after swallowing the food that was in my mouth. "Cue and I are no more than friends; I promise you that is it. That's where it began and that's where it ends.

"Well how come your number has popped up in his phone several times, why are you calling him?"

I did not know if she had seen my number pop up on his screen before or not, but I am playing the, *"I don't know what you are talking about game."*

"Cue and I are friends and I have called Cue several times for friends wanting stuff from him, you know what I am referring to. There is nothing going on with Cue and me. Have you even asked him anything about your suspicions?"

"She replied, "I have asked him.""

"And did he not tell you why I call him?"

With as much attitude that she could muster she said, "He said, hell no he doesn't fuck with you, that you have been with most of his crew, and that you call him about Eric."

If she was looking for any reaction from my face I am sure she got it, including the smoke that was coming from my ears. For him to tell her that he does not deal with me is one thing, but for him to try to make me seem like a hoochie that sleeps around with any and everyone was absurd. Wait until I see this nigga!

I refocused on Mercedes, whom my eyes had never left but my mind had. "Well if that's what he said which is not true, because I am not a groupie and I can count on my one hand," I said, holding my hand up for emphasis, "How many men I have ever been with sexually and still have fingers left over. So if that was his only way of convincing you that he and I have nothing going on, he is not that intelligent. And if he has already told you that there was nothing, why are you here asking me? Do you trust what I say more than your man?"

"Yes I trust him," she said, "Its women like you that I don't trust. You are always after something that you can't have."

By this time any chance we had of talking was gone down the drain. Cue better be glad that I kept my composure and did not let her know, not only do I have your man, I have your man's first born as well.

I stood up and gathered my purse and said, "You can't blame me for your man's infidelity, furthermore, you are not his wife anyway so if I was fucking him you have no bragging rights boo! And stop making yourself look so damn insecure by always running up in female's faces about Cue." And with that I gathered my bags full of merchandise that her man's money had paid for, and walked off leaving her with her jaws on the ground. This was not high school anymore and my world sure did not revolve around her.

I giggled to myself thinking back to those days which made Cue ask what I was laughing about. I turned towards him and squeezed him really tight and said, nothing just thinking about something our crazy son did yesterday which led us to a subject we loved talking about, and that was our son. Cue loved Quincy just as much as I did, and no matter what, we would always have that special bond because we were linked to the one person we both loved more than life itself, there was nothing Mercedes could do to ever change that.

There was once a time that I worried about Cue leaving me if Mercedes ever found out about us. Now I know that he will always be a part of my life because of our son. Although I did not get pregnant on purpose, being a mother has made a great difference in my life. I have strived to be the best mother possible and even decided to enroll into cosmetology school.

Just to think that when I first found out I was expecting I was beyond devastated. I had even thought about getting rid of it. For one thing I was in no position to be bringing a child into this world. I had broken up with the man I was pregnant by a month earlier, and had not seen him, nor talked to him since the breakup. Not to mention, that he was in a relationship with a woman that he took extreme measures to protect from all of his infidelity. So I could only see him being pissed the fuck off at me. Shoot, I was pissed off at myself.

I remember it like yesterday when Cue was told that I was pregnant. I had been trying to convince my girlfriends, Toya, Britney and Ayanna why it would be in my best interest to terminate the pregnancy. I was at my girl Ayanna's house lying across the couch watching television, unaware that Ayanna had called Cue to come over. I heard loud music out front but thought nothing of it because this apartment complex always had people ride through bumping their music, trying to show off their systems. There was a knock at the door. I lazily rose from my comfortable position on the couch and went to the door and opened it, keeping my eye on the television screen because Melanie was just about to find out that Janay was pregnant by Derwin.

"What's up?" A deep sexy voice made me turn my attention back towards the door. My mouth dropped open when I looked at Cue's sexy chocolate ass standing there. I recovered quickly and said, "Hey Cue, what's going on?" He was looking down at me because although I was every bit of 5'9, I was short compared to his 6'5 frame. I could not read the look on his face. One part said he wanted to hold me, another said he wanted to choke me.

"Where's Ayanna?" He asked as he followed me as I headed back to my position on the couch.

"Hey boo," Ayanna said, as she entered the room and went and gave Cue a kiss on the cheek and a hug. Cue followed behind her and as he passed me, he slapped my inflated behind that he loved so much. I just looked at him like, Nigga stop; although I was flattered.

Ayanna's boyfriend Drake and Cue were buddies, and Cue and Ayanna had become really close also. I was still wondering, Why is he here, what in the hell is going on? Because although they called each other brother and sister, and Cue had been to her house lots of times, it was always pre-planned when we were all getting together. He had never just popped up or came by unless something was planned, such as a cookout or card game.

Cue asked Ayanna what was up, and why did she need him to get here before four? He was unaware that he had just answered the questions that were in my thoughts. I sat up on the couch, and pleaded with my eyes, for Ayanna to please not say anything.

She raised her eyebrows at me and tilted her head as to say, "Well you better tell him," which prompted Cue to glance back at me and ask, "Watsup?" while starring at me.

I was livid at Ayanna, she had no right. She knew how adamant I was about this. I had an appointment today at five to terminate this pregnancy; so therefore, she called Cue to intervene because she didn't believe in abortions. Well neither did I, but I would rather do away with it than have it going through life; penniless, homeless, and Cue-less. I know that I would bust my behind to take care of the baby if I did have it, but as of now I had so much going on and so much that I wanted to achieve, and on top of that I want to be a family when I have kids, and this man will never be with me in that way.

"Nothing Cue, Ayanna is tripping about something that doesn't concern her," I said, with my eyes watering.

"She's pregnant," was Ayanna's blunt retaliation. Then she folded her arms and shifted her weight to the left side and just looked at me like, "Now what?"

I lowered my head into my hands covering my face from the shame I was feeling. Ayanna had no right to do this. Who died and made her the Judge, Lawyer and Prosecutor! All of the air had been sucked out of the room and I suddenly couldn't breathe. I felt someone trying to remove my hands from my face, but I trusted my hand and followed my hand, aware of how foolish I must look. I felt my entire body being lifted from the couch, but I still kept my hands awkwardly over my face. I was moving but did not dare look to see where I was going. I felt one of the strong arms leave me for a brief second to open a door, and then I was placed on what I could feel was a bed. I felt the bed go down as the person who had kidnapped me sat down beside me.

"What's up Keisha? Talk to me babe. "Cues voice was soft and soothing.

I just sat there and continued to cry behind my shielded face. How could I have been so stupid and gotten pregnant?

"Keisha look at me," he said, as he attempted to move my hand again, this time I allowed it. I scooted back to the head board and pulled my knees to my chest and wrapped both arms around them to connect my hands. I placed my chin on my knees.

He was looking so darn good sitting there. I wanted to bounce over on him. He was wearing a pair of charcoal grey Nike sweats and a white t-shirt. Of course he was blinged out in a simple white gold rope necklace and matching bracelet. He was smelled of Drakkur and looking like a million bucks in just that plain ensemble.

"When did you find out?" he asked, with his eyes lowered and his voice in a tone to soothe me as if to say, it's ok. All the while, he was looking at me as he rubbed his hand across the back of his neck.

"Two weeks ago," I said softly.

"So why hadn't you told me?" He was speaking so calmly, and those bedroom eyes were making me want him even more.

"Cue, I wasn't planning on ever having to tell you," I said, just as calmly.

"So you were going to just have my baby and not even let me know?"

"I wasn't planning to have it."

His back stiffened as he looked at me for a moment, before relaxing again. Then he said something that I did not expect.

"So you were going to just get rid of my baby just like that? I thought you loved me so damn much?" He looked truly hurt but this is Cue, so I better not read too much into this.

"Cue you have a lady. You and I are not even together anymore, and plus you know my situation. I was really looking out for you, because you and I have joked about this forever. I know you don't want any kids right now and especially not with me. I don't want to cause any problems for you and her because I knew the deal."

He looked at me like he was thinking, is she really serious?

"I tell you what," he said, as he leaned over and placed his hand on my stomach.

"Let me worry about Mercedes and you just worry about taking care of yourself and delivering me a healthy baby.

Mercedes is my problem not yours. And whether you and I are together or not, you do not have to worry about this here," he said, lightly massaging my stomach with his fingers. "He or she is going to be ok. I gotcha."

I burst into tears as I leaned up and threw my arms around his neck, sobbing into his shoulder. He just caressed my back and the back of my head as he repeated, "Baby I gotcha." Cue was accepting, and I was very happy to be carrying his child.

We got back together again and things were great, until my fifth month. His girlfriend Mercedes started nagging him about the rumors again. He called me and gave me a heads up and I allowed him to bring her by to prove a point.

I just sat there and let him tell me in front of his girlfriend, that he had nigga's that would fuck me up for a crack rock, if I did not quit telling lies that he and I was sleeping together. Which we were, but what right did I have to defend myself when I knew the situation when I got involved with him? Truth is... I love this man more than she ever would, and I would not dare put him on blast and risk losing him.

That situation although planned, ended badly. After that incident I did not see Cue but once more before I had the baby. I was so mad at him that I would not even take his phone calls. It wasn't until two weeks before I delivered, that he just stopped by the house to check on me. We had a long talk and after going through the past six months of pregnancy alone, I was more sure of what I wanted for me and the baby, so I laid it all on the line for him.

I told him that all of this inconsistency was not going to happen. I said, that I don't care what he told Mercedes, I don't even care if he told her he had a child or not, but he would take care of this baby whether he chose to be in his life or not. And if he chose to be a part of his life, then that is where he will need to stay, it would not be any in and out. Cue looked at me like WTF? But he assured me that he had planned on always being a part of this child's life. He did not know yet what he was going to tell Mercedes, but for me not worry about him being a dead beat father. To this day, he has been a great father, although he still has not told Mercedes that Quincy is his child.

Chapter Six

(Mercedes)

It had been two days since I had spoken to Cue. Yes, I did talk to him the following day after spotting his car at the "Hyatt" but of course he is the type of man that if you do not actually catch him with his dick in his hand, then he's gotten away with it. After I went off on him about the car being at the hotel; he switched the shit up on me and made me look like the villain. He said that he had gone to ATL to do a pick up, and his boy Eric had his ride. Of course by me not being able to prove that he was lying, he is now mad as hell at me for destroying his Lexus! So what in the hell can I use as a defense? He told me that I was childish, and that I need to act like the professional that I am, instead of a hood rat. He went on to say that he needs some space. I cried, as I begged for him not to leave me. I told him that I would pay for the damages as if that was what he cared about, which was not. Paying for a broken windshield and new tires were like picking a penny up from the floor for him.

I may have been wrong for acting out the way in which I did, everything in me tells me that Cue was at that hotel with a female. After going onto Keisha's face book page, although I cannot say for sure that she was in an around- about- way throwing a stone at me, I am pretty sure, that he was with her trifling ass. The very next day she had posted, "This bitch needs to wake up and see her man for what he really is; a player that plays the game very well, and is very convincing." This tacky ass hoe going to make me go postal on her ass.

I knew Cue was foul and he messed around with other women, but I never could prove it, other than the two times when we first started dating, and he sent my ass running to the doctor for treatments. After the second doctor visit I was done with him and I did not answer his calls, reply to his text or anything for two whole weeks. Two weeks may seem like a short period but when you're use to talking to someone daily even when you are mad, then two weeks is an eternity. So after this, he had promised to be faithful to me, things were great for a while.

Then the rumors started. Some of the rumors actually came from the other females who were saying that they were having an affair with Cue.

Of course me not having any concrete evidence and he being Cue, he always managed to get out of it.

I was debating on whether or not to try calling him again, finally I decided not to. I had called him numerous times over the past two days to no availability. He was really mad at me and I felt so stupid.

I had told myself to not call again, tonight is Friday, and this is the night his club is jumping. I planned to get myself looking hot, and go in the club knowing that I am the bomb. I was going to flirt with all of the guys that had been secretly trying to get with me for years. I was going to show him that I was not sweating him, if he wants to act like he doesn't care, so could I. However, I knew that when he sees me in the club talking to another dude he would not be able ignore me.

I gathered my things together; showered, then headed to the mall. I bought a hot, sexy, silver sequenced fitted mini dress that I would pair with my silver red bottoms. I knew in this dress that Cue's eyes were going to be solely on me. Cue loved to flaunt my high yellow ass off any chance he got, so of course he would not have me in the club looking as hot as I was going to be looking tonight and he is not all on my ass.

When I returned home I shaved my legs, arms, and even decorated my coochie, because if things went according to plan I would be in the strong arms of Cue tonight. After I finished my ritual, I lotioned my body down with my, "Victoria Secret Love Spell" and then lay across my bed to relax my pores.

As I lay there, I thought about Cue and my relationship. I know that it's hard for him, because there are always some gold digging groupie trying to get with him. I knew that Cue loved me and I was going to fight for my man, so if it took me talking to other guys to get his attention, then that's just what I was going to have to do. I will not just walk away and let these bitches destroy what we have. I strongly believe if it's making you lose sleep, then it is worth fighting for.

I would never admit this to any of my friends, but the mere thought of not being in Cue's life, destroys me. I love being his lady. I know that I may not be his only one; however I know that I am his number one. When I go places, people know who I am, and they love to hate on me for it. I can pretty much tell all the women that be on my mans jock when I go to the club, cause they be the hoes that watch my every move or always running up saying, "Hey Cue and going for a hug. I be wanting to say "Bitch, back up!" Instead, I just smile, chill and act as if it doesn't bother me. Never show insecurity, never let them see you sweat.

My friend Tonya is certainly anti-Cue, and she thinks I am the stupidest thing to ever walk the earth when it comes to men. She doesn't realize that while I have seen other guys, Cue is really the first person that I have been this serious with, and for this long. When Cue and I first started dating I was recovering from a bad breakup with Darrell, which whom I had been dating since ninth grade. I met Cue during the summer before I was to become a senior in high school, and he was 21 years old. I had never before dated anyone more than a few months older than my seventeen years, so therefore Cue was like a grown man to me.

I was only seventeen, so the guys I had dated had been immature seventeen year olds also, or whatever age I was when I dated them. So here was this fine, chocolate, specimen who had his own car, own apartment, and money. He showered me with expensive gifts and spoiled me rotten. For a seventeen year old to have a man buying you anything was a plus.

For my eighteenth birthday he invited me to his apartment, which I had to sneak off to, and tell my parents I was doing something with one of my girlfriends. He had dinner on the table, candle lights and soft slow jamz playing somewhere in the back ground of the dimly lit room. Now I don't have to tell you for a young girl, my mind was gone after the first visit.

After we were done eating; we both sat on the couch to watch a movie, and he had his arms placed around me, allowing my head to rest on his chest. He smelled of my favorite fragrance on him, "Drakkur" and the smell drove me nuts.

We talked about all sorts of things. Me not wanting to show my immaturity, thought deeply before I would answer anything. When his hands moved from my back to the gape of my panties, and his fingers lingered there, I immediately felt moisture. And when he lifted my head by the chin and lightly stroked my lips with his, I shivered all over.

What made me stop all these great things that he was making me feel, I have no idea. The thing that impressed me and turned me on the most was when I told him, "I can't right now, not that I don't want you, but I need more time." He looked at me and said, "Well if time is all you need I can give you that. We have plenty of time for me to make love to you, because I am not going anywhere, and I am not letting you get away from me, so time you'll get."

The time was only a week later, because the very next time I was at his house, I was on him like a wild woman. I had fantasized about him all week and one day after I was leaving school, I called him and asked if I could come and see him before I had to be home. He said that he was on the Westside, but give him about thirty minutes and he'd be there. Concerned, he asked, was everything ok? I assured him that everything was fine, I just wanted to see to him for a minute because as I had told him earlier in the week, my mother was making me go with her to Charlotte this weekend to visit my aunt, and I hadn't saw him since last week and I missed him that was all.

He said, "That's what's up, I like that, see you in thirty."

I had to be home by five, it would take me twenty minutes to get to his spot, so that was only giving me forty minutes to spend with him before I would have to head home. I just wanted to look into his dark eyes, and prayed that he blesses me with a passionate kiss before I leave, so I would have something to reminisce about while we were at my aunt's house this weekend.

When I pulled into his yard, I parked beside the black BMW he had at the time, which was a very nice car, especially for a twenty one year old black male. I looked into the mirror that was in my visor to make sure I was on point, and then I exited the car and walked to his door. I knocked, and waited. He came to the door in some red and black Jordan shorts, a fresh white muscle shirt and he only had clean white ankle socks on his feet. He looked at me and gave me a smile showing straight pearly white teeth; his smile was contagious, his smile was seductive, so seductive that I stepped right up to him and put my arms around his neck and kissed him so passionately that his jimmy immediately stood at attention. He pushed the door shut with his foot because his hands were all over my behind. We didn't talk, utter, or mutter the only thing we did was moan, groan and cry out in pleasure as we made passionate love right there in his living room.

Although this had not been my intentions I had no regrets. Cue was all that and a bag of chips. He made love to me in a way that I never knew existed. He was sweet, passionate and strong. He looked me in the eyes and asked, was I ok, when he heard me wince. He asked me did I need him to stop.

"No, I'm fine I said, do you baby."

As his lips stroked my breast it seemed that he went deeper, something I didn't know was possible. I must have felt as if I was scooting, because he stopped everything and looked down at me with those sexy eyes and asked, "Where are you going?" with a sly grin on his face. "If you need me to stop I will" he said, as he tenderly sucked on my neck.

I was breathless, as I said, "No please don't stop, I am loving it."

He lifted his head so that he could look me in the eyes, "If I am hurting you let me know, I'll pull back."

I tried to glare at him in an attempt to save face from the fool I had been acting. This man was bigger than anybody I had ever been with, and he was more mature with his love making skills.

"Baby I can handle you," I said, trying to play the big girl, giving him a sexy smirk. "Like I said," I whispered trying to be grown as I pulled his face to me so I could kiss him, "Do you, I am good."

With this being said he took both of my legs in the fold of each arm, pulled them up to his shoulder and had me hollering like a damn fool! He did not ask me again if he should stop, he did not pull back, as a matter of fact he sped up his rhythm. However, he did continue to look me dead, smack in my face, but my eyes were shut so tight, I did not return the eye contact that I loved. When he had reached his peaked he flipped over to his back in one swift motion, and all I knew is that I was now on top.

I had never been in this position before; I did not know what to do. I just started rolling with him, he pushed my torso up so that I was sitting firmly on him and put his hands on my hips as he moved me. I followed his lead. I liked this, I was feeling something I had never felt before, and I took control. I felt like a cowboy riding into the sunset. Before I knew it, this sensation came over me; I was having a fucking orgasm! I had never experienced this with the other two guys I had been with sexually. My inexperienced ass started to cry, I was feeling so good.

Cue asked, "Baby what is wrong?"

"Nothing is wrong," I said, "Everything's right. I love you Cue."

What in the hell was I thinking? Although it was true, you don't say something like that to a mature man the first time you sleep with him. He pulled me to him, kissed me, and said "I love you to baby girl."

After that brief 40 minute session everything was gravy for us. I was still home under my parent's strict supervision and my friends were pretty much in the same boat as I was, so we were not allowed to go to the clubs nor the fast life circle, which Cue lived. Me being so sheltered, I was naïve to the fact that it was not just me that he was sleeping with. He was having his cake and eating it to. He had this cute eighteen year old, whom he adored and spent a few hours with a week. My schedule gave him all the time in the world, because the only time I could see him during the week was between 3:50, which was the time I would get to his house after I left school, and 4:40, which was the time I'd have to leave his house in order to make it home in time to beat my parent's there.

Yes, he would call me sometimes at night and give me thirty minutes, which was as long as I was allowed on the phone during the week (per my strict parents) and before 9 p.m. on Saturdays. I would go to his pad when I was supposed to be with friends, and chill with him until 8:00 p.m. then head home. When we really wanted some real time together, of course I would scheme up a lie. One night I even stayed overnight at his house after telling my mom that I would be with my friend Christy, who's mom verified, because she thought this was true. Christy later told her that I would not be coming. Cue and I was great, he had no drama from me, because as far as I was concerned we had the perfect relationship. And he was happy with the fact that I was under close supervision, so he could still get out and do his thing, as I would head home before the sun was even set.

When I turned twenty one and was in college and finally free from my overbearing mother, I hit the club scene only to find that my Knight had groupies. It wasn't until he had sent my ass running to the health department a few times, that I realized that my knight was nothing more than a horny dog in heat. And to think that all of this time he had my naïve ass believing him when he said, "If you don't complete all of your antibiotics for STD's even after it's been cured, it will return," and indeed had with him six months later. What my mom had meant for my good had backfired. Cue had a sheltered, naïve fool in love with him and he knew it.

I started having women corner me in the bathrooms demanding to know our relationship. And others that knew from seeing me out with Cue at his friend's cookouts, and gatherings that I was his main squeeze. When I was on the scene I was cutting off their hustle because it was all about me, so I received a lot of wicked stares. I even had one girl come up to me and say, if you are suppose to be his lady, maybe you should do a better job of keeping him out of my bed. I would be at Cue's house and girls would call him constantly. He always had an excuse of some kind. I have heard that he has put girls in apartments, bought cars, and paid their bills, but nothing could ever be confirmed.

There's this one chick name Keisha, who was like a nagging fly that I wanted to swat, she was claiming to be pregnant by Cue. Keisha and I have known each other for years. She knows that Cue and I have been dating since high school, but it didn't stop her from going after him. How could I expect more from trailer trash like her; Keisha is cute, she has a nice figure, but she is no competition to me. She has always tried to compete and always came up short. Anyway, I had heard that she was pregnant and was telling people that it was Cue's baby. Cue was denying that he had ever been with the girl sexually. After threatening to break it off with Cue and taking everything with me of his that was in my name, he agreed that he would confront Keisha with me in tow about the situation.

When we arrived to Keisha's house, which was on a very bad side of town, I almost felt sorry for the girl. How could she dress so nice, hair and nails always on point, and even have a nice looking car, yet stay in a run-down shack like this? The paint was chipped on the house, there was nothing but red dirt where there should have been grass, toys were scattered about the yard, and a worn out sofa that looked flea infested was sitting on the front porch, along with a few other un-matching lounge chairs.

The entire porch was packed with people and I was scared to get out of the car, as a matter of fact I regretted even asking Cue to do this. These people were ghetto and you know they stuck together. I am going to get my ass beat I thought. Cue got out of the car and greeted some of the young thugs that were on the porch, I figured he must have known them from the streets because it was very apparent that they knew each other well. After talking to the guys for a few, he just walked into the house. He was in the house for maybe five minutes, and then he comes back to the door and motions for to me to come in. I acted as if I did not see him from behind the dark tinted windows.

Was he crazy, did he really think I was going to get out of the car in this hood to confront a female about my man on her own turf? He finally came to the car and opened the driver side door because the passenger side was locked. I had made sure of that, I thought I had hit the switch to lock all the doors once he went into the house.

"Come on," he said bending down looking into the car at me.

"I am not getting out of this car to go into her house with her family in there to talk to her about this mess," I said, looking at him like he should have known better.

"No one is in the house; I thought you were such a bad ass, now you want to punk out? You done dragged my ass all the way over here, get your ass out of the car, or I will ask her to come out here, then you can talk in front of all these mother fuckers," he said spreading his hand towards the gang pack, that was on the porch.

I reluctantly, got out of the car and spoke as I climbed the steps to the front door closely behind Cue. I received some weird stares like who in the hell is she, and why is she here? Cue opened the front door and as expected, I stepped into a room that was smaller than my bedroom, yet served as their family room. No surprise here that the furniture did not match, and there was a frozen over air condition fighting for survival in the window. Straight ahead of me was the small kitchen that was smaller than the family room, yet they had managed to squeeze in a dining table, along with the kitchen appliances. Although there was an AC unit in the window the house was still warm and smelled of moth balls and cinnamon, which was not a good combination. The sheet that was thrown over two of the couches to cover the holes had fallen exposing the bad condition of the couches. There was a rusted framed picture of "The Last Supper" hanging crookedly on the wall, and I bet every picture that had ever been given to whomever this house belonged to, had been stuck in the crevices of the frame. The room was dark, and from what I could tell they only had one lamp in the corner for light if needed.

I followed Cue through an opening to the right of the family room. There was no door, although it was a bedroom. This bedroom had a set of bunk beds on one side and a full bed on the other. Not one comforter or spread matched, nor were they coordinated to blend.

There were two other doors in this room so I supposed they were bedrooms also. Cue knocked at one of the doors and Keisha opened it looking cute in her six month of pregnancy; wearing a pair of white leggings and a cute baby blue and white tank top, although it was not a maternity outfit, it fitted her perfectly and it also showed that she was all baby. Only thing that was big on her was her stomach, and it was perfectly round. Her hips stuck out and her breast had grown, but this actually made her look even better. She looked at me. It appeared that she had been crying or fighting back tears. I stepped into the open door behind Cue, to what was Keisha's bed room, and to my surprise, this room was bigger than any other room in the house that I had seen, and it was well lit and super clean, unlike the other parts of the house.

There were two matching twin size beds; side by side in this room, with matching black and white comforters that had hot pink leaves splattered over them. They had black curtains over the mini blinds and hot pink sheers between them. There was a 32 in' plasma television on the wall, right below it sat an entertainment center that housed a cd player, another small 19 in' television that had a game system connected to it, a microwave, and small refrigerator. There was a black love seat at the window separating the two beds. The air condition in this room worked wonderfully, the room had such a comfortable feel that I almost laid across the bed to take a nap.

Keisha sat on what I took to be her bed, and just looked at Cue and I and said, "So what is it you want to know exactly?" then her eyes shifted to me.

Cue rubbed his hand over his head nervously and asked, "Are you telling people that you are pregnant by me?"

Keisha looked at him as her eyes really watered and her lips quivered as she said, "No Cue I have not," tears rolled down her cheeks.

"Well who are you pregnant by?" I asked.

She stood up. "It is none of your damn business who my baby belongs to. It's time for you and Cue both to leave."

I said, "It is my business when you have been going around telling people that your baby is my man's."

"Mercedes screw you and your man, and like I said, Cue get her the hell out of my house!"

"I don't have a problem leaving this hell hole or your tramp ass. You just make sure you keep clear of Cue!" I said, approaching her.

Before I knew what had happened she had slapped the hell out me. She was all over my ass, before I had a chance to recuperate from the smack. Cue pulled her off of me. I jumped up and was about to punch her when she kicked me right in the stomach, causing me to double over. Cue let her go to come and make sure that I was ok, when she turned on him. One of the thugs that had been on the porch, whom I later found out was her cousin, entered the room and asked what was the problem? Keisha said that Cue was holding her to allow me to hit her.

Cue looked dumb found and said, "Keisha, really?"

All I knew was that this turned into something bigger. Cue and Keisha's cousin got into a shoving match.

"Let's go Cue!" I said, trying to steer him towards the door before the other gang members came in.

"I was not trying to hold your ass Keisha! If that was the case I would have, you wouldn't have gotten away from me girl. I was pulling your pregnant ass off of her before you got hurt. I was trying to look out for you're stupid ass. I didn't know she was going to try to hit you!"

After about two minutes of mouth battling, I finally got Cue out of the house. As we were getting into the car, Keisha who was very upset came out on the porch and threw two eggs at his car. One hitting the side of the car, and the other splattered onto the window. Cue hollered, "Girl watch your back, cause I got people that will fuck you up for a crack!"

"Oh so you will put a hit out on me and you know I am carrying your child?" was her last words as Cue quickly tried to close the door to drown out what she was saying.

"What did she say?" I asked, looking at him while tears rolled down my cheeks.

"That bitch is stupid," Cue said, "she's just trying to piss you and me off that's all."

From that point on I never had a problem with Keisha spreading rumors, although she would still come to the club after she had the baby, and she looked great. She never said anything although a few times I did see her in Cues face, "thirsty bitch."

Well I am aiming to fix things with my man tonight and I will tramp over any hood rat that tries to stand in my way. Guess I will lie down and take a nap so I can be well rested and beautified before I make my entrance. I know Cue loves me, that's the reason he is trying to avoid me, because he knows that once he sees me, he can't contain himself from wanting me. Well tonight he was going to have to face me. I was going to do everything in my power to make him take notice, and realize what he was standing to lose.

Chapter Seven

(Tonya)

"Mahogony, I am not going to ride with Mercedes to the club tonight, I don't care what you say. Because you know that if Cue is not there her ass is going to be ready to leave, and if I am paying twenty bucks to get in, I am staying until I am ready to go," I said, as I sat at my vanity filing my nails.

"I know right?" Mahogany replied. "But my question is, when have your ass ever paid to get in the club? And did you know that Cue has yet to call her?"

"Doesn't matter whether I pay or not, it takes more than twenty dollars for me to be looking this good, so your ass just be on time. Yes, I know she hasn't heard from him. Did you see that shit that Keisha posted on facebook the other night? And how did she allow Cue to flip the script on her like that?"

"Well you know how that happened. And of course she can't mention to him about Keisha's post, when her ass is using a secret alias to stalk Keisha on facebook."

"Misunderstood my ass, she knows exactly what was going on. Even if she did not actually place eyes on Cue, he is her man - so some respect should be given somewhere. Whether it be to let her know when he is going out of town, or if another dude is going to have his car parked at a local, frequented hotel, that's parked right on the interstate for any passerby to see."

"You have never lied," Mahogany laughed. "Well are you calling to tell Mercedes that we will just meet her at the club?"

"I already have, so I will see you around ten thirty, because I need a nap girl I am so tired."

"Alright then, don't be late picking me up. You know that I hate sitting around waiting, especially when I am looking like a million bucks."

"I will call you when I head out silly," I giggled, as I hung up the phone.

I so needed to get out tonight and have a great time. It has been a long and frustrating week. I have sat up and baby sat stupid ass for the majority of the week, because her weak ass has yet again let Cue make her feel as if she was the one that messed up.

And then to top it all off, my boy toy Eric was seen going into Red Lobster with some chick. As much as I hate to admit it; and I certainly would not admit it to Mercedes and Mahagony, I have really been bothered. Eric and I have been kicking it for a little over a year now, and yes we have had our fall outs, but we have never gone more than two weeks without one or the other calling.

Sure we have an open relationship meaning that we are not bound to only each other, that we are free to date other people, but we are not suppose to sleep around unless we let the other know first. This rule was made because after a month of protected sex, we slipped up, and in the heat of the moment had unprotected sex. From that point on he never wanted to use protection. I know it is a foolish thing to do, but I felt like if we were only sleeping with each other, what's the harm? And if another relationship got to that point of intimacy, there would not to be any hard feelings, just let the other partner know, We would mutually decide- whether it is time to start back protecting ourselves, or just to go our own separate ways.

Well of course feeling's had gotten involved and Eric has since told me that he loves me. While we have yet to verbally admit that we were indeed a couple all of our actions shows it. He takes me on vacations more than a married man does his wife- he went out and purchased me a candy apple red Ford Explorer for Valentine day- He's at my pad more than he is at his own place- and even calls me if he make it here before I do to see how long I will be.

So how in the hell could he tell me after his ass had been busted- which is a strike with in itself, because if his ass wanted to see other people he was to tell me before hand, and we talk about it. Nowhere in our conversation was it said, that it was ok to tell me after my aunt had saw him with another woman!

So imagine my surprise when I confronted him about this little escapade and he said, "Tonya we are friends we are not a couple".

"Since when Eric?" I asked, looking at him ready to knock his block off. "We have been together for over a year; if we are not a couple then one of us has taken it too far, because everything about us spells couple to me!"

"Tonya you know that we both agreed that we would just have fun and kick it with no strings attached. Why do you want to change the rules now I don't know."

"Eric, we said, that we would let the other person know when we are seeing someone else. And your ass changed the rules when you started staying over at my place every night! You started telling me that you loved my ass, and started cock blocking anytime another man showed some interest in me. Hell how was I to know that these actions didn't change things?"

"Tonya, I do love you baby," he said, as he came closer to me and put his arms around my neck. I haven't slept with anyone but you. I took that girl out to eat that was it."

"I know what you done, but what if my aunt had not have been in the restaurant, would I have known? Hell no! The rule was that you were supposed to tell me before, not after. I don't know about you, but as far as I am concerned that little; I will tell you thing we decided is null and void to me. Don't play the - I thought we had a mutual agreement card with me, because that agreement was shredded when you decided to start telling me you loved me, and started leading me to believe that we were an item! I am sorry that you thought I understood. I am letting you know now, that I can't do this with you if you think we are going to just go back to where we started in the beginning, because now all of a sudden you decide you want to see other people."

"I do love you Tonya, and maybe I was wrong for not telling you. You and I have always talked, and I just feel that I have gotten too serious about you. So before I take it to the next level, I feel I need to see other people to be sure that this is what I want." Eric said, while not really making eye contact with me.

Who in the hell did he think he was talking too? He must have got it twisted. Just because I had told him that his dick is the best I have had, doesn't mean that I just had to have it.

I stepped right up to his face and positioned myself so he could look me directly in my eyes and know that I meant what the hell I was about to say. I know he and Cue are best buds, and he knows that Cue pulls all kinds of bullshit stunts on Mercedes, and her stupid ass just rides it out. Well I am not Mercedes, and I have more dignity about myself. I am not the one to just settle for the ockie doke. I love this man and I cannot just be a friend to him anymore. Either he is going to be with me, or he can take a walk.

When I had his attention I said, "Eric let's call it what it really is, over!"

He tried to make me not break it off, but I stood my ground. It doesn't take all of that; either you want to be with me or not. Don't get it twisted, I loved him but I now understood what Cue meant by "I can still leave you." I am not in the business of keeping no mother fuckers that doesn't want to be kept.

Even though I broke it off with him that night, we have still been seeing each other. I'm just not giving up the goodies. If you want my goodies you have to work for them and earn them, nothing is free not even a sneak peek. Eric knows that I am pure gold, if he wants to experience the gold plated, I'll let him, but he will not get the gold until he is ready to own it. I love Eric and I really do not want to let him go. We will see how this plays out, but I will not wait on him forever. As much as I want to be with him, if a potential mate comes along while he's out finding himself, I have to bounce.

Chapter Eight

(Keisha)

I woke up to find my son Quincy on the floor sound asleep with his Captain America shield on his back. I sat up on the side of the bed and just grinned at my little man. He was the split image of his daddy, no one could argue that. I have been through a lot in my twenty three years, but this little boy here made every troubled mountain I have had to face, seem like ant hills now. My blessing had a heart beat, and I poured all of my love into this little boy. I picked him up from the floor and attempted to remove the shield that his dad had just bought him, from his back, but he grabbed hold and said, "No" through sound sleep. So I just laid him on my sisters bed and thought, I'll try again before I leave for the club.

I went into the living room to see what everyone was doing, and as usual there was a card game going on and the room reeked of cigarettes. My mother was telling my aunt and the neighbor from down the street to get their asses up as she smacked down a deuce of spade. Laughter erupted from the sideline guest who was waiting to get in the game. My aunt Judy was in the kitchen frying up chicken wings in which she was selling sandwiches with lettuce and tomato for three bucks. I asked her to make me a sandwich as I passed by to go into my grandmother's room.

My grandmother was sitting in her bed with her back to the headboard reading her bible.

"You bout done gramps?" I asked, not wanting to interrupt her if she was just starting.

"Yea baby" she said as she closed the worn bible and sat it on the night stand beside her bed. "You going out tonight?"

"Yes ma'am. I just got out of the shower getting ready to eat something real quick before I head out. I haven't had anything all day," I said, as I climbed on the bed beside her.

My grandmother is my love and joy. She is the epiphany of a strong, wise black woman. My grandfather died when I was fifteen and although he left my grandmother with a house that was paid for and a little change; she allowed her freeloading, not wanting anything or a clue as to how to get anything children, go through her money. Although all of their children were grown, my grandmother was still left to be a single parent. Out of the five kids that they had, only my aunt Shaunice who is the baby and only three years older than I; is the only stable one.

Shaunice is now twenty-six and went to college right after graduation at Johnson .C. Smith. She graduated with a degree in education, and she now teaches in Charlotte. Shaunice and I are very close and she is the one that makes me want to have more. She says the world is much bigger than the Avenue. Speaking of the hood we were raised in. She and I often sat on the phone and gossiped about our unstable relatives, and laughed about the most recent events, as I fill her in on what has happened. Quincy and I go and visit Shaunice regularly just to get away from here sometimes.

My aunt Judy, who is a year under my mother although she is married and has a job at the hospital working in housekeeping, still puts her burdens on grandma. Every time her and her husband, Uncle Tim, gets into any kind of argument, here she comes.

Then there is my mother who is forty-one and has always lived at home with her parents. My mother has never had a job where taxes was actually being taken out, so when my brother reaches eighteen, and she can no longer get assistance from the government, I don't know what the hell she's going to do. And the only man of the siblings is my uncle Ray who is thirty-five. I think that explains why he is so spoiled. He works for the City but never had any money two days after he got paid. He is what we called a functioning alcoholic. And my grandmother really acted like his shit didn't stink. He would run in the house on Fridays after he had gotten paid all happy because he knew that he was about to get his drink on. He would give my grandmother the fifty dollars that he gave her weekly for shelter, electricity, water, food, and to wash his clothes. He'd give me whatever he had borrowed from me throughout the week as always. I never had a problem lending to him, although I would make him beg for it at times, but he always paid his debt. He would hand out a dollar or two to his nieces and nephews, then he'd shower and be out. When we saw him again, which would usually be on Sunday afternoon or when the money ran out, whichever came first, he would be broke and tired. But you had to love Uncle Ray; he was witty and actually very intelligent. If he got himself together he could do great things.

Last but not least is my aunt Jackie, who is thirty-three, stays right next door to grandma in a two bedroom house with her five children. She's trying to survive off of her job as a Laundry Attendant at the hotel right up the street in walking distance from the house. And she probably could if she stopped hanging out with my mother at the club house every Friday and Saturday night. But as of right now she has several extension-cords running from her window into grandma's for power. Who does that?

I told her and grandma that she has been using our power for over a month and that she needs to at least go half on our electric bill. Of course aunt Jackie complained that it wasn't fair for her to go half when we all stay in the house and use the electric, so all the grownups in the house should split it. My sister Tamera and I, being the only ones that will speak our minds to her, told her that was some BS. The bill has always been high, but it wasn't this high until you started running your drop-cords!

After a heated argument she is now not speaking to Tam or I which is fine by me, because all she ever talks about is borrowing money anyway. She came over last week rolling her eyes as she walked past me and plugged back in the drop-cord that I had just unplugged and walked back out of the house.

Needless to say, that by the time she got back to her house, the lights were off again. She came back over beating on the door because I had locked it and she could not get back in. She stood on the porch looking through the window calling me all kinds of lowlife bitches

"I'm low life and you're the one sitting over there in the dark? Pay your damn bills and quit freeloading!" I said, looking at her. I know she was pissed because I was all in her face and she could not hit me because the screen/window was dividing us. I had my knees on the couch and my elbows were rested on the back of the couch that was pushed up against the window. I had my chin resting on top of my balled up hands with a cocky ass smirk on my face. Hell I would have been pissed too.

"Keisha I am not playing with you, plug back up the damn drop-cord my kids are over there in the dark!" she said.

"Tell them to take their asses to sleep," was my reply, "It's 12:30am," and with that I said, "Goodnight" and closed the curtains.

Grandmother who had heard all of the commotion was now standing in the doorway of the living room. "Keisha why you do that?" she asked with a smirk on her face.

"Because it is not fair that she does not give you anything on your electric bill. She and those bad kids stay over here all day. They're here sucking up all the air from the house, destroying the house and eating up all the food. Then at night she wants to retreat over there when that man gets off and lay up with him using your electricity. Let him give her money to get her lights cut back on if he's going to be sleeping over there."

Grandma just shook her head and said, "You a mess" and headed back to her room saying loud enough for me to hear her talk to God, "Lord help my children to become self-sufficient and less dependent on me before you take me from this place. Because if they have to depend on Keisha, Shaunice, and Tamera, they going to be shit out of luck!"

I laughed, as I cut out the lights and went to my bedroom to call and update Shaunice.

"How's the house coming along and when you going to let me go see the finished work?" Granny asked, because I had not allowed any of them to see the house once the contractors had started working on, and in it. I took them to see it right after I purchased it, so that when the transformation was done, hopefully they too would see what a little fixing up would do to a place. Maybe they would start fixing up grandmas.

I have wanted to move out of my grandmother's house forever. It wasn't because of her, but because it was crowded and always noisy. The rift rafters did not contribute anything to bills except groceries, and that was because they all received food stamps.

My sister, Ray and I were the only three in the house of six that actually gave my grandmother anything on bills. My sister, who is only seventeen and in school even gives her fifty dollars every week. She works at, "Best Burger" a job I once had until I got on Cue's payroll. Being the dependable and reliable worker that I was, I had no problem getting Mr. John to replace me with my sister once I decided to leave. I gave grandma a hundred, which my grandmother loved, and I take it that was one reason she was so upset when I purchased my house. She argued that I needed to continue to save my money, and wait until I could purchase a house that did not need to be worked on and repaired before I could move in. I paid twelve thousand dollars for the small, but roomy three bedroom house. The house was considered to be in the low income area, but it sat on a main road that was not actually in the hood, but a five minute walk would get you right dab in the middle of the action. I was born and raised in this neighborhood, so I wasn't afraid of my people, and to me, the purchase was a steal.

"The house looks great; they finished staining the floors yesterday." I said, speaking of the hardwood floors that I had put into the house.

When I purchased the house it had tattered carpet and cheap tile on the kitchen floor. The bathroom had to be gutted and I had bought all new appliances. I had hardwood floors put through-out the entire house. I planned to coordinated area rugs in the rooms. I was proud of the house. It did not look like the same unmaintained house I had purchased. I had the chipped wood that was on the outside of the house replaced with grey aluminum siding, and I added black shutters to the windows. What use to be a railing free porch, now has wrought iron railing going across and down the now cemented porch, and steps that were once wooden.

I could not wait to move into my house; although my grandmothers four bedroom, two in a half bathroom house was much bigger than my small; three bedrooms, one bathroom house, it was going to feel like a mansion to me, because it would only be Quincy and I

"Can you watch Quincy for me tonight?" I asked, knowing full well that all I had to do was bring him in here with her.

I had purchased grandma a new bedroom suit and a window unit for her bedroom, so she could be comfortable in her own room. Because we often came home to find her lying across either Tams or my bed because our room was so cool and cozy she stated. Not that we cared about her being in there, that was the reason we gave her a key to our room in the first place, but once we would get home she felt as if she had to leave because this was our space. And as much as we would say grandma you can stay, we can pull the hide-a-way bed out that's in the loveseat she would not. So we decided to fix her room up for her so she could have a nice, comfortable place of her own and she loved it, and stayed in her room twenty four seven now.

"Gal you know that baby can stay here," she said, as she reached over to turn on the television. Just bring him on in here before you leave. I leaned over and kissed her on the cheek and said, thanks, then bounced on out just as quickly as I had come.

I went into the bedroom and stood in my packed closet trying to figure out what I wanted to wear tonight. I decided that I wanted to dress up a pair of jeans that accented my every curve.

They were a pair of dark skinny Calvin Klein jeans that lay right on my waist line perfectly. I paired them with a sequenced gold fitted tank top that I purchased from, "NaTasha's Studio of Beauty & Boutique" a very upscale boutique in downtown Greenville. Tasha was a little pricey but for the quality, and limited amount of each item she purchased for her boutique, it was worth it. The thing that I liked about NaTasha's was that you would not have to worry about every hood rat having on her clothes, because she only ordered six of each item. I never had to worry about going into any club or event and seeing two or three people dressed identical to me.

And the service was superb at NaTasha's. You could go in and shop downstairs or go upstairs and have your hair done and a facial. And Tasha herself motivated me so much; she is such a classy, young, black lady. She has a clientele of mostly mid-class to rich white women who loved her. I go into her store often, and can count on my hand how many times I have seen black women in there. They'd rather go to the mall, take the entire outfit off of a manikin, and then be at an event complaining because they have triplets.

I decided to pair the sequenced tank top with a pair of sequenced five inch Hunfew's that I also purchased from the boutique. After I got dressed I stood back and looked at my ensemble in the full length mirror that was housed on the back of the room door. I was trying to figure out jewelry or none when my cell phone rang.

"Hello?" I said, as I turned my rear to the mirror to see how the jeans were flattering my ass.

"We at the club where your ass at?" came Toya's high pitched voice through the phone line.

"Girl I had laid down to take a short nap and overslept. I am getting dressed now so I will be there shortly. Is Cue there?" I asked.

"Yea girl, he's here and so is Mercedes. Honey she is not sitting in V.I.P tonight? Her and those heifers are sitting on the floor with us peasants, "Toya laughed. "And girl I think something is going on with her and Cue, because he has walked right past her twice without as much as a glance her way. And he even came over here to where we are, asking us where you were?"

"You are kidding? " I asked, in disbelief.

While my girls and I never sat in V.I.P even though we could, we were always treated like V.I.P, Cue made sure of that. He made sure that the bartenders kept beverages and whatever else I asked for on our table. Mercedes always sat in V.I.P; she rarely even left the section even to dance. And for Cue to come over to my group to inquire about me, yea something was up. I looked at my cell phone when Toya and I disconnected our call, and whoa and behold I had three missed calls from Cue.

I walked into the club as usual knowing that I was the bomb. I walked past where Mercedes and her crew were sitting, which were only two tables from where my crew and I always sat. *Coincidental?* I think not. Mercedes said something to her girl Tonya as I was approaching, because Tonya's back was to me, but she turned to look me up and down. I put an extra "ump" behind my already fly strut.

Can't say that I don't have time for hater's, because once I realize that you are one... I do everything in my power to piss you the fuck off. They can talk all they want, but one thing was for certain, and that was that they couldn't do anything with this bitch, because she was bad.

Right as I got ready to pass them this guy name Steady grabbed me and gave me a bear hug right in front of where they were sitting. He then stepped back and looked me from head to toe and said, "You just shitting on'nem!" I laughed, and nudged him in the arm as I walked on by. Once I got to the table and greeted my friends, Eboni said, Mercedes eyes followed you all the way over here.

"Let her look," I said as I crossed my long legs extending my fly pumps. I scanned the crowd seeing if I seen Cue. I hadn't talked to him at all today. I had called him several times before he finally text me asking, was Quincy alright. I text back and said, "Yes he's fine I was just wanting to talk to you. He replied, cool; I will call you later. I am in the middle of something right now. That later never came and I was pissed. It doesn't matter how many times I have told Cue and how many times he has agreed with me, he still does that bullshit. But low and behold he calls me and I don't answer or at least call him back within the next few minutes, he acts like the whole world has come to an end. I even text him back about two hours later and said, "Are you ever going to call me back?" -Nothing!-

Steady came over and asked me to dance. Sure I said, as I got up and strutted again past Mercedes and her bougie friends. Steady and I got on the floor and danced three songs straight before I finally headed for the bathroom. Just as I was getting ready to go into the bathroom Cue grabbed me by my arm and pulled me into a corner.

"What the hell you think you doing?" He asked, furious.

"What is wrong with you?" I asked, as I jerked my arm from his grip.

"You trying to play me for a fool Keisha, where your ass been? And how you come in right behind Steady, both of you all late getting here, then you have the nerve to go and dance with him like that in front of me?"

This was all new to me I had no idea that Steady has just arrived at the club. I was even more shocked that Cue himself had approached me rather than send one of his goons to tell me what needed to be said. I could see in his eyes that he was upset, and for him to do this with Mercedes not two rows over, I knew that I had struck a nerve.

"Cue first of all I didn't know that there was a rule as to how late was too late a person could come to a damn club! And as far as Steady is concerned, I have no idea why he was so late you may want to ask him," I said, as I raised my eyebrows.

I could totally understand why he thought something was shady here. Because while Steady is one of the four copartners of this club; he and Cue are mutual but not buddies. Through Eric, they are mutual friends.

Steady doesn't feel as if he and Cue are close enough that he can't try to screw Cues girl. He has been on me since I came on the scene, and he knows that Cue and I see each other on the side. He was the one that told me that Cue had proposed to Mercedes; also any other thing that Cue has done that he thought would make me hate him.

"Where you been Keisha, your girls been here since eleven, your ass come strolling up in here at one? " He said, squinting his eyebrows questionably.

"Cue I was at home asleep. Maybe if you had bothered to return my calls, you would have woken me up." I said, sarcastically. "I was out with your son and his friends at - Jumping Joes- earlier today. I even tried to call you from there, to see if you wanted to stop by and enjoy some fun with your son, but remember you never returned my calls?"

Cue now satisfied, noticed Mercedes walking in our direction. He slapped my rear end as he turned to walk away, and said, "Keep Steady out your face."

I looked sideways at him, as he walked off with a smirk all on my face. *This guy is jealous,* I thought to myself tickled to death. And although Steady was just as fine, Cue had nothing to worry about. I had loved and fantasized about Cue before he even knew my country ass existed, well at least before I knew that he knew that my country ass existed anyway.

I use to sat back in the cut and just admire all of his greatness when we would be at the club. My girls and I would watch as he and his boy Eric who was also tall, if not taller, would stroll through the club. It was as if time stood still as they made their way through; greeting and shooting the breeze.

The ladies would be showering them with mad love. While the fella's would be dappin' them up, doing their guy hug thing, and shooting the breeze. I on the other hand had not as much even spoke to him, less on try to approach him for a hug as all the other groupies did.

One reason was that I knew he was Mercedes man, and although I was not afraid of Mercedes, she had a lot of mouth and we did not quit see eye to eye. For some reason everyone she dated in high school always want to get with me; whether it was while they were together or after. I never dated any of them while they were together, but-I did entertain them after they had broken up.

She has always seen me as competition. She had a little envious spirit when it came down to me. Mercedes was generally in the club, so I did not want any confusion about a man that I knew, was already taken. I carried on and tripped and had fun with my friends. We were always taken care of while in the club by some of the other hustlers.

I remember when I finally got my second chance to talk with Cue after he had gotten out of jail; it was not even at the club which would have been expected, because that was the only time that our paths ever crossed.

One Sunday afternoon my grandmother asked me to run to Bi-Lo to get her a jar of relish. I had just put on my white Hollister sweats with a big purple t-shirt that belonged to my fifteen year old brother, who was twice my size. I was lying across the bed enjoying being lazy.

I really did not feel up to going but who could, nor would ever tell granny no. I jumped up and grabbed my keys. My plan was to just run into the store, in what I had planned on sleeping in. As I was getting ready to leave, my little three year old cousin ran up to me while his brother was chasing him, and grabbed hold of my white pants with ketchup all on his little hands.

Cursing to myself, I wanted to wring his little neck. I was mad but couldn't be mad at him, I loved this little boy so much, plus I didn't need a child abuse charge.

I went into the room and pulled out my low rider Hollister jeans and threw on a white fitted t-shirt and slid on my white Hollister flip flaps.

As I exited my ten year old- Toyota Corolla, that I had worked and saved for while I was in high school, I heard whistles coming from a Crown Vic. The car was painted like a Captain Crunch Cereal box; they even had the bar-code on it. I waved at the clowns hanging out the window trying to get me to stop so we could exchange numbers. I just smiled, and quickly went into the store. I thought to myself how do you get more ghetto than that? All of that major advertising for a company who didn't even know their country asses existed. And they were riding eight niggas deep. I was giggling to myself as I searched the aisles for the relish, thanking God, nonetheless, that I had decided to put on some clothes. I had picked up the jar of relish and was heading down the aisle to the checkout when I saw none other than Cue, looking confused at some can good in front of him. It was like seeing Jesus Christ in a grocery store. I was thinking, in all of his glory he does his own grocery shopping? I suddenly became interested in a can of beets that his magnificent body was blocking. I had to say, excuse me and act as if I did not even notice him as he said, excuse me and moved over a little. I bent down and picked up two cans of beets. As I was bending down I could feel this tower of a man hovering behind me, and if my thongs were exposing the way I imagined they probably were, I knew he liked what he was seeing. I thanked God once again that I had decided to change clothes. Thank you Lord for little boys with ketchup on their hands, I thought.

Keisha, right? He asked, with a look on his face that was asking was he correct. I about lost my freaking mind; *He remembered my name*! Breathe girl, breathe! I had to tell my brain to send air to my lungs because I was about to hyperventilate. I became a mute for a Mississippi second. Thank God, I was still bending down looking at all kinds of foreign mess, because I would have made a complete ass of myself. Once my blood started to travel back to my brain, I recomposed and stood to face him for the first time as if I was just recognizing him.

"Oh, hey Cue. Long time no see," I said, looking up at him into those gorgeous eyes.

"So you do remember me? Why don't you ever speak to a brother when you see him then, why's that KEI-SHA?" He said, putting a strong emphasis on my name, exposing that sexy ass smile I remembered so well.

I placed my hand on my hip as I extended it out and said, "When do you not have an entourage around you for anyone to get close enough to speak? The first time I saw you since you picked me up from work that day was last Saturday. I was going to come over and speak, but your fan club was so thick." He chuckled at my sarcasm.

"So where have you been hiding?" I asked, knowing damn well his ass had been locked up and had just gotten out. I had been going to the club every week since I heard he had come home hoping to bump into him. However, he had not been out, at least not at the clubs where I was on Saturday nights. Last Saturday, he happened to be in the club, but I could not make my move because everyone else was.

"*Man--,*" Cue said rubbing his hands together, "I had caught this bullshit charge. I have been in the damn joint for the past year."

"*What?*" I knew I hadn't seen you around. I thought you had got married on me and was locked down," I joked.

"Hell yea, I was locked down that's for damn sure," Cue laughed. "So- all bullshit aside believe me," He said looking directly at my hips. "If a cutie like yourself wanted to get in," He paused a second to add more effect to what he was about to say as he looked me square into the eyes, and said, "You won't have a problem at all, entourage or not. And from what I hear your girls Toya and Eboni have such a tight ring on you that a man has to go through two interviews before they will even allow you to give up the digits."

"Oh word?" I asked, giving him what some say is my - devious crooked smile. Don't tell me this man has been scoping me all along, and here I thought that his head was so far up Mercedes ass that he couldn't dare see me.

"Yea it's my job to scope out all the fine women and see what their about," he said, while rubbing his hand over that sexy ass goatee that he sported.

Someone must have cut the air off in the grocery store because I suddenly got hot as hell. I was sure sweat was not pouring down my face, but there was certainly something moist trying to seep through my panties. Thank goodness, I had on these tight jeans. I removed my hands from my hip in the mist of the excitement and realized that I had nothing else to do with them, so I placed them back. Since I did not have anything intellectual to say, I just said, "Yea right" and had the audacity to walk off.

I got to the checkout line and thank goodness that he was still in tow. If he continued to hang around, I would probably be born again before leaving this store. I don't think that I had ever praised and thanked God, as much as I had since being here today.

"So… Keisha, are you seeing anyone?"

I placed all the shit I had picked up on the checkout counter and secretly prayed that; a couple of cans of beets, mushrooms and sauerkraut did not cost more than a dollar fifty a can, because I only had a twenty and my ass had just came in to get a jar of relish. While I stood there being fast, flirting with Cue, I had nervously picked up 2 cans of mushrooms, 3 cans of beets and 2 cans of sauerkraut. What tha hell?!!!

I turned to Cue as the belt started pulling my merchandise to the cashier, "No, I am not, you on the other hand are, aren't you?"

Damn, there he goes with that sexy sly smile again. If he flashes those pearly whites at me one more time, he and my ass is going to be up on this checkout counter with me in a missionary position.

"I have a friend," he said.

"So does Mercedes know that you and she are just friends?" I asked.

It didn't matter to me at this point if they were friends, lovers, or married, if Cue wanted my number... My number he was going to get. I have been in love with this boy from the day he walked onto the set. Look at him standing there looking like he can be sopped up with a biscuit. And if this mug squints those bedroom eyes at me one more time, or licks those plump sexy lips towards me one more *time*... I had never been one to sleep with a guy right off the bat or sleep around period for that matter, but this man could surely get it any way or anytime he wanted it.

Once I got home I dropped the bags on the kitchen table and headed quickly to my bedroom. My sister Tamera was on the phone talking to her little boyfriend, so I had to beg her to let me use the phone. She said five dollars or either you wait another fifteen minutes. I did not have but eleven dollars left from the twenty I had, when I went to the store. Payday was not for another two days. I had to bribe her by telling her I was going to ask, "Was she talking to Mike?" Problem being that Mike was her ex-boyfriend, whom her current boyfriend could not stand. She laughed, and said, "I hate you" but told her boyfriend she would call him back in ten minutes. I promised her it wouldn't take me long (I lied). Tamera and I always got along great, even when we were bribing one another for the phone or anything; it was always funny, where someone ended up coming off the line or dime.

Eboni, girl call Toya and Britney on the three way. I have something to tell you all," I squealed into the phone, as I flopped backwards onto my bed about to burst.

"What is it?" Eboni asked excitedly not even knowing what she was excited about.

"Call Toya and Britney first, because I can't go over the story again," I said, knowing full well that I will be telling this story a few more times today.

My grandmother entered the room with the sauerkraut, mushrooms and beets in her hand and asked where did I want these? She knew that I bought food to store in my room if it was not intended for the entire house to consume. Anything you put into our kitchen was free gain. Too embarrassed to tell her that my ass was nervous while I was talking to this fine brother; and needed something to occupy my hands to keep me from looking awkward, I started picking up shit. I told her that the grocery store had them on clearance, so I just picked up a few cans in case she could use them.

"Well thanks,'" she said and turned around going back to her task of cooking.

Once they all were on the line, I screamed, like a teenage girl, "Guess who I just saw at Bi-lo?

"Who?" They all asked in unison.

"Cue!" I screamed.

"Ok?" was Ebonies hesitant response.

"Did you talk to him or something?" asked Toya thinking the same thing as Eboni.

"Not only did I talk to him he asked for my number!" I squealed. "He told me that he had been checking me!"

"Shut the heck up," Britney said.

"Are you serious?" Came Eboni.

"Girl he was all up in my cornflakes. He even mentioned you clowns by name."

I gave them the run down and we were all screaming like teenagers. After talking for about an hour on how they wanted to be hooked up with this friend or that friend, we finally hung up the phone. It wasn't until three days later before he finally did call, and we immediately kicked it off.

Chapter Nine

(Mercedes)

The silver sequenced dress that I had purchased was doing more for my curves than I anticipated. Hell the dress was almost perverted it hugged my curves so nicely. I wished that I was at least two inches taller. My five inch peep toe $300.00 silver HunFew's, made my 5'5 frame look to be at least 5'9. The form fitting bottom half of my dress, stopped at an almost dangerous location just below my butt cheeks. It made my legs look a mile long. As we greeted Ty and Quan the bouncers that monitored the front entrance, I overheard Cameron, who is the person in charge of checking for I.D's and scanning say, "Damn, Cue better not ever slip up!" rubbing his hands as if he was getting ready for dessert.

We made our way through the club headed towards the back of the club to find a table. We generally sat in V.I.P but tonight I decided that I would give Cue a dose of his own medicine. I would not be sitting where he has always designated for me to so that he could keep an eye on me. We found a table not too far from the bar and had a seat.

Syria one of the waitresses came over and asked why we were sitting out here and not in V.I.P? I told her that we just wanted to be in the center of everything tonight. While V.I.P had everything from its very own beverage bar to finger foods that were not served in the club, it was secluded. It was surrounded with a thin sheer material that allowed you to vaguely see out, and people from the outside could not see in, because it was so dimly lit by only tea-light candles, that served as center pieces on the tables. All the ballers and ballerettes were in and out of the V.I.P section, while all of the fun was mainly going on outside of the curtains. The only way they even knew you were in V.I.P is that you made an excuse to step outside of it for some reason. For me to come up with a reason to Cue was slim to nothing, because there was a small dance floor and private bathroom in the V.I.P section. Although a lot of people that occupied V.I.P would go out just to fraternize and dance on the large dance floor, Cue frowned upon this with me. Tonight was going to be my night.

"I like it out here a lot better than V.I.P." Mahogany was saying, as she swayed to the music.

"Yea, your ghetto behind would." Tonya said, glancing around scanning the room. Tonya lived for V.I.P's. anytime we planned to go anywhere, Tonya's first question would be can we get a V.I.P, how much is V.I.P or can we get a V.I.P hook up? You may as well forget about her standing in lines, that was none- existent in her world. One night we had tickets that were very pricey to see Prince and because there was a long line, Tonya goes past everyone to the front and told them that we had V.I.P tickets. After they told her we would be shown to the V.I.P section once we got inside the club, meanwhile, we must also wait in the two mile line. Tonya gave her ticket to the person standing there in line waiting to purchase a ticket and vowed to never again come back to this establishment. Yet, she has the nerve to call me bourgie.

"What are you three doing amongst us common folk?" Tank asked as he bent down to hug me.

"How are you doing handsome?" I asked, ignoring his question as I gave him a tight hug.

"Good now that I've gotten some love from the sweetest lady in the room." He replied, as he looked over at Mahogany. Tank and Mahagany has been seeing each other for maybe three months now. Mahagany has been upset because he originally told her that he did not have a girlfriend, that he had a friend only, and that they were not committed. So after seeing him for a few weeks with him wining and dining her; treating her like the queen that she thought that she was, she began to develop feelings for him only to find out later, that he and Shanieka were a little more than friends. Tank had failed to share that they had an apartment together; two children, one was eight-years- old so that alone tells that they have a history and now the ay have baby that is nine-months, so this told that they still shared passion. Mahogany was done with him, and he's still begging and telling her he wants to be with her. With her feelings being so deep into it, she kind of settled. Our friend Tonya has given her down the road for this. I don't condone having affair with someone you know has a significant other, however I understand how Mahogany feels about this man. Mahogany did not just settle, she was deceived and her feelings for him are very strong.

Tank went over and gave Tonya a hug, before he practically lifted Mahogany from the chair as he squeezed her.

"Let me go Tank, you are wrinkling my jacket." Mahogany said, as she pressed out her jacket with her hands.

"Where are the rest of your clothes?" Tank asked, while looking down at her revealing those beautiful mile long legs that were peeping from underneath the black and white striped blazer she was wearing, with a pair of cut off blue jean fringed shorts, a red cami, and five inch red Louboutin's. The ensemble had a conservative, edgy, look which was nicely put together.

Before Mahagany could even respond, Tank already had her hand leading her to the dance floor. For Tank to have a woman, you would never know it by the way he is all over Mahagany anytime she's in the building. And then maybe it's because his main lady Shanieka was the type of girl that did everything he asked her to. She was never in the club so this gave Tank too much freedom. I knew of at least eight women before Mahagany that he had affairs with. Hell, I didn't even know his butt was even almost married the way he ran around here with different women.

"Here comes Ms Thirsty," I said, to Tonya. Keisha was coming in our direction to the table where her and her thirsty friends always sat. She looked over at me and made direct eye contact for every bit of five seconds and then smirked. This bitch here is the reason I need to stay out of the clubs before I ended up with a case. I come to this club because it was supposed to be upscale, and my fiancé owns it. However; with rift raft like Keisha, and her hood rat friends, I may consider going other places. Truth be told, she really gets under my skin, and it is very rare for someone to get to me.

I watched as she headed to the dance floor with Steady. Why all these men were always on her jock I couldn't understand. Keisha had nothing going for herself other than the fact that she had a nice figure, dressed her ass off and I am still trying to figure out what hustler is keeping her in the latest pair of Hunfew's which were not cheap, and that Chrysler 300 that she pushed. Although her car had nothing on my Mercedes, I knew that she had no job, so who was footing her bills?

She had no class but hid it behind her nice clothes, fine car and maintenance. I had two nice cars, a very upscale townhouse and a wardrobe that would make the first lady jealous. My fiancé bought a lot of these things for me, but I could also afford it myself. Unlike Keisha's freeloading ass, I worked every day.

"Have you seen Cue yet?"

"Girl you know his ass behind that damn curtain," Tonya said, while rolling her eyes.

"He still hasn't called you?"

"No, but I'm good," I said, lying. I missed Cue even more than ever.

"Speak of the devil." Tonya said, as Cue was heading our way.

Apparently, he had not seen us. As Keisha was coming off of the floor from dancing with Steady, Cue pulled her to the side out of sight.

"What the hell is he doing?" I said out loud to what was meant for only me. I was praying that Tonya and Mahagony had not seen what had just happened, they were always on me about Cue enough. As my luck would have it, they had, and they verbalized their thoughts.

"Why in the hell is he grabbing on her like that?" Mahagony asked, all the while looking at me accusingly like, "Bitch what you going to do?"

I got up without thinking, I was so mad. What business did he have with Keisha, because from what he always told me he doesn't even talk to the girl anymore. Keisha came from the dark corner that Cue had her in as I was approaching. She looked up at me and gave me a look that said, "You need to put a leash on your man."

As I got to the spot where Cue had grabbed Keisha, he was just coming from the corner. I shoved him back into it.

"What the hell you have to talk to Keisha about?" I said, fuming.

Cue stunned from my sudden appearance was looking at me with an opened mouth like, "What the hell?"

"I seen you pull her into the corner," I said, as I poked him in the forehead with my forefinger. "What was that all about?" I was practically screaming.

Cue attempted to move me out of his way as if he was dismissing himself without an explanation, this infuriated me. I started striking him in the back and grabbed his neck to pull him back. Although he came back, it was on his own free will because there was nothing my 5'5 petite frame could do to hurt or stop him. He grabbed my arms and held them down in front of my torso with one hand.

He pointed his finger in my face and said, "Mercedes chill the fuck out cause if you put your hands on me again, expect for me to retaliate." He hissed through grinded teeth as the veins in his neck pulsated.

Water formed up in my eyes as I said, "Cue what is this with her, why do you keep doing this to me?"

He let my arms go; he placed both of his hands on the wall behind me creating a barrier around me. He looked down at me and said, "Mercedes you got to stop being so jealous and thinking because I talk to women I'm fucking them. This is the main reason that you and I need to chill, I will not let you dictate who I can talk to. Just because your ass wants to be all bourgie do your thing, that's not me."

"Cue this girl has caused us more problems than anybody, so why would you keep letting her in?"

"Keisha is no threat to you baby. I promise you that, she is just cool people, we just trip that's all. I don't even really talk to her it's just that she heard that we were broke up, and she been talking shit. I was just fucking with her that's all. She is not my cup of tea. Either you accept me for what and who I am, or we need to chill." He said all of this while still standing with the barrier around me. The smell of his cologne was making me want to jump on him and make love to him right here.

"Cue I love you more than I have ever loved anyone. I just can't keep going through the same old drama. So maybe we should chill for a while," I said, surprising myself. God knows I did not mean one word of what I had just uttered; I was praying that Cue took the bait.

Cue removed his arms from over me, folded them against his chest as he stood back looking at me. "So is that what you really want?" He asked.

"No, but that's what I am going to settle for. I want a man that I can be with more than once a week if needed, you are not ready for that kind of a commitment. When I'm having a rough day I need someone who is going to hold me and tell me it's going to be ok, or just to be there to talk to me. I never get that from you Cue, so since its other women you want so bad, I'm setting you free. You can have whoever you want.

I attempted to walk past him; he pulled me back with one hand. "So is that what this is all about, you wanting to get with other dudes?"

"No, it's about me wanting some form of security from the dude I am with."

Cue looked at me like he was just seeing me for the first time. Maybe he was. Knowing that he may just stand the risk of really losing me for good, I am hoping would be enough to shape him up. Make him realize that I was a dime, and all those other hoes that were all on his jock, were only nickels.

Cue stepped back and held his hands up as if he was being held up and said, "Cool, if that is what you want to do, do your thang. I want stand in your way." He turned and walked off without even looking at me, as I was calling him back.

I went to the bathroom to get myself together then headed back to the table where my girls were sitting.

"What did he say?" asked, Mahogany.

"Girl I don't even want to talk about Cue right now, fuck Cue," I said looking around to see who I could ask to dance. One thing was certain; no one was going to ask me, because everyone knew I was Cue's woman, so the only other men I ever danced with were Cue friends. They just wasn't going to cut it tonight, I needed to make his ass jealous.

I was on the dance floor with Marcell who was shocked that I walked up to him and started a conversation. We weren't talking about anything deep, however, my body language said otherwise. I don't think we had ever had a conversation at all before other than speaking in passing.

Marcell and I danced for maybe three songs before we headed off the dance floor. As I was going back to my seat, I spotted Keisha coming out of V.I.P with Cue. They both were laughing. I got up to go over there, and Mahogany said, "Sit your ass down! Fuck Cue and Keisha; do not make a spectacle of yourself. I know it hurts, and he knows that it hurts you that's why he is doing this crap, to get under your skin. Don't entertain his ass!"

Mahogany spoke with so much authority and anger in her voice; I did as told. I knew that she had my best interest at heart. I sat back down and just as quickly got back up, running for the bathroom. The tears were about to come, there was nothing I could do to stop them.

I was in the bathroom stall letting the tears flow, while I tried to smother my whimpers. Everything within me wanted to kill right now; kill Cue, kill Keisha and kill the fact that I care about his sorry, deceitful and conniving ass. What was it with those two that he could not let go of, what did Keisha have that I did not have?

Mahogany calling my name made me get myself together and come out of the stall. She looked at me with heart felt eyes as she handed me my makeup kit that she'd retrieved from my purse. Friends like this are what were important. They know what you need before you even ask. As harsh as

Mahogany could be, she always had my back and my best interest at heart.

"Thank you girl," I said, taking the bag from her and patting away my tear stains with the face powder. After I reapplied my eye liner, I looked at Mahogany and smiled.

"Get those tears out girl, after a few days you will be all cried out, ready to start the healing process. You know that tears means that you are only releasing what is boggling you down."

Lord, I silently prayed, that she was right.

Chapter Ten

(Cue)

I was on the block chilling with the guys as usual, nothing much popping today, pretty quiet. With me being the type of person that loves the fast life and everything about it, I never want a dull moment, even when I am just chilling.

I pull out my I-phone and called my baby Keisha. Keisha may not be my main girl, but she was definitely someone that I was never going to let go. Yea, I had plenty of other women, but Keisha is my baby. Do I love her as much as I love my chick Mercedes? I can't say that I don't love Keisha even more than I do Mercedes, although I could never let Keisha know this. Keisha is a street chick, and she has my heart. No one would ever guess that of all the fly, educated, and conservative chicks that has thrown their panties at me, that this chick Keisha would have my heart. Keisha knows how to cater to her man and make him feel like a king. She knows her role and she plays it to a tee.

I remember times when Mercedes didn't want to give up the goods I would just call Keisha and say, "I need to feel you baby." Keisha's response would be; my place, yours or a hotel? Then one time Mercedes called herself holding back on me, and we got into a huge argument so I stormed out of the house and called Keisha to ask her to meet me at my spot. Keisha beat me there. I walked into the house to her in a sexy ass gown, as she handed me my favorite drink, plus she had chicken wings on the stove frying.

Why would I give my side piece a key to my pad? Keisha was cool; even if I pissed her off and refused to see her again she wouldn't show out. Unlike a few chicks I had seen in the past that wanted to blow up the spot because they were hot, Keisha would ignore my ass. Whenever, Keisha saw Mercedes and I together she'd speak and keep it moving. If it bothered her it never showed. Plus she was funny as hell; I always knew I was going to have a good time when we were together. Above all else, she had my back. That is why, whatever Keisha wanted or asked; I made sure she got.

Mercedes is my Boo- I love the fact that she is down for me and I know she loves me. Mercedes controlling ways is what turns me off. She wants you to lay around with her ass all the time. I love Mercedes but she doesn't excite me the way Keisha does. I ask Mercedes to suck my dick and it's like I asked her to climb Mt Vernon. Keisha on the other hand I don't even have to ask, if anything I have to pull her up when I'm ready to wax that ass. If I wake Mercedes up in the middle of the night wanting to make love, she complains about me breaking her sleep and goes on about being too tired. Keisha just rolls right over as she says, "Let's do it boo so I can get some sleep," and that is only when she is dog tired.

I ask Mercedes to fix me a sandwich in the middle of the night, she looks at me like I am crazy before saying, "You better take your ass into that kitchen and fix it yourself, while you're at it fix me one too!" as she turns her back and jerks the cover up to her chin going back to sleep. I ask Keisha to fix me a sandwich in the middle of the night; she gets up, hit's me in the head with a pillow and that's only if she's tired and say, "Lazy ass," as she heads to the kitchen to fix my sandwich then hollers back and ask, "What are you drinking?"

Having sex with Mercedes is good but she just relies on the fact that men have told her that her stuff was good. She doesn't yet understand that because it is good, doesn't mean that you don't have to put in work to make it the bomb. I enjoy making love to Mercedes because, she is my lady, I do love her and like I said, she has that good good.

Sex with Keisha- Whew! It's out of this world. If I could bottle up what she does and sell it, I would be a millionaire! Keisha has skin that is as soft as butter, her hands feels so good on my body as she caresses it. I love the way she massages my back while she is underneath me and caress my face as she kisses me. The way that she loves me, as if that is what she was put here to do, no matter what I ask her, she is down for it. I have called her in the middle of the night because I have got wasted and she came to pick me right up, after Mercedes selfish ass had said to me, "Cue, baby, its four a.m. Just stay there until morning, I don't feel safe coming on that side of town during these hours. Mercedes has a lot of lip yet, scared as hell. The very thing that I love about Mercedes; is that she is strong minded, smart, and doesn't take any bullshit, those are also the same things I hate about her. I want my woman to be strong; I also want my lady in all of her strongness; to be smart enough to know when to keep her mouth shut, let the man be the man and lead, especially when he's leading you forward and not backwards.

Keisha can be a ball of fire like no other woman I have ever met when she's mad. Yet, she is smart enough to at least pretend to be submissive and keep her mouth shut when it's not necessary for her to have the last word. I guess this is why she has me crazy about her ass. Not to mention that Keisha is a great mother to my son.

"What's up boo?" Keisha purred into the phone before I even could say hello.

"Just sitting over here chilling. What mini-me doing?"

"Sitting here putting together a workbench he bought at Wal-mart and it looks more like a chair," Keisha laughed.

"You are not helping my boy girl?"

"He won't let me; he said he's got it. You know how he thinks he can do everything himself. Cue I wish you could see this, "so -called -work -bench" it is hilarious!"

I chuckled, listening at how tickled Keisha was about it. "Woman leave my son alone, he say he got it then he got it. Ask him if he can take a break and talk to me?''

"Quincy, your dad is on the phone; can you take a break from your hard work and talk to him for a minute?" Keisha asked as she pulled the phone away from her ear.

"Yes, I can take a break," he said pronouncing it as "bake" I chuckled, as I imagined him wiping his hands on his carpenter jeans that he had demanded Keisha buy. He says they are his work clothes. I don't know what it is that he was going to do for a living when he grew up, with the way he liked to build and make things and that imagination of his; I just hoped that it was something that was going to make him a ton of money.

"Hey daddy, fix me a sandwich mommy."

"What kind of sandwich Quincy? And say please."

"Peanut butta and jelly please. What's up daddy?

Nothing much man just out here grinding, your mom said you're working hard over there building you a new work bench. What you going to make after you finish it?"

"I'ma make you a skateboard for your birthday."

I silently laughed, and asked, "A skate board Quincy?"

"Yes sir. So you can ride your skateboard to the club so you can save gas."

I had to remove the phone away from my ear as I tried to hold back the laughter. He had been in the car with me last week when I went to the gas pump, and complained about how high the gas was. I had said I am going to have to get me a bike to ride if this gas keeps getting higher, highway robbery!

"Cool man," I said, as I placed the phone back to my ear. How are you going to roll out with me on a skateboard?"

"I already have a skateboard remember, you know Grandma Glenda bought it for me?" He said it like he was annoyed that I did not remember that my mom had bought him a skate board.

"Oh so you going to skateboard with me, what if you get tired because you know when we roll out, we roll for a long time?"

"I am going to put a hole in mine and yours so you can hook mine to yours when I get tired."

His imagination tickled me to death, anytime I wanted a good laugh, I could always count on Quincy and his imagination.

"Well what about if your mom wants to go with us, are you making her a skateboard too?"

"*No daddy,* mom can't skateboard she will mess up her toes. You can put her on your back and I will be in back to catch her if she falls."

"Hold on a minute man," I said, as I removed the phone from my ear again and laughed. I told the guys what this boy was saying; we all had a good laugh.

"Alright then man seems that you got it all figured out. Well, let me know when mine is ready."

"Okay, you want to talk to mama?"

"Yea man, love you dude."

"Love you to daddy."

Keisha gets back on the line and says, "What's up papa?"

"You, what ya'll gettin' into today?"

"Whenever he finishes his chair," Keisha was saying, Quincy cut her off,

"Work bench mama not chair!" hollered Quincy.

"I meant his work bench," Keisha said, sarcastically "We are going to get something to eat. Why what's up?"

"I was going to ask you and Quincy to come hang out with me tonight, and you can cook your man some dinner."

"Quincy do you want to go over to your dads and stay tonight?"

"Yes!!!" hollered Quincy, he loved to stay over at my house.

"Cool. Well I should be there around ten, so go ahead to the store and have my dinner ready when I get there woman."

"Whatever! I'll see you when you get there crazy ass."

"Bye baby," I said, mimicking her.

"Bye boo, she said, mimicking me.

I hung up from Keisha and placed a call to Mercedes.

"What up girl," I asked.

"Nothing," she said, like she was so depressed.

"What's wrong with you?" I asked exhaling, already regretting that I had even bothered calling.

"Nothing just sitting here bored?"

"You want to go out and chill for a while?"

"I really want to just chill at home tonight Cue, why don't you come over here?"

I looked at my watch, it was now 4 pm. If I headed over there now I could chill with her until about nine, and then head out. Getting out would not be a problem because she knew my life style and I could always use that I had some business to take care of, but it still would not stop her from bitching.

"Ok I'm headed over, you want me to pick up something to eat?"

"Yes, go buy the Chop House and get me a sirloin and Caesar's salad."

Just like her to always want a meal that's at least twenty five dollars or more.

"Alright, be there in about an hour."

When I got to Mercedes house she was laying on the couch watching life time. She jumped up, ran over to kiss me, as she took her bag of food from my hands and skipped off to the kitchen. I went into the bedroom and stripped down to my boxers. By the time I had got back to the living room, she was sitting on the couch Indian styled, with her food rested on her knees with a glass of wine, eating.

I flopped down beside her as she looked over at me and leaned in and kissed me saying, "I love you."

This is what she lived for. As long as I was here she was fine. Mercedes would be content staying right here in this very room for a whole week, without ever going outside of it as long as I was here. We vacationed for a week in Jamaica a few years back. I tell you it was like pulling teeth to get her out of the condo we rented to sight see and do excursions. I told her that I had not spent all of that money to come over here to sit in a house all day, hell we could have rented a luxury house in our area for that. Her reply was that she never has me to herself like this when we're home, so she wants to enjoy me as much as she could now, because once we're back home its whatever, whenever again. I understood her logic, but hell what else was there to do but look at television? We had already done everything else, now I wanted to get out. As much as I loved her ass, it wasn't that much to keep me hemmed up with her ass for a whole seven days. Either we get out, or she was going to find herself by herself.

I took Keisha to the Bahamas' a month later. I couldn't keep her ass in the hotel long enough to do half the things I wanted to do with her. Her ass wanting to go shopping, get massages she even bribed me into getting a manicure and pedicure, which I have now grown accustomed to. How her ass found a nude beach, I had no idea, but I loved running behind her thick ass on it.

After Mercedes had finished with her $30 meal she placed her box on the coffee table, pulled my arm up, leaned back and nestled her head on my chest and exhaled. I rubbed her back as we continued to lay there and watch the, "Man Bashing Network" I know we watched two movies straight before I tried to get in the goody bag, she said, "We have all night baby, this movie is good."

I don't have all night I thought to myself, there was no way I was going to be sitting here with your ass all night long on a Friday night watching some shit that didn't interest me in the least bit. And then on top of all that even if we did wait until bed time, as good as the sex was, she was still only a one time fuck. It would be no resting up and getting some more in a few. My appetite was nasty, and when I wanted it I wanted it. So if I want you to roll over again and you give me lip about it, I'm bouncing, and going to get it from somewhere. Mercedes wanted to get married. I couldn't see how we could be married and live happily ever after. I do want to settle down in about ten years or so, but my lady is going to have to be submissive to me. I am not controlling at all, I just want whoever my wife is going to be, to worship the ground that I walk on, because if she does that then that means she's going to love to make sure that all of my needs are met. Just a few basics are all I ask; clean house, cook dinner, take care of herself and sex me when I want it. If she performs those duties I will give her the world.

Mercedes and I must have dozed off, when I woke up it was 10:30 and she was in my arms sound asleep. I lifted her and carried her to the bedroom. I laid her down and undressed her and started to kiss her when she pushed me away and said, "Cue why we can't not just lay here and let me sleep in your arms? I am so tired. I promise you that I will take care of you in the morning."

I got up, put on my clothes, as she rested up on her elbows watching me, she said, "Oh because I am not in the mood to have sex tonight that means you have to leave?"

"I'll see you in the morning when you're in the mood," I said, as I picked up my keys and headed for the door. Hell I was already late meeting Keisha and my son, and I was willing to be even later just to please Mercedes because I knew they were at my pad and they were good, but I be damned if I leave them waiting just to sleep beside her ass all night.

"Cue, come back please." She was pleading as I went out the door. I sure wasn't up for talking about this shit all night. Without realizing it, she had just made what I thought was going to be a difficult task of getting away from her tonight, so much easier.

"Daddy's home!" was music to my ears as I opened the door to my house and my little mini-me came running like a bat out of hell and jumped into my arms. I cannot tell you how much this little man means to me, he makes me feel like a man and I know he depends on me and that alone makes me feel great. I can't wait until I can enroll him into sports. He is going to be a beast; he loves basketball and football. When he comes and stays over with me that is all this boy wants to do is play ball.

He was ratting his mother out as I locked up the door because she would not let him bring his work bench over to the house with them. She walked up and started tickling him in his sides and said, "Oh you're telling on me little one?" He wiggled and giggled as she continued to tickle him and stood to her tip toes to peck me on the lips.

"You ready to eat baby?" She asked, as she turned and headed back towards my kitchen.

"Starved" I said, as I started following behind her watching how good her ass looked in those Hollister cloth capri's that were hugging her every curve. Keisha lived to take care of me and I loved that about her. Anytime I asked her to come cook me dinner she would not hesitate, she's very submissive to me and that is why I love her so much. It's worked all these years, so why try to fix it now? One thing is for damn sure and that is that I loved this girl more than I should have allowed myself to. I let my guard down in the mist of all the fun she and I was having, she crept into a space in my heart that I haven't even let Mercedes get to.

When Quincy and I got into the kitchen Keisha was placing a bowl of chicken wings on the table, alongside, a bowl of French fries. She had sliced up some tomatoes and had a bottle of hot sauce and ketchup on the table beside a huge pitcher of homemade lemonade.

"Dang girl!" I said, as I slapped her ass. Quincy giggled and said "Daddy you're nasty!"

I started tickling him as Keisha fixed our plates.

"So what's been going on man?" I asked Quincy as I broke off a piece of chicken to put on my bread that Keisha had layered with Mayo and tomatoes.

"Just working man; trying to build this bench so I can make me a go cart."

"Oh lawd!" Keisha said trying to play my son. "Quincy you told me you were making your dad a skate board?"

"I am mama," Quincy said with exasperation. "I am going to make me a go cart first so I can drive to the store and get everything for the skateboard," he said like Keisha was foolish for not knowing this already.

I just lowered my head and pretended to be concentrating on my food, while trying to hold in my laugh. Keisha kicked me from under the table.

I looked up at her and said, "Darn babe does he have to spell everything out for you? That should be common-sense. Of course he would build the go cart first, anybody would know that. He has to have transportation to get back and forth. I guess he's tired of asking you to take him everywhere." I joked.

"Right daddy," Quincy agreed while putting up his hand to high five me.

"Both of you knuckle heads are tripping," Keisha said as she got up to get more ice. "And Cue you do not need to be entertaining him on this ridiculousness because he will think that it is ok for him to go off by himself."

"I'm a big boy my grandma said it. Big boys can drive to the store by themselves."

"You're a big little boy but you are not a big boy that can go anywhere by himself. And whenever; if ever, you finish your little project, I wish you would leave out the yard, less on off the street without permission or by yourself. Do you understand Quincy?" Keisha's eyebrows were arched up in attack mode.

I stopped eating and looked at her scared for my son myself. She had gone from playing too serious in ten seconds flat. The look on her face told me that she meant business. If Quincy wasn't scared, I sure as hell was scared for him. I had never seen or heard Keisha talk to our son with this much force.

Quincy gave me a look that was saying "Can you clear this up and tell her it is alright?" I just lifted my hands in the air and said, "Buddy, I got to be with your mom on this one. You have to let her know when you get ready to go off. You can't just leave without permission." Shit, he wasn't getting me on her bad side tonight.

Keisha walked by and popped me in the back of my head. "No, you tell him that he can't go off by himself period Cue!"

"Girl he knows that, he's a big boy." I laughed, as she dropped an ice cube down my shirt.

"Daddy can you help me build my go cart?"

"Sure man that would be great, when you want to start?"

"Tonight," Quincy said matter of factly.

It was now my time to look for Keisha to jump in and say something like, "Well not tonight, it is late and you have to go to bed." I was the parent that rarely said no to Quincy. Instead, she lowered her head in the same fashion that I had earlier, trying to conceal a laugh. So I kicked her ass underneath the table.

"Well welcome to my world," she hissed through clinched teeth. "I have to deal with this over the top imagination every day."

Quincy who had his chin resting in the palm of his hand, and elbow on the table was looking from his mother to me trying to figure out what we were whispering about.

"Well buddy it's pretty late and the stores are about to close so let's go tomorrow."

"Ok, well wake me up early because I don't want to be working late."

I looked at him and said in shock, "What tha?" Keisha and I both just laughed.

"I can't," Keisha said waving her hands.

We sat at the table with Quincy entertaining us for another thirty minutes before Keisha ushered him off to bed.

After Keisha had got Quincy settled she came into the living room where I had turned on the basketball game, straddled over me as she started kissing my neck and licking my earlobes.

"Girl you better stop before you start something," I said, while massaging her bottom.

"That is exactly what I want to do," she whispered into my ear as she proceeded to stick her warm tongue into it.

About two hours later she was lying in the cradle of my arm running her fingers threw my chest hairs. "I love you Cue."

"I love you to baby," I said, as I massaged the back of her head.

"Can I ask you a question and you not get mad?" She asked looking up into my face.

Oh shit here we go with the questions, which really came as no surprise to me. Keisha was always pushing me to tell her how I felt, as if she didn't already know. I tell her ass I love her all the damn time.

She had her head lying on my chest looking up to me. I looked down at her and exhaled as I said, "Shoot."

"Why you say it like that?" She giggled as she playfully smacked my face.

"Because you always start getting deep after I lay this good loving on you. I am going to have to stop giving it to you because you start tripping."

"Whatever knuckle head," she laughed. "I wish you would try to cut me off from my baby."

"What's up? Spill it." I said, ready to get this; Yes Keisha I do love you- Keisha you are not going to lose me over with. I don't know why she was so damn insecure, if only she knew the real deal. She worries so much about Mercedes. If I ever did decide to get married; if it wasn't to Keisha, it would have to be someone damn close to her. Right now I am trying to get my mind right. Mercedes she just doesn't have the mentality of the person that I want as a wife. I am every bit of a man and so is her ass. She runs that mouth so damn much. And don't let me raise my voice at her. Shit we are going toe to toe!

Keisha is much bigger than Mercedes size wise. Mercedes is like 5'5 and Keisha's around 5'9. However, Keisha will never challenge me the way Mercedes petite ass does unless I am really just being an ass. I have picked arguments with Keisha simply because I had a bad day. She will just look at me and say "Baby I haven't done anything. I don't know what your problem is but we are good. We are not going to let whatever happened on the street's come into what we have here." She will even go on to apologize or ask what she can do to make my mood better. Try that shit with Mercedes ass and its, "Nigger, I don't know what hoe done pissed you off; but you can take your ass back to her with this damn attitude!"

"Cue I know you love me I just need to know exactly where we are going in our future. I mean how long are we supposed to continue like this?" Keisha continued.

"Keisha don't I take care of you?"

"Yes but," she started as I stopped her by placing my forefinger on her lips to shush her.

"Just answer my question. Do I make you happy?"

"Yes baby."

"Did you not know my situation when you started fucking with me?"

"Yes," it was very softly spoken, but it was a yes.

"Are you tired of me?"

"No Cue, I want to be with you, you know that."

"Then why are you trying to change lanes when the traffic seems to be flowing smoothly?"

"Cue do you expect for me to be your jump off for the rest of my life? I want to be with a man that can do things with me in the open. We have a precious son in there that deserves to have two parents to take care of him."

"Keisha he does have both parents. What the hell are you talking about? And you are definitely more than a jump off to me you know that."

"Your son is your little secret Cue! You're so called woman," she said holding up her two forefingers as to quote, "knows nothing about him. You say he means the world to you so how do you wake up every day knowing that you can't openly be the father that you want to be? You're keeping your child a secret. Who really means more to you him or her?"

"Damn you Keisha! How dare you say some bullshit like that?" I said, getting up from the bed. "I spend as much time as I can with my son. I provide for him and he knows that his dad loves him. You know I love that lil man more than anything! Mercedes or no other woman is that important to me. If it came down to it; I have no problem with Mercedes knowing. There has not been any problems in three years so why in the hell are you trying to make it one now?"

"Because I have been with your ass for almost four years Cue. I am not getting any younger. I want to know whether I am even an option in your life for the future."

"Keisha I am not getting ready to settle down anytime soon. So if marriage is what you are looking for right now you're with the wrong dude. Do I want to lose you? No. But I will not allow you to make me commit to something I am not ready for. Hell no!"

Keisha's eyes watered up as she looked at me and slowly nodded her head as if to say she understood. She got up from the bed and strutted her naked ass into the bathroom. I heard her turn the shower on as I sat at the corner of the bed and just starred at the closed bathroom door.

Keisha was progressing a lot. She had just purchased a small house that she was remodeling for Quincy and herself. I know that she was a great saver of money plus she took very good care of my son. I had never known a woman to love a child as much as she loved that little rascal. I think she showered him with so much love because of how much she loved me. I loved her for that; because I know cats that I am close with who has babies by the most trifling women. They constantly have to worry about their kid's well being; I don't have that problem with Keisha. If I know nothing else, I know that Quincy is good.

I stepped into the bathroom and into the shower with Keisha. She did not hear me come into the bathroom and jumped when I opened the shower door to step in. She had both her hands placed on the wall and her head was slumped between her shoulders. I placed my hands on her shoulders and pulled her to me and kissed the back of her neck.

"Keisha just know that you are not just anybody to me, you mean a lot to me. I don't want to lose you baby. I just need you to be patient with me."

She turned to me and nodded her head as she laid her head on my chest and put her arms around my neck. I felt her softly whimpering as I massaged her back and tried to ensure her that I was not going anywhere.

Damn, I need to do something and do it fast.

As Keisha and I got out of the shower I peeked out the bedroom window because lights were illuminating it. Mercedes was pulling out of the drive way. Apparently, she had been knocking. We were in the shower so we did not hear her knocks. She either thought I was that mad and just ignoring her, or either she figured I was not yet home. She could not see into my garage. Whatever her thoughts, I was just glad she decided to leave. Mercedes must be really upset because she never rides over to my house without talking to me first. Thank goodness that she doesn't have a key, she is my girl but I knew with my lifestyle, and her way of thinking, that I better not had given her butt a key to my pad. I picked my phone up and noticed that she had called me ten fucking times, plus left ten fucking messages. The last one stating that she had called my boys and no one had seen me, so what in the hell was I doing?

This girl here, I swear was only making me want to get away from her ass more. She was really making me second guess her ass. One thing that I don't like or appreciate, is a female taking the liberty upon themselves to just pop up thinking they are going to invade my space. I never pop up at her house although I could. It's a respect thing. I always call letting her know that I am on my way, even if I am only five minutes away.

Chapter Eleven

(Keisha)

"Girl why did you not tell me that Eric would have my ass like this?" Britney was fussing at me through the phone.

She had been kicking it with Eric for a few months and was really feeling him. And from what Cue told me he was feeling her as well. He was driving this fool crazy when it would take him hours to respond back to a call or text she had put out to him.

"You never asked fool. And how was I to know. I have never fucked with him and neither am I close to anyone other than you that has fucked with him?" I laughed.

I was sitting on the side of my bed filing my toe nails before I actually went to the salon to have a pedicure tomorrow. I know I am special; but I had one to chip and you never know who you may run into. I had to always be on point.

"You are having a great time with him aren't you?"

"Yes, but I can't deal with this bipolar thing he has going. I have never been with a man that wasn't all on my ass especially when I am all on his. And when you're a fast typer, ten minutes is too damn long to wait on a fucking response!"

"What the hell?" I laughed at my crazy friend, "Britney you knew that he dated Tonya, so I do not know why you are tripping now."

I am tripping because his ass knew he was dating Tonya when he first started trying to get into my shit. He was dotting every I and crossing every T then, so he could sure as hell do the same now, ain't shit changed! If Tonya was all of that he should have told me that from the start, rather than making it seem like they were not official and just friends! He should have not been the one to decide, "Oh I'll have Britney fall in love with me first, and then spring Tonya on her."

"Fall in love? Really Britney, you are in love with him?" I was totally shocked because Britney is a hard ass and her motto is, "Play them before you get played, leave before you are left," so for her to say that she loved Eric, after only a few months, was huge.

"Well Britney at least you have a little stability. You know that you are going to be with him every Friday night if you want to be. At least he has designated that night just for you. I wish I knew when I was going to see Cue a certain day. I am always surprised when he says "Let's get together" and goodness forbids he sets something up a day or two ahead of time, I would think he's about to propose!"

Britney laughed at my sarcasm and said, "Well you are use to that mess, I am not. And I do not want to get use to it. The thing is, I know he is really feeling me, he's said so himself. I don't understand what his problem is."

I was laying in my bed still waiting on Cue to arrive who was now three hours late. He had told me while we were on the phone earlier that he would be over here around nine. Here it is about to strike midnight, not only had he not shown, he also was not answering his cell phone or returning calls. I have dealt with this, as Britney said, forever. I always waited whether patient or not. As long as I allowed this, he would always do this to me.

"Britney do you feel up to going to the club tonight?"

"You're not going to wait on Cue?" Britney asked. I could hear the surprise in her voice.

"I am always waiting on Cue, and he may or may not show. I have wasted my Saturday night on his ass; I am tired of this mess. I mean he could at least return my calls or let me know if he is still coming. He is three hours late, not answering calls, or returning calls.

Well let's do the darn thing, Britney said, all excited. She too was sitting home depressed over Eric's ass. Cue and his smooth ass friends had a way of doing everything to make the ladies crazy over them, and then start acting like fools.

I put on a pair of skinny jeans and cuffed the bottom. I slipped on a cute off the shoulder, tan, loose fitting, silk shirt that had elastic at the bottom of it. I decided to wear my leopard print, Christian Louboutin's that looked like a boot with cut outs. I must say that I was loving this ensemble; cute, sexy and conservative. Britney was sitting in her car waiting on me when I pulled up. I waved at her as I passed by her car to find me a parking spot. When I walked back up Britney was standing at the steps that led up to the club looking hot.

"Scared of you *girl*, you're looking *cute*! Are those the Hunfew's that you were telling me that Eric bought for you?" I asked, referring to Britney's attire. She had on some super skinny, super low cut Levi's. A cute black fitted sweater that sat across the shoulders exposing her awesome shoulder blades and small waist line. Britney's waist was so tiny that her hips was always overly exposed, baby had back. She was wearing some multi-colored Hunfew's that had more black in them than any other color.

"I do what I do," she said as she pretended to be dusting the dirt/hate from her shoulders. "Yes girl, you know I only have two pair of Hunfew's. The black ones that I bought and these," she laughed "Your looking pretty spiffy yourself I must say," she said as we made our way up the steps and into the club.

I noticed Cue and Eric going into V.I.P. I was furious. I am at home waiting on this dude and he is in the club? He could not even call and tell me that he would be there after, or was not coming? There is a thing called common courtesy. I walked right over to V.I.P; opened the curtain and came eye to eye with both Cue and Mercedes. I walked right on in because I could do that. I was always welcomed in V.I.P. I just chose not to be there because for one, it was away from everything. The real party was on the floor as far as I was concerned. And secondly, Mercedes bougie ass along with her friends, were always up in there. Britney and I walked over to the bar that was in the V.I.P section and took a seat.

Lance the bartender asked, "The usual baby girl?"

"Yes, boo," I replied.

As Lance went off to fix my drink, I swirled around in the swivel bar stool to face the dance floor. Mainly to focus on the couches that sat on the other side of the dance floor where Cue was sitting with Mercedes and her posse. As always, Mercedes was looking dead at me. I could tell she was not too happy with my decision to come up into V.I.P tonight. Hell, she's probably wondering just how come I do get so much special treatment;

although her mind was clearly telling her, she just didn't want to believe it.

Lance finally came back with our drinks. I'm pretty sure she noticed no funds were exchanged, as always, because your man has it. Eric was sitting there beside Tonya looking like a child that had been caught with his hands in the cookie jar.

Britney and I decided to just have fun. We got up to go to the dance floor alone when Keisha Coles "Enough of No Love" came on. Our dancing alone was very short lived. Steady who I did not see come in, came over and started dancing with the both of us. Then another guy that I did not know came over to relieve Steady from having to handle the both of us, and pulled me around to dance with him. He and Steady gave each other a high five as we all switched up. All eyes were on us. We were having a great time, as we danced the next five or six songs.

The .D.J was boosting the four of us up saying shit like, "It's a party right here... Now this what I'm talking about...Get it Keisha... go Britney... Alright I see you Steady...You blinding me Maceo." So that's his name, I thought making a mental note to remember it. "You can't handle Keisha, Maceo." Once I felt the sweat rolling down my face, I knew it was time for a bathroom run. I told Maceo I needed to go cool off. He asked what was I drinking, and said he would get me a drink. He and Steady went to the bar, while Britney and I headed to the bathroom. But not before catching the cutting eyes of Cue and Eric.

When we came from the bathroom, we went to the bar where the fella's were sitting and hopped up on the bar stool. We all were laughing, talking, dancing and having a great time. We eventually had danced up an appetite and ordered some chicken wings. My phone vibrated alerting me that I had a text. I picked it up, read the stupid shit Cue had just sent me saying, "Go home," and placed my phone back on the counter and continued to talk.

Who in the hell did he think he was, better yet who in the hell did he think I was? I was at home nigga, waiting on your ass, and you're up in the club with your bitch. "Fuck Cue" was my attitude right now.

Steady had the bright idea that we should go over to the couches, to get off these hard ass bar stools that we had been sitting on for the past hour. I actually was good and really did not want to be that close to Cue. Britney was like great, more than ready to continue to make Eric's ass jealous. We took our drinks and I walked squarely, as Britney danced her way over to one of the empty couches. When I tell you if looks could kill, we all would have been dead within eye range! We sat there bold as ever. Britney nor I was afraid of Mercedes or any of her friends. Steady and Maceo, was obviously respected as well, by the way Cue and his boys small talked with them.

We were sandwiched between Steady and Maceo. Cue, Mercedes, Eric and Tonya were sitting in the same position diagonally from us. We were close enough that we could hear each other if we listened hard enough over the music, so of course I kept my conversation innocent. Not Britney's ass. She flirted just as hard with Maceo as he was flirting with her, clearly letting Eric know that she could replace him quick, fast and in a hurry. I was not sitting all up under Steady as Britney was Maceo. Steady must had schooled Maceo while Britney and I were in the ladies room about his crush on me, because when we returned suddenly, Maceo was very interested in Britney.

The four of us continued to trip the entire time, while our counter parts across the way were cutting us with their eyes. I knew that if it was not for the fact that Mercedes was here in the club tonight, that Cue would have showed his ass. I also knew that it was not over and that he was going to blow my ears up when he finally could get to them. But hey, I was ready, because I had a few choice words for him as well.

I was so busy laughing at these fools that it did not dawn on me that Mercedes may have purposely kicked my foot as she walked by to go to the bathroom. When I felt my foot being nudged; I looked up as she was passing and thought, "I know this bitch did not just kick me on purpose?" I voiced my thoughts to Britney.

Girl Mercedes scared, no fighting ass ain't kicked you on purpose," Britney laughed.

I toyed around with the idea and came to the conclusion that it was accidental, then thought, "But why in the hell did she have to walk so close to me?" I noticed Cue get up and walk out into the main area. I was pretty sure he would be right back; there was no way he would leave Mercedes and I both alone to long unsupervised. He knew that she liked to start shit, and I liked to finish shit.

I was talking to Britney when Mercedes came back through and this time there was no mistaking that she nudged my foot purposely. I was not looking directly at her, yet I saw everything she did as she prepared to approach me. I saw as she made sure that she would be close enough to hit my foot as she walked by, when there was plenty of room for her not to be that close to me. She pretended to be all into her conversation with Tonya as she stepped on my foot. Before I knew it, I took that same foot and side kicked her ass with it.

Mercedes turned to me trying to act all shocked and innocent. She very may well have been shocked that I kicked her ass, she surely was not innocent.

"Yea, I kicked you. Your yellow ass has walked by me twice and kicked my foot," I said, calmly yet very boldly. I noticed Eric get up and haul ass out of V.I.P, I presumed that he was going to warn Cue about what was transpiring but by the time he got back, I would have waxed the floor with this bitch.

"I did not kick you Keisha. And if I had accidently stepped on your foot that was very immature of you to kick me rather than ask if it was done on purpose, which it was not." She was talking very professionally as if to make me seem beneath her.

"Whatever Mercedes," I said, waving her off with my hand. "The first time you did it, I let you get away with it and thought shame on you. The second time, I knew that it was no accident. If I had let you get away with it, then the shame would have been on me. You knew what the hell you were doing. The smart thing for you to have done would have been for your ass to walk in the direction you sat, not out of your way all up in my space." I had a few drinks in me and was ready for combat. I had been wanting this bitch for a minute anyway with all the shit she's been running around in the street talking about me and my son.

She was standing there saying something which was only a blur to me, because I was concentrating on taking out my two karat diamond earrings that Cue had bought me for my birthday. As soon as I got them out, I placed them into Britney's awaiting hands and went to punch Mercedes who was backing up. Cue grabbed me from behind, picked me up, and carried me to the back office. All the while Mercedes and I both were screaming at one another.

Once Cue got me to the back room he practically threw me onto the couch that was there and started yelling at me. "What the hell is your damn problem, you out there acting like a fucking hoe and now trying to pick a damn fight for something stupid? You really do need to grow the fuck up Keisha or you going to fuck this up for us." He hissed this last part between clenched teeth. I take it so that Mercedes and those out front to not hear. "I don't know what your problem is Keisha, you got it all and you want to trip? Keep your ass in here until I get back!" He looked at me through piercing eyes as he turned to leave the room.

I was so startled by his reaction. His words pierced my heart so badly that I could not even defend myself. Why in the hell was he so mad at me, what in the hell had Eric went out there and told him? I was sitting out there minding my own business and enjoying the company that I had. They were the ones over there mean mugging us. She was the one that walked by me not once but twice and kicked my feet on the sly. Did he want me to just sit back and let his girlfriend do and say whatever the hell she wanted to me, and I do or say nothing? I am the mother of his child. I felt that I have dealt with more than enough from both Cue and Mercedes. I respect them and their space, I am more than loyal to his ass, I stay in my lane and I do not spazz out on him in front of anyone, whether Mercedes is around or not.

The longer I sat there the madder I became. Why in the hell was I allowing him to treat me this way? I call him, he hardly ever answers, nor does he call back until he is good and ready. When I questioned him about this he said, that when he's out working he's normally occupied with his business and if he cannot talk he just doesn't answer. I asked, well what if it was an emergency or something with Quincy, because apparently my ass wasn't that important to him, if he felt that he did not have to answer my calls. He had the audacity to tell me, that if it was an emergency to just text him. Then most days I go two, three days before Quincy or I hear anything from him. Yet he wants me to be faithful to him. If I am going to be faithful to only you, a man that has a girlfriend, you could at least respect me enough to answer my calls and not let two and three days go by before you get back to me.

Despite what Cue may think of me, I am not crazy. Just because I may not be all college educated, and prissy like Miss Thang in there, I do have goals. I am no dummy and just as smart. Fuck Cue was my mentality at this point, as I got up to leave this room. Who does he think he is?

I opened the door to the office and Britney was talking to Cue as I walked up and took my purse from her arm and said, "I'm out." I turned to leave and noticed Mercedes and Tonya was still sitting there. I was sure that he was out here getting rid of her ass, and that was why he told me to stay put. So what in the hell did he call himself doing? Putting me in time out or something? Fuck Cue!

Britney came running out behind me calling my name. We stood outside of my car and talked about what happened. Britney said that she told Cue what had happened, and although he did not say she was lying, that he did insinuate that he could not see Mercedes purposely doing that. She said she told him that the first time she did it I had told her that I thought she had purposely kicked me. We both decided it was an accident. Then as she was coming back through, we both watched from the corner of our eyes as we had planned to do. We saw that she got as close as she could to the couch we were sitting on, and as she passed she stepped on Keisha's foot. She said, Cue was just shaking his head and said something to the fact that this area in V.I.P is tight, especially where the coffee tables are located, which happened to be the area that we were sitting in. Either Cue just doesn't want to believe it or he is just plain out stupid, Britney was saying. It was as if he tried to justify it for her. Britney said that he also told her, "I love Keish, you need to talk to your girl, and she needs to stop tripping."

"Whatever, tell Cue to get over himself. Mercedes and my beef was long before his ass came into the picture."

"Keisha he is so nervous, he's like Britney you need to talk to your girl. Tell her to just hold on and stop jumping to conclusions. I was coming to pick her up tonight, I was about to leave right before ya'll came in. Mercedes called saying she was coming to the club, so I had to hang around for a minute so she didn't get suspicious."

Britney said she told him; he should have called and told me what was going on. She told him he had me at home dressed and waiting on him and he wasn't even answering or returning my calls. And that is why I was so mad. She said his defense was, that Mercedes was sitting beside him and he couldn't answer or text. Britney and I both knew that was not the truth. As much a Cue was out and around in the club, he could have if he wanted to. He just felt that I wasn't that important and he would deal with me when he was ready. That is what pissed me off.

"Do me a favor Britney?"

"What girl," Britney asked suspiciously.

"Go tell Cue that I said to kill himself. If he needs any help doing it to call me, I will be happy to oblige."

"Shut up your just mad," Britney said smiling "Let's go get something to drink at Korkies."

After telling Britney that I would meet her there I went to my car. My mind was made up over something as simple as this. Out of all the bigger things that I had dealt with during our relationship, this here is what made me finally say, "Fuck it." I was done waiting on Cue, I was done being ignored by Cue and I was done being second to that bitch ass Mercedes. If I keep letting him treat me this way, he always would.

Chapter Twelve

(Mercedes)

"My baby wears an S on his chest because his name is Superman." Just who in the hell was this whores baby. And when did she ever spend time with him? Because every time I see her, her ass is up in the club always in my man's face. I was on the passenger side of Mahogany's car looking at Keisha's facebook page. We were headed to Cleveland Park, it was Sunday afternoon and the park was the place to be.

Although we could not say for sure who she messed with, because I had never known her to mess with anyone except for her son's dad, whoever he was, but she does have very whorish tendencies. I say that because she is always in the club wearing her damn clothes so tight I know that she must keep a yeast infection, and she is always flirting with all of the guys that she thinks may have a dime or two including mine.

I scrolled on down her page hoping to see a picture of her son that she keeps so anonymous on facebook. Most parents have their children plastered all over their page, not Keisha. As a matter of fact, that is one reason I created a fake page after Keisha had given birth, so that I could get a glimpse of this child that everyone had so much to say about. Some said that he looked like Cue, others said not. I know that it was not Cue's child; I just wanted to see him. You can imagine the disappointment I had once Keisha had accepted my friend request, and there was not one picture of the baby on her page.

I was thrilled when one of her friends asked her on facebook, to post pictures of the baby; they would love to see him. Keisha responded that she would inbox her. That she did not want his face floating around cyber space. Who in the hell and what in the hell did she think she had, a million dollar baby that paparazzi was going to pay her a million dollars for the first photo of?

Dang this park is jammed packed shrilled Lynn, who was in the back seat of the convertible with Shonda. Lynn is Cue's one and only sister we are very close, although she is shady. She has been my girl sense before I started going out with her brother, but she will defend him to no ends, even when she knows that he is wrong.

When people were talking about Keisha possibly being pregnant by Cue years ago, Lynn defended him. When I caught another girl driving one of his cars, Lynn defended him. When I had to take my own ass to be treated for gonorrhea, Lynn defended him. So needless to say, there was no use in counting on Lynn to spill any dirt to me.

We had come to stand still traffic as to be expected on Sunday afternoons here in the park. Which was fine by us because we had a full tank of gas, and we were in Mahogany's drop top, black Mercedes that was almost, as nice as mine. Sitting in traffic you could people watch, gossip about the half necked hoochies, and flirt with the guys as they passed in their freshly washed whips.

"Look at Keisha and her ratchet crew," Mahogany said.

I logged off from her facebook page. I knew that there was no way Keisha would know that I was on her page, I just did not want anyone to run up on the car and happen to notice it either.

"I don't see what Cue or any man see's in her," Mahogany continued.

Mahogany seemed to hate Keisha just as much as I did. I was sure it was because of Nick. Nick had been Mahogany's first love when we were in high school, and when they broke up he went after Keisha. Mahogany confronted Keisha about going to the movies with him. Keisha made her look and seem really petty; I must say so myself. She asked her did they still date because if they did she would back off.

What could Mahogany say? Because they were not dating; he had broken up with her controlling ass. Keisha told her that she was free to go out with whoever she wanted, and unless he was her boyfriend she had no business acquiring about they done or where they went. She told her that he had said that he was no longer seeing her, and that was good enough for her. She did not owe her an explanation, because she was nobody to her.

"Cue does not mess with Keisha," Lynn said, defensively. "Get the hell off my brother."

"So you accompany your brother on all of his booty calls?" Shonda asked Lynn. "I don't care what you say whether he mess with her now or not, something has happened between the two of them at one point or another."

"I don't need to, I know my brother plus we talk. He has no reason to lie to me, so go back to sleep Shonda. Maybe she's rolling her eyes because she knows that her name is forever in your mouths."

Before Shonda could reply to Lynn, Lynn pointed out Steady who had just parked and got out of his Cadillac. Shonda called his name, when he realized who it was he jogged through the traffic over to our ride. He dapped me, Mahogany and Lynn then looked at Shonda and snared up his nose rolling his eyes imitating what girls do.

"Whateva Nukka," Shonda said, rolling her eyes back at him. "I called you back last night and you are the one that did not answer the phone."

"You must have had me confused with your other nigga, he said, playfully slapping her on the face. "And what the hell do you have on?" Steady asked, tugging at the top of Shonda's strapless shirt.

Steady has been trying to get with Shonda for the past year. Finally she broke and went out with him. After that first date she called and told me that she could not do it. He was so charming and she could not afford to be falling in love with a man that has made it clear that he was in no position to leave his girl just yet. Although Shonda continued to go out with him it was not more than that, and this drove Steady crazy because he was use to women throwing there thongs at him. Shonda would never allow herself to go through the stuff that I went thru with Cue. I wish I was as strong as she is.

Steady asked Shonda was she going to call him tonight. Promising that she would, he said for us to be good and he jogged back across the street to his whip.

Lynn said aloud, "Damn I would fuck the hair thin on his thighs."

Mahogany reached her hand towards the back for Lynn to give her five. Shonda and I just laughed.

"He is fine ain't he?" Shonda cosigned.

"And your ass scared of him," Lynn continued. "See someone wet behind the ears like you would not know what to do with a fine specimen of a man like Steady. You're to sudity, he needs some hood booty," Lynn laughed giving Mahogany five again like Mahogany knew anything about being hood.

"I am not scared of Steady; I am scared of my feelings. You know I work hard to keep my feelings separated from my emotions and when dealing with a guy like Steady? No I will just pass, let them other women deal with the headaches I am good."

"Didn't anyone say that you had to fuck him," Lynn said while waving at someone she knew. "I am just saying that this nigga has plenty resources and you need to take advantage of them."

"He has plenty of women too," Shonda said.

"And he has plenty of money," Mahogany added. "As long as he is breaking you off pretty and don't have his other whores running in your face every five minutes Mahogany said, glancing over at me as if saying, like this dummy here, let him."

"And how long do you clowns really think that this man is going to do that without me putting out? Yea, he will at first because he is trying to get my treasures, but when he finds that the key to the treasure box is lost at sea, he will go elsewhere."

"Shoot Leon still spends all of his money on me, and he gets the treasures." Lynn said.

"Fool your fucking Leon," Shonda said to Lynn.

"I am saying before I started," Lynn laughed.

"Lynn you held out for what? Three weeks? I asked.

"Whether it was three weeks or three days the fact is that he was spending and he still does spend," Lynn said, defensively.

"Yea, he spends, I will give you that," I said. "However, did things not change once he got the goods? Yeap, he flipped on your ass after he had you saying, goo-goo – gah-gah over his ass. Then the calls started becoming less frequent and the hook ups. So don't front like you held out until you got him where you wanted him, when the truth is, he let you hold out as long as you wanted, because he knew that when the time did come that he was going to whip that ass." We all laughed, as Lynn pushed the back of my head.

"Forget all of that," Shonda said, "Things are not how it once was back in the day. There's some harsh mess transmitting now that you cannot get rid of. Back in the day if your man gave you a STD you curse his ass out, go to the health department, and get pills to cure it. But most of this mess they have going on now is incurable. I love me and the life I am living, I am not about to let no bullshitting, can't be faithful man, cut it short behind his mess."

I laid my head back onto the head rest and closed my eyes as I listened to Shonda and the crew go on about infidelity and STD's. Shonda could always get me to thinking and feeling some kind of way about my own personal relationship with Cue. While I know that Cue is a liar and a cheater, I loved him. I have told him over and over again that if he is cheating on me please be smart enough to use protection, don't you ever bring anything home.

I opened my eyes to see who it was that had called Lynn's name. Keisha was standing on the side of the road leaned against her Chrysler 300 along with two of her girlfriends who I despised as much as I did her. Lynn said hi to her, but she acted like she really did not want to speak. Lynn is a trip, I bet when I am not around she probably be all up in Keisha's face.

"Did anyone ever find out who was her baby's daddy?" Shonda asked, leaning up to the front looking into the rearview mirror fixing her hair.

"I heard that it was that guy named Rome, who had moved down here a few years back from New York that everyone was after. Remember, he ended up going back up north," Shonda said.

"Well I sure hope that Cue is not messing with her ass anymore."

Mahogany really had a way of pissing me the heck off. It had never been proving that Cue had ever fooled around with Keisha. Mahogany speaks as if it was a proven fact. Neither Mahogany nor I could really prove that Keisha sleeps around, but Mahogany loves to insinuate it.

"Why didn't he ever get a blood test anyway, whether she said it wasn't his or not, if you know you had been there during that time any decent man would have had a test done."

I was about two seconds from jumping over there on her head. I don't know what her fucking problem was with Cue. It's as if she tries to get under my skin, she knows how I feel about the whole situation and she knows that I do not believe that Cue and Keisha actually slept together. True, I believe they flirted around, nothing more.

"Why would you need a blood test if you haven't had sex?" I asked, looking at Mahogany, letting her know that I was not appreciating her accusations.

"Whatever, Mercedes. Your stupid ass just in denial. If Cue would fuck Tamisha, he surely would fuck Keisha. Pussy has no jurisdiction with Cue. They can be hood, ratchet, preppy or bourgie. As long as they have a body on them, that is his only requirement.

I was about to show her ratchet when she looked over at Lynn and asked, why wasn't she saying anything all of a sudden.

"You seem to have everything that you don't know, figured out. So I'm was just letting you continue to make a fool of yourself. The way you carry on about my brother makes me wonder if you want him or something," Lynn said.

"Speak of the devil," Shonda said, knowingly solving what was about to turn into a blowout. Mahogany had tons of mouth, and Lynn would not take much of her lip before punching her in them. Cue's Denali which was stuck in traffic also, was coming in our direction. I immediately got butterflies in the pit of my stomach. It never ceased to amaze me at how after all of these years, that he still had this kind of effect on me. Some female waved him down and went running up to his car. Traffic had begun to move slowly on their side of the road. Cue and the girl were conversating holding up the few inches that the cars could move. When the girl finally walked away from Cue's truck, he moved up in the space allowed. He was now side by side with us and did not even notice because he was busy calling out to Keisha. Keisha looked over at us and then looked back at Cue without budging. Cue called out to her again. Lynn reached up over the back seat and blew the horn to get Cue's attention. I was so mad that I wanted to put her ass out of the car and tell her to ride with her darn brother. I got out the car and started walking over towards Cue, who was looking like a deer caught in headlights.

"So what is it that you want with Keisha?" I asked, folding my arms across my chest waiting on him to answer.

"I was just speaking to her Mercedes don't trip."

"Cue I get so tired of you always acting like you and Keisha are just mad cool, if you're so mad cool why does she have such a problem with me your woman? If you want that girl you let me know now and I can bounce. I do not understand why you keep bothering this girl that has caused so many problems for us.

I turned to walk away and ignored Cue as he was calling out my name. Keisha was looking at me with a smirk on her face so I asked her did she have a problem. This heifer going to say, "No, but it seems as if you do. And believe me; you do not want another one, not with me anyway."

"Keisha you are not worth my time, I have something that you want, and you don't have a damn thing that I want."

Keisha started walking over towards me. I was glad when Cue pulled me back because I did not want to fight the ghetto heifer.

"Girl you do not know the half of what I have," Keisha said, knowingly, "And believe me you could not even compete."

"I am tired of this mess Cue, either you tell me something or leave me the hell alone. It's always something with you and this hoe! I am tired of it! You tell us both right here, right now, who do you want?"

Cue just looked at me and shook his head as he started to walk off. I jumped in front of him and hissed, "I mean it Cue. If you can't tell me in front of this hoe that you do not want her, it is going to be over. I don't care how hard of a time I may have getting over you, I will get over your ass and believe me you will suffer the consequences."

Before Cue could respond to my threat, Keisha had punched me in the jaw as she proclaimed, "I will show you a whore, bitch!"

It took Cue and Eric to pull Keisha off of me. Cue took me to Mahogany's car and said, "Take her home now!"

"Girl what in the hell is wrong with you?" Shonda was hollering louder than Cue had.

Mahogany, who was embarrassed, started letting the roof top to her convertible up. I guess so that no one could just gawk dead in on us. I felt ashamed as it settled in on how badly I had acted.

"Girl you just made a fool out of yourself straight up," Lynn chimed in. "You never act like that when the other woman that you suspect your man of having an affair with is around. You should have known better than that!"

"I can't believe this happened Mahogany said. You just acted worse than they do. You gave Keisha leverage. You acted pathetic Mercedes, what got into you?

Thanks a lot guys!" I said, through trembling lips. They were right but did they have to tell me just how silly I made myself seem. My stomach churned as I imagined how immature I just made myself look. I am twenty five years old and have a lot going on for myself, yet out here acting like this. I pray that none of my co-workers happened to be out here to notice my behavior. Damn what is wrong with me? This man has me doing things that I would not ordinarily do, and it's not cool.

Once I arrived home I went straight to my master bathroom and filled my Jacuzzi tub up with hot water. My body was aching and my head was hurting. I stood in my double mirror and held my head down as I seen my face. That heifer had scratched me from the bridge of my nose over to my ear. And although I cannot recall the punch she had to have punched me in my eye because it was throbbing and starting to discolor. "Shit!" I said, to no one.

After I got my mind together and body relaxed, I got out of the tub; dried off, put lotion on, and slipped into a cotton gown. I placed a call to Cue. Of course he did not answer, sent me straight to voice mail. I know that he rejected the call because it rang twice and then I got the recording.

I lay across my bed and cried, trying to convince myself that I did not act up too badly, but nothing could justify it. I had just made a fool of myself. I even tried to convince myself that I didn't care, knowing that I actually did care. I pulled out my I-pad and went straight to Keisha's page on facebook. She had posted, "Stupid ass got her damn skin in my nails!" She had over forty comments and they were all talking about me as if I wasn't seeing this. Well actually I shouldn't have been seeing this. Torrie said, "That bitch needs to realize that she is just the girlfriend not the wife, and she has no bragging rights." Sherry stated, "If she tries to fight everyone that Cue talks to, she may as well invest in boxing classes, and get prepared to use those skills daily, because Cue is very outgoing and he talks to women all the time." Tracy wrote, "Doesn't this make twice that you have beat that ass in less than a week? She must be a pain freak." The message that stuck out to me the most although it was not even close to the cruelest came from Lynn. "That was just crazy; you had every right to whip that ass Keisha." Lynn was the only one of my friends that did not know that I had a dummy page to observe Keisha's. I knew that Lynn could not be trusted. Lynn even asked Keisha about her son and how was he doing. Then she said something that struck me as odd. "I miss them cheeks can't wait to see him again."

Chapter Thirteen

(Mercedes)

I rolled off of Cue exhausted! I do not know what that was all about but Cue made love to me, screwed me and whipped my ass during that session. And there was something very erotic about the way he was spanking my ass and he knows that I do not get down with all of that kinky stuff, but my baby had me begging for it.

"Dang girl you rode this horse like you were a fucking cowboy," Cue said pulling my head over onto his chest. Don't tell me that you been holding back on me all of these years? He said jokingly.

"Well shoot you never loved me the way you just done either, so who has been holding back on whom?" I asked raising my head from his chest to look into his handsome face. "Everything I know I was taught by you so I just go with your flow. Obviously though judging from this session you haven't taught me all that you know," I said as I playfully squeezed his chin and pulled at his goatee.

Cue had called me around four in the morning and said that he was on his way and for me to unlock the garage.

Although my girls scolded me on my actions they still decided that they would feed me. The girls gave me their advice and opinions on how to handle Cue. Mahogany said; do not let him dictate this relationship anymore. Cue has been telling you for years that he was going to marry you, so if it's really no one else but you, give his ass an ultimatum. Marry your yellow ass or bounce!

I was excited nonetheless that he was coming over; normally whenever he gets mad at me about something crazy that I've done I may not hear from him, less on see him for a few days.

Once inside the house I went and made both of us our favorite drinks and sat down on the other end of the couch away from him, but was turned facing him.

"Cue I am going to just say what I feel and you can take it from there," I looked at him for approval, he just nodded very slowly.

"I know that I sound like a broken record but I have had enough of you making me look like an ass," he attempted to interject, but I stopped him. "Let me finish."

I do not know what the problem is that you will not keep Keisha out of our life, but it is apparent to me that you are either infatuated with leading her on," he again tried to speak and I again stopped him.

"Cue you are all of that and I understand women throwing themselves at you. You have money, power and great looking so what's not to like? I have a problem with you not being able to be faithful and understanding that you do not have to screw everything that comes your way. I do not trust you as far as I can throw you, and you still feel the need to sow your royal oats after seven years together so why waste my time. I would rather just let it go, get over it and move on rather than years from now saying woulda, shoulda, coulda."

Cue looked at me after I paused and asked, sarcastically, could he speak now. I said, yes using my eyebrow and a slight nod and twitch of my lips.

"I have told you so many times Mercedes the deal with Keisha, but your envious ass keeps letting her get to you. I repeat and I am tired of telling you this, I am not seeing Keisha. If you want to let Keisha get to you and break up what we have that is on you. I love you and I want to be with you, I do not want you to leave me, so once again just tell me what do I have to do to prove my love to you?"

"Let's get married," I blurted out while looking him right in the eyes.

The way Cue's eyebrows dipped I knew he was in shock. He looked at me as if I was a Martian.

"Seriously Cue what is the problem, you say you are not seeing anyone else. You claim that you do not want anyone else, and you have promised me that I was going to be your wife for years, so why not just do it? Because truth be told that is the only way I am going to believe that you really love me the way that you claim that you do. Unless you have something to hide, then why not?"

Cue just looked like he was deep in thought, as I am sure he was, and he said, "Let's do it."

I was in total shock. "Are you serious Cue? Don't be playing with me because you know that I am dead serious."

Cue made his way closer to me and told me that he was serious, that he was tired of playing games. I have nothing to hide Mercedes, and there is no one else. I love you and if this is what it's going to take... it's not like we weren't going to be married anyway, so let's do it.

I jumped over on him and gave him a long passionate kiss. It does not get any better than this as far as I was concerned.

I kissed those soft lips as my hand explored his magnificent body. I whispered into his ear that I loved him so much as my tongue found its way into his ear canal. I couldn't wait for everyone to know that I am Mrs. Cue Davis. My soft breathing aroused him; before I knew it he was undressing me and began to take me to the clouds. In one swift move he had flipped me over while he was still inside of me and had my legs draped over his shoulders. I looked up into those sexy brown eyes and whispered again, I love you Cue so much, I can't wait to be your wife. Cue did not respond verbally but he indeed did physically. He passionately kissed me to drown out my moans that were becoming intense. I just held on for dear life as he stroked me in a way that I could no longer take, but rather than ask him to stop like I had so many times in the past, I just held him tight and allowed his tongue to smother my screams. I loved this man, and he just didn't know what I would do to keep him.

After round two we lay embraced, and although I was sore as hell I still massaged his area knowing full well that this would arouse him again. He squeezed my shoulder and asked, "Dang girl I haven't satisfied you yet?"

"Baby you know you always satisfy me. I just love feeling on your sexy body that's all."

"Well handle your business then babe, it feels really good, I just wanted to know if you needed more before I went to sleep because you know I can oblige you?"

"Don't I know," I giggled. "You're good baby you have more than handled your business as you always do, so get some sleep I love you."

"I love you too baby girl."

Cue was sleep in a matter of seconds and I continued to massage his body and think about how this was perfect. I would cook, clean, iron and love this man to death just to have him with me on a daily basis. I was no dummy. I knew that my baby was a hot commodity and I could not honestly blame the other females for coming after him because if I wasn't his lady I would have come after him my damn self. I mean what was their not to like? He's smooth, fine as hell, a damn good love maker so no boredom there and the list just goes on. I needed to strategize because I am so ready to settle down with this man and birth this man's first baby. I just want to share so much with Cue and to have his child I feel would complete us. Of course I could do that because we do not use protection, but my family would dis-own me if I dared to have a child out of wedlock.

I continued my strategy as I showered alone while my King was in my bed where he belonged sleeping like a baby. Cue had been at my house basically all week spoiling me. Of course he was in and out, but he had been turning in every night at my house since last weekend, and I was loving and taking advantage of it. I had not been calling him every five minutes once he left I was just playing my cards right. When I heard the garage door open as he pulled in late at night I would either greet him from the couch where I was watching television, or if I had already turned in to bed with a, "Hey babe." I had not questioned his whereabouts and I even went as far as asking had he eating and if the answer had been no, I would fix his plate.

I know that I had a gem on my hands and I knew that if I did not start showing him that I recognized what I had that I was going to be ass out, and I could not allow that to happen. I was thinking that Cue had to be feeling some sort of way because he had been at my crib all week although he does stay at my crib a lot, but never before had he stayed six days in a row. The most he had ever stayed was two consecutive days, not counting the two weeks he stayed when he was in hiding until he got his name cleared.

I walked back into the room and went to the side of the bed Cue was laying, and kneeled on the floor beside him and just looked at him hoping he would open his eyes. His phone startled me as it began to vibrate on the night stand which caused me to look at it. The number appeared on the screen, although the name said unknown, I recognized this number as Keisha's so I answered. "Yes?"

"Can I speak to my daddy?" said the sweetest little voice.

"I'm sorry baby you have the wrong number."

"Ha said I got tha wrong numba," I was a little confused as I disconnected the call, although I did not have Keisha's number saved anywhere I could have sworn that was her number. I could not swear by it so I let it go but my mind was still on the cute little voice of the child that asked so sweetly could he speak to his daddy. I could not wait until Cue and I could have a child.

The phone vibrated again after I laid it down and I noticed that it was another unknown call and I figured that it was the little boy again trying to reach his daddy, but before I could reach for the phone Cue turned over and picked up his phone and looked at the screen and placed the phone back onto the night stand. I did not question him because I was working on my insecureness. He like most other people does not answer unknown calls because these telemarketers are ferocious now days.

"I want to go to the mall and pick out my ring. Are you game?" I asked, tugging at his chin.

"That figures," he said playfully pushing my hand away. "Let me shower real quickly."

"Are you serious baby?" I squealed like a child.

Cue came over and kissed me and said "Yes, I am very serious babes."

While Cue was showering I slipped into my black gotcho's with a black form fitting button down blouse and my black and pink Hunfews that Cue had just bought me a few weeks ago. I loved these shoes that crisscrossed all the way up to my calves so they really looked extra nice with the gotcho's. Cue finally came out of the bathroom fully dressed. I guess he thought I would take advantage of that magnificent body again if he paraded around me nude again. He had on a pair of 501 Levi's paired with a white t-shirt that hugged that massive chest and those sexy arms that had "No Limit," written across the chest and some fresh white Nike Air Max that I knew had to be worn for the first time today. My baby just breathed sexy from the way he dressed to the way he walked with those bowlegs.

"You ready, let's do this," he said pushing me from behind, towards the door.

"You are so violent," I said as I turned around and smacked his hands down.

Cue picked me up and threw me over his shoulder like a bag of potatoes and walked out the door with me all the while popping my rear end, and it was hard. I was kicking and punching him in the back to let me down but my punches were merely kisses to him. He unlocked the car door with one hand while still holding me over his shoulders with the other arm, and then he dumped me in the car and said, "Buckle up," as he closed the door and walked around to the driver side of the car.

"You make me sick," I laughed. After he got in the car and I smacked him on the arm. "You're going to be sorry once I start taking my karate classes," I teased.

"Baby girl you're going to need more than a few karate classes if your little butt ever expects to hang with me," he said cutting his eyes over at me with a sly smile on his gorgeous face.

The way Cue even looks at me gets me all hot and bothered, he has been with me all week and making me want him all the more. I laid my head back on the head rest and closed my eyes still strategizing my next moves. I felt Cue's hand touch mine and squeeze it, I returned the embrace as I opened my eyes and looked over at him.

"You ok baby?" I asked softly trying to sound as sweet and innocent as I could.

"I'm good," he said squeezing my hand again.

"Can I ask you a question and you try to be honest?" I said, as I rested my head back against the headrest.

"Oh gosh," Cue exhaled. "What is it Mercedes?" He said in a dragged out tone.

I playfully punched him in his arm, "How can I find out what I need to know if I don't ask?"

"What Mercedes?" Cue said dragging out the words still picking with me as if I was aggravating him which I probably would be after I asked my question. However I needed to know because I was so tired of all the rumors that I was hearing, this has been going on for years and I needed some closure to it. Every since Keisha and I had our altercation at the club last week the rumors had gotten worse.

"What is the real deal with you and Keisha? I know you told me in the past that you and she was just cool people, but I have been hearing a whole lot of mess this past week I find it ironic that all of this with Keisha had died down, then all of a sudden the same rumors from different people starts to resurface. I want to move on but Cue I need to know the truth about you and Keisha, have you ever messed around with her?"

Cue had his left hand steering the car and his right arm was rested on the arm rest to the point where he was leaning over towards me. He looked over at me and asked me did I really want to know the truth and if I thought that I could handle the truth. My eyes immediately watered up because I knew exactly what his truth was.

"Yes Cue," I said in almost a whisper.

"See Mercedes this is exactly the kind of bullshit you do that makes me want to keep my distance. You always asking these off the wall questions like you so damn hard and can handle anything, and then time you may think the answer is not going to be the one that you are looking for, you want to bitch up and cry!"

Cue's words stung more than the confession that I think he was about to make. Yes I wanted to know the truth, because for four years now that is all I ever heard was Keisha and Cue this or that. At one point they were even saying that her baby may be Cue's and we found out that it was some guy from New York's child. But the entire time she was carrying that child that is all I ever heard, even after Cue confronted her in front of me the rumors still did not die. However I knew they were rumors because I heard it straight from Keisha's mouth when Cue took me to her house to confront and ask her was she telling people that she was pregnant by him and she said, "No."

Although Keisha had nothing on me as far as I was concerned, I must admit that I was a little jealous of her. I can't even explain it because I had everything going for myself and she still stayed home with her parents or whoever occupied that shack that they called a house. She had no job but somehow managed to stay fly in a nice ride and clothes. I have to admit that she can dress her butt off. She has a very nice figure, and that is what makes the guys twirk to her ghetto ass.

Last week in the club the way she bounced up in V.I.P like she belonged there and tried to take over really pissed me off. And since I am only being honest with myself; I will admit that a part of me may hate on her a little, because although her and Cue may not have anything going on, I sense that he is attracted to her. I have caught him a few times watching as she passed by us in the club, or talking to her when he doesn't know that I am in the club. I do not know why I feel threatened by her at times because Cue would never leave me for the likes of someone like Keisha.

"Cue I have enjoyed you spending this week with me and we have said that this was basically starting over for us and we were going to just move forward, so whatever you have done in the past it's fine. I just want you to love me now and be faithful to me because I am faithful to you," I said, with my head still rested back on the headrest as I wiped the tears that I had tried to fight from rolling down my cheeks.

Cue palmed my thigh with his hand and squeezed it as to comfort me. "I love you Cede's don't get it twisted, I have done a lot of fucked up shit. But I am done playing games and I am not going to lose you over no bullshit."

My heart gradually became normal again, and although I did not let it out so that Cue could hear or see the relief, there was a sigh of it. I could deal with anybody but Keisha I hate her ass with a passion. I hate the way Cue acts when she is around as if she may have something on him, and I just don't get it. I know they are all cool because Keisha and her friends are the wild, love the liquor houses, out there type of girls, and they get high with Cue and the other guys also, but something just does not sit right with me about their relationship. I have even tried to go to the liquor house and hangout with Cue just to show him that I can be a fun person also, but that life was just not me. Leave smelling like a barrel of cigarettes and chicken. And then the crazy looking people that go in and out of that place? I decided to just be who I am, and he'll have to just continue to love me for that.

"You worry about the wrong darn things; instead of putting all of your energy into Keisha, imagine where our relationship would be if you channeled some of that energy my way? Keisha and I are just cool peeps that is it."

I looked over at him and said, "That is all I have ever heard is that you two were just cool, but if you are so cool why does she have such a problem with me?"

"Maybe it is the way you act Mercedes," Cue shrugged his shoulders, "Hell I don't know. You're the type of person that doesn't let anyone in your circle that hadn't already been there. You don't mingle with anyone but the people you know when you are out, everyone else you give this stank ass attitude. So maybe she has been on the receiving end and that's why she doesn't like your ass."

I pinched his hand that was still resting on my thigh. We both laughed as he continued to go on imitating how he claimed that I act when I am out, which was all lies as far as I was concerned.

Chapter Fourteen

(Keisha)

It had been a week since the incident with Mercedes at the club and the park, and also a week since I had seen or spoken to Cue. For the first two days after the incident he had not bothered to even contact me at all, and I did not try to contact him either. On the third day he sent me a text that said, "Have my son call me." Little did he know that he was making my task of getting over him so much easier and further showing me that I deserve someone better than his ass.

I dialed his number and passed the phone to Quincy. When I heard Quincy say, bye daddy, love you too, this would have normally been my time to talk, but under normal circumstances Cue would have called and asked to speak with his son rather than text, so by him texting this message to me told me that he still had his butt on his shoulders. I was in no mood to be trying to take it down so I took the phone and disconnected the call.

It was apparent to me that Cue had just taken Mercedes word at what transpired that night and ran with it, and if he did not feel that he owed me a chance to explain my side and why I done what I done then to hell with him. Each day that went by made me madder and madder, and I made up my mind that I would not under any circumstances call Cue not even if Quincy needed something I have money saved I will handle it myself.

As I sat on my bed watching Quincy play his play station, I thought back over the years that Cue and I had been on this roller coaster ride. Cue was very good to me and I know that he loved me; however, I still for some reason cannot fathom how you can say you love someone and not care enough about their feelings to contact them and see what is going on in their head, Especially when you know their feeling some type of a way.

For the past four years, my whole being has been wrapped around Cue and what Cue wanted. Sad to say but although Cue has a woman and has messed with other women as well I have never cheated on us. I have gone out with other men but never once crossed that line.

I sat and wondered what was wrong with me that I had so little self esteem to wait on a man that would always have me waiting? I have a wonderful child who adores me, great family and friends although some of their shells are a cracked, they stand by me. I am getting ready to become an independent woman who can hold her own. Forget sitting around waiting on Cue to dish out. I am going to find me a job and finish remodeling my and Quincy's home and just live.

"Quincy do you want to go to the beach?" This was very spontaneous, I had not even thought about going to the beach until just this second.

Quincy turned his head so fast to look at me that he could have gotten whiplash.

"Yes! He screamed jumping up and running over to me.

It was Saturday and I had no plans to go anywhere near the club tonight or in the near future. I had told myself that I would quit making myself available and expansible for Cue. And until I get my house and life in order the way that I wanted it to be, that I would stay away from the club scene. This was a new improved Keisha.

Although it had not been planned, the idea of the beach gave me a boost of energy, and brought me out of the slump that I was trying so hard to keep under cover for the sake of my child. I quickly packed Quincy and my clothes and told my grandmother that we were going to be with a friend for the week. I did not want my cousins or anyone else asking to go that is why I lied, and secondly I do not know if Cue will come by after not seeing me in over a week or not, but if he does let him wonder. The least my family knew, the least they could tell.

Quincy and I arrived at the beach in record time and checked into our room and hit the beach. This was just what the doctor ordered, because I had been down in the slumps for over a week, and all my free moments were thinking about Cue. I had practically gone five hours without Cue crossing my mind other than an afterthought. After hours of fun in the sun we returned to the room to shower and dress, and headed to this restaurant called "Wieners" that I must go to anytime I come to the beach, because they have the best foot long hotdogs and chili cheese fries.

Quincy and I were sitting inside the restaurant eating when I took notice of this very handsome guy walking by. If my son was not with me I would have followed him until he took notice I thought to myself. I t was something unique about this man, while he was indeed fine as hell he had a persona about him that spoke educated, class and confidence. I could tell that he was no street man although he had a look that said money, and a sexy roughness about him, but no this man had a job. If he wasn't a pro ball player he sure had the body frame of one.

This was the kind of man that I needed. I did not know him but he just did not seem as if he played any games. Why did

I never attract men of this caliber? Maybe I am hanging around the wrong places I thought to myself, maybe I need to branch out, spread my wings and do different things. As Quincy and I was heading out of the restaurant this fine specimen of a man that I had been mesmerized by since I saw him passing, was coming in with two other guys. Although they were not as nice looking as he was, their demeanors still screamed confident and got it together. He held the door opened for Quincy and I to exit and said, "Hey beautiful." I blushed, as if this was news to me that I looked good and said, "Thank you," as I walked through the small gap his magnificent body had left opened for me.

Quincy and I headed across the street to "Ripley's Believe it or Not." I was thinking about the man that I had just encountered, during the entire Ripley's experience other than when I snapped back to reality to answer a question, or to seem interested in something Quincy was pointing out. I do not know whether it was because I was having withdrawals from Cue or what that had me tripping about this man that I did not even know, and probably would never see again in my life.

As Quincy and I were exiting I noticed him through the glass door before we got out the door, standing against the wall texting or something on his cell phone. I assumed that his friends were in line purchasing tickets. "Dangit," I screamed to myself, "Why couldn't we have been in here at the same time?" I was really upset at how my fate was going with this guy; I was really considering purchasing more tickets. I even asked Quincy if he wanted to go back in, and he said no, that he wanted to go to the beach.

As we exited the double glass doors I was face to face with the mystery man who looked up as the doors opened. He rose up from the wall and said, "Hey, hope you don't think I am crazy or that I am a stalker, because I promise you," he said, rising his arms in defense, "that I am neither," he laughed. "I just thought you were a very attractive young lady and I did not want the opportunity to pass for me to introduce myself to you." He extended his hand and said, "Hi my name is Grant."

Dang where was he from, that accent was sexy as hell. At first I thought New York maybe, but his words were so precise and pronunciated he had to be from an island. "Keisha," I said taking his hand. "And this handsome fella here is my son Quincy." I said emphasizing son, and watching him closely to see his reaction. Needed to let him know off the bat that I came with company, so if it's a problem doesn't matter how fine you are, you had to bounce. He did not flinch. Instead he withdrew his smooth manicured hand from mine and extended it to Quincy, and leaned down and said, "What's up man?"

Quincy being around his dad too long and picking up on all the slang said, "Nuttin much."

Grant totally ignored me for about three minutes while he and Quincy talked about the go-cart that Quincy is supposedly building. And of course throughout the course of their conversation Grant threw his head back in laughter and glanced at me quite a few times like, "Where in tha hell does he get this stuff from?" I just smiled and shrugged my shoulders, only Quincy. After he was done being entertained by Quincy he turned his attention back to me. We got the usual questions out of the way. Are you married, Do you have a man, Where are you from? To my amazement he too was from down by my way. I lived in Greenville and he was raised in Columbia, SC about an hour and fifteen minutes from Greenville. However he now lived in San Francisco, California, but his family was still in Columbia. I was thinking well this is not bad at all, at least we could hook up when he was visiting with his family every now and then, and depending on how well things went I was game for making the trip to Cali. I was full speed ahead and we had not even exchanged phones numbers yet. Calm down Keisha you fall too damn fast that is why you're always getting caught up. I had to remind myself.

As I knew we would, we wound up exchanging numbers and promising to call each other sometime and see what happens. He told me that he was an architect for a company that built submarines and tanks for the military. He was born and raised in Jamaica before his family moved to the states and in Greenville when he was in elementary school for his dad to expand his family practice. He attended college in Virginia and liked the area and decided to reside there. His father was also a doctor and he had one sister and his mother was a school teacher in Greenville. So his sister ended up going to school in Greenville County rather than Spartanburg County because his mother wanted her in the district with her, but he had always attended school in Greenville County. When he asked me what did I do; I felt stupid and beneath to tell this fine, educated man that came from a family where education obviously was very important, that I was just a mere bootleg hairdresser who was doing hair from my grandmother's kitchen, or whatever client I was doing kitchen, I had no career. He probably only dated women that were just as educated as him and the only thing that I possessed was my high school diploma. I lied and told him that I was a cosmetologist which wasn't extravagant but was a career, and although it wasn't true, it wasn't totally a lie either because I have been doing hair for years. He did not need to know that I wasn't licensed yet.

"That's what's up," Grant said, shaking his head as if saying, "Yea, I can dig it."

"Well Grant it was a pleasure meeting you and hope to talk to you in the near future, but let me get this young man to the beach," I said referring to Quincy who although was not being interruptive or rude was becoming restless, I could tell by the way he was using my arms as his monkey bars. I could have stood there and talked to Grant for the rest of the day, but I felt that I needed to be the one to end the conversation, just feels better when it is closed on my time and leaving him to wonder if I am really feeling him, and not to mention I did not want to give him the opportunity to ask questions about the verizon of my cosmetology business, that I would have to further lie to him about. We said our goodbyes and Quincy dapped him up and we were out.

Wow if nothing else special happened to me on this trip meeting Grant was more than enough for me. Although no promises were made he did seem interested enough in me, shoot the man waited outside while I was on the Ripley's tour. I would say he was very interested, why do all of that if he did not expect for us to at least talk on the phone to see where this may lead. I was excited to see what would happen with the two of us in the future. I felt like I must really play my cards right with this one because this man seemed to have all his cards right, and if I wanted to be any part of his life, I had to at least be showing where I was getting mine in order as well. Things were about to change for the better in my life. Who knows where this may lead maybe for once I have finally met a man that is worthy and would be grateful for my love.

As Quincy sat playing in the sand with his bucket and shovel I took advantage of just how smart my I-Phone 5 really was and googled cosmetology school information. I found that I could pay $45.00 and take a braiding test to get licensed for hair braiding. I sat right there and filled in all the information and paid the fee, and it immediately gave me a date to come to State Boards to test. Although hair braiding was not something I liked to do I was the bomb at it. I tried to not braid hair as much as I had in my younger days, my thing now was cutting and dying and I was a self made professional at it. But the logic behind me going ahead with the hair braiding license was so that if things were to escalade with Grant and I, and I was ever asked to produce or show proof, I would have at least this braiding license. Conniving I know, but I had lied to this man and although my plans are to still go to cosmetology school and become official, I needed to start with what would be quick and now. I was excited; this trip had motivated me to start making moves.

Although I hated Mercedes with a passion I must say I often found myself so envious of her because she had this great career, and really did not need Cue's funds at all. She lived this lavish life with her friends jetting all around this country and that country just enjoying life. Although I did just as much, it was always on Cue's dime, and truth be told if Cue cuts me off, I would be miserable working an Average Joe job trying to make ends meet. Yes it was high time that I started making moves for Keisha and Quincy. I was going to the State Board and hopefully get this braiding license, and as soon as I got back in town on Monday morning I was going right over to Greenville Tech to register for cosmetology. I had always dreamed of having my own salon. I got excited thinking about all of the positive moves I was about to make. The house that I had bought as is, for a few grand was almost ready for Quincy and I to move into and I just this moment decided to turn the small room that was off the back porch into a small salon. Apparently whoever build the room intended for it to be a screened in small porch, but over the years of no upkeep the screen had been torn away, but the wood foundation that covered the bottom half of the porch was very sturdy. I had a plexi glass put where screen once was and I too had planned on using it as a screened in porch, but now the 15 x 12 room had a whole new meaning for me. I lay there on my lounge chair and visualized the salon set up. It definitely wasn't big enough to have more than one or two people in waiting for services, so I figured appointments only and do not come prior to fifteen minutes before your schedule appointment. This definitely would not be a traditional salon where people could come and just sit around and gossip, because space would not allow it.

The room was big enough for one washing bowl, two dryers and two or three waiting chairs. I would have a window air condition unit installed and for the winter months I could basically just open the door that led into the house from the porch to allow the heat into the small room. Actually I could do the same for the air, but with me being as hot natured as I am, I needed to make sure that I was extra cool while I was working. I was so hype I was ready to cut this trip short and head back home to get busy.

After a fun day in the sun Quincy and I retired to our room. Once I got Quincy bathed he fell out on the bed and never woke back up until the morning. My baby was so exhausted. I was glad when Cue sent a text yet again saying, "Have my twin call me." I happily ignored the text and did not even feel the need to respond. One, because it had been four days since you last sent a text requesting to speak with your child. Two, It was 11:30 pm. Why would you call a three year old that time of the night and expect for him to be up? I covered my baby up and went and took a long hot bath in the Jacuzzi tub. I laid my head back against the rear slant of the tub and closed my eyes and let the jets pound into my back and thighs which I had rested on either side of the tub. I thought to myself this is the life, the most important person to me was in the bed sound asleep after having a marvelous day at the beach. I was relaxed and sipping on a cold glass of Moscato. I must have stayed in the tub longer than it seemed because when I got out of the tub I had ten missed calls and two text messages. Four of the calls were from Cue and both of the text was from his assuming dumb ass. The text he sent after the one where he had asked for me to have Quincy call him said "Have my son to call me now please." He sounded calm but I sensed a little sarcasm. The next text said "I don't care what you are doing but you can let me talk to my son."

I laughed to myself as I listened to his voice messages. He started out with, *"Keisha have Quincy call me."* Then, *"I don't know what's your problem but I need to talk to my son let him call me."* Followed with, *"You acting really stupid how in the hell you going to leave with my son and not tell anybody where your ass is? You being very juvenile right now I thought you were better than that. Call me!"* I thought, "Oh now I need to call you, not your son call you? Go to hell Cue," I said as I deleted the message. The next message was, *"If you are laid up with some nigga and you can't call me, you really foul Keisha, that is some bullshit. I been worried and thinking about you all week and you can't even* call *and let me know that everything is ok. Is this the way you want to do things. Every time things don't go your way, you going to just disappear and not answer your damn phone?*

Call me and just let me know that ya'll are alright, aight? Love you." I fell back on the bed and hit nine to listen to the message again this shit was funny.

I called my grandmother to check in with her and asked had Cue been by. She told me that he had come by earlier today and then again tonight. She said he seemed worried when she told him what she knew, and that was that Quincy and I was spending the week at a girlfriends. He inquired on where, who and why. And my grandmother being just as smart of an ass as I am said she told him don't know, didn't ask and she is grown. If you were so concerned with her and Quincy you would have tried to come by and check on them prior to letting a week go by Cue. Keisha is hurt and she needed a break, and even if I did know where she was I wouldn't have told you. My grandmother was straight 100 all the time, I think that she was probably the only person that intimidated Cue besides my mom who had a way with him when she was mad other than that he took her for a joke.

Ms. Margie, Keisha was so mad at the time and I know how she is so I just thought that I would give her time to calm down. She was on some different shit that night, I mean stuff and you know how she is. I f I had tried to talk to her she would have ignored my calls or hung up on me, I been dealing with Keisha I know how she is. My grandmother told him "And I have dealt with Keisha all of her life and I know that Keisha has a heart of gold and she loves you to death, and I also know that you hurt her pretty bad and she is really fed up. The worst thing you could do is give her too much space to think about it and get over it, because then you are pretty much history son. So you keep ignoring and trying to play hard ball you are going to strikeout. She is tired Cue and frankly I have seen it coming I am surprised it took her this long. I have told her that she needed to move on, because she is a special, and she should not have to come second to no one. But I can talk all day long, but until she's sick and tired of being sick and tired she's not going to do anything about it. But Cue I think baby girl is tired.

After grandma and I got off the phone I was so happy about her and Cue's conversation. Gosh I loved that woman more than life itself, she was my ace. I decided to text Cue. I was going to keep it simple and although I was very giddy inside I would give him no indication of this.

My text simply said, "Quincy is sleeping that is the reason I did not have him call, but he is good and I will have him call you tomorrow."

His reply was, "How are you, and where are you babes?"

I decided it was time to turn in. I turned my phone off after calling gramps and giving her the direct number to the hotel in case of an emergency. I lay in the bed and thought this was perfect, let him feel how I have felt all these years. The rest of the week seemed to fly by, and the fun part of it all was listening to Cue on my voicemail beg. I did let Quincy call him the next day as promised, after I told him to not tell his dad our whereabouts. Although Cue did ask, Quincy looked at me and said, "Mom, dad asked where are we?" I asked Quincy loud enough for Cue to hear me, "Quincy are you having fun?"

He said, "Yes, lots of fun!"

"Are you ready to go home?" Quincy looked at me confused not knowing my aim and said, "Ma, you said we have two more days. I don't want to go home."

"Quincy we are not going home, we do have two more days, just wanted to ensure your dad that you are ok and having fun." I said.

"Daddy I am having fun me and mommy, we will be home in two days ok?" Quincy said.

"Tell your dad bye and you will be home Saturday."

"Yes!" screamed Quincy, as he said, "Bye daddy, see you Saturday so we can finish my go cart. Love you." Quincy hung up the phone.

I received a text saying, "Are you ready to talk to me?" from Cue. I replied back, I wanted to talk to you nine days ago but you went to Mercedes rescue and comforted her and left me to wonder and deal with the bullshit on my own. I have nothing I need to explain now I am good. I have gotten over the hard part and you weren't there for me. Cool runnings. Call me Keisha. I never called and I never allowed Quincy to call for the next two days either. Cue was blowing me up and I must admit I liked it.

Chapter Fifteen

(Cue)

I have never wanted to hit a girl as bad as I wanted to beat Keisha's ass right now. Her ass just up and left town with our son without as much as a kiss my ass Cue. I had called her for three days before her ass finally even accepted my call and then she was short and would not tell me where she and my son was. To keep my mind off of her, and from flipping out I had just been kicking it at Mercedes house all week. Now she wanting me to move in with her ass, made me take a key that she had been trying to get me to take for years now, that I had refused to take.

I love Mercedes and all, but I can't say that she is the one that I would want to be with for the rest of my life, she doesn't excite me like Keisha does. And that bullshit that she pulled with Keisha at the club the other week was just foul, she doesn't know yet that I know what went down, but we have video surveillance thru out the club. I watched the tape and seen her nudge Keisha's feet, not only once, but twice. After I watched the tape, I tried to call Keisha to apologize, but she was so angry I guess that she wasn't taking any of my calls.

This has been a hell of a week for me. I was missing Keisha and my son like crazy. Mercedes was all over me eating up the fact that I was turning in to her house every night. She mentioned marriage more than once throughout the week. As I have been telling her, I am not ready to settle down when I am ready she would be the first to know and she just hopes that it is with her. All the crazy shit she has been doing lately really has me thinking about something's and I am just feeling her out.

I picked up my phone to call and see if I could get Keisha on the phone again, she had tried to reach me earlier this morning but Mercedes was all in my face so I had to ignore the call. I was mad as hell because I wanted to talk to her so bad. Keisha answered after the third ring, I was beginning to think that she was going to ignore my call again as she had been doing all week.

"What's going on Keish?" I said calmly not trying to get her hairs standing, because if she got in a defensive mode, I would never get to talk to her.

"Nothing Cue, you want to talk to Quincy?" Her tone was as nonchalant as she could have possibly mustered.

"So it's like that now, all communication is to be only about Quincy, you have nothing to say to me?"

What in the hell was I thinking because she went ballistic! And after listening to her wrath about the chains of events that had taken place over the past two weeks, I had to admit that she was 100% right. She ranted on about how I never thought about how she must have been feeling, and how I just automatically assumed Mercedes is perfect, so her tells of what went down must be the truth.

"Keisha I tried to call you and talk to you, you are the one that was ignoring my calls," I said trying to fix myself up a little, but she quickly tore me back down.

"Your lanky ass did not bother to even try to contact me until three days after all that went down, I was at home going through hell not knowing what you were thinking, and the way you took her defense at the club that night made it no easier for me Cue. I have done nothing but love and respect you, and I am always the one that gets no respect from you. I have stayed in my lane and just tried to be there for you whenever you need for me to be, I take damn good care of your child, and don't even sweat the fact that you are hiding him from her ass. And this is how you treat me?"

"Keisha you know I love you and you know I appreciate everything you do. It's just that shit was crazy that night and I was mad when you came up in V.I.P and them nigga's was all up on you, yeah I was jealous. And then when all that other non-sense popped off I was really taken it out on you because I was so upset with your ass. Baby it had nothing to do with Mercedes but everything to do with you and me."

"Cue you man handled me in front of her, and everyone, and took me to the back and demanded I stay put like I was some kind of dog. Then you go back out there and allow her and her friends to continue chilling. And then the very next day whether you believed that she purposely kicked my feet TWO times at the club, you WERE at the park and witnessed the shit that she started. But you never reached out to me, you went to comfort your precious, can't do any wrong, shit doesn't stank Mercedes. You basically told me fuck how I feel because you never once reached out to me!"

"I was talking to Britney trying to find out what had happened. I was going to tell Mercedes ass to leave and then I was coming back to talk to you." I said defeated.

"Coming back to get in my shit," Keisha interrupted.

"No I was going to talk to you, but you wouldn't know because your high strung ass couldn't follow instructions. And then when I did try to reach out to you after what went down in the park your high strung ass had left town!"

"Whatever Cue, that was a few days later so just stop. I am not your damn child and I am done being your groupie. I love you to death and you know it. But this past week has really opened my eyes to a lot of things about our relationship. I know that I will never fully have you, so it really is what it is, and I need for you to remember that."

"What tha hell does that suppose to mean Keish?"

"I am saying that you have a girlfriend, and I have been totally faithful to a man that can't be faithful to me."

"Keisha your ass knew about-"

"I am not talking about Mercedes Cue! What about all these other hoes you have been sleeping around with? And not only that why in the hell should I not see anyone else? You have your cake on the side and crumbs outside of that. I am tired of always being on the lower end of your totem pole. I am saying; that this is what it is. If you hear about me and someone else, you have no right to get upset, you deal with it the way I have dealt with you and Mercedes for all of these years!"

"Bullshit! Your ass probably done already met someone that is probably where you were all damn week. Let me find out that you had my son with you while you were laid up with some nigga. And how you gonna compare some nigga you just meeting, to me and Mercedes. Hell your ass knew I had a girl when we started seeing one another; your ass is the one that was saying you didn't care if I had a crazy ass wife, we could still work something out. Your ass was the one saying you didn't give a damn about Mercedes that I was the one you wanted not her. Now all of a sudden your ass wants to switch everything up?"

"Cue you know how long that has been, did you really expect me to continue playing your groupie forever?"

"Whateva man, I am not going to argue with you about this right now, where is my son?"

"He is at the house with granny, you are welcomed to go by there and see him if you want."

"Where are you Keisha?"

She hung up the phone without a word. What in the hell is wrong with this girl? I can understand her being mad, hell I can even agree with her because she has dealt with a lot from me more than Mercedes ever has. Keisha has been my ride or die chick for real. She deals with me ignoring her at random, other females approaching her about my whorish ways, and although I provide greatly for Quincy and Keisha, she is the one that does all the extracurricular activities with Quincy. I do scoop him up and ride out with him every now and then, but because no one knows that he is my son, I can't just take him to Chuckie Cheese, Cleveland Park, Zoo or any of those public places unless we are out of town. And I do take him out of town often but not as often as I would like to.

Don't get me wrong because I love that little man more than life, and I have came close more than once in telling Mercedes that he was mine. I can't keep doing this much longer because Quincy is growing up so fast, and he loves anything pertaining to a ball. Football, basketball, soccer and baseball and he gets' it honestly, because I was an all around athlete, and I can't wait until I can get him signed up for his first little league sport. I already coach him on different aspects of the games.

I came to the realization a long time ago, that no matter how long I wait, or how it comes about, that Mercedes is the one that is going to be hurt. I had even considered just breaking up with her for real the next time she tripped. It has been a heavy burden on me every since Quincy has been in this world. Things could be going smoothly between me, Keisha and Mercedes but then I would think about my little man, and how much I loved him, and the pain would bear down on me of how I am keeping him a secret. I made a U-turn and headed to see my son.

Chapter Sixteen

(Keisha)

Who does Cue think that I am? Does he not realize that every dog has his day? Does he really expect for me to carry on in this form for the rest of my life? I am sick and tired of being sick and tired and while I am not ready to let him go just yet I am going to start living and stop giving in to his demands. I make myself to available for him and from here on out if I have made plans, they will not be cancelled because he decides to call me at the last minute and say "Let's hook up."

I have to admit that I was pretty shocked that he remembered the statements I made when we had first started seeing one another, yet he can't remember what year we started dating.

And then this nut had the audacity to tell me that he wasn't going to argue with me, and dismiss me. Then in the same breath ask where I was? Get the fuck outta here. Little does he know Keisha has had enough.

I was headed to pay a deposit for my lights and water now that my house was ready to be moved into and I was planning to be moved in this weekend. Cue knew nothing about what was going on with my house because he never asked. He gave me the money to buy the house probably figuring that it was just going to be something to keep me busy, not thinking I would actually move in. Anytime I would ask him for money for something I was having done to the house, he would hand the money over to me saying, teasingly, "Don't be wasting my money, if your ass ain't going to really move into that house." Boy was he going to be shocked when he finally got the chance to see the finished product, it was a lot of work and money but my house was spectacular and it was all mine no mortgage or anything. People thought I was crazy when I first bought it, so glad I did not let the naysayers disrupt my vision.

I had went on Monday and enrolled in cosmetology school and would be starting in a few weeks. If I went full time I could be finished within nine months and since Quincy went to daycare in the mornings that was my plan. It was time to put things into action, I am secretly hoping that Cue will get the drift and maybe be with his son and I one day. In the meantime I was going to play my role, get all that I could from him and stack my chips as I go to school to get my cosmetology license. Hopefully he would still be generously providing when I was done with school because I would surely let him open up a shop for me.

After I paid my deposits I rode over to see the final touches of my house once again. Although this house was every bit of thirty years old, it looked as if it had just been built, the inside even smelled brand new. Actually in a sense I guess it was because there were new floors, cabinets and a few of the walls had been replaced. The wall that separated the dining area from the living room had been completely knocked out giving the room a more opened look.

I had a sense of pride as I climbed the steps to my front door. I had already brought three white rocking chairs over last week and put on the front porch each had a small white table beside it. With my house facing the main road, I figured that my grandmother would be over here a lot sitting on the porch reading her newspaper being nosy. The wrought iron railings gave the house a warm look. I had hung two firms on either end of the porch, and I also had mosquito repellants underneath each chair and a candle on each table. Although the mosquitos did not appear to be that bad on this side I just had to be ready in case.

On the inner wall of the porch I had a black long container that lined the wall perfectly and inside of that container were seat cushions for the rocking chairs and mosquito repellant spray, more candles and even two throw blankets. I had created a house full of comfort.

The guest bedroom, although at this point was only going to have the twin bed in it, that I was bringing over from my room at granny's was going to be so inviting that my guest may never want to leave. I was going tomorrow to get my things that I had been buying over the course of three years out of storage and moving it in. I was forever putting something on layaway and my sister, granny, mom and whomever else knew what I was doing use to just shake their heads. Now three years later when they walk into my nice home they are going to think "Well wasn't she really smart." I was buying furniture before I even had a home, my plan was to eventually get an apartment, little did I know that I was going to be buying a fixer up home and paying cash for it.

My first purchase had been a nice solid maple canopy bed and dresser that I fell madly in love with when I saw it. The four poles were all extra large and square in shape. There was wrought iron crisscrossed above it and along the sides to place your canopy drapes, mine were going to be pulled back like curtains all around the four corners. I paid more for the drapes than I had anticipated, but what the heck this furniture and décor I planned to have for years. I opted on a red living room suite rather than the leather one that I had first fell in love with.

The red gave a bold statement and the multi colored red, black, yellow and tan striped throw pillows gave me plenty of options. And I could always purchase solid colored pillows if I wanted a change. My six people dining room set and china cabinet I had purchased at a yard sale for two hundred dollars. I knew I had gotten a steal with this one because this table was solid oak and huge and heavy, each of the six chairs had arm rest. It took a act of congress just to load it onto my uncle's truck to transport it to my storage building.

I am beyond excited about my new place, when I unlocked the door and walked in I had to stop, drop and pray right then and there. God had moved marvelously in my life and showed me so much favor and I had no idea why, but at this moment I was suddenly overwhelmed with all that was about to happen in my life and I had to give credit where credit was due. I know I have a long way to go but at this moment I knew that I was going to be alright. After I finished giving God his due praise I got up and walked around my house.

The house was only twenty three hundred square feet but to me it was four thousand. I walked into the only bathroom that the house possessed and just imagined how good it was going to look once I brought in the black, red and white décor. I had a huge flower arrangement made for the wall to wall counter and I also had a small table that had storage at the bottom of it for magazines that would be in there. I had red, white and black rugs for the floor. The rugs were black and the border was trimmed with red and then white. There would be a black plastic shower curtain that a red cloth curtain would hang outside of tied back with white and red polka dotted tie backs. I had candles of each color and towels and wash cloths that would decorate the silver racks that I had installed.

I was in such a trance walking around my house visualizing how everything would look that by the time I realized that my phone was ringing Cue had hung up. I started to call him back and decided that I would wait until I got home. I was enjoying myself all alone, and I was not ready to let him take me out of my real life fairytale just yet.

As soon as I pulled up to granny's Quincy came running out the door with a guitar strapped around him. Where in the hell did that come from? I thought to myself, someone must really hate me. He came running down the steps as I bent down to kiss him and ask, "Well, where did you get this from cowboy?"

"My daddy bought it for me, and he bought me a drum too!" Quincy was pulling away at the strings making a lot of loud awful noise. I am going to kill Cue I thought, and the next time Quincy and I go to his house I am going to take it over there and let him listen to this mess all day and night. Quincy makes enough noise, he doesn't need anything to help him out he is good at what he does all alone.

As Quincy and I entered the house my mom just looked at me and shook her head.

"When are you moving again?" she asked, jokingly.

Quincy had torn their nerves up already with the drum and guitar. Luckily it was just one drum not the entire set but with Quincy it did not matter, he was good with making any instrument sound like he had the entire marching band.

I laughed at my mom as I flopped down on the couch beside her and asked how long was Cue over. She told me that he had came in and talked with her and Granny a while until Quincy saw a commercial on television, where there were watches in the McDonalds Happy Meals and he just had to go. So he took him to McDonalds and brought him back then left shortly after. I asked whether he asked of my where abouts, and of course he had. They did not tell him; they said that I did not say where I was going; I only asked if they could watch Quincy.

I went into the bedroom and looked at all of the boxes that I had lined up on the walls, and decided to pack what I could into the car and carry them over to the house, I was so excited. As I was packing the boxes into my car, my uncle pulled up behind me. I had never been so glad to see him, and I took advantage of his arriving home early and asked him to pack the remainder boxes on the back of his truck, and transport to the house for me. Of course when my granny, mother and aunt saw what we were doing it turned into a family affair. I was happy that they would get to see the finished product of my house, although I had planned on waiting until I had everything in and done before I brought them over.

When we pulled up to the front of the house, my grandmother who was in the car with me exclaimed, "Did they tear the old house down and rebuild? This is a totally different house chile." I beamed at the excitement that was covering my grandmother's face. I felt a sense of pride. The once old tattered wood house was now a white vinyl sided, and black shuttered black wrought iron railing beauty. I could not have been moving into a better place as far as I was concerned. I was in love with this debt free house that God had blessed me with and I was going to treasure my mansion here on earth.

"No ma'am, just a lot of remodeling," I said as I unhooked my seatbelt to exit the car. I was eager to hear what my mother was saying to my uncle and aunt as they were walking back and forth in the front admiring the porch.

When I got over to them my mother was saying, "They done a good job; gosh I cannot believe that this is the same house." She was talking to her brother and sister and did not realize that I had approached and this made me feel even better. They were actually proud of my little house.

I walked up the steps and unlocked the front door with pride. I was overwhelmed with happiness as they went from room to room beaming with excitement about how great the house had turned out. My mother acted as if she was about to cry which really touched my heart, because hopefully they all were recognizing now what a little remodeling and work could do to any old house. We were at the house longer than anticipated because they were all just as excited as I was and by the time we had decided to leave, dishes were in their proper places, my bathroom was completely decorated, and most pictures had been hung. They had already planned to have Thanksgiving dinner here and marveled on about how great the cookouts would be in the yard. And just as I had predicted, Granny was saying how she could not wait to sat out on the front porch with her coffee. I hadn't anticipated the coffee part, but just how early was she planning on coming to my house I asked her laughing. She replied that she hadn't planned on leaving.

Once we were back in the car I picked up my phone as it was on the last ring; the missed call was from Cue. As I looked at the phone I noticed that there had been three missed calls from him. Good I thought to myself, hope he is feeling all that I feel when he ignores my butt. As soon as I pulled in front of granny's house Cue pulled in right behind me. I could not help but to blush, is this nigga serious? I took my time exiting the car and walked to the rear of my car to the passenger side of Cue's car and got in. This was the first time that I have seen him face to face in almost three weeks, and my body was yearning for his touch, but I played it cool. Although it was tough because he was sitting there looking like a million bucks in his dark denim jeans and white Sean John shirt with red embossed writing and a red Adidas jacket with red and white shell toe Adidas kicks.

He was apparently sizing me up also; even though I only had on some dark hip huggers, a sloppy black sweater and my black Polo, lace up boots. I knew I was eye candy to him and he hadn't had what he called "The Gold Mine," in almost four weeks either? Shoot I knew this mug was drooling because he has told me time and time again that I am the best he has ever had.

"What's up Keish, come clean with me is there someone else you want?"

"No Cue not really anyway," I decided to play with his mind a little and see where his feelings really were. I had not met anyone, well at least not anyone that I was willing to replace Cue with, except for Grant. I had not yet heard from him since that day at the beach, and neither was I sweating it because he made me realize just how much I wanted to get things in order in my own life. So if he waited another year before he called me then things would be great although I certainly wanted to talk to him, but I figured the longer he doesn't call the closer I will be to my goals when he does.

"Oh so you have met someone?" Cue's jaws were twitching although he was trying to play it cool.

"Yes Cue, I have, but before you get all bent out of shape let me tell you it is nothing, we are just talking and that is it."

"Keisha for you to admit to me that you are seeing someone else it has to be something to it, so tell me what's up?"

Do I tell him I met this guy at the beach last week and talked to him for every bit of only twenty minutes, we exchanged phone numbers, and I was really feeling him but he has yet to call me?

"Cue to be honest with you I don't know what is up with him and me right now, we are just trying to get to know one another."

Cue kind of lowered his head as if he was in thought, then he looked over at me and asked, if I would be honest with him if he asked me something. Of course I would, what do I have to lie about, because little did he know, I haven't busted a grape in a fruit fight yet.

"Were you with him last week?"

I swallowed before I said, "I was not with him, but I did see him while we were at the beach." Ha, I did not lie. And now he is probably thinking this shit is serious if he came down to the beach to hang out with them.

"Keisha? Cue's confidence level had dropped, "I love you and all and you know I want you in my life, but if I find out that you have been laying up with some dude all week with my son I am..."

I cut him off so fast that he was even shocked. "Who in the hell do you think I am Cue?" I spoke a little louder than I normally do, but oh well. "You know that I don't even lay up in the bed with you if Quincy is in the bed with us and you're his father, do you really think I am that trifling to do it with another man? Let's say what this is really about since you want to be so damn honest. It's not about whether Quincy was with me or not, it's about whether I finally decided to give the goodies to another man after all of these years of only giving them to you!"

I don't know what the hell I was thinking or who the hell that I thought I was talking to, but I regretted making that statement as soon as it exited my lips. Cue's jaw bones were flexing so hard that I knew that he was about to strike my ass. He cranked the car and pulled off with me still sitting there. My first instinct was to open the door and jump out because he was surely taking me to some rural area to either kill me or beat the shit out of me and leave me for the wolves to finish off. Cue has never before struck me and I have never before felt threatened that he may, but tonight was different I was actually sweating bullets.

"Baby where are you taken me, Quincy is at the house and I did not ask anyone to watch him." I said very sweetly.

"Your granny is at the house and everyone else, you know they are going to watch him so don't trip," he said not taking his eyes off the road to even glance my way.

"Cue you are the one tripping how you going to just take off with me in the car and not allow me to get my phone or purse?" I had left both in my car when I got into the car with Cue, how in the hell was I to know that he was going to jack me. "And my car doors are unlocked!" I thought this would surely detour him because he knew that in the neighborhood I lived in they will jack you while you are watching, so a purse in a car seat and no one around was a thieves dream.

Cue passed over his phone to me and said "Well I guess you better call your mom or somebody to lock your car doors huh?"

I took the phone and called Granny and asked her to have my sister go and get my purse and phone from the car, and lock the doors. I was with Cue and would be back shortly, (I hoped) and could they keep an eye on Quincy for me. My grandmother said that she would tell my sister and that I knew that Quincy was ok.

Cue did not say a word to me the entire trip to his house, although I was able to breathe easier the longer we rode I was still uneasy. I had never before admitted to Cue that I was seeing anyone else, although I had never slept with anyone else, I had indeed gone on a few dinner dates and vacations. My thought on the matter was I loved Cue, but why should I not explore other options every now and then, because who knows where Cue may land and I am going to be married one day whether it be to Cue or not.

I have played second fiddle for four years to Mercedes and while I know that Cue cares for me sometimes I just don't know how to read him. Just when I feel that we are moving forward and I am relaxed, Mercedes may call while Cue and I are together and just listening to their conversation cuts me deep. He no longer tells her he loves her as they hang up if I am around; it's just that sheltering tone he uses when speaking to her that tells me he cared about her. I have questioned myself over time and time again as to why I care so much about what he does with Mercedes, and I knew from the start that she was there. I have no answer for it. I guess a part of me will always envy her in some way or another.

Cue must have hired a landscaper to come out and plant the shrubbery because I know there was no way on earth that he himself had done all of this yard work. His yard was always nice and neat but there were no flowers or anything just a nice green bare yard, but tonight it hosted shrubbery along the porch and yard lights that eliminated onto the shrubs. "The yard looks nice baby," I said as he came around and opened the car door as he always has done most times, aiming to lighten the atmosphere a little.

I stood behind Cue as he fumbled with the key trying to find the key slot in the dark. I looked up at his broad shoulders twitching and thought "Damn I love this sexy ass man." Once he successfully unlocked the door he stood to the side for me to walk in and I thought what is he going to do hit me in the back of the head? I headed towards the living room as he locked up the door, I had decided that I would sit in the recliner because on the table beside it, housed all of Cue's brass what-nots that I certainly could use as a weapon if this nut decided to trip. As I was going towards the recliner Cue grabbed me from behind; I was about to panic until I felt his plump lips on my neck.

I turned to face him and his eyes told it all, he wanted to do what grown folks do and I wanted to oblige. It seemed as if it had been an eternity since I had been in my baby's arms, and it felt like it had been years since he had had any, or at least any that was good. He wore my ass out, but believe me he was worn out also by the time it was over. As I lay on his side with my leg draped across his, I massaged his chest and stomach, as he rubbed my back with his arm that was confined under me; I told him I loved him.

"Really Keisha? I find that hard to believe. How can you say that you love me and that it is me that you want, but yet you can go and spend a week with another man?"

"Cue I did not spend a week with him. It wasn't even a whole day; just a few hours, and that was it, real talk."

Cue was looking at me like he wanted to go through me. "Ok," he said, shaking his head as if to say he was giving me the benefit of the doubt. "Let's say that is true, but the fact still remains that you entertained him. You opened the door to allow him to think its ok, and he's going to keep trying, so now what?"

I'll just let him know that I am not ready to go there with him, I am trying to work it out with my baby."

"Are you really that naive Keisha, baby I thought I had taught you better than that? Look I know the game and I am a man that has been around and know how we think. Baby you can't be giving nigga's nothing to feed on."

I could not see Cues face because of the way I was lying on his chest unless I looked up to his face which I did not, but there was something extremely sexy about his tone and the way he was talking to me. Although he was trying to play it cool and not show jealousy it was very clear that he was. It was things like this that confused me with Cue, just when I thought that he was wanting out he would come around and love me like he could not live without me.

"No Cue, Bae, I am not that naïve. It was just that I did not know what was going on with you, and I had not heard from you in almost a week, and even when you had text me, it was simply to say have my son call me. I thought you were done with me as much as I hated it, but you know I am not in the business of keeping no nigga's that doesn't want to be kept no matter how much I may love you."

"That's your problem Keisha, your ass always assuming, I have told you over and over when you assume, you only make an ass of yourself, and cause confusion that is not needed."

"Cue well what was I suppose to do?"

"You were supposed to be the woman that you holler that you are and ask, rather than assume. My not contacting you had nothing to do with you. It was just a lot of shit was going on and I was trying to figure out a game plan. If you loved me the way you claim you do you would have contacted me rather than running off to some other nigga."

"So in other words you're saying that although you hadn't called me to say hey or anything for that matter all week, I wasn't supposed to assume that you were upset with me and done with me? Even an Keisha I just can't deal with you right now but give me a minute would have been sufficient, but you left nothing for me to go on, other than the fact you were with her. That is all I knew."

This mug has definitely got to be shitting me he must think that I am really naive. Little does he know that shit was about to change, he can role with it or bounce and I wanted him to role with it. I am just tired of always having to wait, I am not asking him to leave Mercedes, but it is not going to be always on his time anymore. Because I was tired of being rejected, I had stopped initiating our hook-ups. Although he always gave me a valid excuse whether it was a lie or not I still felt rejected when he couldn't come on my time. So he had trained me I guess to not ask, so therefore he had me just where he wanted me. Waiting on him to want me, and then we hook up all of that shit was about to change.

"Keisha you know how my schedule is and that week was just one of those weeks. After all that shit went down at the club, I left town the very next day to handle some business. And then when I got to Florida it was chaotic and we were in Miami, so you know how we do in *Miami*."

I giggled at how he said Miami, as I crawled over on top of him and said, "Yea babe, I know how you do in *Miami*," I mimicking him as I kissed his soft lips and moved over to his neck. I ceased this as a perfect opportunity to lay my new ground rules while I had him under me moaning. I planned on taking full advantage of this opportunity to lay it on him like I never have and if he doesn't follow my rules; he would only remember how good it was tonight and continuously crave me.

"But I am sure Mercedes heard from you while you were in Miami?" I said as I kissed and licked from his neck to his shoulder blades.

"So did you baby," he was feeling so good that his words were dragged out.

"No you text me for me to have your son to call you."

Cues hands were rubbing up and down my backside caressingly as he said "Keish you knew I wanted to talk to you girl, you knew Quincy was just a ploy to get to you. Your stubborn ass just called and passed him the phone and disconnected after we were done without saying anything to me," he moaned.

I laughed to myself, because he was so right, and I knew when he had sent the text that he thought that I would be on the phone as usual trying to make small talk, but not that time.

"Well Cue this is the bottom line," I said as I stopped kissing him and rested my chin on my arm that I had draped on his chest so that I was looking him directly in the eyes. "I love you, I am madly in love with you, but it's time for me to start loving myself more. I am tired of always having to be second to everyone and everything else in your life. I am not going to play this game with you anymore."

"What the hell are you talking about Keisha?" Cue asked cutting me off. Although his tone was still pleasant I could tell he was aggravated. "You knew about Mercedes."

"And I did not say that I was expecting for you to leave Mercedes, not yet anyway," I said with a smirk letting him know that eventually he would have to make a decision. "What I am saying is that every time I call you wanting to hook up you always have an excuse, but when you call me I need to drop everything and come service Cue. If you're going to play this game play it right. I sometimes have needs even when you don't; I sometimes just need to see you when I need to see you. I need for you to start being more flexible when it comes to me."

"Keisha you need to stop," Cue said as he closed his eyes so he did no longer have to look into my eyes. Hell I knew what my eyes done to him. "I do come when you ask sometimes; don't try to act like I never do what you ask. And to be honest he said opening his eyes back because he thought he had me, "You never call me and say babe I need to see you or babe I need to feel you."

"I never ask anymore because I got tired of always being rejected," his eyes closed again. I couldn't help but to laugh as I eased my way back up to his lips and softly kissed them and asked, "Do you still really want me baby?"

Cue flipped me over to my back as he arched his body over mine. He steadied himself with the palms of his hands, as he looked down on me. "Keisha listen to me, I have always wanted you babe. I am with you and risking everything because I chose to. I can't stop loving you and I will not allow you to stop loving me. Just stop assuming every time that you can't reach me that I am out with another woman. Believe me baby between you and Mercedes, despite what you may believe, I am not a superman and my sex drive is good but I can't handle all that I use to handle anymore," he teased.

"I have been with you for four years Cue, I know what you can handle," I said as I pulled his face to mine and kissed him. I just want you to want me as much as I want you. Just agree that you will try to do better for me please."

"A verbal agreement is as good as the paper it is written on, let me just show you," Cue said as he succumbed to my kisses and groping. I knew I had this man right where I wanted him. I just needed to figure out how to channel him away from Mercedes. As for right now I was just going to continue to play my role only step it up a little and make him see that I could be his life partner. I will give it a few more months, but right now I was just enjoying how my baby was making me feel.

Chapter Seventeen

(Keisha)

I was lying on my couch just thinking. I had no television on, nor music. I had been all in my feelings and crying the majority of the night. Friday night when Eboni called me with the news that she had saw Mercedes going into Hunfew Bridal. A very upscale bridal shop that will custom design a gown for you, my heart was shattered. Yes, anyone can go into a bridal shop and inquire about gowns, but at Hunfew you had to make an appointment just to get in and talk with a designer. When you scheduled the appointment you had to be prepared to pay a $100.00 non-refundable deposit that would apply towards the design of your gown; however, if you decided not to use their services, the money was just for their consultation and time for coming in to see you. So who would do that without wedding plans? Eboni also noticed a huge engagement ring on Mercedes finger.

After a little investigation I found out that Mercedes had not been consulting about a wedding gown, that she had already had her gown designed and that she was going in for a fitting so that the gown could start being made. To make matters even worse she had already paid for the Orthodox where the wedding would take place. Information was steady flowing in to me all of a sudden. I found out about the Orthodox through a friend of mine who is a Facebook friend of Mercedes that called me and asked, "So Mercedes has finally convinced Cue to marry her huh? I had no idea that you and Cue were not seeing each other anymore after all the shit you two have been through together."

Because she was one of those friends that I talked to whenever I needed a favor or information she had no idea just how much shit I had been through with Cue. She did not know that my son was Cue's although she was one of the ones after seeing my son asked, "You sure you are not lying about who this child's father is?" playfully.

When I inquired about how she found out she told me that Mercedes had posted on her Facebook page that she had found and paid for the venue for the wedding. She did not mention when the wedding was going to take place but over the course of the week she said that Mercedes had posted so much about being stressed, and trying to find a caterer amongst other things, so this let her know that it had to be soon.

At this moment I was glad that mom and Granny had Quincy. I had busied myself with moving into my house this weekend and had not been out the entire weekend thus far, or heard from Cue. I was having my own little pity party and had no plans to even go out for our Sunday evening dinner as the girls and I always have. I was relaxing on my couch watching "Toya's A Family Affair" when Mahogony called asking if I was coming to Wild Wings. My thoughts were -Dang it's Sunday already? I had been so consumed fixing up my place and trying to figure how I was going to handle this marriage thing that it hadn't even dawned on me that I had not even talked to my girls. I noticed the missed calls when I settled down each night but by then I was tired and usually just turned in. I decided that I needed to get with the girls to get my frustrations out and let them motivate me to keep it moving.

My phone beeped and I looked at the screen, it was Cue. I sat there staring at the phone debating if I could hold it together if I talked to him. Just as I decided to answer, the phone stopped ringing. I decided to go and get into the shower and call him back later. Soon as I turned the water on the phone started to ring again. I went to the dresser where my phone lay and it was Cue calling again. I said a short prayer for strength before I answered.

"Hey," I said, really low.

"What's up Keish, where are you?" Cue asked.

"I am at home, what's up? I asked, in the same tone.

I sat on the edge of my bed, crossed my legs and rested my chin in the cup of my hand. My heart was suddenly rapid and my stomach had knots in it. I had been nothing shy of faithful to this man for four and a half years, and this is how he was going to do me?

"What's wrong baby?" Cue asked sensing that something was going on from my tone.

I decided to just play my role and not lash out on him just yet about this marriage. As mad as I was, and as badly as I wanted to rip him a new one, I still had to strategize, and make sure that my shit was straight before I completely cut him off. If he was planning on marrying Mercedes he would definitely be missing my ass, because it would completely be over with for him and me.

"Nothing just tired that's all. Look can I talk to you later?" I asked throwing him all the way off base, because for me to be the one to end the call with him was unheard of. And as far as I was concerned, at this point, the only thing that Cue and I could discuss over the phone was our son. Our son was not what Cue was calling to talk about, so if he wanted to talk to me it was going to be face to face, because I wanted to watch him squirm when he realized that I knew his plans to marry.

"Something's wrong I can tell. Talk to me Keisha," Cue asked concerned.

"I will talk to you when we can sit down and seriously talk face to face Cue."

"We'll meet me tonight."

"I'm really not in the mood to talk tonight; can I have a rain check?" My attitude was not the one Cue was accustomed to. I always leaped at every opportunity to be in his presence.

"Just come and talk to me or at least let me hold and comfort you," Cue said.

"Cue I am not in the mood for frolicking," I said as if I was irritated, but truth was I wanted and needed him badly right now.

"Baby we don't have to make love for me to hold you. I can tell that you're just in a bad mood. I just want to hold my baby and hopefully after we talk you will feel better that is all." Cue's voice was so low and soothing that my eyes watered up again.

"Can you pick me up? I really don't feel like driving," I asked, figuring that if Cue picked me up that he could not dismiss himself from me when he felt trapped, or got mad about how the conversation was going.

"Yeah babe I will pick you up I'll be there around nine is that cool?"

"Yeah that's cool and please be on time," I said.

I hung up the phone and went to take a good hot shower. I had no idea what Cues plans were but I sure would be finding out very soon. Mercedes just having a ring I had no problem with, hell I had three of them myself. Mercedes going in to see about a gown, I have a serious problem with.

I pulled around the corner to Granny's house, and Cue had beaten my ass there. "Fuck!" I said as I hit the steering wheel. I still had not told Cue that I had moved and was not planning on it just yet. And I knew that Granny or my mom has probably already told him that I was around at my house. That was why I wanted to get here before he did; I knew I should have called them.

As I was climbing the steps to go into Granny's, Cue said, "Hey sexy."

I turned and he was sitting in his car. "You hadn't been in the house?" I asked with a seed of hope.

"Naw babe I just pulled up," he said as he locked his car door and walked around to where I was standing. "Where you been?"

"Nigga I have told you that I am grown and don't be questioning my every move, I don't question you," I said as I turned my back to Cue and walked into the house.

Quincy ran towards me and as I stooped to give him a hug. He ran right past me to Cue screaming, "Hey daddy, lemme show you what I got," he had Cue's hand leading him into the kitchen.

"Well dang can I get a hello or something?" I asked a little more jealous than I wanted to be.

Cue looked back at me and said, "I said hello to you when you got out of the car," and winked his eye.

Quincy turned around and ran back over to me and gave me the biggest hug and sloppiest kiss. And turned and went right back to Cue. I took this opportunity to tell my family to not mention the house to Cue yet. My grandmother looked at me confused, while my mom just shook her head and said it's your biz, handle it the way you want. You got twenty dollars I can spot so I can go to bingo? She just looked at me waiting on an answer.

"Yes mother," I said, as if she was getting on my nerves. "Cue and I was getting ready to ride out and I was going to ask you to watch Quincy," knowing very well that my grandmother or sister would watch him.

"Girl you know that mother or Tamera will watch him," my mom said taking the thoughts right out of my mind.

"Keish come here," Cue said a little urgently.

I walked into the kitchen to see what precious moments that I may be missing out on. Quincy had found a baby snake and taken a shoe box and made a cage. He had put dirt, grass and worms in it. He had also taken a spray bottle and filled it with water and was showing Cue how he hydrates his new pet by spraying the water into the cage directly onto the snake's face.

I yelped and jumped behind Cue.

"Girl this snake is more afraid of you, stop being a sissy," Cue teased.

"Did that lil MF," I asked while pointing towards the shoebox, "tell you that it was more afraid of me?"

Cue laughed at me as he went on to ask Quincy how long had he had this snake in the shoe box? But was looking at me with his eyebrows squinted, his facial expression saying, What tha' hell?

"I found him yesterday, he fell out the tree by the porch and bumped his head," Quincy said proudly.

I turned and faced the living room to address mom and Granny. *"Ya'll let him bring a snake into the house?"* I asked trying to be calm but very surprised that they would allow him to do this. I mean it could have been poisonous for all they knew, and no matter how small, a snake was a snake and I hate them and anything that resembles one including worms.

"What snake gal?" Granny said getting up from her recliner to come and see what I was talking about, my mother in pursuit.

"Boy where you get this from?" my mom asked Quincy frowning.

Quincy told them the same story that he had just told his dad and I a few minutes ago. My Mom and Granny were just as shocked as Cue and I were. This boy had had this baby snake for almost twenty hours and no one knew it, until we came over. They said they saw him come in and get a shoe box and rush back out the door. When they asked him what he was doing, he only said making a cage. Because Quincy is always making something and has such a creative mind, no one thought twice of it.

I looked at Cue and said, "You handle this, and let me know when you have. I am going into the room."

Cue called me a punk as I walked back to what use to be my bedroom to wait on him to let me know when the situation was resolved. I could not even stand to look at snakes and to think that the mother had to be around somewhere made me shiver. I would be going to buy some lime to lie around and put under Granny's house tomorrow for sure.

After about thirty minutes Quincy came into the room with a kid's meal and said, "My daddy said come on so we took the snake and put him in the river' it was fun. Daddy said he going to find his brothers and grandpa."

I bent down and hugged my baby and I told him to never pick up anything else without first letting us know what it was because if that snake had bitten you it could have hurt you badly. He told me that his dad had already told him and that he will ask Granny or Mom to pick it up next time. Like that was really going to happen in this life time. I warned him to not even get close to anything else like that without an adult around, he agreed. This little boy here was all boy, he loved climbing, building and animals, any animal. I kissed him goodnight and left him watching his favorite DVD.

When I got in the car Cue started shaking his head grinning. He was telling me everything Quincy was saying about setting the snake free, and how he himself was actually scared to death of snakes but it was something about protecting him that made him put away his fear. Cue was really touched by this, as he was saying "Keish, I'd die for that boy, that's my man, I love that dude."

I looked over at him and he was slowly shaking his head as if he had just received and epiphany of some sort. I knew he loved Quincy if not more than I; we were surely toe to toe. So that is one reason I never could understand why he had not owned up to him with Mercedes, because I know how much I loved Quincy, and no man would stop me from being the full time parent that I wanted to be. Cue is a great dad and as far as Quincy is concerned, Quincy could never call Cue and absent parent; Cue see's him at least twice a week sometimes more. And when he does have me bring him to his house, he stays home with him all day. He and Quincy just chill together unless I decide or am invited to hang around. Quincy loves being with his dad.

Cue pulled up to, "The Block" a cozy restaurant off Augusta Rd. It was very expensive so we never ran into anyone we knew here and rarely any blacks at all. We were seated at a table in the back, and what we both loved about the block was that all tables were booths with very high backs. No one could see you unless they walked right up to your table as the waitresses/waiters do. It was intimate, and each booth had its very own lamp on the table and you could dim or brighten it to your satisfaction. Needless to say Cue and I was always in the darn near dark which was great.

After the waitress took our drink orders and left, Cue looked at me and said, "Ok let's talk, watsup?"

I shifted in my seat to where I now had my legs crossed underneath me, and I leaned up to the table and asked as calmly as I could, "When were you planning on letting me know that you were getting married?" I couldn't have planned it better myself, my eyes watered up.

Cue choked on his drink, although he tried to play it off, I saw how his throat pulsated and his eyes strained, as he tried to get the liquid to go down the right wind pipe. Then he cleared his throat and sat with his back straight to the seat and said, "Keisha all this mess happened so fast, I agreed but I did not tell her ass to start planning. Before I knew it she was rambling on about this wedding and then her mom and aunt starts calling me all excited and shit. I know that this makes no sense to you but until you have witnessed how they already look down their noses at me because I am not all college educated like them, you wouldn't understand why I could not reverse it."

I just sat there looking at him with tears rolling down my face. He leaned over to touch my hands and I immediately sat back to the seat so that I was out of his reach. Not willing to let him off the hook so easily with his lame excuse I just put it out there to trap him so that he would have to come clean with me and answer my question.

"So you are really going to marry Mercedes?" I asked really softly through trembling lips.

Cue suddenly found something on the table that caught his interest because he stared at whatever it was the entire time he spoke as he answered me.

"Keisha I don't want to get married, at least not now."

"But you do want to marry her?"

Cue finally looked up at me and again went to touch my hands that were on the table. I pulled them off the table and placed them in my lap.

"Answer my question Cue, what exactly are you going to do?" That damn thing on the table had his attention again.

For the first time ever in the time that I had known Cue, he was speechless. No matter how bad our arguments had been or how much he had messed up, he always had a voice in the past. Tonight he was as mute as if someone had pressed a mute button to silence him.

"Keisha I do love you and I hope that you know that," Cue said as if the life had been sucked out of him. "I just don't know what to do or how to get out of it at this point."

"See this the bullshit I'm talking about," I said angrily. "It's always pity Cue. Someone's always doing your ass wrong." What in the hell do you think that you are doing to me? I have been down with your ass, really down with your ass for four years and this is how you repay me?"

Cue's eyes watered up as he sat there looking at whatever in the hell he had been looking at since we had been talking whenever he felt stuck.

"So this is it for us hunh? Is this also it for your son to or do you plan on telling your wife about him?" I asked not being fair, but hell neither was he.

Cue looked up at me and let the tears roll down his face. I had only witnessed Cue cry once in four years. One being when he saw his son for the first time. I remember being so mad at Cue because he had yet to come to the hospital, and I was thinking so this is the kind of father that I am going to have to deal with if he ever comes around at all? I had Quincy on a Monday afternoon at 7:20 p.m. Cue did not see him until Wednesday after we had come home from the hospital. His excuse was that at hospitals you never know who you may run into, and since Quincy was our little secret, he did not want to chance coming and some motor mouth be there visiting me and run with it. So this is why you couldn't call either I asked being sarcastic. I was home in my bedroom when Cue unexpectedly walked into the room. I had not bothered calling him other than when I was on my way to the hospital, hoping that he would show up for the birth of his first and only son. And then I called him after I delivered this beautiful healthy 8 lb 10 oz baby boy knowing for sure that he would come running- No show. When Cue walked into the room I did not even acknowledge him. I just glanced at him when the door opened and directed my attention back to the television. He popped the bottom of my feet as he was passing by and asked, "What's up sexy?" and went right to the basinet. I watched as Cue gently lifted Quincy up smiling, and his eyes watered up. At that moment, any ill feeling that I had for Cue, left.

Lost in my own thoughts, I heard Cue say, "You know me better than that, how dare you ask me a crazy ass question like that?" Cue hissed angrily at me. "He is my son. Whether you and I are together, or Mercedes and I, no one will ever stop me from loving or being a father to our son. He is a product of you and me, conceived out of love. I am happy that you decided to carry my seed. It only made me love you that much more. Every time I would see your growing belly, I would be like that's wat'sup."

I was beginning to feel a certain kind of way when Cue said this, but then thought- whatever! Don't let his words, though sweet, side-track you. "So are you planning to tell her before the wedding or after?" I asked sarcastically.

That damn thing on the table whatever it was had his attention again.

Cue looked awkward. "I am going to tell her Keisha, I have wanted to anyway a lot lately. The timing just is never right especially with how envious she is of you already anyway."

"So this is real huh, she wins?" I was more saying than asking.

"No baby she hasn't won, I just got myself in some fucked up shit. I love you and I don't want to lose you babes. I just gotta figure this mess out."

"How in the hell did you get yourself into this fucked up shit? You had to have asked her because I am not for a second going to believe that after all these years of her trying to manipulate, trap and threaten you into marrying her ass that she suddenly just decided to plan a wedding and set a date! Really Cue?"

Keisha it happened when you took Quincy and left town and I could not get in touch with you, I was just so upset at the time with you," Cue started, but I cut him off because he was not about to make him proposing to Mercedes my fault.

"Hold on you are not about to put this mess on me. You are the one that asked her to marry you, not me. Own up to your shit Cue!"

"I'm not blaming you Keish. I'm just saying it happened when you and Quincy left. I had been with her all week and I had been trying to get in touch with you and my mind just wasn't right. Mercedes was there and she was being everything that I needed her to be at the time," Cue said shaking his head as if he really could not believe how it happened. "I was just feeling some kinda way about all that had happened with you her and me. I needed you and my son really badly. I didn't know what you were thinking; whether you were done and moving on or what. By day three with nothing from you I was just mad I guess, she asked and I was like fuck it may as well. You may not want to believe that you had nothing to do with it, but truthfully Keisha you had everything to do with it. Not your fault but just telling you where my mind was when I agreed."

I just sat there stunned and speechless. Did my retaliation back fire on me with such vengeance?

"Babe it's not your fault," I guess Cue took the death stare I had on him as me saying are you really blaming me, but actually I was really blaming myself at this point.

"I know this is my fucked up shit. I do love you and I still want you. Man I don't know what I would do if I lost you Keisha."

I cleared my throat and said, "I tell you what Cue since you seem to be stuck between a rock and a hard shell right now. I'm going to give you your space. What you need to do is figure this out without me on your back hounding you about whether or not you have worked your way out of this mess." Cue went to shaking his head no and was about to say something but I asked him to let me finish.

"If you can't figure out a way to tell her that you do not want to marry her which is bullshit to me because we're talking about a marriage here not whether you're going to have chicken or chops for dinner, then you go right ahead and marry her. I promise you that you will have no problems from me as bad as it may hurt. But I will say this; Quincy loves you to death and I love him to death. Before I let you desert our son who is attached to you, it will be the death of you! I don't give a fat babies ass whether you tell Mercedes about him or not, but you will not suddenly become absent in his life. You continue to play your role and we have no problems."

I had become so enraged that I did not realize how aggressive my tone had become, until I saw the deer in head light look that Cue had on his face. Blame it on maternal protection because all I knew is that I said what I meant and I meant what the hell I had said. If he thought for one minute that I would let him hurt my baby- I would take matters into my own hands and spill my guts to everybody and that includes- Mercedes, that mom and aunt, which he tries so hard to please. And I was not beneath putting his ass on child support.

Cue had me in a place that could be fatal for him. I have loved him, had his child, been faithful and I felt betrayed.

"Keisha what kind of a man do you think that I am? I love that lil rascal. Quincy and I are going to be straight, and you and I are going to be good to babes, just let me get out of this mess." Cue reached over the table and took my hands into his as he leaned over the table and kissed me real softly on the lips. "I love you Keisha and I won't lose you."

Does he really think that if he carries through with this that I am going to deal with him in that way? I was feeling so bad right now I just needed him to hold me. "Can we leave now; I really want to just lie down."

Cue looked at me as if he just wanted to squeeze all of the pain away. "Yea," he said putting a hundred dollar bill in the folder for a seventy dollar check. "Let's go home, or do you not want to be with me tonight?" he asked with pleading eyes as he stood by my seat waiting for me to get up.

I did not even try to stop the tears from flowing down my cheeks. "Let's just go please," I said, as I got up and walked off. Cue placed his hands on my lower back and I melted underneath his touch.

Once in Cue's car I turned the radio up to listen to the Quite Storm. I was already into my feelings and Kenny only took me deeper into them. Keisha Cole's" "Enough of No Love" was playing and I just cried more. I was wishing that by some miracle Vetsa Williams "Congratulations" would come on next, Cue would shit on himself. I just wanted to be swallowed in pity. Cue reached over and grabbed my hand and squeezed it tightly; I just lay with my head back on the headrest, eyes shut and let Kenny the Mac Miles carry me away. Cue took it upon himself that I was going home with him because he was heading towards his house and I was glad of it. This was not even about him tonight; this was about me and my needs.

My phone rang the next morning and I lifted Cues arm from my waist and rolled over to pick up my phone. I looked at the clock and it was 11:43 a.m. Cue and I had basically slept the morning away. I noticed the call was coming form Granny's, I answered figuring that it was my mom or Granny calling to check on me.

"Hello?"

"Hey mommy, where you at?"

"Good morning baby," I sat up in the bed. "I am at your dad's house but I will be home in a little while ok, what are you doing?" I said quietly to not wake Cue up.

"Why you and daddy didn't take me with you?" Quincy asked whining. "Daddy said I could stay all-night. Where daddy at? Let me speak to him."

"He is asleep Quincy. I did not know that I was going to stay overnight, your dad and I went out to eat and it was late when we were done so I just came over to his place," I lied.

"Well wake him up and tell him to come get me?" Quincy demanded.

"No Quincy daddy has to work this morning he will pick you up later. Ok?"

"Why you can't wake him up so I can talk to him for a minute? Pleeease mommy?"

"He is going to bring me home in a minute and you can talk to him then ok?" This little boy here was a piece of work.

"What does he want?" Cue's voice was raspy because he was just waking up but it was still sexy as hell.

I looked at Cue who still had his head on the pillow but was looking at me through half closed eyes. I removed the phone away from my ear and covered the mouth piece so that Quincy would not hear Cue or I. Whispering, I told Cue, "He's mad because I stayed overnight without him. He said that you had told him that he was coming to stay overnight." Cue reached up and took the phone from my hand.

"What's up man?" Cue exhaled as he spoke with his eyes all the way closed now and listening to what Quincy was saying.

Cue wasn't getting much in because all I was hearing from this end was basically; yea- un- hunh- ok.

"Man I told you that I would, I'll get you tonight when I am done working, cool?"

"Yeah man I gotcha," Cue exhaled again.

"Yeah Quincy," Cue said, becoming frustrated.

"Ok man."

"Yeah Quincy."

"Yeah man. I love you too."

Cue never opened his eyes as he passed the phone back to me and said, "That boy been here before I swear." I checked the phone to see if Quincy was still on the line but he had disconnected.

"What was he saying?" I asked smirking, with Quincy you never knew.

"You mean what he didn't say," Cue said pulling me over to him.

My question went unanswered as those juicy lips lightly brazed mine. Last night had been great. We made passionate love, we held, touched and caressed. We talked, cried and the love making became even more intense. Cue looked down on me at one point and said, "Do you really think that I am going to lose all of this?"

Chapter Eighteen

(Cue)

"Eric man hit me up when you get this message, Keisha knows about the wedding man." I disconnected the call and ran my hand over my head as I headed towards my barber. What in the hell had I gotten myself into I thought. Damn if Keisha had only been answering her phone a day sooner I wouldn't be in this predicament. Dammit, I thought to myself. My phone began to ring I reached up on my dash which held my phone holder and looked at the screen, it was my boy Eric. As soon as I answered the phone Eric started going in without as much as a, what's up?

"How the hell Keisha find out man, don't tell me that your conscience finally got the best of you? Eric said sarcastically.

"Hell naw man, I ain't told her shit. I don't know how she found out but she has. Man she is so hurt right now."

"Are you surprised, how did you expect for her to feel nukka? This girl been really down with your ass. Keisha is in love with you and she loves you for you, not what you can give her. Hell yeah she's hurt," Eric said as if he was getting mad, "you're about to be a married ass man."

"Man I know but I guess I didn't expect her to be like this. Man you know Keisha is my heart and I don't want to lose her over this bullshit. She said that she was going to back down, I can't let that happen."

"Cue you have less than two months so you better think fast or let me know something before I go and put this grand down for this expensive ass suit your high solutin fiancé got us wearing. Better yet you better tell Daryl, because if he goes and get that suit and your ass try to renege you won't have to worry about Keisha or Mercedes, because Daryl will kill your ass." Eric laughed.

"Man you ain't lying," I laughed at Eric speaking of our boy Daryl, who is not in the game and works a 9-5 job so his money is sacred to him. "Hell I told him that I would pay seven hundred leaving him to pay three, and he's still talking shit!"

"Damn right," Eric said. We suppose to go Thursday to get fitted and pay the deposits. You better know something by then or your ass getting married whether you want to or not. Because after my money is spent and especially Daryl's, you're going to be a married man." Eric said getting a kick out of all of this.

"Man I'm glad you are being humored at my expense. I need advice not your damn jokes."

"Nukka don't get mad at me because your dumb ass was getting some good sex and messed around and said Marry me."

I laughed, "Nigga I done told your ass that I did not ask her that while we were having sex, she asked me to get married. Damn, why is that so hard for you to understand?"

"Whateva nigga, you were fucking her and she was throwing it on your ass really good and your dumb ass popped the question. That's the scenario that I'm sticking to and telling everyone that ask what made you want to get married all of a sudden. Logical to me fool."

"Go to hell dude, where you be?"

"Just pulling up at Sue-Sue's, getting ready to take these nigga's lunch money." Eric said.

"Oh word? I'm coming to take yours then," I said making a u-turn to head over to the Westside.

"Yo' ass need to be heading over to Mercedes house to tell her that you don't plan on marrying her ass." Eric said, getting a real kick out of his humor. "Does Keisha know that this execution- I meant wedding is about to take place in seven weeks?"

"Naw man she don't know that shit, she can't deal with that right now. I'ma tell her, just trying to find the right time that's all. Damn man, of all the bull crap you and D.J ass does; why am I always the one in some shit?" I asked.

"Because your dumb ass is the only one that thinks with the head that doesn't have a brain, but don't worry about Keisha, I will make sure that she is good literally." Eric was always kidding me about wanting Keisha, which I don't doubt, but a line that he wouldn't dare cross.

"Whateva nigga, Keisha is off limits to you remember that," I said as I looked over my shoulder to switch lanes so that I could get from behind this slow car. "I'm headed your way now to take your lunch money to give Quincy so he can buy his sandbox."

"Quincy will never get his sandbox if he's waiting on you to win the money from me, bring me your money nigga." Eric said boasting, because he had just won fifteen hundred off of me last Saturday.

"Whateva clown see you in ten," I said as Mercedes was beeping in.

"What's up babes?" I asked.

"You are, I miss you," Mercedes moaned.

"I know you do," I kidded with her, but I knew that she did, any time I was away from her ass she missed me.

"Are you coming by tonight?" she asked.

"You want me to come by tonight?" I asked playing with her, of course she wanted me to come by, when did she not.

"You know I do. I cannot wait until we're married so I will no longer have to hope to see you when I turn in at night because you will be turning in to me every night."

This made my stomach drop, damn this did mean that I would be staying at her place every night didn't it? What the hell! I love her and all but this marriage thing may not have been thought through too well, I mean I am the type of guy that needs my own space, I don't like being hovered over. Mercedes and I was going to have to really talk, she might try to tell me a time that I need to be home at night. While I will not disrespect her, I am still a grown ass man and I am not use to anyone dictating my moves. And Mercedes was so damn bossy, spoiled, and thought the world should revolve around her that I could see her trying to lay down some rules. Now Keisha on the other hand she would be like, Ok love; see you when you get home, because her ass will want to go out too. I guess that is why Keisha and I vibe so well. She does her own thing and when I catch her we're cool. She never sweats me or call me twenty four seven on my whereabouts.

I was telling Mercedes that I was going to play cards and that I would call her when I was on my way over when my phone beeped again, it was Keisha. I told Mercedes that I would talk to her later let me take this incoming call and clicked over.

"What's up babe you missing daddy already?" I said into the receiver.

"Yeah daddy, I miss you, are you on your way to get me?" asked Quincy.

Oh damn; I had forgot that I was going to have Quincy tonight when I told Mercedes that I would be over to her place. "I'm coming in a little bit man, where is your mom?"

"Gone over to her house," Quincy responded.

"Gone over to who's house?" I asked Quincy, pushing the phone closer to my ear to hear him.

"She at us new house," Quincy said.

"It's our, not us Quincy," I said correcting my son's language. "What she doing at the house this time of the day?" I asked Quincy while making my second u-turn for the day to head over to Keisha's.

"I dunno, she always goes over there. She like it I guess. Are you still coming to get me?"

"Yeah man I will be there soon, ok?"

"Ok, bye daddy- love you."

"Love you too man."

Although it was only five forty five it was dust dark outside so I don't know what Keisha would be doing at a house that had no electricity this time of the day. I picked up my cell phone and called Keisha, and the phone went directly to voicemail. I left her a message pretending that I was calling because I was on my way to get Quincy, and wanted to make sure that she was home, or if his bags were packed. Keisha called me back ten minutes later, just as I was pulling into her yard.

There was a light on somewhere in the rear of the house because I could see the glow seeping through the mini blinds that were on the windows. I sat looking at the house that Keisha had transformed from a shack to a mini mansion. I was really impressed and proud of her.

To think that I laughed at the shack that she had brought me to see that had, "As is $12,000.00" spray painted right across the wood peeled white house in orange paint. And it was paid for; it was actually hers with no mortgage, bank loan or personal loan I know because she coursed me into reluctantly buying it for her. Not that I did not want to buy a house to put Keisha and my son in, I just didn't want to buy this shack that she had presented to me. A sense of pride went through my body; my baby had her own home. This house was something that she could one day pass down to our son.

I was still confused as to why Keisha hadn't mentioned that the house was complete to me unless maybe the inside still wasn't complete. I had only been by here twice prior to today, and that was when she first brought me over to see where she wanted me to invest my money, and another time when she was in traffic court and was not able to get over to let the contractors in and asked me to come by the court house to get the key and let them in.

My cell phone rang, it was Keisha. "Hey, what's up, Quincy bag ready I am on my way." I said while still sitting in the parking space in front of her house.

"Yes he's ready, how far away are you?" She asked as I was backing out of her yard.

"About ten minutes," I told her, when in actuality I was not even two minutes away from her Granny's house. Keisha's house was maybe a ten minute walk but only a two or three minute drive to Granny's. I parked at the top of granny's street by the park where I could see down off into the alley for when Keisha arrived. I knew that she would not be coming from the top of the street where she would pass by the park, because it was more convenient for her to come through the tunnel from where she stayed, because as soon as you came through the tunnel Granny's house was to the left.

Keisha must have ran out her door before we even hung up the phone because as soon as I parked on the side of the road and killed my engine, her 300 whipped from under the tunnel and halted in front of Granny's house. I watched as she jumped out of the car and took the steps two at a time and dashed into the house. I cranked my car back up, coasted down the hill and parked behind her car.

As I knocked on the door I could hear Quincy running through the house screaming, "That's my daddy, that's my daddy, I'll get it!"

Although my mind was boggling with what Keisha was doing, I could not help but smile hearing my lil man's voice and excitement that it carried. Quincy flung the door open and leaped into my arms so fast that I had to drop the bag that was carrying his shoes that I had bought him, to keep from dropping him. He was talking a mile a minute as I stepped over the threshold and kissed Granny and Doretha on the cheeks greeting them. Keisha had one cool family. I could actually say that I really liked all of her family from her cool younger brother and sister, to her aunts and uncle who was all just real about theirs. Her mother I personally knew because she was a different type of hustler, and always kept it 100. Even her grandmother who I had a hard time with at first but learned that if you are on her good side, then you had no worries. I remember one day I bounced over to see my son, at the time Quincy was about six or seven months. Although I broke Keisha off nicely for Quincy I wasn't as active a father as I should have been. Don't get me wrong I loved my son and when I had not seen him in a few weeks my heart yearned every time I would pass church street knowing that my son was just down the street. I would normally be on a run every time I passed and the timing just wouldn't be good for me to stop. So I saw him as often as I could, well whenever it was convenient. I must be honest and that had turned to sometimes once a week, sometimes once every two weeks or month.

The particular day that granny had got into my shit I hadn't seen Quincy in almost a month. I came in as I always had and spoke to everyone and granny started in on me. "Where have you been Cue, streets got you too busy to come and see about your baby?" she said looking at me with her neck cocked to the side as she lifted her left eyebrow when she asked the question.

"No ma'am, I know my son's good I talk to Keisha on the regular it's just that I have been busy working and trying to get some things together for this barbershop I plan to open."

Granny reached over and pulled the sheet that was covering the hole in the couch back up and tucked it. "So do you mean to tell me that it is ok for Keisha, as a mother who is trying to get her beauty salon up and running, it's be ok for her to not see her child for a long period of time?" Granny was looking at me like I was crazy. "Just because you give Keisha money does not replace you being there to bond with and teach your son how to be a man. Sonny next door does not have a pot to piss in nor a window to throw it out, but you know what I like about Sonny?" Granny paused for me to answer.

"What do you like about Sonny?" I asked Granny exasperated.

Granny gave me a "don't try to be slick" look before she continued. "Sonny only gets a mere $178.00 a month on disability, and Melanie only receives $126.00 a month from disability benefits for their child. That boy he can't do much financially for his child but he is more of a father than you have been." I tried to cut in but Granny cut me off and said that she was talking and I need to just listen.

"That boy walks up to the daycare everyday; volunteers his time for forty minutes and then walks back home. Then he walks back up there at the end of the day and picks up his child and keeps her until Melanie gets off of work and come and picks her up. That day care is based on income so they only pay ten dollars a week but he pays it out of his lil $178 a month rather than have the child sitting at home with him all day. He could easily save his lil money and keep that child with him but he'd rather have his child learning and interacting with other kids."

"Granny," I started, but just as Keisha always does, she shushed me with a shake of her head and her finger in the air.

"Cue you have the means to be a great dad. You have transportation, that boy doesn't. You have money, Sonny doesn't. But you'd rather run the streets rather than put some quality time in with that precious son of yours? Lucky for you Quincy is still an infant and you have the time to bond with him. But I'm telling you now that it will be a cold day in hell before I let you bounce in and out of my house on your own free will after going weeks without seeing that baby. You either be consistent or you stay the heck out of his life. If Keisha wants to be stupid and let you come in and out, then she better find somewhere else for you to do it. Do you hear me boy?"

"Oh you want me to really answer?" I asked, being sarcastic.

Granny looked at me and shook her head before saying, "I asked you a question didn't I? I swear I hope that Quincy doesn't get his smarts from you."

If it wasn't for the fact that Granny was the backbone, and everyone loved her so you better not dare disrespect her, I would have told her exactly what I thought of her lil lecture. Granny has five kids. I wonder would she have been singing this same song if Mr. Dextor had taken off leaving her to raise all of them kids they had without money, only giving of his time. Sonny's lazy ass can work, he just played the system and faked that his back gave him so many problems so that he could get disability. And Melanie was not at all happy about that lil

$126.00 a month she received because we all hung out in the same spots, she just had no choice but to deal with it. I mean, like she said, what could she do if that is all that the state said that he had to pay. His black ass wasn't doing nothing else and could not get around fully anywhere else because he didn't have transportation, so I guess the daycare was the highlight of his boring week. But since this was Granny and I did like the old fart I just kept all of that in and said, "Yes ma'am, I hear you and I will do better." I had, I started making it my business to come by everyday at first really just being sarcastic, see how much granny would like me at her house every day, however I did want to see my son as much as possible too. Then I got into a routine where I came at least once a week sometimes twice just depending on what was going on, but I never again let an entire week go by without seeing Quincy.

I walked into Keisha's room and she was lying on the bed as if her ass had been there for hours. "Where you been?" I asked, swatting her curvaceous ass with the palm of my hand.

"You nasty daddy," Quinton said tapping my leg with his hand laughing.

I grabbed him into my arms as I sat on the corner of the bed and started tickling him.

"Nowhere just here chilling, why you ask?" Keisha said, looking down the bed to where Quincy and I were.

"I thought I had just seen you pull in as I was coming down the hill?" I said, still tickling Quincy.

"Oh I ran to the store," she said.

I stopped tickling Quincy and just stared at her. Why in the hell was her behind lying, why did she just not say, I was over at the crib taken care of some stuff? She acted like she did not notice me staring at her as she tried to keep her focus on the television. Her ass probably did not even know what the hell she was watching because it was a Spanish show, language and all was in Spanish and Keisha talked no Spanish at all. Her ass probably didn't even know what, "Gracious" meant. This told me that this whole entire set up was just a prop to throw me off to think that she had been here watching television the entire time.

"Why you looking at mommy like that?" Quincy giggled. "You silly daddy."

Keisha looked at me when Quincy asked the question and asked, "What?" In an annoyed voice.

"Nothing," I said, shaking my head and started back tickling Quincy. "You ready man, where's your bag?" I asked standing up.

Keisha got up from her position on the bed and reached to the top of their curtain covered closet and pulled down Quincy's Pittsburgh Steelers overnight bag. Keisha was not a football fan at all but she knew that I was a diehard Steeler fan. She has always bought Quincy everything Steelers. When he was a baby and I would have him with me in the few places I could take him without Mercedes finding out about him, he would have on his Steelers gear. Keisha had him bottles, pacifiers, socks and even my daddy bag was Steelers. My son and I repped hard!

Keisha pushed the bag into my chest as she followed Quincy and me out of the room and into the living room. Quincy was running around saying his goodbyes and love you's to everyone, as Keisha stood closely behind me waiting on Quincy to finish so that she could walk us out. When we got outside I strapped Quincy into his car seat and watched as Keisha bent down into the car with her rear end sticking out to give him a goodbye kiss and tell him to behave. When she stood back up she was right on my crotch that was yearning for her again even after all that we had done last night. Keisha always had this affect on me. She looked down at my crotch and shook her head as if she was saying "Do you ever get enough, get over it."

"Sure you don't want to come and hang out with us tonight?" I asked in desperation.

"Cue what did I tell you this morning? Play fair, this is hard enough for me so don't push me please. You two have fun and take care of my baby," she said, as she opened the door and stepped back into the house closing the door behind her before I even got into the car.

Quincy and I had stopped and picked up some wings when Eric called seeing where I was. I told him that I had forgotten that I was picking Quincy up, so I had to go scoop him real fast and now we're headed to the house.

"Oh you got lil man? Let me talk to him," Eric asked.

"Hello?" Quincy said, trying to keep the phone from slipping from his ear.

I think all Eric was allowed to say was, "This is Eric," because after I heard Quincy say, "Hey uncle Eric," I don't think he took a break from talking anymore, until I said, tell uncle Eric that you will talk to him later. When I took the phone back from Quincy, Eric was laughing.

"I don't know what y'all are going to do with that rascal," Eric laughed. "He told me that I still owed him a dollar, and he needed it to put in his piggy bank."

"Yeah I heard him," I laughed. "Don't play with Quincy about his money man he's ferocious. He asks me about that lil dollar you owe him all the time. I meant to tell you that you had better pay up before he puts a hit out on you."

"What ya'll getting into," Eric asked still laughing at Quincy.

"Nothing just picked up some wings and going to the pad to chill."

"Well tell Quincy I will be over later to have the game system ready so I can see if we can break even over that dollar. He's trying to break me," Eric joked.

I told Quincy what Eric said and Quincy got excited. "Tell him he gone owe me two dollars and I want my money tonight."

Eric had played Quincy in some game where they raised a family or something. You cooked and played with the kids all kinds of mess to earn points. I did not have the patience for that game. Now when it came to basketball and football I would play that game with his lil butt all day. I did not go easy on him just because he was three. His little butt talked and acted like he was a grown man, so I played him like he was a grown man. He talked just as much trash as I did while we played the game, but he was no competition for me. Keisha argued one night that I should be ashamed of myself how badly I beat him, and that I should let him win every now and again. I told her in the real world unless your born rich, lucky or own your own shit, ain't nobody going to give you shit you have to earn it. I am teaching him how to not give up and fight for what you want.

Once we got home I got Quincy's bath and put him into his Steelers pajama's this must have been a new pair because I had not saw these before but they were nice. He even had the Steelers bedroom shoes. I have to ask Keisha to hook me up with some of this gear. We sat down at the coffee table to eat our wings and salad that I put together real quick that only consisted of lettuce and tomatoes, but Quincy did not care he only ate the salads for the dressing anyway. As soon as we were done eating Quincy was ready to play the game before I could even clean up the mess he had made. I was tying up the trash bag when the doorbell rang and Quincy hollered, "Daddy I think Uncle Eric at the door you want me to get it?"

I ran out of the kitchen to stop Quincy from running to the door. Although Mercedes had never come by my house unannounced but once since we'd been together, you never knew with her. If she had I would have had a bad attitude with her and may not even have let her in even if she called and I answered, I would tell her I don't pop up at your house so you don't pop up at mine. Now go home and try this again. Now if Quincy wasn't here it may go a little different. I would still make it known that I did not appreciate her just popping up at my crib without calling.

I looked through the peep hole and it was Eric. "Your right Quincy," I said as I opened the door for Eric just as Mercedes was pulling into the yard. It was too late for me to close the door and pretend that we were not there because she had already seen us. "Oh shit!" I hissed to Eric, "Mercedes."

Eric turned and looked as Mercedes was cutting the car off. "I'll take Quincy to the back, handle this man," Eric said, as he looked at me like he was disgusted. "You're his dad, he shouldn't have to hide."

Eric loved Quincy and had been telling me every since Quincy had been in this world, that he wished that he had a son like Quincy. Apparently, Eric was only shooting girls. He loved those three girls to death and was a great dad but he wanted a son so bad. He thought Quincy was everything that a son should be and he was right.

He was tough, he loved sports and my son had swag. Seriously Quincy was too cool to only be three years old. My son had mad swag.

I heard Eric ask Quincy to take him into his bedroom and show him the scrap book that he had put together of himself again. I stepped outside to talk to Mercedes. She got out of the car smiling, but my face was cold.

"What's up baby?" she said, standing on her tip toes to kiss me. I let her peck my lips before asking, "What was she doing here?" She said that when I did not show up that she was worried and that she had called me and my voicemail picked up so she decided to ride over to see if I was home and what happened.

Damn I should have just took her calls and told her some lie. "The guys and I are playing cards tonight I had forgot all about it when I told you that I would be over until Eric called and said they were getting ready to head over. I was planning to call you but got sidetracked and forgot all about it until you come pulling up."

She looked at me like she was a little upset and said, "Whatever Cue, fine. I will just go in your room and watch television until you guys are done," she said, attempting to walk past me and into the house.

"No Mercedes not tonight baby," I said, grabbing her arm pulling her back. "It's going to be all the guys and really it's not the same when women are around even if you are going to be in the bedroom. They will feel as if they have to whisper or not talk freely as we usually do. I'm sorry but you're going to have to bounce tonight baby girl," I said, tugging on both of her ears playfully to soften the rejection.

She looked a little uncomfortable and let down. "I promise you that I will see you tomorrow," I said, putting on a puppy dog face and extending my lower lip out pleading for forgiveness. She punched me playfully in my arm and said, "Stop silly, you get on my nerves. You and your boys play your little stinky cards and you better be ready to spend the day with me tomorrow," she said, as she slipped her arms around my waist and squeezed. I escorted her back to her car and playfully spanked her ass and said, you better just be ready for me tomorrow.

I went back into the house. Eric and Quincy were still in the back room. I walked back there and opened the door and Quincy was screaming; In your face nigga! They were playing one of the older basketball games that Quincy was a beast at.

"Man sit down, it ain't over," Eric argued.

I went and sat down beside Quincy and watched as he beat Eric 118-93. Eric wanted to play again but Quincy said, "Naw man I want to play football, you can't beat me." Eric looked at him and then looked at me shaking his head as to say, "I do not know what to say about this boy here, he is too much and too grown to be only three," and that he was. Where he was always respectful he said some stuff that you would not believe a three year old would say or much less knows.

He and Eric put in the football game and as always an argument pursued as to who was going to have the Steelers; Eric just liked to get Quincy started because he always let him have the Steelers when it was all said and done. But what Quincy said had Eric and I both doubled over laughing.

"Man you ain't even a true fan, you aint even got on Steeler gear, get outta here," Quincy said.

Chapter Nineteen

(Lynn)

Good afternoon, my name is Sonya Jeter and I am the wedding Director. We are brought here today to rehearse for the wedding ceremony of Cuedricus Davis and Mercedes Drummond. This is a magnificent occasion and I am here to make sure that it is as beautiful as the love that they have for each other.

I looked around the church fascinated and amazed at how much money had been put into this wedding that I knew for a fact my brother was not really ready for. Although I knew that Cue loved Mercedes, she was not the right companion for him. Cue was outgoing, playful and fun. Mercedes kept her circle very tight and was always so serious. They say opposites attract, but this one was going to blow, I just knew it.

I looked over at my brother who was talking to Eric and D.J, his two best men, he looked alright, but I knew that he was only playing the part. Unlike other grooms, Cue had his black ass at home last night no doubt crying to our mom. They both were hemmed up in her room talking half the night. I was not allowed in the room. I figured it had to be about this wedding and what he had gotten his stupid ass into. I did not get to talk to mom this morning because everyone was running in every direction to get this or that done before the wedding.

I can't believe that Cue is actually going to go through with this, because he told me a month ago that he wasn't. The next thing I knew a rehearsal date was here. So unless he planned on dying tonight or skipping town in the morning, it appeared as if his ass was going to be married by this time tomorrow.

"Lynn," the wedding director called my name taking me away from my thoughts. I jumped up and went and stood beside Troy who was going to be my escort for tomorrow. She lined us all up accordingly to our escorts, and then she went over the process of how we would walk into the church and out. We only had to run through the drill twice and we were professionals.

After we were done rehearsing we all retreated to the basement for dinner. From the way Mercedes and her mom had the dining hall in the basement decorated one would have thought that the reception was going to be held down here. There were red linen table cloths covering each table with white strips crossing over it forming a lower case T. In the center of the table where the T crossed there were huge vases with all sorts of wild flowers flowing from it. On each of the four tables there was a bottle of chilled wine in a wine crate along with mixed chocolates. They served us prime rib, shrimp, mashed potatoes and string beans. These were the best ribs I had ever had. I was thinking what are they going to serve at the wedding reception? But then again the wedding party was only a group of twelve so maybe that is why she went all out for the wedding rehearsal dinner.

I should have known better with Mercedes high sudity ass. After a magnificent wedding we were chauffeured by limo over to the reception which was held at the Orthodox. When we walked in to a clapping audience I was mesmerized by the amount of flowers they had in this huge room. If you thought the flowers at the wedding were extravagant, they had nothing on the reception hall. We were introduced through a curtain of white lilies that were stringed together and had to be held open as our names were called out. We walked down a walkway that was lined with white and red roses and lilies. When we came to the end of the walk way we were standing directly in front of the table for two that Cue and Mercedes would be sitting at. On either side of their table were long tables, enough to seat ten people at each table for the wedding party. On Cue's and Mercede's table, there was a huge glass vase that had at least four dozen of red and white roses cascading from it, and there was a small buffet on either side of the vase as was the wedding party tables. Where our vase wasn't nearly as big we had just as many roses in the three vases that served as center pieces for our table. There was a small vase with a dozen red roses on one end, and in the middle another small vase with red and white roses mixed and on the other end another small vase with another dozen red roses, same pattern for the other wedding party table opposite us. In between each of these vases that were on the table was our very own private buffet that consisted of: macaroni & cheese, rice pilaf, green beans, potato salad, chicken, ham, shrimp kabobs and dinner rolls.

Ok, we had our own private buffet so we should fix our own plates right? Wrong! Each wedding party table was assigned a waitress who fixed our plate for us and kept our drinks refreshed. Each table also had three bottles of champagne on it for the toast as well as each of the guest tables were assigned a waitress/waiter for every two tables making serving very fast and no one had to wait forever to eat. As I continued to look around the room from where I was sitting, I noticed what reminded me of an Alice in Wonderland game box in the rear. It was decorated with pink and white flowers cascading everywhere. Flowers were coming from the ceiling hanging down over the table. There were small, tall, big and tubed candy dishes everywhere. The dishes were filled with all sorts of candy from hard to chocolate. There were nuts, Twizzler's, Skittles, you name it. There was another table in the center of the room that was a chocolate station. There were three huge fountains one held milk chocolate, one white chocolate and the last one dark chocolate. There were plates lining the table that had pound cake pieces, pretzels bananas, strawberries, apple slices and pineapples.

Then, there was a table on the other end that held a huge ice sculptured swan that had tons of shrimp floating around in the water. On the other side of the same table was different levels draped with a table cloth and had all sorts of sushi on the platters. There were all sorts of sauces to for dipping the shrimp and sushi. That table along had to cost them close to a grand if not a grand. The candy station and chocolate station did not come cheap either. Looking around and trying to estimate the cost of this entire get up just in the reception hall alone I estimated about ten thousand if not more. For someone who wasn't really serious about being married Cue had dropped a pretty penny. I'm sure Mercedes parents paid a good portion, yet I knew that my brother had come handsomely out of the pocket as well. They were going to Hawaii on their honeymoon for an entire week, courtesy of Mercedes' mom. My mother bought the cake, well gave three hundred dollars on it once she found out that the cake Mercedes had chosen was thirteen hundred dollars. My mom actually cursed and said "I could feed my family for a year with thirteen hundred dollars and she wants me to spend thirteen hundred on a damn cake? Cue better think twice about this one."

When I told my mother that Mercedes' wedding gown had cost six thousand dollars to have made, I regretted it soon after. I thought that my mother was going to blow a head gasket! But once I saw Mercedes walk down that aisle I understood why. I am not saying it was logical but it certainly was unlike anything that I had ever seen before. She was already beautiful, but coming down that aisle, she was nothing short of stunning. I looked over at my brother and he had tears rolling down his face. I didn't know whether they were tears of joy because he was finally making this woman that he had been through everything with his wife, or that he could not believe that his dumb ass could not come up with a way to get out of it before this day arrived. Either- or- it looked sweet to all who was watching, whether they knew the truth or not.

I must say that this was one of the most expensive, gorgeous and fun weddings that my country ass had ever attended. And when my boo Leon graced me with his appearance, shit really got popping then. Leon had regretted that he would not be able to attend because one of his mom's friends had passed and he was going to have to drive his mom to North Carolina to be with the family. His mother decided that she would stay the week instead of come back home only to return in three days for the funeral so he dropped her off and was able to come back and get dressed in time to make the reception. We danced and drank until almost midnight before retreating to the hotel room that was across the street from the Orthodox. I felt that we had both drank too much and did not need to get on 85 to drive home.

Cue and Mercedes had a suite in the same hotel although they were on a different floor. They had left their own reception before anyone else because they had to be at the airport by seven for their flight to Hawaii; however, we enjoyed every bit of what they missed. Cue seemed so happy as he kept his arms around Mercedes as they walked around saying their goodbyes. Even during the reception when they were doing the toast, cake cutting, first dance and garter throw he seemed to be enjoying himself, either that or he deserved a Oscar award for his stellar performance.

I called Keisha last night out of curiosity, really to see if she had any clue about this whole thing. While she knew that a wedding was being planned I could tell by the way that she talked that she had no idea that the wedding was the next day. She told me that she and Cue had not been getting down like that for over two months now, she said that she had told him to figure out what he was going to do and she was going to just step back. He had been coming by to see or pick up Quincy and she admitted that he had tried more than once to get her to sleep with him. She had stood firm. She said that she was tired of this mental roller coaster ride that Cue had her on and either he was going to get it right or she was getting off, no longer putting her life on hold for a man that would allow her to do so as long as she was naive enough to do it.

I felt really bad for Keisha and I had intended on telling Cue just how wrong he was. Not that he was wrong for marrying Mercedes, but for not being man enough to let Keisha know that he was doing it. Just like Mercedes, Keisha had been true and stood by his side. I think he at least owed her that much regardless of how badly it may have hurt her. I didn't want to imagine how she was going to feel once she finds out that he went through with it. Cue should know, that there is nothing like a woman scorned.

My mom had told Cue a few weeks back that it was his life, and that she did not care how he lived it as long as he done right by Quincy. If Mercedes was who he had planned on spending his life with, then be a man and take her and talk to her, and let her know that this is your baby. If she loves you the way she claims to it will be hard, but she will forgive you and eventually get over it. If not, let her bounce because your child should be the most important thing to you right now. I had no idea what Cue was going to do or when he was planning on telling his now wife, that he has a son by the one woman that she hates more than anything. All I knew was that the "Ish" was about to get all the way real and I just prayed that I was around when it did.

I like Mercedes and all but she is so out of touch with the real world. She has no sympathy for people with struggles. Her thing is everyone had a choice to make whether it is to finish school, go to college, have a child out of wedlock or work at a restaurant. She snarled her nose up at people so much I am surprised it's not stuck in that snarl. I told her that I had not planned on having my first child at the age of seventeen the shit just happened. She responded that if I knew that I was not on any birth control and had unprotected sex then what had I expected.

One day we were at the soup kitchen that her family owns and someone had brought in a bag of clothes. There was this lady at the soup kitchen picking up food to take back home to her family when she overheard the lady asking Mercedes if they would like the clothes. Mercedes told the lady that they did not do clothing at the kitchen, only food, but she would take them to her friend who runs a community center, who had a clothes bank that sold clothes at a very low price, and donate them to them.

The lady who had brought the clothes over said there are a few coats and some nice pants and shirts in there that my daughter has outgrown, they are size twelve's. Mercedes thanked her and the lady left. The other lady who was a soup kitchen customer asked Mercedes if she could look through the bag because her daughter wore a size twelve, and she was a single parent of five and could use the clothes. Mercedes told her that she would have to go over to the community center because they were not for her to give away, she was suppose to take them to the center, not realizing the lady had heard the entire conversation.

I asked her what was the difference whether you take them to the community center for the less fortunate or give them to someone that is right here who's telling you she could use them. Mercedes told me that people always wanted something for free. If she knew that she could not afford to raise five kids without handouts, then she should have thought about that before she kept having them. I told her shit happens and if you got out of your country club environment and went out into the lower income areas and hung out some, you would maybe understand.

"I did not go to college and get my degree to hang out in lower income areas," Mercedes said, with her lips in a disgusted curl. "I can't support nor take care of everyone who made bad decisions, and it is certainly not my fault. No one told any of them to have these kids that they can't afford." She turned and placed the bag on the table in the back of her, and started back packing the small brown paper bags with food that they were giving to the needy, which consisted of a bag of rice, two cans of peas, can of evaporated milk, dozen eggs, pop-tarts and a loaf of bread. I have to say that what Mercedes family went in together and done on a weekly basis for those in need was grand, but the things I heard them say after all the people were gone- keep your damn food. They're going to bust hell wide opened. They were so out of touch with the world, so what you had a good education and you all could each afford to give the one hundred dollars a week to buy the food to distribute. Their intentions were good, but if your heart wasn't in it, you may as well have not done it at all.

Of course I was the friend only friend of Mercedes that never went to college. But if you asked me, she and her friends were all ghetto chicks just fronting to be classy. Her other friends had money, careers, houses and nice cars just as she did. I still lived at home with my mother and worked at the manufacturing plant about two miles from the house, although my car was new and very nice, it was only a Honda Accord to them. They never verbally said anything negative about my car, but in conversations when we were talking about different things about cars, I've heard a time or two that you don't have to cover luxury insurance you are lucky. Or I wished that I could get thirty dollar oil changes, or my car only take premium. Yes, they had a roundabout way of trying to tell me that my car was not up to par with theirs. I only dealt with them when I could not find my fun friends to go out with. Mercedes seldom came over to our house at all, but now that she and Cue were married I was pretty sure that she would be over a lot more and, "whoa" to her boogie ass around my mom. After spending a day around my mom and aunts she would either shape up, pretend to have shaped up, or keep her ass away.

Chapter Twenty

(Keisha)

I don't know what that was all about last night, but I tossed and turned all night long. I dreamed that Cue and I were on an island making love all over the island. I had trained myself to not think about Cue as much because I had made up my mind that it has been over two months, and he still hasn't gotten his shit together and I was done waiting. His sister had called me a few days ago and I had voiced my feelings to her and she agreed that I should move on; I had waited long enough.

I got up and took a long hot shower and called over to Granny to see what Quincy was up to. He asked had I talked to his daddy and I reminded him that his dad was going out of town, and said that he would be back next week. Quincy asked if he could call him and I told him we would later. Quincy was getting to the point that he wanted to be around Cue all the time. I told Quincy that I was getting ready to go to the flea market and asked if he wanted to go with me? He asked if I would buy him a dog and when I said no, he said then no he would just stay at Granny's and play with his friends. This little rascal was a mess, I told him that I would see him when I returned and we may go to Frankie's Fun Park, of course that meant I would be taking his little friends also.

I was walking around the flea-market picking up some great things for my house when I ran into Alana. Well Alana ran into me because she ran up on me so fast I almost punched her. I said, "Girl, don't be bouncing up on me like that," laughing.

Alana laughed with me and asked, "So how are you?"

"I'm good girl, just going to school and trying to get my salon opened," It was something about the way she looked and asked me was I ok, as if I had recently lost a loved one or something that did not sit well with me.

"Oh you are in school? Great! Where are you trying to open your salon?"

"I bought a house."

Alana pressed her lips together and raised her eyebrows giving me a, that's what's up, nod.

"And the back porch is the length of the house and it was already screened in so I am having it closed all the way in. It's just going to be a small shop enough space for only me to work in."

"So where is your house?" Alana asked. I knew she wanted to know how in the world I could afford to buy a house. They would really shit bricks when they found out that it had no mortgage.

"It's on Church St, right in front of the hotel," I told her," feeling proud that I could say that I had bought a home, was in school and getting ready to open up my own beauty shop. I thought that I was doing pretty well for myself; although I had yet to find a job my bank account was pretty stacked. Thinking about how Cue's generosity and my conservativeness with handling a buck. If Cue threw me a grand to go shopping, I put at least five hundred of it into my savings if not more. Once I had told Cue that I needed to get Quincy some winter clothes and he brought me over five hundred dollars because that was all he had on him at the time and said that he would bring me the rest later. By the time Cue came by the next day with another five hundred I had already shopped and got everything Quincy needed and only spent two hundred and ninety dollars. So needless to say the rest of it went into my account. Hell I did not know in Cue's line of work how long he would be around leaving me to care for our son all alone. So although Cue may think that I need him, I really don't my chips were stacked, at least enough to care for my son and I until I finished school and opened my salon if needed.

"That is great Keisha," Alana said. "So how do you take care of your bills? Are you working?" Alana did not even beat around; she just dove right into being nosy.

"I get child support from my son's dad and with me being in school I get some refund money so I'm making it."

"Dag' I get child support and work too and it is hard for me to stay above water, with paying rent, lights, phones, water and groceries? Girl be just be glad that you only have one child," Alana said.

"Well my house is paid for, I paid cash for it. It was an "As Is" purchase and I just remodeled it," I told Alana. "So I just have my cost of living bills."

I could not read the look on Alana's face as surprised, jealous or proud. "So what about your car payment?" she asked speaking of my Chrysler 300 which was only a year old.

"Oh my car is paid for, Cue paid my car off not long after he bought it," I said matter of factly.

"Dang well at least Cue got you set up nicely before he got married. After all those years you two were together he owed you that much. I can't believe that he finally married Mercedes. Since my cousin's boyfriend could not go to the wedding at the last minute I got to tag along. Girl they spent some money!" Alana was talking but I was having an out of body experience. Did she just say that Cue had got married and that she had actually witnessed the wedding? I started getting dizzy, all of a sudden the entire area where she and I were standing started to spin and my legs punked out on me. I caught Alana as I was going down. Alana screamed for help as she grabbed me by the waist and helped me to stand. She was saying "What's wrong Keisha, what's happening?" I looked at Alana with tears filling my eyes, I so wished that I could have reacted a different way but I was hurt beyond grief.

Alana helped me to a bench that lined the wall while one of the vendors who had witnessed me going down, came over with a cup of water for me. Alana was holding the cup to my lips for me to sip the water as the man was asking was I ok or should they call 911? I could not speak clearly but I did a good job of signaling him that I was fine with waving my hand, "No." After about what was only three minutes but seemed to be an eternity, I was able to partially regroup and gave Alana this bogus excuse as to why I had nearly collapsed. I told her that I had taken some medicine for an ear affection and it said that I was supposed to rest once I took it but I came on down here and suddenly just got dizzy. Not wanting Alana to know that I did not know that Cue had gotten married and also wanting to know that I understood her correctly I asked, "So you say the wedding was really nice?" trying my best to act as if it was not affecting me.

She went on to tell me every detail of the ceremony and reception. I listened attentively as Alana slowly killed me. Finally

I had enough and I told Alana that I would talk to her later that the medicine was affecting me and I really needed to get home and lie down as I had been instructed to do in the first place.

"You look flushed," Alana said looking at me with concern. "I can drive you home and bring someone back to get your car," she offered.

"No, I'll be fine," I said waving her off. "I just need to get home and I will be just fine, call me later," I said trying to sound as if everything was alright.

I waited until I had got out of the parking lot and cursed and cried all the way home. Instead of going to Granny's, I went to my house and lay on the bed and cried until I had cried myself to sleep. I must have been exhausted because when I finally did wake up it was almost 5 p.m. My head was hurting so badly that it was hard for me to stand. I finally got myself up and went for my phone to call Quincy. Thank goodness that granny answered the phone because I was really in no mood to talk and explain to Quincy why I could not take him to Frankie's today.

"Where have you been gal?" Granny asked. "We have been calling you all day, worried about you."

"I'm fine granny I just really don't feel good, and I have been sleep. I am sorry I did not mean to sleep this long at all, I just woke up."

"What's wrong with cha?" Granny asked concerned.

"I just have a bad headache, can't seem to shake it. I suppose to take Quincy to Frankie's Fun Park but I just don't feel up to it granny," I had started crying again alarming granny.

"Come on over here and get your rest so I can take care of you," Granny said worried. "Don't you worry about taking that baby anywhere he will be just fine, he's always going somewhere."

"Granny I just want to sleep, I think that I'm going to take this medicine and see if I cannot sleep it off," I told her knowing very well that this would not be slept off.

Granny gave in and told me to just get some rest and not to worry about Quincy because she would take care of him. I knew that already, I never worried about Quincy as long as he was with granny. After I promised to call when I woke up and we said our love you's. I went into the kitchen and fixed me a package of oodles of noodles and curled up on the couch with my blanket listening to Pandora.

I sat there and pondered and rehearsed over and over how I would handle this. The angelic side of me said to just let it go, stick to your task to do what you have to do to better yourself for you and your son. The conniving side of me said to wait and see how long it would be before he came clean and told you the truth. In the meantime milk him for every penny you could get before he knows that you know. Then the hood side of me said wait until their back from their honeymoon take Quincy and knock at the door and ask, "Why did you not invite nor have your son in your damn wedding?"

I cried and cried until I could not cry anymore. My phone was constantly ringing but I was not up to talking to anyone right now, I just drowned in my own self pity. Cue had made himself loud and clear. Mercedes would always be there no matter what he felt about me, I was not the one he saw spending the rest of his life with. She had won the battle and killed me without lifting a hand.

Finally the, "I Don't Have Pity Parties Angel" appeared and asked me, *"So bitch, what you going to do now? Are you going to continue to be down with that Low down Dirty Bastard after he has clearly let you know how he feels about your ass. His punk ass didn't even respect you enough to tell you that he was getting married to the love of his life."* She was a bit harsh but I continued to listen anyway as I cried. She went on to say, *"You should have left his ass a long time ago, look at all the shit that he has taken you through. He has humiliated you in front of Mercedes by bringing her to your house, when you were pregnant with his child to ask why you were lying. Then he told you that he could have you knocked off for some crack. He doesn't show up to the hospital when you delivered his child, which alone said that he cared more about Mercedes finding out than he cared about you or his child. He dissed you on your birthday when the two of you were supposed to have been going to ATL for the weekend to celebrate, because Mercedes showed up at his house demanding that he choose between her or his friends, and he chose to stay and appease her. Remember he did not even bother calling to tell you plans had changed, and your dumb ass sitting there bags packed waiting on him. And even if he had called and told you what was up, which he didn't, it should not have made a difference, it was your weekend not hers. He has messed around with other women and you have caught him, or they have approached you with the news. The damn list could go on and on. Keisha you need to finally face reality, Cue has no respect for you. So what- he gives you money, would he be so generous with the money if he actually had a real job? He probably would only give you child support and say bump all the extra's, if he even gave you the due child support.*

I had no idea where this angel came from or if she was really an angel at all. I couldn't argue with the fact that; she was right, and had me mad and ready for war. This betrayal hurt deep to the core but I had to regroup. I still did not know how I was going to approach the marriage situation with Cue. I had a few more days before he would be back from his honeymoon, and hopefully by then I would have had a visit from the "Logical Angel." The few things that I did know was that I was going to finish cosmetology school on schedule, open my salon, and be able to provide for Quincy and I in case this whole thing gets ugly once Mercedes finds out, and he may chose her over his son. I thought I knew Cue, but his actions lately have proven that I do not know him at all. However, I have no problem with putting his ass on child support if I needed to.

My phone rang again and I looked onto the screen it was an unknown number with an area code that I did not recognize. Thinking that Cue may have taken a walk or someway got from under Mercedes, I decided to answer.

"Hello," I said, grabbing the phone that was slipping because I was trying to hold it between my neck and ear while I fixed another pack of noodles.

"Hey sexy lady, how are you?" asked a very deep, sexy voice.

"I am good," I said, narrowing my eyebrows thinking, Who in the world is this? "I'm sorry, I did not get your name," I said.

He chuckled, and even his laughter was sexy. "How soon we forget, this is Grant," he said, not playing the guessing game and I liked that, showed maturity.

I was so glad that Grant could not see my face as I beamed so hard that I almost had to cover my lips to keep the squeal that was in me from coming out.

"Hey you, long time no hear," I said. I had not heard from Grant since the beach and that had been months ago. I thought that he had lost my number or just wasn't interested.

Grant chuckled again, "I know right, I have to apologize to you for not calling sooner. When I got back home we had an emergency situation at our Germany office and guess who they sent off to correct it?" he said, like it was not something that he had wanted to do.

"It's cool," I said, "I have been so busy lately these days anyway with school, and trying to get my house in order," he cut me off before I could finish what I was saying.

"So you're saying that you haven't had time to think about a brother and to think that I have been thinking about you since the day I met you," Grant said, trying to sound wounded.

"Stop with the flattery Grant, if I had been on your mind so heavily you would have called."

"Baby girl believe me, you have been running all through my mind. The only reason that I hadn't called is because of the roaming charges and the hour difference. Plus, I was so busy over there and disgusted with being there, I decided to just wait until I was back in the states to reach out to you."

I smiled feeling like a high school girl all over again. "Well better late than never. So what's going on with you, and when did you get back?" I asked.

"I just got back last night, so nothings been going on but Germany. Glad to be back home I have a few things I need to share about Germany this week with the owners and then I'm taking two weeks off. I would love to see you sometime in those two weeks."

I could not contain the blushing or the giddy tone when I said, "That sounds good to me, would love to see you again."

"Would you really?" Grant asked, as if he was surprised that I wanted to see him.

"Why you say it like that?" I giggled.

"Oh nothing, I was only hoping that you would be down for seeing me, wasn't sure if you really wanted to I just went out on a limb and put it out there," Grant laughed. "Well that's great, what is your schedule like the weekend of the twenty third?"

Although I knew that my weekends were always free I ended up doing something the entire weekend, my activities had been spontaneous. I asked him to let me look at my calendar, and I do not know what probed me to say that that weekend would not be good for me. It was weekend after next and I had absolutely nothing at all planned. I wanted to see him and I had thought about him also over the months, I tried to dismiss him as a "Can't miss what you've never had" factor due to the fact that my feelings were hurt that he had never called, but he still would creep into my mind every so often. I guess this was the, "Don't Appear Desperate Angel" that had urged me to say I wasn't free that weekend.

"Ok," Grant said, as if he was disappointed. Well I am going to visit with my grandmother in New Hampshire the weekend before that and I will be going back to work on the twenty sixth so I was hoping to see you while I was on my two week's vacation. I'm off on weekends but with us opening up this new plant, it's going to be hard for me to travel because I am overseeing the whole thing. Maybe after we get everything up and going I can take some more time off," Grant said.

I could have kicked my own ass, two weeks were going to be long enough for me after hearing his voice, and now he's saying that after the plant is opened he can take some time off. That could be up to a year for all I knew, I was really considering recanting my statement that the twenty third wouldn't work for me, and telling him that I could just reschedule my appointments. I did not want to come across as dropping my plans to please a man. I had done that with Cue and although I had no plans, Grant did not know that, and I was not going to suggest changing my make believe plans. This, "Don't Appear Desperate Angel" wasn't shit, messing up my flow.

"I hate that. I would love to see you. How soon before the plant is opened?" I asked, out of desperation.

"It should be up and running in about four months."

Four months wasn't a year, but it was still four months, and I wanted to see him before then if at all possible. I was just going to leave the twenty third as it stood for now and then maybe in a few days call him back and tell him that the plans had changed, and see if he still wanted to see me.

"I don't know how comfortable you are with it but if you are willing to fly up here to me, I will cover your airline ticket," Grant said.

Oh gosh was he serious, did he not know that I would be on the first thing smoking? I have always wanted to visit California.

"Why wouldn't I be comfortable Grant?" I asked, trying not to let my excitement show. "I mean I know that you can't judge a book by its cover, but you do not seem like a threat to me, plus you have too much going for yourself to risk your freedom over doing something crazy. I'm good." I said.

"You darn skippy," Grant said. "But I just had to put it out there because I do not want to put any pressure on you to come. So if you are good with it how about the weekend after the twenty third I think that is the thirtieth?"

The "Don't Appear Desperate Angel" came into my head again saying, *"Ok, you see he wants to see you, so just go for the weekend after the thirtieth. He will agree to any weekend you say at this point. Paint the picture that you are a busy woman and have a life, men love women like that, you know the ones they have to chase?"*

"Fuck you bitch," I told her. "Move outta my ears!" Not going to let this opportunity pass by again I quickly said, "I think that would be good, but let me get back with you on it early next week. Need to make sure that my mother or grandmother do not have any plans, and are able to keep my son for me that weekend," I said knowing full damn well that a babysitter for Quincy was never a problem, but again I had taken a little of the, "Don't Appear Desperate Angel" advice, but this time I controlled her ass and what came out of my mouth.

"Sounds good to me," Grant said, excited. "Speaking of Quincy where is he?"

If he was trying to impress me, he succeeded. He actually remembered Quincy's name after all these months. "He's with my mother and granny," I said. They have that child so spoiled it is hard to get him home these days. Plus there are a lot of children around there for him to play with. My house is located on a main road, where there is a lot of traffic and there is not many children around for him to play with. My mom and family only lives around the corner from me, so he is over there a lot."

"Cool, well tell him I said hello, will you?"

"Sure I will. Well I will call you sometime next week as soon as I talk to them and confirm." I said, basically ending the conversation.

"So I can't talk to you anymore until next week?" Grant asked, playfully. "And you want to end our conversation now? Damn am I that square?" he laughed.

"No stupid," I said, laughing, I thought you were ready to end the conversation, so I was just telling you that I would get back with you once I talk to my mom and them, before we hung up the phone."

"What did I say Keisha to make you think that I no longer wanted to talk, tell me so that I will know not to say it again," Grant kidded me.

"Whateva Grant. I guess when you said to tell Quincy hi, I thought you were getting ready to hang up, charge it to my mind and not my heart please." I said, laughing.

"I'll let you slide this time," Grant laughed.

Grant and I stayed on the phone for another two hours talking about everything under the sun. It wasn't until my granny called me that I realized that I had supposedly been sleep for over three hours. I asked Grant to hold on while I took this call and I told granny that I felt much better which was certainly no lie and that I would be over as soon as I got dressed. Heck I was even going to take Quincy and his crew on to Frankies. I clicked back over and wrapped my conversation up with Grant, which took another thirty minutes. We were still heated in conversation but he respected the fact that I had a date with Quincy and the crew and promised to call tomorrow and we disconnected.

I was on another level while I watched Quincy and his friends play at Frankie's. My mind was totally on Grant in fact I had not really even thought about Cue since Grant had called. Grant was exactly the kind of man that I needed in my life, it wasn't so much about the fact that he was educated, it was the fact that he worked hard for what he had and he talked with respect for me. I could not believe that he had offered to fly me up to spend a weekend with his fine ass, the only problem that I could see was keeping my legs shut tight, because there was no way I was giving up the goods no matter how much I wanted to.

Grant was a keeper, and I was going to handle this relationship very fragilely.

I had already asked mom and granny about keeping Quincy for that weekend, and they said what I already knew they would say, "Of course." I was still going to wait until Monday to tell Grant that it was a go, today was Saturday so Monday would be just fine. Once I dropped Quincy's friends off at home Quincy and I went home and got ready for bed it was after eleven pm. Quincy had just come and hopped in my huge bed with me when the phone rang. I picked up the phone while kissing Quincy's cheeks without even looking to see who was calling and said, "Hello?"

"Hey babe's what y'all up to?" It was Cue and he was talking really low and sounded sad to me.

I still had not decided how I was going to deal with Cue yet and I really did not figure that I would have to talk to or deal with him until he got home from his honeymoon. Cue stayed in Spartanburg, Mercedes stayed in Gaffney and I stayed in Greenville. Greenville was twenty to thirty minutes to Spartanburg. Spartanburg was twenty to thirty minutes to Gaffney, so Mercedes and I stayed almost an hour away from one another. So I guess he figured that since the only time that Mercedes and I paths crossed were in the clubs, and very seldom we may run into one another at the mall or something. Cue knew we surely did not have very many mutual friends besides the clubs, and none that would be at their wedding that I would know to tell me about the marriage. He figured he was safe until he could decide how to tell me. I decided that I would not let on that I knew anything just yet so I said, "Nothing much, we went to Frankie's and just got settled in to bed," I was talking really low.

"What is he doing?" Cue asked talking as low as I was, and I do not think it was because he may have been in another room and did not want Mercedes to over hear his conversation, he really sounded tired and sad.

"He's right here; do you want to talk to him?" I asked, looking over at Quincy, but he had knocked straight out. "Never mind he's asleep," I said. "So how's your trip going?" I asked.

"It's fine I guess, just tired and ready to come home so I can see my lil man, I miss him," Cue said.

"He misses you too," I told him.

"What about you?" Cue asked.

"What about me?" I asked knowing very well what he was talking about. What kind of game was he playing, not even a week into your marriage and already trying to see if you can still tag me along?

"Do you miss me?" Cue asked, and his voice sounded desperate, as if he needed me to miss him, to want him.

"Yes Cue, I do miss you, but it is what it is, I'm going to have to accept it and keep moving."

"Keisha I love you, despite what may happen just know that I do love you, and I miss you like crazy, and really do need you in my life." Cue sounded as if this was a life or death thing to him. Well his ass should have thought about that before he said, "I do."

Not wanting to go into this with Cue or even play him and ask had he came up with a way to get out of this marriage thing I just said, "Let's talk when you get back, is that ok with you? I'd rather not talk about this right now, and especially not over the phone." I said.

He said that was cool and reminded me again how much he loved me and we ended the call. My soul was sad again because truth was, I loved him too, but he had made his decision, and I had not been his choice, and even if he went and divorced her next week, the damage was done. I had cried my last tear.

I found out accidently that the love of my life had got married on me without bothering to tell me anything. I thought about all the hurt and pain that I had experienced in my life, but nothing compared to the pain I felt over Cue marrying Mercedes. When Alana told me about it I actually felt as if someone close to me had died without me having a chance to say goodbye. I had no idea how my life was going to change with Cue no longer in it, he will be a permanent fixture in my life because of our son, but he will definitely not be my lover again no matter how much I may miss his ass.

I let my mind go back to Grant. I was not longer waiting on my Cue. No sense in wasting time over a married man. I thanked God for a couple of things as I lay there thinking about all that had taken place in just this one day.

I had accidently found out that the love of my life had gotten married without bothering to tell me anything. I thought about all of the hurt and pain that I had experienced with Cue over the years, but nothing compared to the heart wrenching betrayal and pain of him marrying Mercedes. When Alana told me about it I actually felt as if someone very close to me had died without warning or giving me a chance to say my goodbyes.

I had no idea how my life was going to change with Cue no longer in it. I know he will always be a part of it because of the son that we both adore and share, but he will never share my bed again, no matter how badly I may miss his ass.

Chapter Twenty One

(Mercedes)

I was running late to work. Cue and I had just got back from our honeymoon on Friday, and had been so busy the weekend visiting with family and friends that insisted that the newlyweds come over for some sort of brunch, lunch, or dinner. I had not gotten any rest since being back. When Cue and I finally got to snuggle together last night I was asleep before my head hit the pillow. We had had an exhausting, yet very fun week in Hawaii. And we had a great, yet tiring weekend since we had come back from our trip. My alarm went off at 6:45 a.m. I hit snooze and turned back over and cuddled under my husband and slept another hour in a half. I woke up at the same time that my ass should have been at work!

I had called into the office to let them know that I was running late and would be in shortly. Shoot I was the HR manager their asses were probably hoping that I wasn't coming in at all. I drove a hard ship, and I did not put up with slackers because although we did not get paid by production, the size of my bonuses most certainly did.

When I got to the office I was greeted with two bouquets of flowers that were on my desk. I read the cards that were attached. One was from my office staff with the sweetest message. The other was from my parents and brother; they had given me no clue about this last night at dinner. I went into my office and sat the wedding picture that my mother had printed and framed on the counter in back of my desk, and she had had me a name plate made that had Mercedes Davis on it that I placed front and center of my desk. Although I still needed to go to the Social Security office and Highway department to make it official; from this day on I was demanding to be addressed as Mrs. Davis. "I had waited a long time for this," I laughed to myself.

It took me a minute to get into the working mode as I sat at my desk twirling my pen and talking to Tonya on the phone about how great the week had been for Cue and I. We made plans to meet for lunch before we disconnected and then I called my husband to remind him of how much I loved him. My morning flew by with me playing catch up with all that I had missed being gone for the past two weeks. I had taken the entire week from work the week prior to the wedding just to make sure that everything was according to plan and to clear my mind. I do not know what I was thinking when I suggested meeting for lunch with Tonya today of all days, but I hurriedly flew across town to dine with my buddy.

Tonya and I had just ordered our lunch when in walks who else but Keisha. For some reason my heart leaped. I do not know whether it was because I had not seen her in over six months since the incident at the park, or that she was in my neck of the woods. I never run into her other than at clubs or special events. Nonetheless she looked absolutely stunning. Not that she needed to lose any weight, but she looked to be about ten or fifteen pounds thinner. She was wearing some super skinny jeans that even looked expensive, along with an army green long sleeve thin sloppy sweater with an infinity scarf that had army green, orange, yellow and black in it. And she had on some bad low ankle cut suede army green boots with a wedge heel. Keisha always dressed really nice but this outfit was really flattering on her I had to admit. For some reason I was thinking I am so glad that Cue isn't here to see her. I had to stop the negative thoughts that were popping into my head.

"I wonder what is she doing up here in Gaffney?" I said to Tonya

"I have no idea," Tonya said sizing her up. "I love those boots that she has on though; they would go great with that sweater I bought from Macy's.

As if someone had overheard Tonya, this lady walked up to Keisha and asked where she purchased those boots, they were slamming. Keisha smiled and thanked her before saying that she had ordered them from Armani New York. But I just left the Gaffney outlet and they have some very similar to these there at a fraction of the price. Keisha was telling the inquiring lady, and answering our question as to why she was all the way in Gaffney this time of the day.

Tonya immediately went to Armani from her phone to see if they had them. I continued to watch as Keisha was telling the lady that she was embarrassed to say what she spent on them, but go to their online store you will find all that you need to know, Keisha laughed.

"I know this bitch did not spend eight hundred dollars for those shoes, who in the hells payroll is she on?" Tonya exclaimed once she found the boots on line. We both looked back over at Keisha and her feet. As if Keisha herself heard us she said to the woman, "I spend a lot on shoes. I have a bad shoe fetish, it's ridiculous. Every time I tell my boyfriend that I saw a pair of shoes that I like he exhales," Keisha laughed. The lady said, "Well apparently you have very good taste in shoes and men if you have a man that can buy you shoes that cost a couple hundred bucks."

Tonya and I sat and looked and listened as they talked. Keisha had yet to see us sitting right behind her at the small circular table. I looked at Tonya and said, "Well there you go. She's on her boyfriend's payroll."

"Nothing but a gold digger," Tonya said shaking her head. I knew she was hating because so was I.

"I know right, get your own," I said as I raised my hand to give Tonya high five. Truth was the both of us secretly hated on her. We worked our butts off for what we had and what we wanted, but it was the girls like Keisha who had everything without having to lift a finger that bothered me the most. And these dumb ass men seemed to run after and sweat them with a vengeance.

After Keisha had gotten her order to go she was standing at the condiments tables getting ketchup when she noticed Tonya and I. She looked directly at us before rolling her eyes and turning to leave.

"I don't care what Cue says, there is no way that I believe that something has not gone down with that girl and him at one point or another," I was saying to Tonya. "She tries to mess with me and has too much animosity towards me for there to have never been anything between the two."

"I know right?" Tonya replied. "But does it really matter now because you are Mrs. Cuedricus Davis," Tonya put her hand up for me to give her high five and we both laughed.

"Tonya I cannot believe that I am his wife. I know it sounds crazy, but I really did not expect for Cue to really go through with it so soon. How about I had our wedding picture put into the Greenville newspaper also. So that all of those thirsty hoes will know that Cue now has papers on him and to back the fuck off."

Tonya and I sat there laughing and talking for the next hour before I told her that I really needed to get back to work. I stopped by the bank and Keisha was in the line for the teller and I ended up standing right behind her. She just glanced back as she felt someone come behind her, we were less than two feet away from each other and this heifer lifted her eyebrows and snared up her nose before rolling her eyes and turning her back to me. She was certainly a bold bitch I thought to myself, but I did not say anything because I was not about to entertain her ass.

She was called to one counter and I was called to the counter beside where she stood. Although I had come to the bank to make a deposit, I used the opportunity to make Keisha aware that I had gotten married by asking the teller what I already knew. I asked loud and clearly, "I got married last Saturday and my last name is now Davis," I said pronunciating the Davis very clearly, "I was wondering what I would need to do to have my last name changed on my accounts?"

Keisha had her back to me so I was looking to see if she was listening which I was pretty sure that she was, because the teller who was serving her glanced over at me also and asked, "So you got married? Congratulations." So even if Keisha did not hear me she certainly heard the teller. I could not have planned it better. "Yes, last Saturday," I exclaimed.

"So pretty soon I guess you will be getting ready for those babies you have been wanting?" Keisha's teller asked.

"Yes mam, I want at least two. We plan to start as soon as possible." I said loving every bit of this. Keisha was still with her back to me although she was totally hearing everything. "Can't wait to have my husband's kids; he loves children. Can't wait to have a son for him to play sports with and a daughter for me to shop with," I laughed. After Keisha was done with her transaction she looked at me, put a devilish smirk on her face and shook her head as she walked off. It was as if she was almost laughing at me. Oh well get over it; Cue was mine. As she said before, that girlfriends did not have bragging rights, now I had papers, so in your face Miss Thing.

Chapter Twenty Two

(Keisha)

When Cue pulled up to meet me with the money that he was giving me to start the closing in process of my back porch, it was all that I could do to not break into tears. Mercedes actions today had made me want to get really ratchet. She just did not realize how close she had pushed me into pulling out pictures her husband and our son had taken together right there in front of her bank friends where she was boasting, and letting her know our secret. Every bone in my body was ready to do it and the "Get Her Ass Angel" was boosting me on. But God- Jehovah Jireh- Jehovah Nissi- allowed me to let her reign in victory... this time. Dang Hawaii had been mighty good to him because he was looking quite spiffy and his dark skin was glowing. I refused to believe that it was an "I'm happy glow" I knew better than that; because there was no way that he could be happy, especially knowing that shit was going to be hitting the roof really soon. I stepped from my car and walked over to his Denali. From the way he was eyeballing me the entire stretch to his truck, I knew that I was looking like a million bucks.

"What's up babes?" Cue asked passing me an envelope before giving me a hug like he never wanted to let go.

I finally stepped away and asked, "You tell me what's up?"

"You are," he said rubbing his hands together to warm them up. "Where's Quincy, he been missing his old man you say?"

"He's with granny, and yes he has," I said dropping the envelope into my purse. "When are you going to come and get him he's been saying that he wants to come and stay overnight all week?" I asked, simply to hear his excuse. It dawned on me last night how was he going to spend his alone time with Quincy like they use to do at his crib, or was Mercedes going to allow him to still stay out all night now that they were married, I doubted that very seriously. So Quincy's time with his dad was on the line already and I was not going to let Cue off the hook easily.

"I just got back in town Friday. I have some things to get in order, but I'm getting ready to head over that way now and see him. I missed that rascal. I missed you to," Cue said trying to seduce me with those sexy dark eyes, as he bit down on the bottom of his plump, juicy, soft lips. A part of me wanted to just fall into his arms crying and asking "why did he do this to me?" The other part wanted to put a dagger right into his heart so he could feel the pain that I was feeling.

I decided to go along with Cues little game and just see how controlled was this marriage thing, to see if he still was allowed out after hours. "I miss you too babes and I am horny as all hell," I said, putting my sexy on.

"Well let's go to my crib now!" Cue said rising from his position where he was leaning back on his car excitedly.

"Whoa cowboy. Why the rush?" I said, putting my hands out to hold Cue back from attacking me. "I have a lot to take care of today and so do you. I can just come over tonight and spend it with you. This way we will not have to rush just take our time and do what we do," I said, winking at him seductively.

Cue did not do a very good job in covering up the fact that something was wrong. He stuttered clumsily as he said something about tonight not being good for him because of Eric. He went all the way left with something that made no sense to me at all; before he finally got it together and gave me a spill about Eric using his pad. My man was slipping. Little did he know that he was going to wish to slip into a very deep dark hole by the time all this shit came to light.

"So you're telling me... that I cannot come over to your crib tonight because Eric who has two cribs of his own, is using your place to entertain one of his groupies. Is that what you're really telling me Cue?" I asked, looking at him sideways.

"Yeah man. This dude talking bout he don't want this particular chick knowing where he stays so asked if he could use my place," Cue said like it was ridiculous to him also. "Said that she be tripping and might start stalking him."

"So you're going to allow him to have the crazy chick think that your place is his? So if she decides to go ballistic- what the hell," I shrugged my shoulders, "Go to Cue's place and show your ass. Burst out his windows and slash his tires. Hell shoot up the place if that's how you're *really* feeling. Lord forbids that your son is over at your house when she decides to go pyscho," I said, sarcastically as I proceeded to walk off. "Fuck it Cue. Do your thing I'm good."

"Keisha?" Cue caught up with me and stood in front of me with his hands resting on my shoulders. "Babe, I know it's crazy and I wasn't thinking when I agreed. You're right. I'll tell him he can't use my place, but give me a few and I'll let you know what's up with tonight, ok?" Cue pleaded with his eyes.

"Ok," I said, giving him a don't bullshit me look.

Cue leaned in and kissed me lightly and then looked at me as if he was trying to figure out what was different with me. Little did he know I had had all week to think, cry, kick and scream. As much as I loved him and as much as I wanted him, I'd be damned if I let him see me broken and bent all out of shape when this shit hit the fan. No time to worry about Mercedes right now, I was on a mission. Hell, her ass should have not been so quick to jump the gun when she knew it was loaded and needed a release. She pressured him into marriage thinking that this would detour some of the groupies; but little did she know I was not a groupie. I had a special place in Cue's heart and I shared a life with Cue just as she did if not a better life with him. And above all else, I was the mother of his child. So yea, the hoe had every reason to worry about this one.

I wondered what excuse Cue would call me with, because I knew he would. There was no way he could justify to Mercedes his staying out all night, so of course as usual I would be the one getting the short end of the stick tonight and it was fine with me. I had no intentions of getting with his ass anyway. I just wanted to see him squirm and see what excuse he would have.

I jumped in my freshly detailed 300 and rode my pretty ass away from Cue feeling proud of my heart and mind. That was not as hard as I had imagined it to be. This week had given me the time I needed to regroup. I never imagined that Cue would immediately come back to town ready to rumble. Mrs. Davis must not be putting it down the way she thinks she is. Only a week into their marriage and Mr. Davis already wants some more of Keisha. Bitch please. I will always be a factor. It's going to take me to make myself a non-factor. Humph, you better ask somebody.

I headed back to Greenville to meet the man that was going to close in my back porch. I made a stop at Home Depot to pick up two lanterns that they had on sale to put out by my driveway at the street. I was talking to a floor clerk about the lanterns when I noticed D.J walking in my direction. The sales associate and I was wrapping up our conversation, but I needed him to stand there and talk to me until D.J had at least passed. But the associate was already walking off leaving me less than 100 feet away from D.J on an aisle that only he and I occupied. I decided to just pretend to be looking at other light fixtures hoping that he turned around or walked passed me. I do not know why D.J has never cared for me. I have never been anything other than nice to him.

"What's up Keisha? How are you doing?" D.J asked as he approached.

I looked up as if I was just noticing him. Although I was really startled that he spoke to say the least. "Hi D.J, I'm good. What are you doing in this neck of the woods?" I asked, not knowing what else to say.

"I stay not two miles from here," he said as if I should have known.

"Oh really?" I asked, raising my eyebrows as if I didn't know, which I didn't. I don't know why I thought that you stayed in Spartanburg," I said, shaking my head.

"Nope baby girl, I live here. Just because Cue stays in Spartanburg does not mean his friends have to stay there also," he kidded.

I just grinned and said, "*Whateva* - Well it was good seeing you, take care."

"When was the last time you talked to Cue?" D.J asked. I immediately knew that he was fishing.

"I just saw Cue, what you haven't talked to him?"

"Yea, we went to Bailey's today for lunch." I guess he wasn't either expecting an answer, or figured that I would be suspicious as to why he asked, because he immediately changed the subject and started talking about Quincy. Which talking about Quincy was pleasant for me- I could talk forever about that little boy. After about five minutes of talking I finally said, "Speaking of, I really need to go and get him. I know he probably has torn up their nerves."

D.J laughed and said "You might be right, that rascal can talk. Well dap him up from Uncle D.J." It was what he said next that almost made me pass out as much as it did blush.

"You look great Keisha, which you always have. Damn... I've always envied Cue for getting you first."

I looked directly at him to see was he bullshitting me. His face said serious as a motherfucker. I would have never thought that D.J had the hot's for me. He spent so much time avoiding me. While he had never said anything mean to me; it was his actions around me. When I did use to try to conversate with him, he'd just bluntly answer my questions and not even attempt to try to make more conversation. Eventually, I too stopped. D.J was really a Hot Tamale and although I knew I was just as fine as they came- he seemed so out of my league. And it really did not matter because he was Cue's friend. But trust and believe when I would see this dude out, my friends and I would be mesmerized on just how fine he was.

"Yea, yea I hear you Mr. Mean. Thanks though, that means a lot coming from you."

"What does that suppose to mean, coming from me?

"Because, D.J… can I be real with you?" I asked, with a smirk.

"I don't like anything but real, come on with it."

"You have always acted like I got under your skin. You have hurt my feelings so much over the years, although, I kept it to myself. But I never knew why you did not like me." There it was out.

I have had the hot's for your ass every since you bounced onto the club scene, but Cue beat me to you. Hell, if anything, I hated on Cue's ass because he knew I was feeling you. Don't get me wrong because Cue is my boy and he's been there for me like no other, but I even told his ass that you could have been Mrs. Mullings. If he knew he wasn't trying to make you number one he should have let you be. Baby you better than a sidekick. Cue cares a lot about you I know that, but you over Mercedes any day in my book."

"Wow," I said, really shocked and flattered. "I would have never known you felt that way really. Well thanks for enlightening me," I faintly smiled.

"Any time. If you ever need to talk just call me. I know you wouldn't rock the boat and I'm not asking you to, but you have my number. And Keisha this conversation is A&B, C doesn't need to know about it." D.J said.

"D.J regardless of what you may believe, I am really not the author of confusion. I would never tell anything to come between you and Cue's friendship. You told me what you felt in the past, no harm done. Just too bad I didn't know this prior to fucking with Cue. But just so you know, I am more than flattered but I could never mess with one of Cue's friends despite what happens with Cue and I."

D.J shook his head up and down and said, "I can dig it, and I can respect that. I just wanted you to know why I acted the way I acted towards you. Remember you asked the question. But it really had nothing to do with you. I am just a straight and narrow guy. And with the way I felt about you I just thought it was best that I try not to get to giddy with you because I didn't know what I might have done, and not wanting to cross my boy. So I just kept my distance. I have nothing but love for you baby girl know that. I did not realize that I was coming across as rude or mean. Not built like that, I'm sorry."

"Thanks D.J, you've made my day." I do not know what made me hug him but I immediately knew that it was a mistake. The way he squeezed me, how strong his body felt, and good he smelt. Whew, I had to exhale and step away. "Good seeing you, talk to you soon."

"No doubt," D.J said. Leaving me thinking what in the hell was that supposed to mean. I could never mess with one of Cues acquaintances. He and Cue were boys, and just because I made a mistake by fucking with Cue, I will not make a bigger one to overshadow it by fucking with his best friend. While I liked the attention he was given me that was as far as it was going to go. Come on, I may be a side chick, but I have morale's believe it or not. I could not help but laugh to myself as I walked off, leaving D.J watching me do so. Guess the saying is true; one word from the right person can erase many bad actions from the wrong person.

Chapter Twenty Three

(Britney)

"Keisha my ass is pregnant!" I cried, into the phone to my best friend. "What am I going to do, how did this shit happen?"

"What tha' hell? Oh my gosh; is it Eric's?" Keisha asked.

"Yes, it's Eric's. I haven't been sleeping with anyone else since Eric and I have been kicking it." I had other friends, but I had been monogamous with Eric for a while now.

"O.M.G!" Keisha said slowly pronunciating each letter. She was so extra, I swear. "Have you told him, what did he say?"

"I haven't told anyone but you yet. I am too scared to tell him. You know he has made it clear that he wanted no more children right now. He may think I did this shit on purpose. And shit was going so good for us right now," I continued to cry.

"He can't blame you totally Britney. Why was he having unprotected sex if he was 100% sure he wanted no more kids right now? Hell he had to know by going in raw that the chances of you not getting pregnant were slim!"

"Keisha I have been on the pill since I was sixteen. I have never gotten pregnant before. Hell, I even thought that by the time I decided to have a child I would have to be off the pill for a few years." I paused to blow my nose. "Shit I have never even missed a dosage, so I don't know what the hell happened."

"Didn't you say something about having your pills changed a while back? Maybe that had something to do with it."

"I told you about them changing my pills last month, but that was only two days that I didn't take them because I had to wait for my cycle to start. And I wasn't even intimate with Eric until after I had started back on the pill."

"Well there you go," Keisha said. "You know if you have sex it says to use protection. And further more you know Eric is with Tonya, so why are you having unprotected sex with him anyway?"

"Hell you know Cue's ass is with Mercedes and other women- but you still have unprotected sex with him!" I retaliated.

"Britney, I know this is weak and lame, but truth is I trust and would bet that Mercedes is not sleeping with anyone else but Cue. And I know that I am not sleeping with anyone else but Cue. So if anything comes in we both know that Cue brought it in. Which this is no form of protection but I have been having unprotected sex with Cue's ass for so long, there was no way in hell that he would settle for me saying "I want to start using protection" without making him think that I was sleeping around. He claims of course that of all the women that he has fucked around with that Mercedes and I are the only two that he's had unprotected sex with since all that shit went down years ago with the STD's. And I really believe him. I just know Cue. Britney you don't know Tonya like I do Mercedes. You have no idea what kind of person she is as far as sleeping with other guys, that's all I'm saying." Keisha said.

"And you know Mercedes like that, is that what you're saying?" I asked, sarcastically. "Listen Keisha shit happens. What's done is done and your lecture is not going to change a thing about it."

"You're right and I'm sorry. So what are we going to do, when do you plan on telling him?"

"I don't know what to do; he's coming over for dinner. He wanted some of my famous jerk chicken. I am so scared."

"Don't be, Eric may be mad but he will get over it real quick. Shoot, this might be that son that he wants so badly," Keisha said trying to make light of the situation. Of all Cue's friends, Eric had to be the most down to earth and coolest of them. Eric was a fun person but he was all about his. He had three daughters who he adored, and he was a great father, so while I understood Britney being upset because of the timing in her life right now, Eric's child would be taken care of no doubt.

"Keisha you do not understand. This man and I have talked so much about this. Yes, he may get over it but he's going to be mad. He doesn't want any more kids right now!"

"So what is your solution then? Because I do not know what to tell you. Do you want to go through this pregnancy? Tell me what role you need me to play to help you and I will play it."

"I am not aborting my child Keisha if that's what you're worrying about. I just need to figure out something that's all. I can't tell Eric right now until I have a master plan. I need to first make sure that we are stable, that he will lose sleep without me, because I'm not even going to lie to you. I will lose sleep without him."

"Wow, it's like that? Britney I know you're crazy about Eric, but you never let any man get you to the point where you have insomnia behind them. Yes, there has been a few that you were crazy about and I had to listen to you rant and rave for weeks because the relationship did not work out for one reason or another, but you always kept moving as if no dirt was on your shoulders.

"Yes Keisha, I am in love with this man. And I do not want to lose him behind this or have this alter our relationship. Do you know that Eric and I have yet to have an argument or disagreement after all these months?"

"Really?" Keisha asked in shock.

"Really, I mean he's done things that I wanted to check him on, but I felt I had no right because I knew the situation when I got into it. Like that night at the club how they were all lovey dubby it bothered me, but hey what could I say? It comes with the game. I just try to not always be accessible to him when he wants because he's not always accessible to me when I want. I try to keep him guessing just as I am. But he has really gotten past my steel curtain."

"Well damn," Keisha laughed. "Eric is a good guy, and I can understand how you have allowed yourself to fall for him. But don't play yourself thin because you and I both know Eric, and we both know that he's had his share of women, but look at how he treats you compared to some of the others we know he's been with. I think he's really feeling you as well, so don't get to down about this pregnancy."

"Speaking of the devil, that is him calling now, let me hit you right back after I'm done talking to him," I said.

"Cool, do that," Keisha said and hung up.

"Hey baby, what's up?" I said, sweetly.

"Hey boo, got some bad news," Eric said sadly like he was dreading saying what he was about to say.

"What?" I asked alarmed.

"I'ma' have to take a rain check on tonight, something important came up."

I smacked my lips. I needed to see him tonight. Not that I was going to tell him about the baby, but my emotions had been up and down since finding out that I was pregnant. I was looking forward to his company and needed it tonight.

Sensing my disappointment, Eric said, "Baby I'm sorry, if this wasn't so any important I would cancel. But it's something I have to do. I will make it up to you I promise. We can hook up tomorrow if you don't have plans."

"Did you forget that tomorrow Keisha and I are going to see Mike Epps? Are you going to be all night? Maybe you can come over later when you're done?" I was desperate, ordinarily I'd said fuck it, and do what you gotta' do. But I really needed him tonight.

"Naw', it's going to be really late when I'm done," Eric said.

"What's really late Eric, I'm trying to see if we can work something out. I have had a rough day," My voice started wavering and given in that I was near tears. "And I just was really looking forward to seeing you tonight," I stopped before it really broke down.

"What's wrong, what happened?" Eric asked truly worried.

"Nothing, it's just been one of those days. Just seems that nothing has gone right for me. And I just kept going strong because I knew that at the end of it, I was going to be with you and now this too."

"Brit-Brit I'm sorry baby to have let you down. But baby trust and believe if I could get out of this anyway I would. I promise you I am all yours on Sunday unless you want me to be waiting at your crib when you get back from seeing Mike tomorrow?" Eric said trying to make me feel better.

"Humph, Sunday is fine Eric. Guess I have no choice and I apologize for being selfish because I know your business requires things to be handled unexpectedly at any given time. I'm just all into my emotions right now, but I will be fine. Take care of your business and I will talk to you later."

"You sure you're alright with this?" Eric asked.

"Well Eric I don't think it would matter one way or the other, you have to do what you have to do, right?"

"Yea, but don't think that your feelings doesn't matter to me because they do. You are very special to me and you know that. I just hate that I can't hold my baby tonight and caress all your cares away."

"So do I," I exhaled. "But I'm sure they'll be other times that I'm on an emotional coaster," I said making light of it.

"And I plan to be there for you."

"I'll hold you to that."

"So what are you getting into tonight?" Eric inquired.

"Nothing now. I guess I'm just going to watch some television and sleep."

"Ok, well I'll try to give you a call later," Eric said. I knew that I would not be hearing from him anymore tonight but I said, "Ok, do that," and we hung up.

I was so mad! Eric and I had these plans since Tuesday night and hell it had been his idea. I picked up the phone to call Keisha back.

"Hey what's lickin' chicken?" Keisha said.

"Girl...he is not coming!" I told her the story and then went on a rant about how pissed I was. Keisha suggested that we go and see the new movie that was out by Tyler Perry, since neither of us had any other plans for a Friday night. We had first thought about going out to the club but decided that we'd wait until tomorrow since we were planning to go out after seeing Mike Epps. So a movie and dinner it would be for us tonight. I told Keisha that I would call her as soon as I was dressed so we could head out at the same time and meet at the movie. Keisha asked that I just come to her place after I was dressed and we could just ride together. I told her that would be cool, since I hadn't got a chance to see her new place since she had moved into it yet.

I went into my walk in closet to decide on what to wear. I knew Keisha's ass was going to be dressed to kill but my black BCBG sweat suit that had BCBG written across the ass in silver sequence was going to be my attire for tonight. I threw everything out the drawer trying to find my sequenced tank top to wear under the jacket only to finally find the tank top hanging in my closet. I wore that with a pair of white Air Max that Eric had just bought me last weekend. Put on my silver jewelry and I was out the door.

When I thought to even call Keisha to let her know that I was en-route, I was halfway to her house. She said "Girl I told you to let me know when you left your house that way I could jump in the shower, just hard headed!" She laughed. She told me that she would put the key under the flower pot on her back porch for me to just let myself in; she was going to shower.

I pulled up to Keisha's house and was in awe of how nice it had turned out. When I let myself in through her back door I was speechless, as I stepped into her kitchen. I strolled through every room except her bedroom amazed at how beautiful and tastefully everything was done. From the expensive looking borders lining the walls, to the beaming hardwood floor and furniture, Keisha had outdone herself. I knew Keisha had taste in clothes but I guess because this was her first rodeo in her own place, I never knew she had decorating skills like this. If Keisha indeed did all of the decorating, she had a new business endeavor in which she should pursue. Her home was warm and inviting. I loved the oversized pillows she had in the window seal. There were two huge bay windows in her living area. The one facing the road had a huge floral arrangement in it, along with huge brass book holders, and three books in between them. And on the other side of the floral arrangement she had a large brass elephant. The other bay window which was facing the side of her neighbor's house and yard which happened to be landscaped beautifully with flowers and large water fountain. Keisha had placed a pillow the length and width of the window, not sure if she had had it made especially for the window or lucked up, but it fit perfectly. She had two other throw pillows in it to rest your back. And there were tons of books in the book case that was built in right under the window seal. Keisha who loved to read had created her own little reading bungalow, using her neighbors beautiful yard for scenery. It was perfect.

Keisha came out of her room surprising the heck out of me in only a pair of boot cut jeans which was rare for her, a black sloppy sweat shirt that hung from one shoulder, and a pair of black polo boots. She was chilled, cute, and comfortable looking.

"Girl I cannot believe that this is the same house!" I exclaimed.

"I know right? They did a great job didn't they?" Keisha said looking around amazed herself.

"Yes, they did," I said, walking past her to go into her bedroom. "And you decorated and furnished the hell out of it."

"Thank ya- thank ya," Keisha said proudly. "I like it."

Her bedroom was probably the most fabulous room in the house and believe me the rest of the house was laid. She had really out done herself when picking furnishings and decorating her bedroom. She had created her own haven. After showing me around the bedroom and all of the little perks within, we decided that we had better bounce. The movie was starting in ten minutes and we needed to get in the long line they always had for popcorn.

As Keisha was walking out behind me to go to her car she said, "You know your ass working that BCBG?" Keisha was always on me about having such a small waist and huge hips.

She was built just as nicely if not better but she always said that she would pay to have a waist like mine.

It was after eight by the time Keisha and I got in line for the movie and the movie started at 7:55. We prayed that previews had been long and maybe we hadn't missed too much. We made our way into the line for popcorn and low and behold we were side by side with Eric and Tonya! Eric looked like he could have shitted bricks when Keisha got his attention by saying, "Hey Eric, how are you?" totally ignoring Tonya.

Eric looked over to see who was speaking and all the blood in his face had drained by the time he said, "What dup ya'll?"

I rolled my eyes and turned my back to them without speaking, as Keisha said, "Nothing much."

I told Keisha to get me a Sprite and a bag of Sour Patch Kids I was going to the bathroom. I walked off headed for the ladies room making sure that my ass was jiggling and doing what it does. Giving Eric an eye full of what his ass was going to be missing.

Chapter Twenty Four

(Cue)

I went by Granny's and scooped up my son and hung out with him for a minute. Afterwards I took him to see my mom so she could spoil him. He was asking if we could go see his uncle Eric or D.J. I called D.J and he was headed to the A. He said to tell Quincy that he would stop by and see him tomorrow. "Really D.J, don't be lying to my son," I said tripping. While D.J. was crazy about Quincy he had never been to Keisha's house to visit with him. One time when I was running behind coming out of the A I had gave DJ Keisha's number to call and ask her to meet him to scoop up Quincy for me. DJ, Eric and I along with the kids were all flying to Disney. Keisha and DJ played phone tag for about an hour before they finally hooked up. Other than that whenever he saw Quincy it was because Quincy was with me. He would come over and scoop him up from me to ride out with him, or take him to some chicks party they were having for their child. D.J had no children, but he and Eric spoiled Quincy.

"Man when have you ever known me to lie to that boy?" D.J laughed; knowing exactly why I was asking. "Tell my godson that I will see him tomorrow when I get back."

"Ok," I said skeptical, but relayed the message to Quincy anyway. Quincy said "Bet it up."

"Did he just say "Bet it up?" D.J. asked.

"Man—this mug is liable to say anything," I laughed.

Well Quincy, Eric is not home I can tell you that now, so we will catch him next time cool?"

"Cool beans!" Quincy yelled. "Where is Uncle Eric at?"

"He had to go to work," I lied. Eric had called me earlier saying that Tonya wanted to go to the movies and he had forgotten that her birthday was this weekend, and had made plans to hang out with Britney tonight. I asked did he have to spend Tonya's entire birthday weekend with her and he said no, but she wanted to celebrate it tonight because she had to go back to work on Monday, and that she wanted them to enjoy their time without her having to worry about getting sleep.

So after he called Britney and cancelled their plans, he called me back and said that he felt so bad. He asked me to call Keisha and find out what was going on with Britney, because she said that she had had a bad day and that she was really upset that he had to cancel their plans. I told his ass that he didn't have to cancel, he chose to cancel. After he cursed me out, he demanded that I just do as he asked and find out what was wrong with Britney.

I told him hell no, because I'm trying to figure out a way to get out of this shit with seeing Keisha tonight and still had not. So my plan was to pull a -no call- no show. I had done them plenty of times before; she always got over them after a few days of giving me the silent treatment. So if he wanted to know what was really wrong with Britney, he was going to have to call Keisha himself.

"You ain't shit man," Eric said. You been away with Mercedes ass all week- and you stiffing Keisha tonight also for her? You ain't had enough of that ass in a week? You been hemmed up with her on an island and in her bed. Why don't you just be straight with Keisha and let her know your ass has gotten married, and your trying to do the right thing by your wife, and that is why you can't come to her tonight." Eric was loving this shit a little bit too much.

"Not even about trying to do what's right. It's the fact that Mercedes is not going to go for me staying out all night and coming home in the morning. And if I have Keisha come to the house her ass is not going to deal with me getting up at three leaving and not coming back."

"So you're on curfew hunh? Well actually 3 a.m. is not all bad Cue. I could do a lot with that if I was married," Eric laughed.

I thought Eric's right. I could swing this. Just have Keisha meet me at my place and have one of my boys call me around 2:30 and say I needed to handle something. Tell Keisha to lock up if I wasn't back before she left. And if I was lucky I just may be able to get up from Mercedes around nine and say I have to run out a minute and run back to the house and wrap it up with Keisha. Yea, that would work.

I called Keisha for two reasons; first to let her know that I was getting ready to drop Quincy back off at Granny's, and second to let her know that tonight was a go. Keisha's phone went straight to voicemail. After I left her a voice mail just saying I was taken Quincy back and wanted to know what time was she coming over tonight, I received a text from her saying; I had not heard from you and made plans, so I will just talk to you later. What in the hell was that all about? When did she start making other plans because she had not heard from me? Keisha was on some different shit these days.

I text her back and asked "What kind of plans have you made?" She replied "At the movies with Brit." I asked, "Just tell me one thing and I will leave it alone. Are you really with Britney?" Keisha has never put me off before for a friend. I understand that they may already be at the movie and I did not expect for her to pick up and leave. Ordinarily she would have said, "I will call you after the movie so we can hook up." Tonight she left nothing for thought. No plan to call later or nothing. What in the hell was really going on?

She replied back, "I am watching the movie Cue and I am not about to entertain you while I do so. Ask Eric if you don't believe me, he's here with Tonya."

I almost ran off of the fucking road. I read back over the text to make sure that I had read it correctly and indeed I had. If Eric was at the movie with Tonya, and Keisha was at the same movie with Britney… Ooooh shit!

After I dropped Quincy off I sent Eric a text that said, "You in some quicksand aint'cha nukka?" He replied back "Fuck you man, this shit ain't even funny. I feel like shit right now. I can't even begin to tell you one word they done said thru out this whole damn show!" I laughed out loud in my car and replied, "Damn playboy, you slipping." He replied "Fuck you man, get you some business!"

I could not stop from laughing- this dude! And he really was feeling Britney too, and Britney was not the type of girl to put up with no bullshit. He should have never lied to her I thought. But who was I to talk I was holding two of the biggest secrets from both women that I cared about.

Well I was good for tonight. My question had been answered. Keisha was at the movie with Britney as she had said and not with one of these other scavengers that were lurking after her. I was going home to my wife and get some sleep and strategize for tomorrow. I was upset that I couldn't see my baby tonight, but tomorrow I most definitely would. Shit, I may even tell Mercedes that I had to make a quick trip to Florida to handle some shit.

Chapter Twenty Five

(Keisha)

Britney ended up staying at my house last night because we were up late talking. I told her that she may as well stay over rather than going home this time of the night, well morning because it was well after midnight. We had a few drinks and although I tried discouraging her not to drink, she said she really needed a drink, so I fixed her's light.

Britney was so hurt over Eric being at the movie Last night with Tonya. It wasn't so much about him being with Tonya; she said it was the fact that she let him know how important it was for her to see him last night. She told him how badly she needed him and how her day had been, and he lied to her. She said if Tonya was all that to him then he surely did not need her and she was done. I don't know what Eric's circumstances were or why it was so important to take Tonya out last night. I did know that Britney was not the one to play with. If Britney said she was done, Britney was done. And from the pain I seen in her face and heard in her voice, it was a done deal for Eric.

Eric had called and text Britney this morning a few times apologizing over her voice mail. Britney had not even responded to one voicemail or text message yet. He messed up by first saying that it was Tonya's birthday weekend and he had forgotten. He said that Tonya insisted on celebrating last night because she had to work Monday, and wanted to enjoy it without having to worry about getting up early. Britney felt that she was put on the back burner which she had been. And although she knew she was involved with a man that had another woman, it doesn't make it any better. I asked her what was she really going to do, does she really want to be done with him as she verbalized so much last night? And her answer was simply "Yes."

"So when are you going to tell him about the baby?" I asked.

"I don't know," Britney looked off towards the window with tears streaming down her cheeks. "I don't know what I am going to do Keisha," she said softly.

I got up and went and sat beside my friend and hugged her. We both sat and cried together as she trembled and sobbed. I knew she was releasing it. That is just how Britney operated; she may not shed another tear after this day was over. I wished I was half as strong as she was. After maybe about five minutes she pulled away and looked me in the eyes and made me promise not to say anything to Cue about her being pregnant until she comes up with a plan. I promised.

My cell phone which was on the coffee table started to vibrate. I picked it up to look at the screen to see who was calling. It was Eric.

"It's Eric," I said to Britney.

Answer, but do not tell him that I am here.

"Hey, what's going on Eric?" I said trying to sound like I was just waking up.

"What's up Keisha, have you talked to Britney this morning?"

"No, not since last night, I guess I need to call her because she was really upset."

Man--- that was some jacked up shit. I know she's mad but unless you know Tonya… Keisha, Brit is my baby and I ain't gonna lie, when I saw ya'll last night and the hurt in her face I wanted to die."

"Trust me, she wanted to also." Britney was mouthing what are you talking about? What is he saying? I put up my forefinger smiling, signaling her that I got this. "She felt like you chose Tonya over her when she really needed you the most. She just had a terrible day yesterday all the way around. So yea, she was very emotional."

Britney looked at me grinning and gave me the thumbs up.

"What was going on yesterday that made it so bad for her? She mentioned it to me but she never went into detail about it."

"She woke up yesterday feeling sick but went on to work anyway. She had to leave work and go to the doctor because she started feeling worse. Then her family called her and said that her grandfather had been admitted into the hospital with chest pains. And you know her grandpa is like her father, he raised her. Her not being able to leave to go until tomorrow when she gets off of work because she is on this new job and still under her 90 day probation period. She was just overwhelmed. Then when you called and cancelled on her…" I just shook my head as if Eric could see me doing so, but he got the point.

"Damn – I had no idea," Eric sounded sad. "Well what did she say about us?" He asked.

"She just said she thought she could do this, but she doesn't think she can. She was ok with your setup as long as it wasn't in her face, and this was just to in the face. You chose who was more important to you and did not consider her feelings."

"Hell I didn't know what she was going thru, she never said!" Eric was anxious. "It wasn't that Tonya was who I wanted to be with last night but Britney knows that Tonya and I are together. I can't always be with Britney every time she wants me to be. There are going to be situations that come up in Tonya's and my relationship that I am going to have to take care of first before getting to Britney. That doesn't mean I don't care about her or how she feels; that's just how shit goes when you're involved with someone who has a main chick." Eric exclaimed. I regretted that I had put him on speaker phone because he had unknowingly put the last nail into his own coffin.

"Well you need to talk to her," I said feeling defeated my damn self. "Maybe she is not cut out to play the side role."

"She means more to me than that Keisha, just like you mean a lot to Cue. I have had plenty of women on the side you know about and some you don't, but Britney is one that can get anything I have. She is not just sex to me. Hell if Tonya and I were ever done she would be my lady."

"What? Really?" I raised my eyebrows looking at Britney who was beaming. "Call her Eric and talk to her and make her believe all of this. I'm on your side, I understand. I have been in this game for a minute so I know how she feels and some are just not built to play it, hell I wasn't. It took a while for me to understand and not go off every time Cue reneged on me. I know I was better than that now that I look back over everything, but when you love someone you put up with a lot. I'm finally at the point where I'm tired of being tired." I was talking to Eric as I did my girlfriends. I had forgot for a second who I was talking to. Eric and I talked for a few more minutes and he said he would call her and we hung up.

"So what do you say to all of that?" I asked Britney beaming myself.

"Sounds good and all but Keisha I'm done. Like he said... If Tonya wasn't in the picture. However, Tonya is in the picture. I knew she was, but now I also know that I am not cut out for it. So I have to do what will keep Britney sane."

"Britney I admire you so much. It has taken me four in a half years to get to this point where I feel that I can move on. I always knew I was more than a chick on the side but I allowed myself to be that. Do you know he married Mercedes two weeks ago?"

Britney's expression was priceless. I always new, but at this very moment I knew that Britney and I had a bond that could never be broken. Britney had tears rolling down her face before she even got details. Britney hugged and comforted me before she even asked questions. She felt my pain as I relived everything that had happened over the course of the past two weeks. She was upset that I had been going through this all alone.

"Fuck Cue. Girl I know you love him but I swear if you continue to fuck with him after this... Girl he has nothing to say to you but, "When can I get my son or what does my son need." Britney was mad as hell. "Fuck Cue and fuck Eric. Girl we are so much better than this and together we can overcome this. Let them have their women, we don't need them."

Hell she had gotten me all fired up. I was doing fist pumps in the air by the time she finished with her lil speech.

"I don't think that I am going to tell Eric about the baby Keisha," Britney confessed.

"What... what you mean you ain't gonna tell him? What are you going to do?"

"I'm going to have and raise my baby alone. I do not want Eric in my life at all, and if he knew about this baby, he may or may not make a skeptical of being there. I have to do what I feel is right for me and mine. I don't know if he'll even want to be a part of this child's life especially with what he is trying to build with Tonya. And I'm sure as hell am not going to take a risk on my child having an in and out father, I'd rather it not even know that one exist."

"Britney, you have to tell him," I pleaded. "That is not even how Eric operates. He has three daughters that he adores-hell he even loves Quincy to death," I exclaimed.

"Yes he has three daughters by a girl he dated all through high school, two of them while they were still in high school and the third one later. Here it is eight years later, and remember that chick he was messing with a few years ago he made have an abortion. I am not aborting my child under any circumstances, and he may decide well if that's what you want to do then I'm out. I can't risk the rejection; I can do this and that is what I plan to do."

"Wow… It's your body, your baby. I just hope you have a change of heart before this is all over. I think every man should know if they have a child, now if they wish to be there for the child or not is totally up to them. You did not make this baby alone and you should not have to raise it alone. Hell he knew the risk you were taking by having unprotected sex whether you were on birth control or not. I don't agree with your decision, but I totally support you in it."

"Thank you," Britney said. "Right now I just don't want him to know. Who knows? I may eventually change my mind."

"Britney being realistic, you know he's going to find out that you're pregnant eventually."

"Keisha I am planning on moving to Baltimore to help my grandmother take care of Grandpa if he makes it. Things are tough on her right now in her old age, and people don't do what they should to help. You know, pop in and out, and every time she needs to go somewhere she say they have a million and one excuses. Grandma and I have been talking about this for a few weeks now, and since this has happened I know I need to go. I put in my two week notice at my job Friday."

Now it was my time to look shocked and start crying. Britney again hugged me and said, "Girl stop, you know we are as thick as thieves; we are always going to see one another. You are my excuse to come here, and you and Quincy can come visit with me."

Britney and I sat and talked for over an hour before she finally left. I knew in my heart of hearts that we both were going to be just fine. We both had a game plan and we both knew exactly what we had to do to achieve our goals. We were now on it.

Chapter Twenty Six

(Keisha)

I needed to make a run out to the mall real fast to pick up some final things for my trip out west to visit with Grant. These past two weeks have gone by in a blur. I had helped Britney pack up and move what she did not give away into storage. We cried as she got ready to get onto the bus. We had just found out on yesterday that she was not four weeks but eight weeks pregnant. I told her that she had better plan on me being there when she got ready to deliver my godchild. She was more than delighted.

Britney had talked to Eric twice over the past two weeks; he had been trying unsuccessfully to contact her. She had not bothered to tell him that she was moving away and made me promise not to tell him either. She confided in me that knowing that she was going back home, made it that much easier on her not deciding to continue on with Eric. She said the distance would certainly not work with them.

As far as Cue was concerned, I was so done with him right now. He still came around to see and scoop up Quincy, and of course he tried his advances in sly ways with me. He made it so easy for me to turn him down, because he had always been trying to get me to come to his place during the day, so that way he could retire home to Mercedes at night as if nothing was going on. Although I had made plenty of trips to his house during the day in our past, this day and time, it was not happening. I be damned if he used me to get what he knew was good and home was no comparison to, but home got all the cuddling. Keep your ass at home or find another boo was my attitude. Every time he asked me over during the day, I always converted to, "Why not tonight?"

He had yet to tell me that he had gotten married, although Mercedes wedding portrait was in Sunday's paper. One of my grandmother's friends recognized the name in the paper as being Cue's government name and told her about it. My grandmother asked me what was going on with Cue. I admitted through tears that he had gotten married. My grandmother hugged and comforted me as she told me- "That this too shall pass." She said, "Cue has a lot of growing up to do so you should be thankful that you are not the one that will have to go through all the changes he's about to go through. You are a beautiful queen who's brilliant. Take your focus off of that boy and stay on the road you are on to success. You have accomplished more in this past year than most do in a lifetime. You're in college, your home and car is paid for in full."

"But Granny, Cue bought the car and house it wasn't me," I said not being able to take credit for buying a house and car.

"Hell yea he bought it because you told him to. Most young girls your age are in apartments and as long as the guy is throwing them a few dollars here and there they are content. But no not my baby, you made him invest in you, and buy doing so he's invested in your future. You are a homeowner; do you know what that means?" Granny asked not expecting or giving me an opportunity to answer. "That means no one can take that from you, you have property. You can use your property for collateral to purchase more property without putting a cent down if you play your cards right. You can rent out the property you own or the new property you purchase for income while the tenant is paying it off for you. When times get hard, lights and water off, you'll still have a roof over your head. That's as long as you keep your property taxes paid that is," Granny added with a smile. "You are about to open up your own salon, chile... to be your age again and have the head that you have on your shoulders, I would have been something else!" Granny exclaimed clapping her hands together.

After Granny and I talked I was rejuvenated and ready for the world again. I was about to go and spend an entire weekend with this fine ass man that I thought I would never see again. I had spent the entire day with Quincy, we had went to the movies and to Frankie's Fun Park, and now we were off to the mall to find me about two more cute tank tops. I had found four cute tank tops and was about to head out of the mall when Quincy spotted the cookie store and wanted a cookie. Of course he picked a cookie simply because it was made as Grover from Sesame Street, and that one cookie cost almost four damn dollars. I was shaking my head digging in my coin purse when Quincy suddenly took off running and screaming, "Daddy!"

I looked up into the direction in which Quincy was running, with my hand frozen inside of my purse, and sure enough - he saw his daddy walking in our direction, holding hands with his wife. I was frozen in line. I had no reflex other than to stand there and stare. I could not move or holler for Quincy to come back. My heart was beating more than a mile a minute and sweat beads immediately popped up on my forehead. My stomach was cutting all sorts of cartwheels. And from the looks on Cue's and Mercedes faces-they were feeling everything that I was feeling. Quincy jumped up into Cue's arms and instinct made him catch Quincy. Something finally snapped in me and I was able to step out of line leaving the cookie.

Mercedes eyes were as big as golf balls and she stood speechless watching Quincy steady talking to his daddy, whom he seemed to know very well. There was nothing I could do but face the inevitable, whatever that may have been, but one thing was for certain, my child would not suffer behind this. I approached Cue and Mercedes and hiked my purse that was falling, back onto my shoulder as I put my hands out for Quincy to come to me.

"What, what," Mercedes words were hammered, *"What's going on here?"* She scratched behind her ear and squinted her eyes at Quincy and Cue and asked, "Cue what is going on, how does he know you so well, and why is he calling you daddy?" she asked looking totally confused but knowing the answer to her question already.

Cue kept Quincy in his arms as he put one arm on Mercedes back to move her to an area where there was not so much traffic to talk. I followed behind them. Cue was at first heading for a bench that was right by the store we were standing by, but after realizing that Mercedes wasn't resisting and as of now being very cooperative he took this opportunity to lead us outside which turned out to be for the best.

"Mercedes, baby I'm so sorry about this but I just didn't know how to tell you about him, I did not want to lose you baby." Cue actually had tears rolling down his cheeks.

"Why you crying daddy?" Quincy asked beginning to cry himself.

I stepped up to take Quincy, but Cue motioned me off as he comforted Quincy.

"So are you telling me all these years you have had a child that you have known about, and obviously have been seeing on the regular because he knows your ass very well. You never once found a good opportunity to tell me?" Mercedes words were stern and her eyes were glaring fire. "All this time my intuition has been right about you and this hoe, and you been making me feel as if I was just insecure?"

Cue had his head down and he had stood Quincy beside him but was still holding his hand. "Mercedes what would you have done if I had told you? You hate Keisha so much there was no way you would have understood."

"Fuck that Cue! The bottom line is that your ass cheated on me with this bitch and produced a child," Mercedes was now shouting. "What is it about this whore that drives your ass so damn much?"

"Bitch?" I said interrupting her, I had let it slide the first time she called me a whore but there would not be a strike three. "I have showed you once what a whore could do, now you want see what a bitch can do? Yea, that's right I have your man's son, his first and only." Cue tried to shut me up but I did not give a damn. I kept talking fuck him; little did he know I was done with his ass anyway. "Yea now it's all in your face just like you tried to put it all in my face when we were at the bank when you and Cue had come back from your trip that you were married!" Cue was stunned. "Yes motherfucker, I knew your ass had married her, that's why I have been putting your ass off! Forget you Cue, you are a liar and you have no remorse for your actions. How you treat another person doesn't matter to you as long as Cue has what he wants. I am done with your sorry ass and I am glad that you're her husband and not mine!" I took my crying sons hand and pulled him away from Cue so that we could leave, but not without first saying, "Cue has always been a father to this little boy and fuck what you know or think," I looked from Mercedes to Cue and said, "And you will continue to be a great father to him even more so now since your little wife knows, play with it if you want to!" And I picked up my son and walked off.

There was a lot of ranting and raving going on behind me but it did not concern me so I kept going. Let them fight it out. I don't care if she leaves, he leaves or they stay together, but Cue's ass had better pick up Quincy as planned on Sunday; that's all I knew. I got in the car and had to take a minute to comfort my child and make him understand that everything was going to be alright. Then had to do a few breathing techniques myself to calm my nerves.

I could not believe how this had all gone down. I imagined over twenty different scenarios of how Mercedes would find out in the past years, but not one of them resulted in Quincy being the one that let her know. That was crazy and ironic at its best.

My flight was at nine in the morning, and Quincy was going to Granny's so that would be one less thing I would have to do in the morning. So after dropping Quincy off, and watching to make sure that he was ok, I said my goodbyes to everyone and left to head home to finish packing. Quincy gave me a kiss and ran across the street to the park laughing with his friends.

I was home packing and filling Britney and Toya in on what had happened. Britney was on speaker phone, and Toya was lying across my bed. We were all in disbelief about today's events. My phone lit up alerting me that I had an incoming call. It was Cue's house phone number; I thought they must have really had it out and she had put his ass out.

"Britney, this is Cue girl. Let me take this I will call you right back." I said.

"As soon as you hang up you better call me!" Britney demanded.

I had not heard from Cue since leaving the mall over five hours ago and really had not expected to hear from him anymore today. I figured that he would be spending the rest of the day crying and begging and we would be the last ones on his agenda.

"What'sup?" I said in a no nonsense tone.

"How's Quincy?"

"He's fine," I said dryly.

"Keisha we going to have to talk, that was fucked up the way you handled that situation today," Cue was calm but I could tell that he was mad and exhausted.

"Oh, really, how so Cue? Is it because I refused to let your wife continue to talk about me and call me out of my name as if I wasn't there or as if our son wasn't present? No, the only fucked up thing about this whole situation, is how you've handled it from the start. If you knew that you wanted to make it work with Mercedes when you found out that I was pregnant, you should have come clean with her then. And If you had been honest with me and told me that you had married Mercedes, I wouldn't be so bitter towards you now. Yeah, I would have been hurt, but do you know how hurt I was when I accidently found out?"

"Keisha I'm sorry. I know I fucked up, I fucked up bad, but what can I do about it now? Mercedes is hurt and it's my fault, you're hurt and it's my fault, but she is my wife and I have to finally be a man and do what's right. I've screwed up enough, so she and I have talked, and if we're going to make our marriage work, and until she can trust me again, from this day forward it's only going to be about my son. You're going to have to learn to deal with Mercedes, because if you need anything or need me to get Quincy, you are going to have to call and talk to her"

What the fuck! Was this motherfucker serious? Does he really think that I needed his ass that much? Did he not know that it would be a cold day in hell before I would ever call Mercedes to set up anything? He apparently did not realize that if he waited on me to call Mercedes to set up meetings for him to see his son, he would never again see his son! And Mercedes' ass better not call me to even attempt to set up shit!

"Cue do me a favor will you," My tone was chilled but I was pissed the fuck off, how dare he? "Put me on speaker phone so that your wife can understand where I am coming from, because I know she has to be standing by you."

"I'm already here," Mercedes said with an attitude.

Oh really, so this was how they were playing it?

"Great. I know you're hurt- and every reason to be. I know I was wrong for sleeping with your man. However you cannot put all of the blame on me," She went to interrupt me but I demanded that she let me finish and then she could have her say. "Cue and I both were wrong," Cue went to interject also, but I shut him down too.

"Unh unh," I said shushing him. "Let me finish please." Cue and I have raised Quincy together for the past three years without an interpreter, and I be damned if I'll bring one in now. Quincy is *Cue's* and mine, not mine and Mercedes child, and it will be a cold day in hell if you really think I am going to allow you to be our median. So Cue if you want to see *your* child, you call me, not have your wife call me. If I need anything for *our* child, I will call you. If you don't want me calling, hell I'll text you. There is no way that I will relay one damn word through your wife. Now do you understand me? Tell me what it's going to be, because I have my child, I see him every day. It's totally up to you whether you do or not."

"Keisha you made your bed hard when you decided to have an affair with my husband, so now you do not have a choice, either you deal with me or you don't deal with Cue at all," Mercedes said with so much authority I thought they had got a judgment. "Cue and I have talked and he has come clean with me about everything and we are going to get through this, so your little surprise did not separate us just so you know," Mercedes charged at me.

"Mercede's you can keep Cue honey, I had already decided to move on. And for someone who is supposedly so smart you are one stupid ass broad. Do you really think that just because I don't deal with you about *Cue's and my son*," I said putting strong emphasis on Cue and My son. "You really believe that you would be able to stop Cue from seeing his son? Girl you obviously didn't pay much attention to the bond they have today did you. Believe me when I tell you, it's a four year bond, not overnight. Cue is an excellent father to his first son. Cue has him spoiled rotten and he has Cue wrapped around his finger. So honey, you can never compete with that. Cue I know that you are not going to allow her to come between you and your son?" I asked just to confirm to this heifer who thought she was going to run this show.

"Keisha, we are talking arrangements here not—"

"Answer the damn question, because I need to know where you stand here." I barked.

"You being stupid, you know I will always be a father to my son, but we are talking about how to make this work for the all of us," Cue said.

"Keisha, I will say this and you can take it anyway that you feel fit. I would never try to come between any father and his child, but this is not just about you, Cue, and the child. I am the one that has had the bomb dropped on me. This much I can tell you for a fact; until I am ready, no one will be here. Just as you expect me to adapt, you're going to have to adapt to the fact as well, that Cue now has a wife. A wife who has been delivered a bad blow and this is going to be on my time." Mercedes said matter of factly.

"So are you saying that Cue will not be seeing his child until you are ready, is that what you are saying?" I asked just to make sure I was hearing her correctly.

"Cue and I have discussed this whole ordeal and Cue is going to support him, but he's going to give me time before he starts coming around, yes."

"Cue is she serious, and did you really agree to this bogus shit?'' I asked angrily and already determining that if that happened I would be the one to make sure that he never saw him again. "And what about Mrs. Glenda, does she know anything about this little arrangement?"

"Mrs. Glenda knows about all of this?" Mercedes asked deflated.

"Does Mrs. Glenda know? Girl apparently your husband hasn't come to clean with you. Not only does Mrs. Glenda know she keeps him every other weekend. She took him with her to Florida for their family reunion last month. Quincy has Mrs. Glenda just as wrapped as he has your faithful husband. And despite how stupid and naïve your husband may be and allow you to think that you can control his relationship with his son, his mother never will. I dare you to take your logic to Mrs. Glenda, or Lynn for that matter. You will get your feelings hurt!"

I heard a phone slam down and knew that it was Mercedes. She knew that Mrs. Glenda wasn't too fond of her ass anyway, because she thought she was so much better than anyone. Mrs. Glenda only tolerated her. From what Lynn told me, Mercedes was scared of Mrs. Glenda because she did not play games. And she did not like the way Mercedes tried to rule Cue.

"Keisha that was messed up," Cue said. "I'm trying to figure out something that would work for the all of us, and you're just trying to cause more confusion!"

"No, your punk ass is only concerned about Mercedes and I don't give a damn about her. That was her solution not yours, and all the confusion could have been avoided if you had told your girlfriend years ago that you had a child on the way.

Not abiding Cue, you two need to go back to the drawing board and you need to grow your damn balls back!"

"Keisha, you have to understand how hurt she is right now," Cue said almost begging me to understand. "This has been a tough pill for her to swallow."

"Hell, I'm not hurt? I am still hurt! So you have totally dismissed how I must be feeling again, huh? Mercedes has you to babysit her feelings, so as far as I am concerned... Fuck her, she'll be a'ight.

"You tell me now Cue what in the hell are you going to do, are you going to let her tell you when and if you can see your son? Because if so, I can spare you the headache right now and you can just sign over your parental rights and I mean it."

"Hell no you're crazy? That is my son, my one and only child, and I am going to always be his father. She's just mad right now but I would never let her or anyone come between me and my mini me. I should bust your ass for even suggesting some bullshit like that Keisha. You know what that boy means to me!"

"Well you need to act like it. You cannot blame me for asking; because that was some "ill will" shit you called me with. And your ass should have known that I would never go for that mess so why did you even bother calling. My days of going along with you are over. I am willing to compromise, but not at the expense of Quincy being short changed. Like I've told you, your either going to be there or not, but there will be no in and out. Are you still going to pick him up Sunday afternoon for Eric's daughter party?"

"Yes I am picking him up, why wouldn't I? You're tripping Keisha. You're going to have to talk to Mercedes eventually, so you may as well get use to the fact that we are married and she is going to be around Quincy."

"Cue I have no problem with her being around Quincy as long as she treats him right. But I will tell you one thing and this is a promise not a threat at all. If I ever hear one word of her ever mistreating my baby---that's her ass and yours too! You better be damn sure that she treats him well, because I will fuck the both of you up about that boy. I trust you and I know you love him. But you better make damn sure that your wife is on board before you take my son around her. Don't forget to pick him up Sunday, your probation period will begin then," I said, and disconnected the call. I wished I had a landline so that I could have slammed it down on the receiver for more effect.

I looked at Toya wide eyed and asked, "Can you believe that mess? Can you believe his nerve?"

Toya, who was dying laughing as soon as I hung up the phone said, "Keisha you know that was all Mercedes doing. That was some stupid broad shit, and you know only a jealous ass woman would have come up with some mess like that. Thank goodness you are not stupid and didn't go along with it."

"Not in this lifetime," I said angrily. "I hold all the cards right now as to what kind of a relationship he has with his son, so why would I settle for some mess like that? They will play by my rules or he can dismiss himself from our lives totally. I have played his way for four years. Did he really think that I would allow his wife to start dictating as well?"

"Girrrrl!" Toya said shaking her head. "That was some juvenile shit. You know that was all Mercedes, I'm just amazed that Cue even bothered calling you with that."

Little did Cue know that any feelings that I had for him now had vanished with that little episode. How dare he tell me that I have to come to the fact that Mercedes is now his wife? Hell I came to that fact when I started letting my feelings diminish for him a few weeks ago. I allowed myself to fall in love with a man that had a significant other. I allowed myself to believe that I was more to him than a booty call. Yes, Cue may have cared a lot for me and done more for me than most other men have done for their side chick. But at the end of the day when the pressure was put on him... he married the one that meant the most to him. I got a lot out of the relationship. I got a house, all mine. I got a car, all mine. I got a swollen bank account that he doesn't know about, all mine. And the most precious thing that Cue could ever give me is a child that I adore, and he is all mine.

I finished packing my bags for my trip to see Grant as Tonya and I talked. I do not know whether this adventure with Grant was causing me not to have time to feel heart break or what, but right now I was just fine. I am excited and ready to start my new life without Cue in it other than to be a father to our son. I am hoping for the best with Grant, but prepping to handle it one day at a time. I will not rush or try to make it more than what it is. Right now we are getting to know one another and I will not allow myself to think that I am his lady. However, I will never again play second fiddle to anyone else. I don't want to hear about no friends, if they are just a friend then you will not have a problem introducing me to them. Thank goodness that Grant has been honest about not having anyone to the best of my knowledge. And by him flying me there to stay with him this weekend, I have no choice but to believe that he is being honest.

I am going to California to enjoy some fun and sun with a very nice, fun, respectful man, whom I respect and have enjoyed talking with over the past few weeks. When I return home I will finish what I started. Finish school, my salon and being the best mother that I could possibly be. And I will always remind myself that I never have to settle for being number two, because I am the prize and any man would be lucky to have me.

No more shady missions for this girl. Something just snapped in me when he said, I had to understand how hurt Mercedes was. Once again I was the one that was supposed to settle and go with the flow. I was tired of always being the one who had to put my feelings aside, having to cope with everything on my own and not suppose to have a voice. Yes, I chose to be with Cue; no one put a gun to my head and forced me into having an affair with a man that was already involved. I made the best of it for four years and got a great son out of it. But for this man to up and get married on me without as much as a phone call to say he was getting married, was just plain disrespectful. Cue showed no respect for me in his actions so therefore; it is what it is. I was a booty call to him that he just happened to have feelings for. Bottom line is that Cue did not play me I straight played myself. I allowed him to use me whenever he wanted, and my stupid ass was so in love that I could not see the bigger picture. The bigger picture was large and clear from the beginning - never settle for being number two, when you could find someone out there that would gladly make you their number one. Yes, I got a lot of perks from being Cue's side chick, but the one thing I wanted more than anything... his main chick got it. I am bitter, but I will be alright. Cue was my heart and my soul, but he will never again see any more of my pain, and I be damned if he will ever see me broken. I do not know what my future holds and I am not looking for Grant to be my rebound man. I just want to enjoy my time with him and hope for the best. I do owe Cue one thing... Thanks to him I will *NEVER* settle for any bullshit again.

Book Club Discussion

Which character did you like the most, and why?

Are there characters or situations you can identify with? Who and why?

Mercedes seems to have it all, even Cue. So why is it that you think she was so jealous of Keisha?

Do you really think that it is possible for Cue to be in love with both Mercedes and Keisha, and why?

What are your thoughts on Keisha, and the way she dealt with Cues relationship with Mercedes?

Did the book evoke you in anyway?

Have you ever had a girlfriend that reminded you of Keisha or Mercedes?

What was your favorite part or scene from this book?

Can you understand why Cue did not tell Mercedes of his son earlier, and why?

Join my fan club on Facebook- Waiting On My Cue Fan Club

If you would like to book Belinda Hunter to join in on a book club meeting or engagement email hunter.belinda99@gmail.com

I'm not ashamed to admit that there was a time in my life when I was Keisha. I was the ride or die, down for whatever, 2nd string chick. I saw so much of my own life in this book and understood the plight of Keisha. I think the real goal for her was to win Cue even though she knew deep down he did not possess the traits to be the man she deserved. He would never truly be "all hers" because, regardless, Cue was never satisfied with one woman. This doesn't mean that she didn't love him; in fact, she loved him more than she loved herself. However, I think the driving motivation often turns from the love you have for the guy and goes more to your will to win his heart just to claim victory over the other woman. I thought the book did an excellent job at portraying the life and mindset of two young women from different backgrounds who shared a common issue; low/no self-esteem. The major difference between both women was the growth in which Keisha displayed. It was the awakening of her spiritual being that began her transformation and aided in her regaining or developing the courage to say enough is enough.

I am dying to read the sequel. I need this ASAP!!!! It is not often where I read a book and relate in such a passionate way with one of the characters. Job well done!!!!!!!

Nachelle White (Diva Book Club, Washington, DC)

NOT COMPLETELY EDITED

Read part of

**No Longer Waiting- My Cue has been
Granted**

Belinda Hunter's sequel to *Waiting on My Cue*

Coming this fall

Chapter One

Mercedes

"Help me to make sure that I understand you correctly. Are you saying that I can't get my son this weekend because if I do that you are leaving the house?" Cue asked with fire in his eyes.

"You can get him if you want to Cue. I am just letting you know that if you do get him, I will not be around this weekend. Plain and simple!" I said, shrugging my shoulder. "I am tired of you jumping every time Keisha calls asking for you to babysit while she runs all over the damn country!"

I am sick and tired of Cue and Keisha. Quincy is a sweet little boy and he is never a problem. But why should I deal with a kid tagging along behind me and my husband every other weekend? Why should I have to look at a calendar to make sure that it's not the weekend that we will have Quincy when trying to plan? Hell I haven't had any kids and I did not know that I was marrying a man that had any either! I get tired of explaining that he is not my child after telling people that Cue and I have been together for nine years; but yet he has a six year old son. And forget me trying to avoid all the questions by claiming Quincy to be mine, because that backfired like crazy the last time I tried.

We were at Shoguns having dinner; and two other families were seated at the big square grill table with us. So, of course in conversation with these other career oriented adults such as myself, I just pretended that Quincy was my child when the lady asked was he the only one that we had.

Quincy piped up. "You're not my mommy. I am my mommy and my daddy's only child. My mommy name is Keisha. You're my daddy's wife."

So what, he was only four at the time. I still felt that Cue should have chastised his little ass for butting in grown folk conversation. But no—Cue argued that no harm or disrespect was intended. I had never been so embarrassed in my life. For the rest of the dinner I kept my eyes on my plate and ate in silence. I was sure that they all were staring at me wondering what kind of dysfunctional family we had here.

"Mercedes you can do whatever you want to do. I am tired of going down this road with you every time my son comes over. It's been almost three years and if you're not over it yet, you will never be over it." Cue said.

"What are you saying Cue? So now you're saying you are choosing him over me, and what Keisha wants you to do over me?"

"Hell Mercedes, Keisha seldom calls and ask for me to keep him, and when she does need for me to, you have this stank ass attitude the entire time he is here. It's not about choosing him over you, but the bottom line is he has never done anything to your ass and he is my child. He will always be my child, but you may not always be my wife if you don't get your act together!"

Cue stormed out of the house slamming the door behind him. I flopped down on the couch and cried from his last words. They cut deep into my soul. Cue and I have been married for two and a half years and I am happy until Keisha or Quincy is mentioned. I have tried my hardest to get the envious spirit out of me retaining to Quincy, but it is so hard.

Cue honored my request when we first got married and he did not keep him every other weekend as he wanted to. However, he would go and see him a few times out of each week, and Cues mother kept him at her house a lot. This too bothered me. It seems that every time we were at Cue's mom's house that was all she talked about was Quincy. I suppose she thought that I was ok with the situation because it had been a few months. But little did she know. Even now every time I look at that cute little boy, all I can think about is the connection that he brings to Cue and his trifling ass momma Keisha. When I see how Cue reacts to him and the love they share it makes me so jealous. And to make matters worse, when I told Cue that I was ready to have a child he asked me to wait another year or so until he got some things in order.

Of course I asked him "Why did I have to wait? You and Keisha did not wait!" This brought on a huge argument that ended with him storming from the house, and my deciding that day was the last day that I would take my birth control. So either he'd use protection or he'd take that risk of me getting pregnant.

Sure enough, not two months after stopping my birth control, I became pregnant. I was ecstatic! Although Cue was upset at first, it only lasted about a week. After that first week he too was happy and ready to bring in this new life. Cue would cuddle with me at night massaging my belly. I loved it when he would talk to his child through my stomach.

I was quick to let Keisha know through a text message that I was pregnant. Although Keisha and I still did not communicate at this point, I saw no harm in sending her a text saying, "Tell Quincy that he's going to be a big brother!" She never responded. Just like her jealous ass.

Three months into the pregnancy I miscarried and I was devastated! Cue tried to comfort me. My mom took the entire week off of work and drove up to spend it with me. She assured me that the next pregnancy would be a success, and that I was still young, and I had plenty of time to carry and birth a house full of babies.

When I lost the baby, it seemed that it made Cue and Quincy even closer. He said that life and being a parent is so precious, and me losing the baby makes him appreciate being a father even more. As if this was suppose to please me; hell, he being a father is what bothered me. I was the one that had been with his ass forever. I am the one that was supposed to be the mother of his first child. Cue just did not seem to grasp the concept of why this was so hard for me. Every time he had to talk to Keisha about anything pertaining to Quincy, my heart continued to chip away.

One night Keisha called the house at midnight to inform Cue that she was going to have to take Quincy to the emergency room because he had been running a fever all day and it still hadn't broken. Of course I took this opportunity to make her look unfit, and as always Cue went to bat for her when I asked, "What kind of mother allows her child to run a fever over a 100 all day and does not bother taking them to the doctor?" Cue's response was, "She has been monitoring it all day Mercedes, and it had went down but spiked back up. Plus her grandmother has been working on him with her home remedies, and she was the one that advised Keisha to take him on in. Earlier when I called to check to see had it gone down, it had." So this told me that he had been talking to Keisha all day, and he had not even mentioned a fever to me until just this moment when Keisha called.

Of course I got up to get dressed to go with Cue to the hospital, although he protested by saying that there was no need for me to go, plus I had to get up and go to work in the a.m. I insisted, and slipped on some jeans and a hoody with my Air Max. When we got to the hospital, Keisha and her family seemed to be having a reunion. Who wakes the entire family up at midnight to come to the hospital? Her Granny, sister, brother and aunt Shaunice who happened to be home visiting was there.

I immediately hated that I had tagged along. Everyone looked at me as if I was crazy although they did speak. This was my first time officially meeting Shaunice and Keisha's sister, but I knew exactly who they were from Keisha's Facebook page. I had met her granny and brother briefly in exchanges when I would ride with Cue to pick up Quincy. Everyone spoke then ignored me the rest of the time I was there, except for granny who tried to include me into certain conversations. Keisha never spoke, nor acknowledged that I was even in the room. Watching how Quincy acted towards his mom made me even more envious. He truly loved and worshipped her to death. Watching Keisha and Cue beside his bed talking and comforting their son, made me want to slap the shit out of both of them.

After it was determined that Quincy was going to be ok, and that he would not be staying at the hospital overnight, Cue and I left. Once in the car I was silent and Cue asked what was wrong with me.

"Quincy did not even talk to me." I said softly.

Oh, my gosh! You would have thought I had blown up the hospital from the way he went off on me. I did not mean it the way he took it. Hell, I knew he was sick. I was merely stating that normally when he is at the house his little ass follows me around talking my head off; tonight he did not even speak.

"Mercedes, grow the fuck up! My son is lying over there feeling bad. He is only six years old. Making your ass look stupid is the last thing on his mind. Hell, I never saw you once walk over to his bed and ask him how he was. You're the grown one and nothing is wrong with you!"

"I am just saying that I felt out of place as it was, and it would have made me feel good if he had acknowledged me, and acted as if he liked me, as he does when he is at the house, that is all."

Cue looked over at me and shook his head before saying, "I swear sometimes that you ain't got a lick of sense. You don't give a damn about nobody but Mercedes' spoiled ass. Life doesn't revolve around you! Get over yourself, this is not about you!"

My house phone ringing jolted me back from my walk down memory lane. I got up from my position on the couch and went to answer it. It was Cue.

"Just want you to know that I have Quincy. He and I will be staying at my mom's this weekend."

"What do you mean; how in the heck are you going to leave your house and your wife to go and stay at your mom's with your son?"

"Well, you did say that you was not going to be around

if I kept him this weekend; and since I am keeping him and you're not going to be around anyway, I figured you wouldn't miss me. So we will be at moms, no sense in coming all the way back to Gaffney when everything I have planned is in Spartanburg anyway. So enjoy your weekend." And with that being said, Cue disconnected the call. I immediately called him back; and he sent me to voicemail.

I lay on the couch and cried. I finally decided to call my mother; she always had an encouraging word for me. She never liked the idea of Cue having a child either. When she found out about Quincy, (which was a day after I found out), she told me to get an annulment. Although she did not mean that because that would bring shame to her little world. She stated that his decision to not come clean with me before we got married was grounds enough for me to not want to be around the child until I was ready. She went on to tell me that Cue's loyalty was to me, not Keisha or Quincy. I was his wife and I was to come first. Cue made his choice in not telling me about his child, but me dealing with the child or not was my decision, and he had to respect it.

Cue and I had been married for almost three months before Quincy first came to the house to stay overnight. And Quincy was precious. I could not help but to like him, although I tried not to get too close to him. He would follow me around the house steady asking questions. Likewise, I threw some questions about Keisha to him. One day I asked him a question about Keisha and he sweetly and innocently said, "My mommy said if you want to know something about what goes on in her house, for you to call her."

"Why did your mom say that Quincy, what did you tell her?" I asked, alarmed.

Quincy shrugged his shoulders and said, "I don't know, call and ask her."

"That's fine Quincy. Just tell me what did you tell her that I had asked you to make her say that?" I asked in a panic.

"I just asked her if her boyfriend ever stay all night because you wanted to know." He said.

I could have shitted in my pants. There was nothing that I could say because truth was I had asked this child so many questions. I never thought that his young behind would remember enough to go back and repeat what I had asked. I thought he answered my questions and then they were lost to the sea of forgetfulness. After that incident, I never again mentioned anything about Keisha to Quincy, and I prayed that Keisha did not say anything to Cue about me questioning him.

My mother picked up the phone just as I was getting ready to hang up.

"Hey baby, what are you doing?" She asked.

I started crying as soon as I heard my mother's voice. How I wished that she stayed closer, so that I could run to her awaiting arms right now.

"Cue left the house to go and stay at his mother's for the weekend with Quincy," I cried.

"He did what?"

I repeated what I had just said, while explaining that I told him that I was not going to be in the house this weekend, because he decided that he would babysit without first consulting with me about any plans that I may have had.

"Mercedes let him be, and don't call him or take any of his calls this weekend. If he thinks he can just run off with his bastard child and leave his beautiful wife for the entire weekend- let him. You are a queen and his hood ass should be honored that you even want to be with his uneducated, no class having butt. You have options you don't need him!"

My mom as I said always knew how to cheer me up. She told me to pack my bags and go somewhere myself where my mind would be off of Cue. After I spoke with my mom I hung up and took her advice. I went upstairs and packed me an overnight bag, and hopped into my new Range Rover hitting 85 South, headed to Atlanta to spend the weekend with my soror Candice.

Once I made it to Candice house, I showered, dressed and we hit the club scene. We did not get back in until 3 a.m. I was tired yet feeling like a champion. I woke up the next day a little after 1 p.m. and we went to Glady's Knight Chicken and Waffles for what should have been breakfast by it being our first meal of the day. Cue had yet to call me; neither did I have any missed calls from him. I felt some kind of way by this, but I shook it off and continued to enjoy my time with Candice.

When I arrived home on Sunday evening I had yet to hear from Cue, and I hadn't reach out to him either. I was home, showered and in my bed watching B.E.T when Cue finally arrived after 9 p.m. He walked into the room as if his ass hadn't been gone the entire weekend without as much as a phone call to me to see how was I and said, "What's up big head?"

"Hey," I said, directing my attention back to the television.

He went into the bathroom and showered, and then came and got into the bed and attempted to put his arms around me. I nicely got up and left the room slamming the door behind me. I would be in the guest room for the rest of the week, I don't know who he thinks I am, but we are not the two and I am certainly not the one.

Chapter Two

Keisha

"I love and miss you to bay," I purred into the phone as Grant and I ended our call.

Although Grant and I have been seeing one another for two in a half years, it feels as if we just started dating. I still smile when I see his name flash across my phone screen, and I still get excited when I am going to visit or he comes to see me.

We both have very busy lives. I have my salon and I'm training students at the vocational school. He is always traveling with his job. We have probably visited each other ten times in the past two and a half years. With me living in South Carolina and him being in California, our schedules hardly ever permit a lot of togetherness.

I am smitten with Grant. He is everything that I could ask for in a man. From the first time I stepped off of the plane to visit him two-in-half-years ago, I knew that I had to have this smooth brother. He greeted me with a peck right on my lips as he took my luggage from my hand. He placed his hand on the small of my back as he escorted me out of the airport and into his waiting Ford F-150 that was sleek as hell. It looked as if he had just driven it off of a showroom floor. However, he said that he had bought it brand new a year ago.

By the time we made it to Grants house which was an hour from the airport, it was after 10 p.m. I could not see the detailing of the house but the lights that illuminated the house showed that it was at least a two story brick home. Once he opened the door and stood to the side to allow me to enter, I was astonished. Just who all stayed in this one room alone? Heck, the foyer was bigger than my living room and he proved that by having a 64 inch aquarium housed against one of the walls. He had all types of exotic fish in it. The opposite wall had two red leather arm chairs with a red leather ottoman between them.

When we got to his common area as he called it, (Living room, I called it) we stepped down three steps into the huge and spacious room. The room was so big that if he had dared to put either one of the two loveseats, or the couch to the wall, as mine were at my house, the room would have looked empty and bare. The furniture was in the middle of the room in order for it to look completely furnished. And the furnishings were of good taste I must say.

"Now this is a house," I said, looking back at Grant amazed.

Grant was standing there looking around the room as if he was just seeing it for the first time himself.

"Yea, I like it," he said. "When the realtor met me to see it, after seeing at least twenty others, some were a lot nicer than this one, but when I saw this one, it just felt right."

"And you stay here alone?" I asked, not believing how huge and beautiful this house was. I had already planned my wedding right in this very room, with me coming down the winding stair case.

"Yes, Keisha, I stay alone." Grant chuckled. "Let me show you to your room, beautiful."

I followed Grant up the stairs, as I continued looking

back over the balcony. I noticed a bedroom downstairs that had a massive poster bed in it that seemed to cover the entire wall. I was wondering was that where he slept.

He opened the door to what I would later say was one of the four guest rooms that he had. I mean this house had five bedrooms and he was the only one living here, so that meant all the other bedrooms were guest rooms- logical to me. The room he was putting me up in had a cream bedroom suit that had a footboard and headboard that was so high, no one could see you unless they walked to the side of the bed. The footboard had a damn television housed in it! WTF... The bedding was garnet and black, and there were enough throw pillows on it to create a king sized mattress on the floor I thought.

On the dresser there were pictures in black frames of him vacationing everywhere possible. Each frame was labeled with a plate of the location it was taken. I walked into the connecting bathroom and it too was decorated lavishly in garnet and black. The flush rug that was on the floor made me want to lay on it. On the counter in a basket he had every toiletry one could need. I could not wait to fill that jacuzzi up and relax in it later.

"Whatever you sell, you must sell a lot of them!" I said.

"Just selling one of my designs a year is enough commission to keep me afloat, imagine selling twenty," he grinned. "I make a decent living I guess," He said, being modest. "Is there anything you need to do before dinner or are you ready to go?"

"Well that depends I guess on where we are going. Since you know, you tell me, do I need to change?" I asked, looking up into his handsome face. Lord please be with me and don't let me turn into a straight up slut and hop this man's Jimmy tonight. I was already yearning for him just from conversation over the past few weeks. He was sweet, smooth and sexy as heck to me, and then to see how this mug was living...

His eyes were so dark and mysterious. Why did he not have a woman? I was going to have to find out more about this man because something just wasn't adding up. Here he was; successful, handsome, well connected and very easy to talk to- yet single. Over dinner, according to him, he had not even been with a woman intimately in nine months. Of course I was looking at him sideways.

"Don't look at me like that," he laughed, as he swiped my nose with his finger across the small circular table we were sitting at.

"I'm just wondering what is up with you? I mean you have it all. Looks, money, intelligence- so why doesn't a woman want your ass?" I asked, turning my head so that I could continue to look at him sideways.

Grant held his head back in laughter. "That's your predestine, I never said I wasn't wanted," he continued laughing.

I took it that predestine must have something to do with assumption. Hell I was going to have to get polished up if I was planning to kick it with Grant, because while his demeanor hadn't been to attempt as to come across as being too intelligent or smart, he couldn't avoid using words that were common for him and the circle he rode in.

"So what's the deal then? Do you have HIV, Herpes, or are you gay? Tell me something" I teased, yet I needed to know. "When was the last time you were tested, do you have your results?"

Grant and I had kidded around over the past few weeks when we would talk on the phone; so therefore, he knew I was playing around with him as always.

"What?" He asked pulling that bottom lip in between his teeth. "Have you changed your mind since seeing all of this man that I am, and now plan on sleeping in my bed with me this weekend? Because if so, I can produce for you everything you need to see. I am as clean as a whistle." He said lowering his eyes, biting on that lip and slowly shaking his head seducing the hell out of me.

I quickly got control of myself and said "Hell no, I am sleeping in the room you designated for me. You think because you flew me up here to see you in your huge beautiful home, and you have me in this restaurant dining with Tom Joyner and President Bush, that I would let you into my cottons that easy?"

"He's no longer President Keisha, he's just George," Grant laughed. "And I thought once you saw him and his entourage come in that would surely make you want me." Grant laughed, although he was just as surprised to see the former president come in himself.

Grant had told me that I was dressed fine for dinner in my black slacks that hugged my rear end and thighs but belled out from my upper thigh down to my feet, silver sequenced tank top and black Hunfews. He was sporting some khakis and polo and so was the former president. Although this restaurant was clearly upscale, it still had a casual feel.

"I have wanted you from the day I laid eyes on you, but that still doesn't mean I am going to sleep with your ass just like that," I said, pressing my lips together and lifting my eyebrows.

Grant nodded his head up and down slowly in agreement and had the audacity to say, "We'll see about that."

"What?" I asked laughing. "Are you planning on forcing yourself on me?"

Nodding his head from side to side he said, "Before this weekend is over I will be the one fighting you off," he said biting the corner of his lower lip again.

Oh shit, I thought. Little did he know, he had me wanting to hop over this table onto his lap right now. Maybe he did know.

"We'll see about that," I forced out as I took a sip of my water.

The waiter came to our table and asked would we like a cocktail, tea or coffee. I asked if I could have a margarita, but Grant said, "No bring her the Corpse Reviver, she may need it," he chuckled.

"Don't make me mace you tonight, because I am strapped with a full can and backup," I laughed.

Grant and I stayed at the restaurant and talked for almost two hours before returning to his house. Once there he fixed us both cocktails and we retreated to the Common Area. By the time my eyes could no longer stay opened I was already nestled in the cradle of Grants arms as if we were a couple. It felt so good there. I really did not want to retreat up stairs but this was day one, couldn't let him predict everything. I said my goodnights and headed upstairs.

The next morning I was awaken to the smell of bacon. I lay in the bed for a second taking in this beautiful room before getting up to go wash my face and brush my teeth. I was debating as to whether I should get dressed or would it be ok for me to go down in my pajamas. After all they were real pajamas, no lace gown or negligee, although I did have those packed just in case. But last night I slept in black silk PJ's. I decided that my attire was fine, after all, hadn't I already cuddled in his arms, so it was safe to say we were doing something that should allow me to sat around comfortably.

I went down the stairs taking in the scenery and followed my nose to the kitchen. Grant's bare back and his own black silk pajama bottoms were to me as he stood over the stove frying up the bacon, took my breath away. He had to work out daily, because these cuts were from hard work not inheritance. But the view from the windows that replaced the back wall was even more mesmerizing. I had no idea that Grant's house was on a huge lake. It was absolutely, beautiful!

"Good morning you," I said, as I walked past him going to the window to get a better look at the lake. I rubbed his back as I passed, his skin was so soft.

"Morning, beautiful," He glanced at me as I passed. "How did you sleep last night?"

"I slept like a queen. Grant, that bed," I said shaking my head. "It was the most comfortable bed that I have ever slept in, no bullshit."

"I know, I have that same mattress on my bed. Hell, it's on all the beds in the house," he chuckled.

I stood at the window just staring out at the lake. "This is beautiful, you really are living that life," I said, more to myself than Grant.

He walked over and stood beside me putting a piece of bacon into my mouth. "Yea, it's nice. Something about water makes me feel free," he said. "When I was young I would sit by the family pool and do my homework, talk on the phone and just think. Anytime I was down I would go out to the pool and the water would tranquilize me," he said, with a look that told me that he was gone back to those days as he looked out at the lake.

"I know what you mean," I said. "I too love the water. In my bedroom at home I have a fountain that sits on my night stand that I turn on at night, and just listen as the water flows as I read. It really relaxes me. I always have said that one day I will have a house on a lake or the ocean. I will spend my day's just writing poetry."

"Really," Grant asked as if he was surprised. "I would have never took you as wanting such a tranquilizing life. You seem to be a city girl and the country life would bore you."

"You don't know me very well. I was raised in the city and still stay in the city, but I am just old fashioned and laid back at heart. I just deal with the life I was giving, for now."

"I can totally understand that," Grant said. "I was raised in the city and stayed in the city when I first moved here. I knew when I got ready to purchase a house it had to be away from the city. Well let's eat, and I will take you to the city," Grant grinned.

After breakfast we both showered in separate bathrooms although he playfully told me that his shower was huge enough for the two of us. I dressed in some loose white linen pants, and a lavender sheer blouse over a white camisole, and a pair of Nine West sandals. Grant looked at me approvingly as I came down the stairs, and we left for a day of fun. I was having a great time, Grant and I just naturally vibed. More than once, I pretended that I was his very happy wife.

We settled at a Mexican restaurant for dinner although Mexican food was not one of my favorites, the restaurant itself was astonishing. It sat high up on a mountain where you could look over into the city. By it being dust dark, the city lights were beautiful.

"Grant, how are you?" came a female's voice.

I looked up and was staring into the green eyes of the prettiest woman I had ever seen in the flesh. This sister had to be a model; if not she had cheated herself. She stood at least 6'1 and maybe a size 9. Her waist was even smaller than my girlfriend Brittney's was. Not that I am a lesbian or bi-sexual but my eyes seemed to always wonder right back to her voluptuous breast. Her hair was cut very close to her head, showing just how beautiful her face was, and her accent was very nice.

"Hello Sky," Grant said as if he really did not want to speak to this lovely lady. He directed her attention to me with turned up hands introducing me to her.

"Keisha, baby this is Skylar. Skylar this is Keisha."

I extended my hand to Skylar, she vaguely accepted it and shook it before directing her attention back to Grant.

"So why haven't I heard from you?" She asked annoyed.

"Skylar I am not going to talk to you about that right now, I am with Keisha."

"I see that Grant, but when will you talk to me because you changed your number and I can't call you. I have been by your house several times and you are never home?"

I sat there cool but shocked. So this was the chick that Grant was telling me about that he last dated. Apparently, she did not realize that he had been out of the country making it even better for him to avoid her. He told me that they had dated for two years and he had planned to marry her. However, he had to leave California to handle another job in S.C for three weeks. He received a call from his frat brother saying that Sky had been with another frat brother the night before at a party. And this frat brother had no idea that she was Grants fiancée as he drunkenly bragged about how she sexed him before coming to the gathering. He said that he had just literally called and broken up with her maybe an hour before he ran into me at the beach. After calling her and breaking it off with her, he called and had his number changed that very night because she kept calling and begging for him to reconsider. Three days later is when he found out that he was going to be going to Germany for a few months. So if all was true, this was the first time in seven months that she had even spoke to him, let alone seen him. Wow!

"You and I really have nothing to discuss Skylar, it's over between the two of us and I would really appreciate you letting us be," Grant said nodding his head towards me.

Skylar directed her attention back to me and gave me the once over.

"What is it that you do for a living Keisha? Are you in architecture also?"

"No, I am a cosmetologist," I said, wondering why I even felt the need to give this heifer a response.

"You're a what? I mean what kind of salon do you own? It must cater to the most prestigious clients, because all women that Grant has ever dated made at least six figures."

"Enough Skylar, either you leave now or I will have security escort you away," Grant boomed.

I am leaving Grant, no need to cause a scene. Just need to know does your beautician friend know how in love you are with me and that we were planning to marry?"

"Yes, I know that you and Grant dated for a few years and were planning to marry. So by me knowing this, you should also know that I know why the prenuptials didn't take place as well. As Grant said… Please excuse us!" I was not loud but my voice carried enough weight that she realized that I had some street in me and was not to be played with.

She looked taken aback, however she regrouped and looked at Grant and said, "Call me," as she walked off. Grant apologized and looked embarrassed, but it was funny to me.

"So those are the kind of bougie women you date hunh? Really Grant?" I laughed. "How could you ever have thought about marrying someone so stuck up? You don't seem to be the type to be with a woman like that."

"That is why you are a breath of fresh air to me. My schedule is so hectic that the only time I really get to meet women is when I am handling company business. The majority of them are so independent that they are very arrogant and more man than I. When my frat brothers and I get together, our outings always seem to be in an environment that attracts these same nut cases. Shoot I was about ready to start hanging at the clubs that had no cover charge and reaped of cigarettes and chicken until I met you." Grant chuckled. "Not saying that all career women are like that, but the ones I seem to attract minus you, are. That is one of the reasons I haven't even bothered dating for a while. I am tired of the ones that think that the world revolves around them."

"Well I can respect your decision to be alone if that's the kind of bougie women you have been dealing with," I laughed. He considered me a career woman- I was flattered.

Grant and I continued our weekend together without another glitch. By the time that he saw me off, I was in love with a man that I had yet to sleep with.

$14.99
ISBN 978-0-615-78376-5
51499>
9 780615 783765